THE SOBER PILL

Sobriety Ain't for Sissies

ROCMO BROWN

Cover designed by Anthony Prieto

This book is a work of fiction. Names, characters, places, and incidents either are products of the author's imagination or are used fictitiously. Any resemblance to actual persons, living or dead, events, or locales is entirely coincidental.

RocMo Brown

Printed in the United States of America

First Printing: Aug 2017

ISBN—978-0-578-74798-9

To Kendra Christine for being the ballsiest woman I've ever known. Thanks for all the inspirati

THE SOBER PILL

PART ONE

2004

It was a long way down. Xochitl had been sitting, motionless on the narrow stone ledge for hours. Raising an arm, she feared, even enough for a quick glance at her watch, would throw her off balance and send her plunging over the side to her death. The valley floor was visible only as a diffused pattern of greens and grays through a thick, whirling mist that lingered hundreds of feet below. She sat rigid with no give, no fluidity, like a boutique manikin hooked by its plaster butt cheeks to a small display shelf.

Nothing grew on the side of the cliff. A sheer granite face, it was practically straight up and down. If she fell there would be no foliage to break her fall. Panic welled up in small waves as Xochitl realized her own flesh and blood butt cheeks were gradually becoming numb. Her back was pressed firmly against the rock face behind her and her fingers were splayed to cover as much of the little ledge as possible. But the cheeks were taking all the weight, and now they were beginning to pay for it with decreased blood flow. Xochitl desperately wanted to lift one side or the other and let the blood flow into her anesthetized buttocks, but there was no room to maneuver. The ledge was too small, less than a foot deep and maybe three feet wide.

Each time her lungs filled with air she had the desperate sensation of being pushed forward. She tried restricting her air intake to shallow breaths but couldn't keep it up for long. Panic caused her to gasp involuntarily, thrusting her forward and making the ledge feel even smaller than it was. Occasionally an ache appeared in the small of Xochitl's back forcing her to relax the muscles. Lacking the reassurance of the rock wall against her back, a wave of vertigo enveloped her and panic raised its unwelcome head causing her back muscles to tighten once again.

The drop looked to be somewhere between three and four hundred feet and Xochitl avoided looking down as much as possible. She had called for help as best she could through her shallow breaths, but her voice had come out small and insignificant. In this remote area it was unlikely that anyone would hear her, anyway, especially since sunset was approaching and most of the day hikers had gone home. This was one of the rare times that Xochitl doubted the wisdom of her self-imposed ban on cell phones. One quick call would have had rescuers tossing ropes over the side in half an hour.

"Hell, the damn thing probably wouldn't even work up here, anyway," she said aloud. "Besides, I'd fall just trying to get it out of my pocket."

It felt good to hear her own voice, reassuring her that for now, at least, she was still among the living.

A 35mm camera hung on a strap around her neck like a stone weight and the longer she sat on the ledge, the heavier it became. Balance was becoming a serious issue and she considered dropping it over the side, but decided against it. Assuming she survived this ordeal, she would need it. After all, she was a photographer, not hugely successful yet, but steadily trudging toward recognition.

Xochitl had rappelled down the cliff face to this little ledge late in the afternoon to insure the best lighting for her images. The bird she was trying to photograph for an article in AWARE Magazine had long since skitted away, squawking indignantly as it fluttered down into the forest below. The article charged that base jumpers, parachutists jumping off the cliffs in this area, were disturbing the breeding patterns of the cliff-dwelling birds. The day hadn't been a complete wash; she had gotten a few great shots before her rope had somehow come loose and fallen away into the misty depths.

The sun sank slowly into the mountains in the distance and a shadow began to creep up the side of the cliff toward Xochitl. She was aware that if darkness fell while she was still on the ledge, her chances of survival would effectively be reduced to zero. There was nothing to fasten herself to, nor anything to fasten with since the rope had disappeared, and sooner or later, against her will, she would fall asleep and slip off the ledge to her death. What would it be like, she wondered, to be jerked into full consciousness knowing it was too late, she was already falling and there was no stopping it now, that there would be no do-overs. Slowly she lifted her right butt cheek, shifting her weight gently to one side. Panic, but only momentary as she stuffed it back down, refusing to let it possess her. She lowered her right side and felt blessed stability once again. With so little ledge beneath her, she needed to be able to feel it, to know how much rock was holding her up.

A loud flutter startled Xochitl from her morbid speculations, and then a snapping noise from above brought her squarely into the present. A multicolored parachute, spread out like a great rainbow, drifted past her on its way to the valley floor.

"Help!" she called, her voice hoarse and choked. Then again, louder "HELP!" The parachutist struggled to turn his head, but his back was to the cliff and he couldn't work his body completely around. Seconds passed and the man managed, by tossing his weight to bring the parachute about until it was facing the cliff. But it was too late. He was some distance below her. He looked up, searching for the voice, but the open parachute blocked his view.

Xochitl, exasperated at missing her chance at a safe descent, clenched both hands into fists, driving them into the hard surface beneath her. She railed at the disappearing chute. "Come back here you son of a bitch," she shouted mindlessly. Her shoulders slumped and she began to slip forward. Panic struck once again and she arched her back, slamming it against the rock wall. "Aaah hell!" The parachute was slowly sinking away from her like some life-giving Atlantis and her momentary hopes of a long, happy life were sinking with it. She had a sudden, irrational urge to jump and land on top of the parachute. She could do it, but that was just foolish thinking. The parachute would lose its lift and she would plunge to the valley floor anyway, taking the base jumper with her.

Unsure what to do, Xochitl followed her instincts. Shoving her back hard against the stone wall behind her, she released one hand from the ledge and fished gingerly into the camera case, gently producing her camera. Bracing her wrist carefully on her knee to balance the weight of the camera, she squeezed off a few blind shots of the descending parachute. Not knowing why. Perhaps it was just habit, perhaps a futile attempt to generate some hope in a hopeless situation. Only people with a future take pictures, she thought. But frustration consumed her and she got careless, failing to notice that her right butt cheek had now gone completely numb.

"Shit!"

She slammed the camera back in its case and the ledge slipped out from under her. It happened very quickly. Resignation took over, shoving all feelings of panic aside as she realized that this was it.

It was time to die.

Xochitl's reaction center, her animal brain, was not ready to surrender, however. She found herself still supported by the little ledge, her left arm, elbow to armpit, held her to the platform like a hook. Instantly her right hand darted around and found purchase on the ledge. Thin fingers slid into a small crack and anchored themselves. Holding her feet against the side of the cliff, she was able, after some trial and error, to stabilize her weight. It was nothing like the good old days when she was actually sitting on the ledge, but it was infinitely better than falling to the canyon floor. Slowly, an inch at a time, Xochitl began to pull herself back onto the little stone platform, keeping her weight pressed against the face of the cliff as much as she could.

Barely had she regained the ledge when the flapping noise came again from above. She raised her right leg and hooked the heel of her shoe on the edge of the stone platform, pressing her back hard against the wall. Struggling to keep her balance, she began to work the other leg into the same position. Knees buckled, back against the stone wall, she was ready by the time the second parachutist floated by. It was now or never. Mechanically, she sprang from the ledge, thrusting with all the power her nearly numb legs could supply, and in short order found herself clinging to the waist of a second parachutist. The man stiffened for only a second and then began to scream like a terrified schoolgirl.

"Calm down. I'm not gonna bite you," she said, struggling to hold on. "I just need a ride to the bottom."

"LET GO!" the parachutist screamed, his pasty face contorting in terror. "You're going to kill us both! Let go! This thing's not designed for two people. LET GO!"

"NO! Sorry Flyboy," she grunted, "not gonna happen. We'll just have to land a little harder than you're used to. We may break a few bones, but nobody's going to die here today unless you do something stupid."

Flyboy immediately did something stupid. Releasing his grip on the ropes, he hooked his thumbs under Xochitl's clasped hands and tried to pry them loose. The chute, now without a functioning pilot, began to careen erratically. She let go with her right hand and reached around the man's body, grasping one of the harness ropes. Releasing her left hand, she swung her body around behind him like a monkey on a vine, pulling herself up enough to grab on to the harness with her left hand. The parachutist began kicking backward with his heels, landing a few good blows to Xochitl's hips and mid-section. Xochitl had been taking kick boxing lessons, along with a few of her friends, for the past year or so and had never found an occasion to use the knowledge outside the classroom. Until now it had been nothing more than an empowerment ritual among girlfriends. As she had been taught, Xochitl's right foot flew up over her head and caught the man squarely in the temple. He sagged, unconscious.

With no one at the helm, the chute spun wildly and darted away from the cliff, then turned and rushed toward it. Xochitl began tugging randomly at the ropes, but with no experience to draw from, the parachute began to spiral. The ground was rising fairly quickly and the now familiar feeling of vertigo was beginning to consume her. She pulled on the ropes erratically as the rock face slid rapidly upward.

And then something worked.

She had no idea what she had done, but the parachute was obviously going slower now, not slow, but slower, and the wild spinning had halted altogether. The ground was close enough to make out smallish details such as logs and individual plants. Xochitl was certain she was still moving fast enough to break a bone or two. A small river flowed nearby and she tugged on one of the ropes, trying to steer the wayward parachute toward it, hoping the water would break her fall.

The man regained consciousness, his eyes immediately grew round as he spied the ground rushing toward him. After a few piercing screams he lost consciousness again. Xochitl was now enjoying some success at steering the chute. She steeled her muscles for the impact. The river came rushing up at frightening speed. Her feet were inches from the surface when the parachute jerked to a halt. She was thrown, feet first, into the water. Her head was submerged and she felt her heels dig into the sandy bottom. Instinctively, she raised her hands, and the camera, perched high over her head and still in its case, remained dry.

Shaken, she waded ashore and sat down hard on the bank. Her drenched clothes must have weighed a hundred pounds, but as long as she was living and breathing and standing on solid ground again it didn't matter. Across the river the parachute hung limply from the craggy remains of an old, lightening-tortured oak tree with its unconscious pilot dangling inches above the water, oblivious to the current nipping at his toes.

"Good," said Xochitl aloud to the unconscious parachutist. "You just wake up that way. Maybe that'll teach you a little something about sharing."

"That was quite an exhibition." The voice came from behind her. She spun her head around and saw that the first parachutist was standing behind her, a blemished young man in camouflage army pants and a sleeveless tee-shirt. "Flying and kick boxing at the same time, pretty Hollywood."

"Look man, I'm sorry if that guy's your friend, but he deserved what he got. We weren't in any mortal danger until he started trying to pry my fingers loose. I'm sorry, but I had to do something."

"Yeah, he's kinda new at the sport," the man said. "He's not such a bad guy, really. I guess anybody would panic, getting tackled in mid-air like that."

"Hey, you do what you gotta do."

"Yeah."

Xochitl groped in her shirt pocket. "You got any paper on you? I have a pen, but my paper got all soggy in the river."

"What do you need paper for?" the man asked.

"I want to leave your compadre a thank-you note."

The man pulled a grocery receipt from his shirt pocket and handed it to Xochitl. "Will this do?"

Xochitl took the paper. "Perfect," she said. "What's his name?"

"Barry. Barry Northrup. It was only his second jump. He's really not such a bad guy."

"Yeah."

She began scrawling on the paper: 'Dear Barry, thanks for the use of your parachute. I couldn't have made it down alive without you. Sorry I had to force your hand, but you just wouldn't behave yourself. Panic is everyone's enemy. Pleasant dreams, Xochitl.'

The man pointed to the scrap of paper. "What's this?" he

asked.

"It's my name," she grumbled, rolling her large brown eyes.

"How do you say it, Ex-oochie-tell?"

"You pronounce it So-chee"

"How do you get Sochee out of all those crazy letters? What is it, Russian or something?"

"Aztec."

"Aztec?"

"That's right, Aztec."

"Those people were pretty gnarly, weren't they?"

"Still are. My people have a long history of human sacrifice. You might want to mention that to good ol' Barry, here, when he wakes up. Let him know what a lucky guy he is."

"Yeah, thanks, I'll do that." The young man turned and trudged away. After a few paces he stopped and looked over his shoulder. "I got tickets to the monster truck rally on Friday, you wanna go?"

"Flattered, but not dating right now," said Xochitl mechanically.

"Well, it doesn't have to be like a date ...I mean ...uh...it could just be like..." The man bit his lip, nodded slowly and began to walk away.

As Xochitl removed her shoes and squeezed the water from her socks, she spied a candy bar wrapper tucked halfway under a rock. "Stupid people. That's what trash cans are for," she mumbled, snatching up the wrapper and stuffing it into her pocket. Replacing the shoes, she began boulder-hopping down the riverbed in the direction of her car. A moment later she stopped and turned in the direction of the hanging parachutist. She removed her camera from its case and squeezed off a few rounds in his direction. Half an hour later, as the sky darkened, she slipped the key into the ignition of her aging Toyota 4Runner.

1944

Alf Sedgwick burst into the world by way of a small oil town in the central valley of California during the mid-1940s, only narrowly missing World War Two. He spent most of his youth grudgingly executing chores relating to the upkeep of his parent's land, 15 acres of dusty rolling desert, furnished with non-functional cars and decorated with scrub brush. His father, who thought of himself as 'a man of ideas,' placed these objects at what he called 'creative' angles and claimed that, taken all together, and observed from the right perspective, they added up to some sort of important artistic statement. Alf let slip to his father that the 'statement' was lost on him.

"It's just a bunch of junk, Dad. It's a mess."

"Well, maybe that's what you see. Maybe you just ain't got no vision," his father would say. "You know, most people only use 10 percent of their brain, and I figure you're using even less than that if you can't see my statement."

Another one of the old man's pass times was collecting piles of discarded pipe from nearby oil fields. The plan was to some-day sell them to a scrap yard down in LA for money. The pipes were stacked into neat piles in more obscure corners of the property. Alf's father was not quite sure about the legal status of the pipe, but, "What the hell, they're just gonna rot away in the fields anyway."

His mother was a substitute teacher who sprinkled her talents among all of the ramshackle oil towns in the area. Most of the nearby towns were fairly small, ranging in size from one pot-holed street with a few suffering roadside attractions to average sized hamlets with at least one supermarket and movie theater.

It was the movie theaters that attracted young Alf's interest more than anything else in the area. Most of the boys in his town kept themselves occupied hunting rabbits or rattlesnakes, but, other than the immediate thrill of shooting a gun, this seemed remedial to young Alf and he lost interest after the first few excursions.

The movies, on the other hand, were never boring. The viewing of a film was magical, like entering into a new world, almost as though he were able to start life afresh each time the introduction credits began to roll. Sitting rapt in the dark, Alf would wonder where each new life was going to lead him. Sometimes he would ride his bicycle up to 20 miles, the hot sun beating on his back, if an interesting movie was playing in a neighboring town.

Alf would earn money for the movies by collecting used pop bottles and cashing them in at the market. Occasionally, though, he would simply steal it, usually from his parents, and most often from his mother. A five-gallon water bottle in the back of his mother's closet was the receptacle for her spare change. The little treasure was intended for holidays and family emergencies, but to Alf it was simply free money. He was careful never to take enough to give himself away and always replaced the bottle in exactly the same position, meticulously aligning its edge with the ring left in the carpet.

Alf didn't much care for his parents and something inside of him enjoyed stealing from them, though he couldn't say why. They treated him decently enough, but somehow, to Alf, the family felt like a slap-dash bunch of acquaintances that, through circumstances beyond their control, happened to be living together under the same roof. Alf felt no particular attachment to his family, or anyone else. He had no real friends and spent most of his free time alone. The truth, though, was that Alf probably would have stolen from his parents even if he had loved them dearly, because Alf just plain liked to steal.

Alf's introduction to thievery had taken place in the third grade. One morning he and an acquaintance had taken a load of empty pop bottles to the market in their coaster wagon and traded them for cash. As they were leaving, they noticed a large stack of wooden crates behind the market. The crates were chock-full of used pop bottles. Alf and his friend quietly crept behind the market and filled the coaster wagon with the bottles from the stack. Then they slinked away and hid nervously in the bushes for an hour.

Eventually, they returned to the market and cashed in the new load of bottles. Then they crept out back behind the market and repeated the process once again. It was easy! Alf was hooked. Later, that afternoon, he went back to the market and spent all of his ill-gotten gains on sweets. His purchases must be kept low-key, he understood, so that his parents would have no reason to inquire where the money had come from. Even in the third grade Alf was smart that way.

One day, when he was 11, after succeeding at a particularly risky theft, Alf rewarded himself by inventing the sugar sandwich, which promptly became his catnip. And then his heroin. The sandwich was simple and consisted of two pieces of white bread with as much granulated table sugar as Alf could squeeze between them. The first time he tried one, Alf sprinkled only a small amount of sugar onto the bread, just enough to sweeten it. But before long a mere sprinkle became inadequate, ceasing to satisfy him. He began to apply more and more sugar to the bread until he could feel the little granules crunching between his teeth.

Once, when there was no bread in the house, Alf lay on his back, attempting to pour an entire box of sugar directly into his mouth. He covered his throat with his tongue and poured until the sugar ran down the sides of his face. Then he began to chew, slowly and sluggishly .

The sugar was sweet at first, but as the granules turned to liquid, it began to taste bitter. Once the entire mouthful was chewed into a thick syrup, Alf began to swallow. Little by little the thick, bitter yet horribly sweet liquid oozed down his throat, causing him to shiver uncontrollably. He lay on the floor of his bedroom, google-eyed and paralyzed with sugar shock, for an indeterminate amount of time. It was only the chugging of the family car, pulling into the driveway that forced him back to mobility. He imagined this was what it felt like to return from a drug trip. It felt dangerous and risky. Alf knew he was flying close to the flame, but he couldn't wait to try it again. It couldn't really do him any real harm, could it? It was just food, right?

2004

Aware magazine occupied the third floor of a five-story office building in Xochitl's hometown of Soda River. June Belby, an elderly receptionist prone to silk blouses and bright lipstick, peered suspiciously over her blue, rhinestone-studded glasses as she heard the *scooshh-weeek scoosh-weeek scoosh-weeek* of Xochitl's wet shoes entering the lobby. She tossed Xochitl a probing look, pursing her lips and pinching her chin as the young photographer sloshed her way across the lobby in her soaking clothes, disappearing between a pair of large oak doors. Xochitl trudged up to an office with the name, Albert Trundell, in bold brass letters on the door, and barged in without knocking.

"WHO THE HELL KEEPS STEALING MY PENCILS?"

Xochitl was greeted by the sight of a gesticulating black man, once muscular, now simply large, with tired yellowish eyes and a thick head of graying hair. He sighed and every part of him slumped. His jowls and shoulders adopted the same downward angle. He was sitting at a cluttered metal desk with three yellow pencils protruding from his hair.

"I couldn't tell you, Boss, but it's gotta be someone close to you."

"Yeah, that's what I was thinking," said Trundell. "Jesus, St. James, what happened to you?"

"I'm trying a new look. What do you think? Like it?" She spun on her toes, striking a pose like a model on a catwalk.

"I've seen better."

18

"Hey, be nice and I'll give you this." She pulled a small canister from the pocket of her flannel shirt. "Pictures of the birds, and the parachutists."

"Nice work. Now go on home and get cleaned up. I have another assignment for you."

"No way, ...tonight?"

"That's right."

"Oh man, you don't know what kind of day I've had. Can't this wait until tomorrow?"

"Not really. But I think you're going to like this one."

"Why, what is it?"

"Some guy..." he fumbled with a piece of paper on his desk, holding it at arm's length and squinting. "...a Dr. Sporkin, has invented the sober pill."

"The what?"

"The sober pill. Apparently you take one of these little pills and it neutralizes any alcohol in your system. It says here it binds with the alcohol molecule and turns it into something non-intoxicating and nontoxic."

"No way!" Xochitl's jaw dropped. "So, you mean I could go out on Saturday night, drink until I've made a sufficient ass of myself and then take one of these little pills and I could drive home?"

"That's the way it looks, yes. Maybe even on a Sunday or a Monday, though being the owner of the business you work for, I'm not recommending it."

"And not get so much as a ticket?"

"I've seen you drive sober, St. James, I couldn't guarantee that."

"How long does it take, you know, before you're completely sober again?"

"About twenty minutes, according to this press release."

Xochitl began clapping her hands together. "Holy shit! Who is this guy? What's his story? I think he's my new hero."

"I don't know his story. Either does anyone else, right now. That's why I'm sending you and Blanchard out to interview him."

"Ernie? You're sending me with Ernie? Isn't this kind of an important story? I mean, Ernie doesn't have a whole lot of experience, Boss."

"He's gotta get his feet wet sometime. I've had him following some of the veteran reporters around for almost six months. He must have learned something in all that time. No, I think he's our man. This is basically just a human-interest story with a little twist of science thrown in. He can handle it. Besides, everyone else is already occupied, and hey, he's got you, with your three years of on-the-job training, looking over his shoulder."

"I'm a photographer, not a reporter."

"You know the drill, St. James. Just take your pictures and elbow him in the ribs if he starts saying something stupid. Now head on home and put some dry clothes on. Meet up with Blanchard here at around 7:30."

"Where is the good doctor staying?"

"Says in the press release he lives in Los Angeles, but he's here in Soda River on business. Apparently, he doesn't yet have a manufacturer for his product. He's meeting with representatives from three or four major pharmaceutical firms, trying to get a bidding war going."

"I see. So this is not a humanitarian effort on his part."

"Hardly. He couldn't make more money if he had the cure for cancer, and he knows it. That's why he's trying to get the pharmaceutical companies to play off each other."

Xochitl turned and walked toward the door. "So, where do we meet this guy?" she asked over her shoulder.

"He's rented a cabin out on North End." Trundell pulled a new No. 2 pencil from his desk drawer and wrote the address on a piece of paper. He handed it to Xochitl, who folded it over a few times and slid it into her pocket.

"Okay boss," said Xochitl, " I'll get on it. This one holds a personal interest for me."

Trundell inadvertently slid the pencil into his hair, freeing up his hand. Seconds later he began frantically searching his desk. He called to Xochitl as she turned to leave, "Saint James? You take my pencil?"

1956

Alf admired a number of movie actors, but his all-time favorite was James Dean. There was something about Dean's tortured loner characters that Alf was drawn to. Dean had acted only three movies before he died, tragically, in a senseless automobile accident, not too far from Alf's hometown. But those three movies were enough to give Alf's life a sense of direction. That and the one time a while back when he'd met James Dean in person. Actually, he hadn't so much met James Dean as eavesdropped on a private conversation. Through pure coincidence Alf had stood behind him at the soda machine in the local gas station. Alf, staring intently at the vending machine, was trying to determine which brand of soda contained the most sugar. James Dean stood nearby talking business to someone whom, Alf decided, must be his agent or financial manager, someone holding an official capacity. Alf had heard people say that, in person, this or that celebrity was nothing like they appeared on the screen, but it carried no weight with him until he heard the voice of his film idol speaking lines that were not memorized from a script. As Alf listened in, Dean was speaking in a worried tone about something. His voice was high-pitched and whining, full of fear. A sort of pleading quality to it.

Man, he sounds really wimpy, Alf thought. After idolizing the macho, lady-killing James Dean on the screen, Alf would never have guessed in a million years that his idle was capable of producing this kind of unflattering tone. It was all too human, and it bothered Alf to think of his idol as a mere human.

As Dean drove away in his Porsche Spider, Alf pulled an off-brand of grape soda from the machine. He sat on the little curb by the soda machine and thought about what he'd just seen. Practically everyone in the world knew who James Dean was, but only a very few people close to Dean had ever heard that voice come out of his mouth. A light went on in Alf's head and he was struck with a realization that would change his life. "You are what you pretend to be," he said aloud, placing the bottle on the ground.

And then he said it again just to make sure he had it right.

2004

Xochitl pulled into her driveway and checked her mailbox. A cool afternoon breeze chilled her skin through her damp clothes. She shivered as she approached the front door flipping through her mail. Bills, or as she called them, the monthly punch in the gut, plus another letter from an ex-boyfriend who just wouldn't lay down and die. At the bottom of the pile she found a pale pink envelope from the City of Soda River. It looked official, so she opened it first. The envelope contained a traffic citation claiming that on April 12th Xochitl had been in the intersection of State and Franklin after the light had turned red and was expected to pay $340 for the privilege. Also in the envelope was a full color brochure explaining the advantages of the new system of red light cameras the city had placed in "trouble" intersections about the town. The brochure claimed that the system had worked in other cities around the country, protecting ordinary, law-abiding citizens from the type of blatant, careless scoff-laws who deliberately ran red lights, endangering innocent human lives, presumably just for the hell of it.

Xochitl was outraged. The incident didn't sound familiar to her at all and she certainly didn't feel like a blatant, careless scoff-law. In her kitchen she fiercely flipped through the pages of a calendar filled with pictures of half-naked firemen, stuck to her refrigerator with a large round magnet. April 12th. That was the day she had lent her car to her friend Marissa for a few hours. Xochitl wanted to call the police station and contest the citation, but there was no time. Dry clothes and a good soak were the priorities. "A good deed never goes unpunished," she sighed.

Drawing the hottest bath she could stand, Xochitl poured a capful of lavender oil into the steaming water and leaned over the tub, letting the fragrant vapor run through her nostrils and fill her lungs. The muscles in her legs began to relax and she sat down on the toilet seat. Soon, she felt loose all over. Weezy, Xochitl's cross-eyed Siamese cat wandered into the bathroom seeking affection or, more likely, food. He rubbed against her legs and purred. She ran her fingers through his fur a few times and scrunched his ears up in her hand.

Forcing herself to her feet, she removed her still-damp clothing. The heat was just a smidgen below pain level as she gradually lowered her shivering body into the water. At first she had the odd sensation of not being able to tell whether the water was hot or cold, but within moments warmth began to penetrate her body and her eyelids grew heavy.

Xochitl's hair was thick and straight. It fell nearly to her waist, and it was black, the black hair of her ancestors. She leaned back, lowering her head into the water. The shiny, dark strands of hair flowed over her shoulders and across her breasts, weaving in the water like a thousand tiny snakes.

Amazing, she thought, a sober pill. My God, how would that change the world? Especially the world Xochitl lived in. It was always difficult for her to say 'when' if alcohol was present and a good time was being had by all. A few of her ex-boyfriends and ex-not-so-boyfriends had resulted directly from those circumstances. It was no secret to her that she made questionable decisions under the influence; still she craved a drink or two in social situations. An innate and well-disguised shyness kept her from breaking the ice on her own. She had been told innumerable times how outgoing and entertaining she was at parties, but in truth that only happened a few drinks in. Worst of all were the times she had driven home drunk. Xochitl, an independent woman with a will of iron, felt somehow defeated if another person had to do something for her. Sometimes this served her well; sometimes it led her to do very stupid things.

Often she wondered if she wasn't perhaps a budding alcoholic. Not that she was driven to drink every day, but once she started it was difficult to stop. At the library one day, she had looked up the definition of alcoholic and had been dismayed to read a blow-by-blow description of her partying habits. Still, she was young, she told herself. Sometimes it took years to learn how to pace yourself.

1993

Alcohol had played a major role in the death of Xochitl's parents when she was 12 years old. Xochitl had spent her early years in Fresno, a large agriculturally based city of high crime and questionable air quality, in California's San Joaquin Valley. One year the city was rumored to have held the title for highest Murder rate in the country. Nobody celebrated that one.

Xochitl's mother, a beautiful, dark-eyed, full-blooded Aztec from the mountainous area east of Mexico City, had become restive during her husband's excursions as a traveling salesman. She took on a job as a part-time bartender to occupy the lonely nights while her husband, Clive, who represented a large dried fruit farm, was away. Her name was Maria and she became one of a pair of bartenders running a small soul-less drinking establishment called The Rancho. Most nights business tapered off fairly early at the Rancho, a neighborhood bar, and she was able to knock off by 11, getting her home before midnight. Francie, the other bartender, a single, older woman in need of rent money and a social life, volunteered to stay each night until closing.

Clive was never gone for a day, or even a week. It was always two weeks, three weeks, or even, occasionally, a month. At first the sex was great each time he returned home. Both were hungry and devoured each other greedily. Eventually, though, the intensity waned and Maria began to suspect liaisons with other women during Clive's lengthy stints on the road.

As a rule, drinking with the customers was not something Maria condoned. They were all drunk, for crying-out-loud. Someone had to stay sober. Someone had to captain the ship. What if a customer passed out, or had a heart attack? Who would handle that? She would have to, and that was that. Though she'd never experienced such an occasion, it made her feel a little superior to know she had her wits about her when no one else in the place, even Francie, could speak without slurring their words.

Suspicion gnawed at her gut as the months rolled into a year and more. As Maria's soul darkened with jealousy it became difficult to socialize with the customers, and as she soon learned, socializing is the lifeblood of the successful bartender. Tips dropped off and some customers began patronizing a bar down the street rather than address an angry, depressed bartender.

One night a semi-regular customer, a handsome ranch worker who wore a cowboy hat religiously, asked Maria to have a drink with him. Her first response was her habitual, "Thanks, but somebody's gotta drive this crazy bus." But, the man, being a cowboy, was persistent, and she was reluctantly flattered by his attention. She felt herself weakening steadily. Hell, it wasn't like she was going to run off to a hotel room with him, it was just a drink for crissakes. Two charming hours later, the cowboy managed to talk her into taking a single shot of tequila with him. It wasn't much, but it was a little chink in her long-standing armor.

Once the ice was broken it was easier for her to have a single drink with the cowboy each time he came into the bar. And then one night she had two shot glasses ready on the counter when he arrived. That evening the cowboy talked her into having another drink with him. And it wasn't hard at all. Two drinks became the new ritual while her husband was away. A few days before Clive's expected return from a sales trip, she would stop drinking with the cowboy. 'Getting her head on straight', she called it. The cowboy would feel warm at these moments, and a little evil. She drank the tequila just for him. They had a little secret together. Just a tiny, little something, but it was moving in the right direction. As for Maria, it wouldn't do at all to greet her long-absent spouse with the reek of alcohol on her breath. She couldn't have her husband suspecting her infidelities with the cowboy, even if they were all in her head.

One night as Clive was due to return home after three weeks on the road, he called Maria at the bar to inform her that, due to circumstances beyond his control, he would be held up another week or so. She hung up the phone angrily, went out in the alley behind the bar and lit up a cigarette, inhaling deeply. She hadn't been an avid smoker until recently, at least not of cigarettes. There had always been the occasional cigar, but that was more of an Aztec thing. A spiritual thing Aztecs did, part of a ritual she occasionally performed for purging her life of unwanted spirits from the Aztec equivalent of Hell, a place called Talocan. She wasn't sure if it worked or not, but it felt good just to do it, as though she had some measure of control over the random curve balls life often threw her. Smoking cigarettes, on the other hand was purely for pleasure. The cigarette smoking seemed a natural extension of life in the bar, particularly on nights when she was drinking with the cowboy. What the hell, she was breathing other people's smoke all night long anyway.

Two nights later the cowboy came in and over the course of his two-hour stay, Maria indulged in five shots of tequila with him. A warm sense of invulnerability possessed her. Her mind felt open and intelligent. They flirted intensely, and when the cowboy left at the end of her shift she had a powerful urge to honor his standing invitation to leave with him. It was the thought of her daughter that kept her from it. Little Xochitl was home alone. She was 12, old enough to take care of herself during the evenings, but not to be abandoned for an entire night.

Arriving home, Maria spotted Clive's bags in a pile on the

living room floor. Apparently his bosses had allowed him to return earlier than he had anticipated. If, indeed it was actually business that had caused the delay. Still, he was home. Through a tequila-saturated haze, she breathed a sigh of relief at not having left with the cowboy.

Clive was asleep as Maria entered the bedroom and she threw herself down hard on the bed, shaking him roughly. "Come on baby, wake up. Mamma's here. Wake up baby boy." She clawed clumsily at his pajama top, pulling a button loose.

Clive floundered into semi-consciousness and flinched from an assault of cigarette and tequila-sodden breath. "Jesus, girl," he exclaimed halfheartedly, pushing her away, "you're drunk."

"I just had a couple," she said, chin pressed against her collarbone, doe-eyes pleading.

"Yeah, a couple of what?" He rolled over, facing away from her. "Sleep it off. I'll see you in the morning."

"Don't you turn your back on me! Talk to me, damn it! Look at me when I'm talking to you!" She began to quietly sob.

Clive groaned. "Look, you're drunk okay. You're not going to make any sense anyway. Wouldn't you rather save it until you have something coherent to say?"

She stiffened, thought for a moment, and then crawled on top of him. "Then hold me, baby." She was slurring now. "I need a man to hold me. I'm young. I'm dying of loneliness. How long do you think I can go without being held? It's been almost a month. Make love to me like you used to. Used to be you couldn't wait."

Head jammed into the pillow, Clive pinched his eyes shut. "Used to be you were sober," he said snidely. He could sense her face right next to his, hear her breathing and feel her quiet tears dripping from her chin, splattering lightly onto his cheek. He felt pity. He felt concern. He felt anything but aroused. There was nothing he could do about it. It simply wasn't there tonight. He had originally been attracted to Maria because of her ferocity and independence. The wife of a traveling salesman needed to be somewhat independent. He knew a little of the history of the Aztec people and had assumed she was a fighter, that it was in her blood. And to a degree it was. But now there was nothing for her to fight against except loneliness, which by its very nature sapped her strength, making her less appealing to him. The marriage he had wandered into had become little more than a cage, an empty room.

For Xochitl's mother, a husband who wasn't present was torture. Every instinct urged her to solve her loneliness problem in the manor of any other independent woman. Each time the cowboy entered her bar a battle waged within her between the forces of loneliness and the vows she had sworn on her wedding day. Her independent spirit took a beating almost daily.

Clive had sensed the change in her over the last year or so. Perhaps it was that job she had gotten. Perhaps it was because Xochitl was now old enough to develop her own interests and was showing some of the same independent traits her mother had exhibited, no longer needing strict attention. Whatever it was, her edge was rapidly disappearing. The sharp, sarcastic wit was all but gone and in its place he found a roundish, pleading quality, something he found himself trying unsuccessfully to manufacture an attraction to.

"Look, just go to sleep, okay. We'll talk in the morning."

She stormed from the room, slamming the door shut behind her. On the back porch, she sat heavily on the railing and lit a cigarette. Smoke swirled lazily through the dim porch light. Restrained tears wiggled through her nearly-closed eyes, eventually forcing the lids open. Then they began in earnest, flowing readily. She buried her face in her hands. Twenty minutes later she was cried out, dabbing her wet cheeks with the hem of her open sweater. The myriad emotions arguing among themselves in her head began to gel, finally coalescing into a willful hard-edged anger.

Sometimes life flew off the tracks and rolled into unexpected territory, she thought. If you were going to make it, you had to deal with change. And that's what she would do. The next time the cowboy came in, by God she would be ready for him. She stomped back into the house, lit the cigarette dangling loosely from her lips.

Clive snored loudly as she entered the room. Her clothes formed a trail to the bed as she tore them off. Crawling into bed, she pulled the covers up to her neck, satisfied that she had finally made a decision. Her muscles grew hard as she sensed strength and independence flowing through her veins once again. Drifting off, she failed to feel the half smoked cigarette roll from her silken, tranquil lips and settle lightly on the feather pillow. Was something burning? Ah well, she would deal with it tomorrow. She would be able to deal with anything in the morning.

Young Xochitl smelled the smoke before she saw the flames. Sniffing, her eyes popped open and she stared uncomprehendingly at the dancing red curtain before her. Immediately, she was in a crouching position on the bed, her mind racing, clicking off possibilities. The entire side of the room that held her door had become a wall of flame.

The fire quickly spread across the carpet toward the bed. Xochitl, instantly lifted her nightstand and tossed it against the window, shattering the glass outward. Enough presence of mind seeped through her panic to allow her to examine the window frame. Large, menacing shards protruded from the windowsill, ready to gash her hands as she made her escape.

The flames grew more intense, spreading rapidly across the floor. Xochitl could feel the heat lapping at her from behind. Gathering the blanket from her bed, she wrapped it several times around her hand and forearm. The glass shards snapped and popped as she pushed against them breaking them loose and flinging them over her shoulder into the crackling fire. Flames lightly danced at her back as she snapped off the last piece and dove through the opening face first. The cool, damp earth felt refreshing as it collided with her hands and face. She rolled a few times as they had taught her in school, then, quickly crawling across the lawn to the sidewalk, stood up and faced the inferno.

Sirens pierced the quiet night as a herd of screaming fire trucks invaded the tranquil street, speeding toward Xochitl's flaming house. Men scrambled in every direction as the large metal beasts skidded to a halt in front of her. How out of place they looked in the middle of this chaotic disaster, with their bright, red paint and shiny chrome. A man dressed in a thick, asbestos coat, the color of cardboard, and a red metal hat threw himself down onto one knee beside her.

"Do you live here, young lady?"

Xochitl nodded in silence.

"Who else lives here, honey?" the man asked, his big hand on her shoulder. "Is anyone else in the house?"

A sudden blinding vision, too terrifying to examine, filled Xochitl's frantic mind. "MY MOM!" she shouted. "MY DADDY CAME HOME LAST NIGHT. MY MOM AND DAD! OH MY GOD! THEY'RE IN THE HOUSE!! THEY'RE IN THE HOUSE!!" She pulled free of the fireman's grasp and ran back toward the inferno. The man bolted in pursuit and tackled her at the foot of the stairs leading to the front porch. She scratched at him, but her nails wouldn't penetrate the thick fireproof coat. He held her firmly to the ground.

A piercing wail rose above the clamor, and for a moment both Xochitl and the fireman ceased their struggle and stared. The front door of the house burst open and a figure, engulfed in flames, stumbled into the open air. Once more the screeching wail stung their ears as Xochitl's mother collapsed and tumbled down the steps leaving a swirling trail of smoke behind her.

The fireman seized Xochitl and rolled aside as the floundering body came to rest next to them. He immediately slapped his hand over Xochitl's eyes, but not before she had caught a fleeting glimpse of her mother's blistered face. Something in the mechanism of Xochitl's mind jammed up at that moment and she went limp, the fight gone out of her.

The fireman picked her up and cradled her in his big arms. He carried her into the street. "It's alright, baby. It's alright, baby," he whispered over and over again.

Spotting a policeman he knew casually from many fires in the past, the fireman hurried over to the cruiser and placed Xochitl gently on the hood. "Eddie," he said, "I need a favor man. I need you to get this little girl out of here."

"What are you nuts, Karl? Who the hell is she?" asked Eddie. "I can't just leave the scene."

Karl leaned in close to Eddie's ear. "She just saw her mother burn to death two feet in front of her face," he whispered. "I want you to get her away from here, Eddie. For her own good, get her away from here, quick...Please."

"Where am I gonna take her?" Asked Eddie, his protest more feeble now.

"I don't know. Take her to the station. It doesn't matter where you take her. Just get her away from here. Anywhere but here."

"I can't take her to the station. They'll know I left my post."

"You got a piece of paper, Eddie? And a pen?"

The Policeman fished in his shirt pocket for a pen and paper. "Why? Here I got this citation book. Write on the back."

Karl took the booklet from Eddie and, placing it on the hood of the cruiser, began to write. "This is my address, Eddie. Take her there. My wife's name is Doris. Explain to her what happened and ask her to keep the girl calm until I get home. I don't want her getting fed into the system just yet. She's just been through the most horrible thing that's probably going to happen to her in her whole life. The last thing she needs is a bunch of suits hounding her with questions. I'll cover for you if anyone asks where you are."

"I don't know, Karl. This is nowhere near procedure."

"Just do it Eddie. Do the right thing."

1974-1980

There are creatures among us who Mother Nature never intended to swim in the gene pool, but Mother Nature, like the rest of us, sometimes falls asleep on the job. One of these creatures was Chester McFadden, a short, burly man of thirty-six with a round, pulpish nose and thinning hair. His eyes, though tired, were dark and penetrating, speaking of an awareness belied by his drooping countenance and the slovenly cut of his wardrobe. One might have mistaken him for a dockworker but for his withered left arm, which was a little shorter than the right, and much thinner with a pink, helpless, childlike appearance. The effect was that of someone having torn an arm off a Barbie doll and stuck it on an action figure of the Incredible Hulk. The arm was an insignificant little thing, really, seven maybe ten percent of his overall body weight, and yet it ruled his entire existence. He was aware of it during every waking moment, and often he dreamed about it.

The arm was something Chester was born with. He had never known anything else. Still, the fact that he was different from his contemporaries was ever present and he longed constantly for some sense of normalcy. Children being what they are, his elementary school and junior high years, from 1974 to 1980, were emotionally brutal. Ridicule and physical abuse were regular features of his school day. Punching bag 101. Not only in the hallways when no one was looking, but also the classroom itself became a battlefield or, more often a firing squad, where he stood cowering as popular children assassinated his self-esteem with words, rubber bands and paper airplanes. No one took notice of his welts, bruises and small cuts, as they were integral features of his appearance.

Occasionally, after school, he would seek shelter under the Mission Bridge, an ancient stone structure constructed by Native American slave labor hundreds of years ago. Chester knew the history of the bridge and was glad those days were gone, because in any society where slavery was endorsed, that would undoubtedly be his fate.

Under the bridge he felt free to let his tears flow uninterrupted. Out in public, though, he developed the ability to dam up the tidal wave residing right behind his eyes, showing nothing, like the stoic front of a West Virginia coal miner. The bridge was his sanctuary, his church, and once a week or so he would climb down the embankment and let his tears flow into the running water of the stream, washing them away to some happier place.

One day as he huddled beneath the bridge, face in hands, a group of Chester's classmates discovered him and stood pointing and smirking from above. "Troll under the bridge," they chanted, and it became Chester's new name. For a time he became known as the Troll.

The name had a nasty sting to it, but it hadn't lasted long. Soon a new, more deliciously cruel name found its way into Chester's life. 'The Fiddler Crab', and that was a name that stuck. It had come about innocently enough. One day, in the sixth grade, Chester's teacher, Mrs. Bartlett, a straight-backed woman with kind eyes and stiff hair, brought in a slide projector and three carrousels of slides from her recent vacation to the Florida seashore. She believed the children would enjoy the slides, and they did. One in particular. The slide that would change Chester's life depicted a small crab with a tiny fragile arm on one side and a huge Popeye-looking appendage on the other.

"This little creature is called a fiddler crab," Said Mrs. Bartlett. "See, he looks like he's playing a violin."

"He looks like the Troll," Someone whispered.

Giggles snorked from the girls.

"Hey Troll, I didn't know you lived at the Florida seashore. I thought you lived under that bridge over by the mission."

"People," chimed Mrs. Bartlett, jumping up and banging two erasers together, "we do not speak ill of our neighbors"

"I thought I saw you walking sideways the other day, Troll. I just thought you were all drunk and shit... you know, like your old man."

Giggles.

Smirks

He darted for the door.

He ran.

1959

In high school, during the early sixties, Alf Sedgwick hadn't been the top student in his class, although he could have been with a bit more application. He was born (contrary to his father's opinion) with a quick mind, though he had difficulty focusing. Essentially a lazy dreamer, he had forged his way primarily on the strength of his considerable wit and charm. He had a knack for drawing a few key facts and phrases from a given subject and was able to talk about it as though he had been familiar with it all his life. All one needed to know, Alf found, was the central concept of a subject. The rest of the details could be invented. He named the invented details "fluff" because they were fuzzy and ill defined, and for Alf the fluff was the easy part. It was the way in which any subject affected the average human being, and this was open to all sorts of silly interpretations. As long as he had a solid grasp on basic human nature, Alf could let his mind go wild. In fact, the wilder the better. The bottom line was, if you had a couple of key nuggets and you knew how to weave them through a big pile of fluff, you were an expert. Instantly. And, oddly, people simply accepted your authority.

Alf became fascinated with people, especially in the area of self-image and self-deception. He spent a lot of time watching them, fascinated with their reactions and rationalizations to all sorts of stimuli. In fact, if there was one thing that Alf did take the time to learn in high school, it was how human beings worked. For one thing, they were all, every single one, unhappy, constantly in turmoil because their world had failed to live up to their expectations.

People knew much more about who they wanted to be than who they actually were. They wanted to live incredible dream lives, but their real lives kept getting in the way. Rare was the person who wasn't trying to cram at least two contradictory worlds into the same life. People would insist on pushing and shoving their lives into directions that the lives themselves had no intention of going. And the people suffered for it. Alf could see it in their eyes.

Once, in the cafeteria at school, an acquaintance, an overweight girl, had confided in Alf that she desperately wanted to be a dancer, but she couldn't stop overeating. Alf, after stealing the desert off of her tray, had informed her that the solution was simple. She must either stop overeating or give up the dream of being a dancer. "I mean *really* give it up," he said. "No hidden desires, no secret hopes, nothing! It has to be completely gone. Erased! The truth is that you're probably never going to stop overeating, anyway, so quit torturing yourself, get rid of the dancing." After this, the girl simply did her best to avoid Alf. She never got any thinner and she never became a dancer.

Alf soon forgot the incident, but not before gleaning a bit of wisdom from it. People were not looking for honest advice, he realized. When he gave them brutally honest advice, they thanked him politely and gleefully continued to torture themselves. They had no interest in being told the truth. They simply wanted their dreams watered and encouraged, regardless of how ridiculous or unlikely the dreams were. Giving up a dream was a big thing, Alf decided. A dream was a huge part of what made people who they were. The person they wanted to be was much more important to them than the person they actually were. It defined them and gave them a sense of direction. Tenuous direction, perhaps, but they seemed to be lost without it.

There were much better odds in getting people to pursue their dreams than in convincing them, for their own good, to give the dreams up. Alf found he could egg people on toward any ridiculous goal they might have in mind and they would lap it up like bums in a soup line. They were actually eager to delude themselves. And then they would thank him profusely, as though he'd done them a great favor.

Alf discovered that he enjoyed pushing people toward unreachable goals. To him, it felt much the same as stealing. The power he exercised gave him an almost sexual thrill. He loved to push people in ridiculous directions and watch as their self-inflicted frustrations mounted and took them over. When they crashed it was like an explosive orgasm for him making him feel superior to his victims and, in his mind, he became the ultimate alpha-male. If that's what they want, he thought, that's what I'll give them - then he'd go somewhere very private and make himself a sugar sandwich.

One day Alf sat drinking a soda and dangling his feet on a low concrete wall near the entrance to his school. He was playing a game that involved making eye contact with random people walking by and cataloging their reactions. Alf wasn't sure why he was passing his time this way. It wasn't an experiment, really, just something he found himself doing. What would people do, he wondered, if he tried to force eye contact with them? Would they turn away, would they glare? It was an interesting question worth pursuing.

The first person to walk toward him was Ingrid Sohndhiem, tall and blonde and untouchable, a beauty of Scandinavian decent. Alf found himself desperately wanting to make eye contact with her. Ingrid, unfortunately, had no desire to make eye contact with Alf, as he owned no football jerseys or fast cars and therefore didn't even register on her radar. When she was a good 50 feet away, his eyes locked on to her down-turned face. He stared viciously, demandingly, powerfully.

Nothing!

Not even a muscle twitch. It was as though he were staring at a movie screen. At 25 feet there was no difference. At 10 feet, still nothing. But, as Ingrid walked past, Alf noticed something unusual. A quick, nervous little blink. Not a full blink, where the eyes close solidly, all the way, more like a fluttery little half blink, as though she were trying to protect her eyes from minor intrusion. He felt his excitement diminish immediately afterward, as though an invisible string that stretched between them had been cut. If the eyes were the windows to the soul, as Alf had read, then Ingrid's widows had just shut firmly against the approach of Alf's soul. Alf didn't really believe in souls as such, but he had definitely felt it…something had died. Very subtle, but it was there. He had felt desire for Ingrid, then the blink, then no desire. Or no, a different type of desire. More like a pining, hopeless desire. All from a little blink.

Alf was disappointed by Ingrid's unspoken rejection, as would be any red-blooded young man. But his disappointment was short-lived. He continued what had indeed become an experiment and discovered that practically everyone reacted in a similar fashion. Even though they rarely looked in his direction, they still seemed to sense Alf trying to make eye contact and pry his way through their windows and into their soul. He would pick a person at random and stare intently at their eyes from some distance. Just as with Ingrid, nothing happened until they were right in front of him, and then they inevitably fluttered their eyelids and he felt the energy die. Male or female, it didn't seem to matter.

Occasionally someone looked straight at him and then snapped their head away quickly, some actually smiled and said hello, but most simply walked by, stared straight ahead and fluttered a little blink. If someone made eye contact, he felt a slight flash of warmth. A small bond was established and the person would have to acknowledge his presence. He found himself referring to these tiny bonds as strings because that's how they felt, like fragile little interpersonal fibers. Alf dubbed the little eyelid flutter 'blinking the strings away'. It was unfailing, every person that didn't make eye contact blinked when they walked by. Alf thought about this for several days, and finally decided that there must be senses beyond the five he'd learned about in biology class.

2004

Time marched on as Xochitl lay motionless in the bathtub with only her nostrils and startling blue eyes above the surface, eyes that grew suddenly round as she realized that the temperature of the water had dropped well below lukewarm. "Oh man, I'm gonna be late," she mumbled through the few remaining suds, "If I don't freeze to death first." Hobbling from the tub, she wrapped a towel around her goose-pimpled body and made a bee-line to her clothes closet, a deep but narrow walk-in affair.

Fifteen minutes later Xochitl St. James emerged from the closet a casual beauty. She wore a short yellow tank top under an open flannel shirt, loose-fitting black denim pants and stylish hiking boots. She checked herself once more in the mirror. Perfect, tough yet fragile. One of the great perks of being a photographer, Xochitl found, was that one's wardrobe was pretty much dependent on one's mood. No uniform required.

The answer machine in Xochitl's cluttered living room showed two messages. She pushed the play button and listened to both. The first was from Xochitl's best friend, Marissa, explaining that she was planning to have coffee at Jitter Central, a local coffee shop, at 9:00 tomorrow morning. Would Xochitl like to join her? The second was from Ernie Blanchard confirming their assignment for that evening. She wrote down the time and place to meet with Marissa and placed it in her pocket.

Photography equipment was scattered haphazardly

throughout the little house. Xochitl rummaged through the piles and gathered up her best camera and lighting gear, placing them into a black duffle bag. She cast a quick glance at the kitchen clock on her way out the door. Seven-fifteen, she might make it, if the traffic was light. She placed the duffle bag carefully into the rear compartment of her 4 Runner and closed the hatch.

It was 7:40 when she entered the building that housed the corporate headquarters of AWARE Magazine. Ernie Blanchard was waiting for her in the lobby, his hands shoved deep into the pockets of his baggy pants, his longish blond hair obscuring a blemish-covered face. He looked lost. "I'm gonna have to take this poor baby by the hand," Xochitl mumbled to herself.

"Hey Ernie," said Xochitl, lifting the duffle bag from her car. "Sorry I'm late."

"Hello Soach," said Ernie, removing his hands from his pockets and pushing the hair from his face. "Don't worry about it, I just got here myself."

Ernie helped Xochitl load her equipment into a company car and they drove out of the parking lot, headed toward the North End section of Soda River.

"Did you get the address?" Xochitl asked. "I left my copy in the pocket of my other pants."

"336 Whitewater," said Ernie mechanically.

"Good. What do you know about this guy?"

"Not a whole lot, other than the fact that he's about to change the course of my partying career. I guess he's here meeting with some prospective manufacturers for his sober pill. The press release didn't say much about his personal life. Only that he lives in Los Angeles and that he developed the pill independently, without any corporate backing. He stands to become a very wealthy man virtually overnight if all goes well for him in the next few days. Most of the big pharmaceutical manufacturers are in on the bidding. Some sort of deal will be struck and life will become permanently better for him and you and me and a couple billion other beer drinkers around the world. I wonder if the pill neutralizes the alcohol before it has a chance to damage your liver. That's an important question, I need to remember to ask him that. Man, Soach, can you imagine just pulling the ultimate all-nighter and then half an hour before work downing one of those pills and showing up stone sober. I'd almost feel guilty. Almost!"

"I think you're a little too into this," said Xochitl, laughing. "Aren't you supposed to be an objective reporter? Maybe you should just stick to the story."

"What do you mean? This is the story. Our own little personal story times about a billion. Everyone who reads about this is immediately going to see a vision of their favorite bar and the last time they had to dig up money for a cab or tried to drive home drunk. People must have felt like this the day they introduced the birth control pill."

"I'm sure men did. Women are still waiting for the male birth control pill that men will actually take when they're supposed to."

"Hey, easy now." Ernie took both hands off the wheel and assumed a defensive position. "I keep a condom in my wallet at all times."

"I bet that thing's been in there for over a year. I bet it doesn't even work anymore."

"Okay, you're on. After the interview, we'll go back to my place and fill it with water. If there's no leaks, you spend the night with me. If there is a leak, we go to your place and I spend the night with you. Fair enough?"

"I wonder if the good doctor has also invented the anti-fantasy pill, because you need one really bad right now. Do you have a photo of this guy? I don't even know what he looks like."

"Yeah, there's one in that folder on the floor by your feet."

Xochitl fished the folder out from between her feet and thumbed through it until she found a couple of photos of Doctor Anthony Sporkin, a black and white head shot and a picture of the doctor standing before a microscope in a small laboratory. "Oh jeez," she said, "he's not the most photogenic guy in the world is he? Looks like I've got my work cut out for me. Fortunately I know a few lighting tricks."

"Oh, that's harsh Soach. Maybe he's got a good looking brain."

"He may very well have the Johnny Depp of brains, but it's his mug I have to shoot. I guess if worse comes to worst I can always manipulate it a bit on the computer. I mean, jeez, look at that schnoz. You'd think the last thing on this guy's mind would be sobering women up. The poor guy's misdirecting his talents - not that I won't take advantage of those talents, of course."

"Of course."

1975

Things calmed down a bit for Chester McFadden once he reached high school. It was only those with a budding career in sadism that continued to tease him. Though there were enough of these about, the numbers were definitely down since elementary school and Junior high. He even made a few friends, acquaintances really, that accepted him as a normal, interesting human being with only a slight physical difference. They often gave him the benefit of the doubt, realizing his condition was nothing but a simple physical deformity. Though due to his timid nature, he still wasn't invited to many parties.

One of his new acquaintances was Elsa Starlighter, a beautiful girl with thick, black, waist-length hair and striking blue eyes. Not a cheerleader or valedictorian, just a girl. Just a beautiful goddess of a girl. Short like him, she was very shapely, with slightly Asian eyes and, he discovered, in some surprising warm and fuzzy way, accessible to him.

She's so open to me. It seems we can talk about anything - history, math... She barely notices the arm at all. Chester was puzzled at her acceptance. He longed to know more about the olive-skinned beauty who was beginning to filter into his thoughts more and more each day. In fact, he was soon driven to know anything and everything about her. He wondered what position she slept in, what she liked to eat, what color her underwear was.

Each afternoon Chester faced a collection of troublesome, immature boys who believed they were older than their years, and who assembled in the restroom between metal shop and Gym. And each day someone had a new story about the girls they'd boffed or porked or rogered. Chester was very nervous using the restroom during their daily pow-wow, feeling like a moving target as soon as he entered. As he stood at the urinal listening, he longed for some stories of his own to tell. He felt wholly inadequate listening to the sordid boasts of conquest by these swaggering, confident boys. Sometimes he was so nervous he couldn't make himself pee. Straining every muscle in his body, he was still unable to produce a single drop. The Stud Club, he called them, and he both hated and envied them.

Elsa, he thought one day as he waited for his urine to flow, *if I'm ever going to have any stories to tell, it'll be with Elsa.*

Facing the mirror in the privacy of his bedroom, Chester fumbled awkwardly with words, trying to generate the perfect line or phrase that would guarantee a positive reaction from Elsa Starlighter. He went through everything he could think of and it all sounded ridiculous. Pointing a finger at the mirror and glaring down the length of his arm into his own eyes he blurted: *You and me are doin' dinner, Baby.* Then, cartoonishly over-cultured: *Wouldst milady carest to sup with me this eve?* They were all forced and insincere. Very un-Chester-like. The problem was that Chester-like was the worst sounding of the lot, involving lots of stuttered words and *uhs* and *ums.* A bunch of confused vultures, circling, with no idea where to land. It was a directionless mess that never really made its point. Perhaps words were not the answer. Perhaps he should pull up to her house in a big, fancy car and nod his head knowingly with one eyebrow raised, his elbow resting firmly on the horn. Except he wasn't quite old enough to drive and he had no big fancy car. One day, surprising Chester completely, it simply slipped out in the cafeteria lunch line "You wanna, maybe go somewhere and, I dunno, do something or something?"

"Sure Chester, let's go to dinner, but do you mind if we bring our math homework? Is that okay? I need some help in that area. Badly"

2004

A slight screeching of tires interrupted the still evening air as Ernie Blanchard spun the company car onto Whitewater Street. "Keep an eye out for 336," he said. It's supposed to be one of those big cedar vacation cabins."

"I wonder why he chose to have his meeting with potential manufacturers in our little town? It seems like L.A. or New York would be much more press-ready."

"From what Trundell told me, he seems to be kind of afraid of the press. He knows that the conservative press will probably denounce him because his pill makes the over-consumption of alcohol penalty-free. Doing the crime without doing the time doesn't sit well with a lot of people. Anyway, he likes AWARE Magazine. He has a subscription and he likes the politics that the magazine represents. He's having the meeting here so that we can be part of the process. He knows we'll present him fairly."

"Oh, oh, there it is...336." Xochitl jabbed her finger at the side window. Startled, Ernie leaned on the brake pedal and the car jerked to a halt. "Back up, pull over," Xochitl barked excitedly.

Ernie glared at Xochitl, brows furrowed, mouth in a doughnut.

"I'm sorry Ernie," she said. "It's just been a long, hard day."

"I guess," said Ernie. "But chill out a bit, though, okay? This is my first big gig and I don't want to blow it. I'll be nervous enough for both of us. You need to stay calm because I'm probably going to need some help from you."

"Jeez, one little slip. I said I was sorry."

"Yes, you did," said Ernie. "I guess I'm just getting nervous already. This interview is what I've been waiting for. I've been working up to this for a long time. If all goes well tonight, it'll be the beginning of a long, rewarding career. If not, it might be my Waterloo."

Two cars occupied the driveway, so Ernie pulled up to the curb in front of the house. Xochitl got out of the car and stretched. Mr. Trundell had said that Sporkin was staying in a cabin, but the word "cabin" was not one she would have applied to the building standing before her. A cabin was a tiny hovel made of logs, with a dirt floor and flap of leather over the entrance. This place was palatial. A beautiful two-story cedar home, three stories if you counted the attic room, with its small balcony window. For all its vastness, the stained wood gave the place a warm, woodsy feel and Xochitl wondered what it would be like to live in this much space. Hell, she could give her cat half the house to roam in and still not have enough furniture to fill the rest. The yard was manicured to perfection with a pathway of heart-shaped flagstones leading from the sidewalk to the front door.

"We should probably go and meet the good doctor first, before we bring all our stuff in," said Xochitl. "We don't want to freak the poor guy out."

"Good idea," said Ernie, slipping on his jacket, finding it upside-down and taking it off again. They walked gingerly along the pathway to the door. Though the curtains were drawn, Xochitl could see that the living room was well lit. On the front stoop she noticed that the door was slightly ajar. She knocked gently, but received no response. She tried again, a little harder. Nothing. This time she rang the doorbell. Silence.

"This is kinda weird," she said, pushing lightly on the door which squeaked open a tiny bit further. She placed her mouth near the opening. "Hello... hello. Doctor Sporkin? Are you home." Turning to Ernie, she said, "This is the right house, isn't it?"

"336 Whitewater."

"And we're on time?"

"Seven thirty."

"P.M.?"

"PM!"

"And he *is* expecting us?"

"Far as I know."

"Look around. Maybe he left us a note."

"I don't see any notes."

"Doctor Sporkin? Hello?" Xochitl pushed the door open all the way. "Hello! We're here from AWARE Magazine. I'm coming in Doctor Sporkin. Don't be alarmed." She stepped into the house and took a quick look around. The place was tidy, only slightly lived-in. The television was off. There was an open book on an oak coffee table in front of a green leather couch. Xochitl thumbed through it, discovering that it was a hardbound notebook. Most of the entries looked like some sort of hand-written computer code, but there were also pages of personal data, addresses, phone numbers, web site URLs. A few pages toward the back contained some badly rendered sketches, mostly of nude women. She closed the book as Ernie walked up behind her.

"What's in the book?" he asked.

"Nothing," she said, "just a bunch of computer stuff and personal stuff. "What's that noise?"

A muted whirring sound permeated the house, emanating from somewhere toward the back. Xochitl gradually realized that it had been in the air all along, but she had only just noticed it. "Come on," she said to Ernie, "He's gotta be here. Help me find him."

1975

Chester was buried in his closet up to his pudgy, lilly-white waist. "What about this?" he mumbled to himself. "Nah, too formal!" *Formal? It's just a homework date...* "Weeeell, not necessarily, it could have potential." *This thing could go further. I can feel it. After all that's the whole point, isn't it? It's not like we're gonna sit around doing homework for the rest of our lives.* "What about this sweatshirt? Hmm...Pink Floyd." *Too Scruffy. I mean scruffy's good, but not for a date...or at least not a first date. Or is it? I don't know, maybe for some dates, but not for an Italian restaurant date.* "No, stupid," smacking the side of his head, "it's a homework date." *Well as of now it's a homework date. But it could turn into something else. It could! Couldn't it?* "Yeah, like what? Marriage? HA!" *I guess it could...lead to that... eventually. Couldn't it? Oh man, I'm getting way ahead of myself.* "Wingtips? Too dressy. Too nerdy, too lame. Jeans? Nah, too common. But maybe that's good." Chester covered his face with his hands. "I'm getting nowhere! Maybe I'll just show up naked and scare the hell out of her from the get-go."

Elsa and Chester met in a small Italian restaurant with checkered tablecloths and wicker covered wine bottles. They munched on bread sticks and passed furtive glances toward each other as they arranged and rearranged their books and papers on the table. The waiter, a sleepy-eyed young Italian man, brought them each water in a squat little glass with crushed ice, two cocktail straws and a cherry.

Elsa's math book went clattering to the floor as Chester

hastily cleared a spot for the glasses. This was his first time alone with someone he had feelings for and it was already obvious that it was not going to go easy for him. His good hand was in his lap, balled into a tight fist so that Elsa wouldn't see it shaking.

What did people talk about when they were alone? Funny, that hadn't occurred to him before now. The normal everyday things seemed out of place here. The surroundings demanded something more. It was strange. He saw this girl every day at school, had spoken to her easily and had even managed to bark out a few witticisms. Yet here, sitting across the table from her in unfamiliar territory his tongue had suddenly grown warts.

She wants to learn about math, well I know all about math. It comes easy to me. I actually enjoy it...God, what a loser. No, not a loser? Was Einstein a loser? Did Einstein ever sit across a table from Elsa Starlighter? What would he have talked about? Math, definitely math, maybe that whole 'playing dice with the universe' thing. But it's so dry, so...cold and bloodless. Still, if that's what she wants to talk about, then that's what we'll have to talk about. Hell, at least it's safe. I can't mess it up too bad.

"So Chester, you seem to be really good at math," said Elsa as though on cue. "Do you enjoy it?"

"Uh, HA! Yeah, yeah! Math is cool," he blurted, "well, not cool...but it has some things, you know, that it does...sort of. Math can do anything, really... well, I guess not anything, you know. I mean you can't move a building or, you know, heh, slaughter a chicken with math, oh hell, heh, where did that come from? Well, there's probably math involved somewhere in slaughtering a chicken, but it's fun, you know, not slaughtering the chicken, heh, the math, and there's all those numbers and stuff."

Elsa frowned slightly and stared at Chester intently.

Chester's eyes were glued to the table, his hand repeatedly wadding a piece of paper into a small, tight ball and then smoothing it out into a flat, wrinkled sheet.

"Yeah...Well, I guess I never really looked at it like that," she said.

"Well, you know, it's just that math is probably the secret of the universe, you know, probably the secret of life or something." *Shit*, he thought, *the secret of life? What an idiot! This is going from bad to worse.* Chester's eyes crossed slightly, glaring downward toward his mouth as it spewed phrases he had no intention of uttering.

Slowly, Chester lifted his gaze from the table and saw Elsa's huge blue eyes staring, inquiringly, at his. The corners of her mouth were turned up in a slight quizzical grin.

Oh Heaven!

"You're acting kinda funny," she said, "Do you like me or something, Chester...? Is that what this is about?"

Oh Hell!

Chester sat helpless, frozen, like an undercover agent who'd just been exposed. He could do nothing but stare into the two captivating eyes before him. Caught like a chubby, lopsided deer in a pair of irresistible headlights. Oceans of bile swooshed in uncomfortable directions all through his knotted, churning insides. What could he say? He hadn't counted on a moment of truth. Not this soon anyway. Sure, he was crazy about her, but you couldn't just go around saying that on the first date. That should come later. Much, much later. The silent stare endured, endlessly, reaching an uncomfortable, not only pregnant, but two weeks overdue, length. It seemed to have taken on a life of its own, and though the pressure was unbearable, neither of them turned away.

Chester felt his blood boil and his self-consciousness reached a critical state. He groped blindly for his water glass. Taking a drink would mask his nervousness a bit and buy him a little time while he maintained the stare and fumbled for a passable answer. He grasped the squat little water glass roughly with his good hand and raised the two cocktail straws to his lips.

By the time he felt one cocktail straw enter each nostril it was too late. Eyes still locked, Chester jerked the glass away from his startled face and discovered that, to his horror, the straws had lodged themselves into his nostrils.

The stare had reached a crisis point. Chester saw the corners of Elsa's eyes grow wide with morbid fascination and the spell was instantly broken. He'd gone from victory to defeat in thirty seconds, albeit an eternal thirty seconds.

Chester panicked. In a last ditch attempt to save face in this now crumbling situation, he began waving his withered arm in front of his face between the two straws and making what he hoped were humorous elephant noises between sputtering, forced laughter. *You can get away with any kind of stupidity if a girl thinks you're doing it on purpose, to be funny. The Stud Club boys said so. I overheard them. After all, stupid has to be better than crazy.*

But when he looked at Elsa's face again, the little smile had vanished. *Crazy it is, then.* Elsa's jaw hung open and her eyes were as round as the cherries in her squat little water glass. *She's not getting the joke. No...see, the straws are tusks and the arm is like the trunk...*It suddenly became clear to Chester that his withered arm flopping all over creation may not appear to Elsa a clever display of animal theater. Indeed it may be disturbing to her, perhaps even frightening.

Panic!

Chester stared transfixed at the little red and white squares on the tablecloth for a few seconds, then rose suddenly from his chair, knocking it over behind him. He bolted through the noisy kitchen, toward the back entrance. The old wooden-framed screen door clattered as he shoved it open, making a bee-line for the dark alley behind the restaurant. But some slovenly restaurant worker had left a cardboard box lying around on the ground directly in his path. Chester's foot jammed into the box and he felt himself spilling forward, head first, into the mouth a round aluminum garbage can. The can was only about half full, or half empty, really, Chester thought briefly, since at present he bore no leanings toward optimism. He plunged in up to his waist. The can, now off-balance, clattered onto its side and rolled over a few times with Chester inside. Frantically, he forced himself to his feet, the can wedged firmly on his upper half, pinning his arms to his sides, and the cardboard box clinging to his shoe. He hobbled, lop-sided and sightless, down the ally.

Elsa ran outside after Chester, looking on helplessly as the little figure thumped and clanged away from her. Something inside caused her to freeze as she opened her mouth to call to him. Oh, poor dear Chester, she thought, he'll feel better if he thinks I didn't see this.

2004

"Xochitl, I'm not staying in here. This is breaking and entering."

"Do you want your interview or not? Show some balls. I definitely want to take these pictures. Besides, we're invited guests. He's expecting us."

Ernie grimaced, stepping hesitantly into the hallway leading to the rear of the house. He glanced around, gritting his teeth. "I don't like this," he said, plunging his hands into his pockets. "I don't like it one bit… What's that noise?"

"I don't know. Let's go check it out," Xochitl said, fixing her eyes on Ernie, daring him not to back out." They walked down the long hallway toward the back of the house, passing a few open doors on the left of the hallway, revealing untouched bedrooms. The last bedroom they passed had recently been used. The bed was unmade and clothes were strewn about the floor. Male and female clothes, Xochitl noted. The noise grew louder as they neared the door at the end of the hallway. Ernie placed his hand on the door, ready to push it open. Suddenly he spun around, back toward the living room as a screeching of tires blasted its way through the open front door behind them.

"What the hell?" Xochitl snapped. She ran back the way they had come and sprinted through the front door just as one of the cars that had been parked in the driveway sped off toward the corner. It slowed briefly, turned right at the corner and was gone out of sight. I hope that wasn't the good Doctor, she thought.

A piercing scream rose from inside the house. Xochitl rushed back into the living room. The scream came again, from the end of the hallway she had just been exploring with Ernie. She darted down the dark hallway, slamming the door open with the palm of her outstretched hand, into a brightly lighted kitchen. Ernie jumped and screamed again. "Man, that's the second time today I've heard one of you guys scream- ing like a little girly-girl," she said, shaking her head in disgust. "What's the world coming to?"

Ernie wasn't laughing. In fact, Ernie didn't move at all. He was staring fixedly at something behind the kitchen island. "What is it Ernie?" she asked loudly, trying to make herself heard over the incessant whirring noise, also coming from be- hind the kitchen island. "What's wrong?"

"The...the Doctor," Ernie stuttered, just loud enough for Xochitl to understand the words. "The Doctor." He pointed limply in the direction of the whirring noise. Then his eyes rolled up in his head as he collapsed to the floor in a faint.

Xochitl scrambled to help Ernie. She rounded the kitchen island and halted in her tracks. "Holy shit!" she barked. Ernie had fallen on top of the prone body of Doctor Anthony Sporkin. Sporkin lay in a crumpled heap on the floor. His right arm raised above his head, was jammed up to the elbow into the pitcher of a whirring blender.

There were little red spots of blood on the walls. Thousands of them! But the floor ... the floor was covered with huge gloppy pools of the stuff. There were bone chips scattered throughout the oozing mess. The entire side of the kitchen is- land was painted with the dark red of Sporkin's blood. Xochitl began to feel queasy, herself. She placed her hand on the drain- ing board for balance, then looked up at the ceiling and took a few deep breaths. "Calm down, Xochitl," she whispered. "Az- tecs are not supposed to be bothered by blood." after a moment she grabbed a drawer handle for support, squatting down, fa- cing the prone figures. She placed her hand on Ernie's shoulder and shook gently.

"Ernie?" she said, her voice shaking. "Ernie, are you okay?" His eyes began to flutter slightly and his lips moved, but his words could not be heard over the rasping whir of the blender. "Goddamit!" she shouted jabbing a finger at the off button on the blender. The silence was deafening.

Ernie's lips moved again. "Call the police," he said. Even in the sudden stillness, Xochitl had trouble understanding his words. "Call the police," he said a little louder, and then he turned his head and vomited.

Xochitl sprang to her feet, searching about for a phone. She spied one hanging on the wall next to the back door. Hurrying across the slick floor toward it, her feet went out from under her and she fell to her hands and knees. She crawled to the wall and grabbed the doorknob, pulling herself up. Snatching the receiver off its hook she stabbed in the numbers, 911 with a bloody finger.

"COME ON!" she screamed when there was no answer. Suddenly, she became aware that the phone was producing no sound at all, not even a dial tone. Dropping the receiver, she ran through the door, down the hallway and into the living room, where she remembered seeing a phone on a small decorative table by the front door as they entered. Xochitl picked up the receiver and placed it to her ear. As she suspected, this one was dead, also. She sat down heavily on the couch for a moment, breathing deeply, collecting her thoughts. Picking the notebook up from the coffee table, Xochitl tore out a few pages, wiping the blood from her hands with the torn sheets. She wadded them up and, stuffed them in her pocket. For the second time that day Xochitl tried to control her panic.

A few slow, deep breaths calmed her nerves a bit. With her new-found clarity, however, came the smell of blood. She hadn't really been aware of it before. She rubbed her temples with her fingertips. "Come on, think!" she said. Suddenly she remembered passing a gas station on the way in, only a few blocks away, just before they had turned onto Whitewater Street. There had to be a pay phone there. All gas stations had pay phones, didn't they? "I'll be back in a couple of minutes, Ernie," she called shakily down the hallway.

1961

After high school Alf hadn't the desire, nor the economic resources, to tackle another four years of academic life. Instead, after much thought, he decided to relocate himself to Los Angeles, which he fancied would equal any formal education in both quantity and quality of learning experiences. His departure from home came without fanfare. "You'll be back," his father grumbled. "They'll eat you alive down there."

Once he arrived in the City of Angels, it didn't take Alf long to understand that his small town upbringing hadn't even begun to prepare him for the emotional meat grinder that was L.A. Here, no one harbored a secret dream. Dreams were worn on the sleeve. Everything was out in the open. Embarrassingly so. There were no qualms about saying you were going to be the next Richard Burton or Elizabeth Taylor. But, Alf noticed, if you wanted these things taken seriously, you announced your intentions with complete, unshakable confidence, as though it were already a done deal and Dick and Liz just hadn't heard the news yet. This was a solid, unbreakable Los Angeles tradition, a rule really, and it was strictly enforced from the lowliest gaffer to the producer on-high.

Even the most basic of Hollywood paeans took some mildly interesting aspect of their life and blew it way the hell up into a huge production number. The object of this omnipresent game was to be higher up the food chain than everyone else in your social circle by presenting a more convincing facade than they had. Though not a strict rule, the facade was nearly always about the film industry. Everyone in town, it seemed, had something, no matter how tenuous to do with the film industry. If you walked a certain movie star's dog, you were higher on the scale than, say, simply having delivered something to that movie star's house. With each new rank came a certain privilege of recognition and standing.

Alf quickly learned as much about the Hollywood caste system as he could. Everyone was apparently trying to attain some sort of 'next level' like in the Free Masons or one of those wacky Eastern religions Alf had read about. Eternal struggle seemed to be the name of the game. Even the most famous movie stars were treading water as fast as they could, albeit with unwavering confidence, in order to retain their positions at the top. They were only as good as their last picture and there was nowhere for them to go but down.

2004

The front door banged hard against the stained cedar wall as Xochitl threw it open and dashed out into the night. Jogging had never been a passion with her, but she could keep a steady pace if she had to. And now she had to. The hiking boots she wore were heavy and stiff on her feet, designed for endurance, not speed. She soon began to grow tired, feeling the lactic acid ache in her thighs. The corner came sooner than expected and she cut through someone's front yard onto Fisherman's Way. The gas station was visible, but it seemed to be farther away than she had remembered. A large lighted sign out front looked to be about five blocks down the road. Xochitl stumbled, but caught herself, finally slowing to a walk in order to catch her breath.

An elderly woman approached, arms encircling a cloth bag full of groceries. The woman gaped in astonishment at Xochitl. "Oh my," she gasped, and raised her hands to cover her mouth, releasing the bag. Fruit spilled out onto the sidewalk and Xochitl instinctively bent to pick it up. "Don't hurt me," the old woman said quietly. "Please don't hurt me."

"What?" Shaking her head, it suddenly dawned on Xochitl that she was covered in Doctor Sporkin's blood. She rose to her feet, dropped the fruit and continued running. The gas station was only a block away now, and she forced herself to keep running, though the ache in her thighs was becoming unbearable. At the station, the lone pay phone was in use by a man wearing a denim jacket and tan workman's boots. His tattooed hand pressed the receiver against his pierced ear.

"Look, Baby, I was wrong. I admit that."

Xochitl tapped the man on the shoulder. "Excuse me, sir. This is an emergency. Can I use the phone?"

The man ignored Xochitl. He continued to talk without so much as turning his head to see who was addressing him. "Listen, Baby, she didn't mean a thing to me. Okay? I was just caught up in the moment. You know how it is. You were a stripper, for crissakes. You should understand. It was just one of those things that just happen."

"Sir, I really need to use the phone," Xochitl said, tapping the man on the shoulder again.

"Just a minute, Baby," the man said into the receiver. He remained hunched over the pay phone, but this time turned his head to one side. "Look, lady, you can use the damn phone when I'm done with it. Okay? Now take a hike."

Xochitl grabbed the man by the sleeve and tugged hard, pulling him around to face her. "I said it's an emergency," she yelled. "Do you understand? Does that make sense to you?"

The man's eyes flew open wide as he saw the blood on Xochitl's hands and clothes. He dropped the receiver and backed away. "Whoa! I'm sorry, man. It's all yours. You okay?"

"Yeah, I'm fine. It's not my blood."

A small, tinny voice came from the phone receiver, "Who are you talking to? Who's there with you? I give up. You can't even apologize without hitting on somebody else. You're pathetic, Greg."

Xhochitl picked up the receiver, "It's not what you think. He'll call you back in a little bit," she said and hung up the phone. She dialed 911 and right away a voice came on the line.

"There's been a murder," Xochitl squawked without listening to the voice on the other end of the line.

"Calm down, ma'am," said a soothing female voice. "What is your name?"

"Xochitl Saint James."

"Where are you located?"

"I'm at a gas station on Fisherman's Way, but that's not

where the murder happened. I'm just here to use the phone."

"What is the location of the incident?"

"It's at 336 Whitewater. You need to send someone over there right away."

"Do you know what happened to the victim?"

"No, I just came across the murder scene. I have to get back. My friend is passed out in the house."

"Who is your friend?"

"Ernie Blanchard. We work for AWARE Magazine."

"Uh huh, I see. And do you know the victim?"

"No, not really. I know who he is. It's Doctor Sporkin, the man who invented the sober pill."

"The what?"

"The sober pill. You take this pill when you've been drinking and a little while later your sober again."

The person on the line was silent for a moment. "No kidding?"

"Yeah, I know. Crazy huh?" said Xochitl with some urgency. "But we need someone to come out there right away. I don't know why it didn't occur to me earlier, but the murderer might still be in the house. Poor Ernie, he's there all by himself."

"Alright Ma'am, someone will be there shortly."

"Okay, thanks. I gotta get back there."

"It might be best to avoid going into the house."

"I have to. Ernie's in there. I think he's unconscious, he can't take care of himself."

The woman on the line uttered some type of protest, but Xochitl hung up the phone and began walking back toward the house. Running would have been a better idea, she thought, but she was exhausted and a growing sense of dread caused her to drag her feet a little. The vision of Doctor Sporkin's body with it's arm jammed into the whirling, rasping blender returned again and again like an obnoxious party guest that wouldn't go home. The whole night was taking on a hazy, surreal quality and she wanted nothing more than to be laying, once again, in her bathtub with her cat, Weezy, stretched out on the rim.

1975

The hot water felt soothing as the shower pounded Chester's rigid body. He sat in the stall and held his head in his good hand. His squat little back pressed against the smooth tiles as the searing stream washed over him. Fifteen minutes under the rushing torrent and he could still smell the fetid stench of garbage clinging to his skin. Forcing himself from the shower, he staggered to his bed and lay naked and still, in a fetal position.

Chester's muted television stared at him from the darkened room, a huge, square eye mocking him with visions of lovely women and healthy-looking men engaging each other effortlessly. He unfocussed his eyes and the screen took on a distant, hazy quality. He was lulled by the movement of shapeless forms on the screen. Chester remained in this position for hours and, at some point, drifted into a light slumber.

Later, as he faded back into the waking world, Chester felt a mild annoyance with a stark blue glow his room had taken on. It was coming from the television, he discovered, late-night infomercial programming. There was a lot of yellow text scrolling upward through a bright blue background. It was traveling a little faster than he was able to comprehend in his semiconscious state. The scene switched to a handsome middle-aged man with a thick shock of shiny, graying hair and a powerful, square jaw, dressed in a well-tailored suit. The man was seated on a stool in front of a small enthusiastic audience. Behind him on a smooth blue and gray, corporate-looking wall, in large gold letters were the words; **YOU CAN DO IT! ANY-ONE CAN!!** An attractive young woman sitting next to the man occasionally turned toward him and spoke. She bore a slight resemblance to Elsa, so Chester, grunting, extended his leg and turned up the volume knob with his toes.

"Anything, Doctor Banders?" the woman asked.

"Anything, Cindy. Anything from the mundane to the impossible. You can accomplish anything you want to in this world if you believe in yourself strongly enough and use as much of your brain as you possibly can. And my book, "ANY-ONE CAN!!" will show you the simple steps you must take in order to achieve complete, unwavering confidence and superior mental and physical power. There isn't anything you can't do if you believe in yourself strongly enough, Cindy. I can't stress that enough." Dr. Banders pinched the bridge of his nose, then turned and faced Cindy. His face grew earnest and sincere. "Tell me, Cindy, if you could have *anything*, I mean if you could have the *one* thing in the world that would make your life a better place to live, what would that one thing be?"

"Well gosh, Doctor Banders," said Cindy, eyes wide, a finger on her lips, "I guess I'd have to say ...financial independence." Financial independence was phrased like a question.

"You can do it! Anyone can."

"Really? Me?"

"Yes, you, Cindy, and millions of other Americans just like you." Doctor Banders turned toward the camera. "Stay tuned while Cindy gives you the information you need to order ANY-ONE CAN! by Doctor Robert Austin Banders." He flashed a toothy, clench-jawed grin, holding it until the scene faded.

Once again the blue screen appeared. This time the yellow type was stationary and the brightness of the letters made Chester's television emit a loud annoying buzz. They spelled out an address. Cindy's bubbly voice was superimposed over the yellow lettering. Both were telling Chester how he could purchase Doctor Banders's groundbreaking book, ANYONE CAN!.

1961

It didn't take long, following his arrival in Los Angeles, for Alf to obtain a job as a short order cook. He applied for various positions at several places and succeeded finally at a shiny little street corner diner called Roolie's. It was obvious to Alf right from the start of his very first day that he was going to need a friend on the inside. Preparing anything more complicated than a sugar sandwich was a complete mystery to him. He had only chosen the job because it seemed like an easy catch, the type of high turnover job everyone took when they first arrived in LA.

Alf had bluffed his way into the job, using his tried and true method of facts and fluff and of course, right away there were difficulties. Being a short order cook was a very fast-paced job and there wasn't much time for a learning curve. Alf was expected to hit the pavement running.

Roolie's had only one waitress and a few waiters per shift. On Alf's first shift the waitress was a tall, sultry, auburn haired beauty with torn stockings and large breasts. Her bright red name tag read: Jessica. During the shift he attempted several times to make eye contact with her, but failed as she continuously blinked the strings away. She placed her tickets on the clip for Alf to read and focused blankly on the wall behind him. Standing at the order window, Alf ran his eyes over her shapely body, starting with her petite shoes and working his way up to the thick, auburn hair framing her exquisite Hollywood face. As his gaze reached her eyes, so dark he could barely discern iris from pupil, she blinked. She blinked the strings away and Alf felt a sudden void where only moments before he had been under the impression he was building a subtle bridge.

After hours of trying to force eye contact, Alf finally gave it up. He would just have to fake this cooking thing on his own and hope that no one died in the process

2004

Xochitl, lost in thought as she approached the rented residence of Doctor Sporkin, was suddenly jolted alert by activity in front of the house. Several men in dark clothing were hefting what appeared to be a couple of large, elongated plastic bags into a waiting van. They looked like the type of body bags Xochitl had seen on the news, but she couldn't be sure in the dark. Perhaps the woman whose clothes Xochitl had discovered had been murdered, also. Her first thought was to approach the men carrying the bags and tell her story, but a sudden instinctual tingling stopped her.

Something didn't seem right.

How strange, there were no flashing lights, no police cars, and medical people always used some sort of stretcher or gurney, even if the patient was already dead. These guys were just carrying the bags by the ends. The van didn't seem to be an ambulance, either. It looked to be a dark purple color, like no ambulance Xochitl had ever seen. And no flashing lights on top. Xochitl hung back and observed from the shadows. The scene was all wrong somehow. It certainly didn't look as though things were being done by the book.

The van pulled slowly away from the curb and drove silently down the street, leaving only one man standing on the sidewalk. As Xochitl watched, a large tow truck rounded the corner onto Whitewater Street and pulled up in front of the company car that Xochitl and Ernie had arrived in. The truck was the same dark purple as the van that had just departed, and a small yellow happy face was displayed on the door along with the words: Smiley's Towing. Again, there were no flashing lights. In fact, the only light at all came from the headlights of the tow truck. The driver turned his engine off and got out of the cab. The man on the sidewalk approached him casually and for a few moments the two spoke in mumbles and whispers as they attached Xochitl's company car to the tow truck. When they had finished, the two men climbed into the cab of the truck and drove off.

Xochitl watched in mute shock as the car containing all of her best photography equipment disappeared down White-water Street. She nearly called out to them angrily, but her instincts once again told her to keep to the shadows. She was confused. Why had they taken the company car? Surely Ernie would have told them that he and Xochitl would need it. And speaking of Ernie, where was he? He should be up and about by now. But the house was in darkness. All the lights had been turned off and it seemed unlikely that the men had come and gone, leaving Ernie unconscious on the kitchen floor. Perhaps he had been taken away in an ambulance while Xochitl was at the gas station. She mulled through various explanations, but none of them quite fit the little bit of evidence she had. A sense of dread engulfed her as she crept toward the darkened house.

The front door knob stayed in Xochitl's hand for a full minute before she worked up the nerve to turn it. It was still unlocked and the door squeaked open into the unlit living room. A few seconds passed before her eyes adjusted to the moonlight glowing through the windows. The living room looked much as it had earlier, except that everything was a bit more orderly. The darkness felt disturbingly normal, as though the occupants had simply straightened up a bit, turned off the lights and gone to bed. She picked up the phone by the door and listened. A healthy dial tone droned into her ears, mocking her.

"This is weird," she mumbled, "and getting weirder." She dragged her fingers along the wall, feeling her way down the hallway. Xochitl pushed open the kitchen door glancing furtively inside. The kitchen was nearly as dark as the rest of the house, but the white walls provided a little reflective moonlight. It was enough light to see that the kitchen was spotless. Not a drop of blood remained. Come to think of it, even her bloody footprints were missing from the carpet in the hallway and living room. Had she stumbled into the wrong house? No. It had to be the same one. The furniture was identical, as was the art on the walls. A powerful, involuntary shiver traveled through Xochitl, from her core to her extremities. "Ernie," she whispered, then louder, "Ernie, where are you? Are you alright?"

The body of Doctor Sporkin had disappeared. For a moment Xochitl entertained the thought that the doctor wasn't dead after all, that perhaps he had simply gotten up and walked away. But that was ridiculous, and what of the thick puddle of blood that had been here, deep enough to make her slip and fall. No one could survive that kind of blood loss. No, the doctor was definitely dead, but who had killed him and what had happened to his body? Obviously the men in the van had taken it, but where to, and for what purpose? She looked closer, concentrating in the dim light, examining every detail she could make out. The floor and walls had been wiped clean of blood. In fact they were spotless. It was as though they had been scoured clean. "How is this possible?" she said to herself. "I wasn't gone more than thirty minutes."

A cold creepiness wrapped its fingers about Xochitl once again and she had the urge to run. If only Ernie were there with her. The whole thing would be so much less serious. He may be over his head in a threatening situation like this, but at least, they could hold hands and be terrified together. Where was Ernie? He obviously hadn't driven away in the company car. Perhaps he'd recovered his senses and bolted out the back door when the men from the black van showed up. She could only hope.

And what if someone else was still in the house? It was possible, maybe even likely. Not Ernie though. If Ernie had run, the chances of his having run further into the house were pretty much nil. Ernie was easily frightened, he would run to safety, and that meant outside.

Xochitl slipped out the back door and disappeared into the shadows of the alley behind the house. Crouching between a fence and a garbage can, she waited another twenty minutes, but the house showed no signs of life. The police had never arrived. A black and white had driven through the alley and slowed as the officer gave the house a once-over. But it hadn't stopped.

Xochitl nearly stood up to flag the policemen down, but her instinct told her she should remain hidden until someone got out of the car and showed some real interest in the house. Her story would sound ridiculous with no body to show them. Without even a blood stain, for that matter, except for the stains on her clothes and hands. She would appear to be the guilty party, though without a body there was technically no crime.

The police car had driven to the end of the alley and disappeared around the corner. Xochitl was unsure whether she was relieved or disappointed. She needed time to think. One last look around and she slunk cautiously out of the alley and began the long walk across town, through the shadows of the tree-lined streets, toward the promising safety of her house.

Once she had put some distance between herself and the murder scene her whole body began to relax and she breathed a sigh of relief. Nearly an hour later the relaxation turned to fatigue. The muscles in her thighs ached and her back had no strength to hold her up. The few hours spent on the little stone ledge the previous afternoon had taken its toll. Every muscle in her body had been strained, and though she had felt all right immediately afterward, it was beginning to tell on her now.

The evening, surreal enough already, began to take on a dreamlike quality. Had the murder actually happened? Had the body really disappeared and the house been sanitized? It just didn't seem like enough time had elapsed for all of that to have happened. Was it possible she had blacked out between the gas station and the house? No, there was no sense of missing time, only of too many events in too short of period.

1961

At Roolie's Diner Jessica had been secretly watching Alf in the kitchen and had seen him fumbling badly. He was trying to figure things out as he went, that was obvious. Alf was a better-than-average looking guy, she decided, and, God knows she needed some distraction in her life after Robert. Against her better judgment, she decided to bail him out. She scribbled a list of definitions for all the abbreviations of the various menu items on the back of a blank check and slid past him in the kitchen, quietly slipping it into his shirt pocket. Afterward her body language softened and she became much more amiable, introducing herself as Jessica Coolwater.

Alf learned on his first day in the restaurant business, that people were always touching one another. At first he mistook it for affection, but soon noticed that everyone was doing it. No employee ever walked by another employee without touching them in some way. There would be a light hand on the back, a soft squeeze on the arm, a brushing of breasts across the bicep, or a little pat on the butt, anything to let someone know that someone else was walking by them, probably with a full tray. What a godsend! Alf considered it permission and had no problem sliding his hands around Jessica's waist and spinning her around to face him at the end of his very first day.

"Thanks Jessica," said Alf. "You know, you really saved my ass there. It's kinda been a while since I did this type of work, and well, I'm a little rusty."

"Oh, cut the shit, hayseed, you've never done this kind of work in your life."

Alf flushed bright red. "Well, I did some stuff back home, but we do things differently there."

"Look, you don't have to lie to me. I don't own the place and I don't know you from Adam," said Jessica. "I'm not even a waitress, not really. I'm an actress. I'm just acting like a waitress."

Alf had no reply.

"It's like this," she said. "I'm going to be the next Elizabeth Taylor, you know, but I'm just not quite there yet. Meanwhile I've gotta eat and pay the rent just like everyone else. That's why I'm here. See, I just come here every day and act like a waitress. Look at these customers. Every one of them brings a little bit of their lives with them when they come in for dinner. So I find myself in, maybe, thirty situations a night that call for my acting skills. I walk into thirty little lives. Someone's dog died, I'm trying to keep my tears out of their food; someone has a baby, I'm their best friend, ecstatic at their good fortune. I can't contain myself. Honey, even Elizabeth Taylor didn't get that kind of training. I'm getting better every day and, on top of that, it pretty much pays my bills. And you, Darlin', need to learn to act like a cook."

"Well, I'm trying. Actually, I thought I did pretty good today for knowing nothing at all."

"Honey, you shat. You wouldn't still be here if I hadn't been helping you out all night. You have no idea how many customers I had to console. Look, why don't you come over to my place after we get off, and I'll show you the basics of cooking."

1975

On the day following his date with Elsa Starligher, Chester encountered her in the hallway at school. He made a clumsy attempt to duck into a nearby classroom, but wasn't quick enough. It was too late. She had spotted him. "Chester, why did you run away last night? You just left me there. Did I say something wrong? I felt deserted. I needed help in math and now I don't know what I'm gonna do. I have a test today and I don't know if I'm gonna pass. Here, you left your book at the restaurant."

Chester fumbled his math book away from her, staring down at his feet. "I'm an idiot," he said.

"You're not an idiot! You're a smart guy. You just need to calm down. Don't get so nervous."

Chester stared at the floor. "Just look at me," he said, displaying his withered arm. "Wouldn't you be nervous if you were out with a really pretty girl and you had this thing hanging off your shoulder?"

Elsa stood silently for a moment, then, leaning toward him, said, "You really think I'm pretty, Chester?" A tiny smile formed at the corners of her mouth. "Maybe we should have dinner again someday soon. Just promise me you won't get so nervous." She gave him a tender peck on the cheek and walked away.

That afternoon at school Chester was dancing on clouds when he entered the restroom. As he watered the porcelain, the usual stories of conquest echoed off the ancient tiled walls.

Someone had dorked a cheerleader, someone else had hosed the head of the debate team. Dorked? Hosed? What the hell was that? Were they making up words as they went along?

"Hey, Crab," one of the boys said, "Did I really see that smokin' little Elsa kiss your sorry ass?"

Chester stiffened as he realized that for the first time he was being addressed directly by a member of the stud club. He stared rigidly at his feet. "No," he mumbled defiantly "she kissed my face."

"Sorry man, I couldn't tell the difference." The boy approached Chester and with his index finger lifted Chester's chin until they were in direct eye contact. Chester's eyelids fluttered furiously. "What's the story with you two? You in luuuv? She develop a taste for seafood?"

Chester was quiet, both frightened and hurt, but soon the two feelings coalesced into a steamy anger. "She said she wants me to...to porp her," he said defiantly.

"To what?"

"Porp her, you know? I mean she really wants me to ploop her."

"Ploop? She wants you to ploop her?

"Yeah."

"What is ploop?"

"You know ...it's ah ... you know."

Laughter.

Stares.

He ran.

2004

At the corner of Fourth street and Trout, in the town of Soda River, there was a large, tree-filled city park with a semi-paved path running through it from east to west, terminating two blocks from Xochitl's house. She greeted the path warmly, like an old friend and took comfort in the familiar medley of fragrances from the trees and bushes, a welcome contrast to the ghastly events of her night so far. In the middle of the park, surrounded by regal, ancient oaks, there stood a stately old gazebo made of redwood slats and painted a sickly bluish green. Some city planner must have gotten a deal on the paint, she thought.

Xochitl wearily climbed the steps and sat herself down cross-legged on the floor of the gazebo. She pulled a small wad of copal, an Aztec ritual incense, and a hand-made cigar from the pocket of her flannel shirt. She lit the cigar and puffed heavily until the smoke surrounded her head. She hated the smell, associating it more with overstuffed businessmen than the spiritual protection she was seeking. But her mother had always told her that the smoke would shield her from the dark spirits of Talocan, the Aztec underworld, to whom she felt particularly vulnerable tonight. Picking up the small piece of copal, she lit it with the smoldering cherry at the end of her cigar and placed it on the wooden floor of the gazebo. Breathing its vapor, she began to hum a tune, more growl than melody, a prayer beseeching the dark spirits to stay away. Xochitl wasn't even sure she believed in dark spirits, but right now she was very much in need of comfort. With the lattice of the gazebo protecting her from view, she curled herself around the little smoking ball and closed her eyes. "Just for a minute," she mumbled. "Just for a minute."

1961

Alf Sedgwick followed Jessica to her apartment after work and didn't leave until the next morning. He learned a little bit about acting like a short order cook that night, but he learned a whole lot more about how to get by in Hollywood.

Alf began seeing Jessica regularly. At her urging, he attended a few auditions for small parts in feature films. The audition process was a learning adventure for Alf. Each audition taught him a little more, usually about what not to do. He soon became fascinated with the audition process and decided to make a regular activity of it. Sort of a hobby.

Getting a part in a film didn't really interest Alf all that much. It was just a necessary sort of report card reflecting his abilities. His true goal involved successfully convincing people that he was something he was not. He wanted to be able to speak with absolute confidence like the people around him. The auditions were simply a proving ground, although, he wouldn't turn down a good role if his abilities won it for him. It was as quick a way to the top as any, it just wasn't the only way. Nor did Alf feel unqualified for the job. No one he met seemed to possess any better credentials for acting than did he. In fact, no one seemed to have any credentials at all. So, if Alf could get there without doing too much work, why not? Why not him, Alf Sedgwick, screen idol?

After perhaps, 50 auditions without a solid bite (other than a small role as a homosexual librarian in an independent film), Alf was beginning to doubt his abilities to appear as something he was not. Discouragement set in and he began to actually want a part in a film. "These bastards are all alike," he complained to Jessica. "It's always somebody's son or nephew that gets the part." Eventually, being no one's son or nephew, he simply resolved to work with more enthusiasm. Perhaps he wasn't pretending hard enough. He must not be convincing. He certainly wasn't convincing the film producers he came in contact with.

"I think you need to do something with that name," said Jessica one evening as they sat around her apartment playing poker and polishing off a bottle of the best wine they could afford on their meager restaurant wages. She was wrapped in a light blue flannel bathrobe, wearing fuzzy pink slippers sporting the phrase, 'Welcome to Hollywood' on the toes.

"What, my name? What's wrong with my name?" He sounded hurt.

"Well, it's not bad...It's just kinda, mmmm, I don't know. I guess not very powerful-sounding."

"You thought it was okay when you invited me home after my first day at work."

"Nah, not really. I didn't really like it even then. I just thought you were kinda cute. And you were new in town, an easy catch."

Alf sat in silence. "Sooo," he said finally, "what would you have me change my not-very- powerful-sounding name to ... Your Highness?"

"I don't know," she said, ignoring the barb. "It's not like you have to change the whole thing. Maybe just the Alf part would do it."

"What's wrong with the Alf part?"

"I don't know. Maybe it sounds a little too much like Alfalfa, you know, from the Little Rascals."

"It's Alphonse," he said indignantly.

"Oh yeah, right, that's much better," she giggled.

"So you don't like the Alf part, huh? Okay, so, maybe Rocky Sedgwick, or Killer Sedgwick, or what about President Sedgwick?"

"President Sedgwick has a nice ring to it," she said. "It sounds kinda regal or something."

"I was just kidding. I'm not going to have people calling me President Sedgwick. I'd be explaining myself wherever I went. I mean, if I got elected president of the United States or the Screen Actors Guild or something, that would be different because everyone would already be calling me President. But to just come right out and call yourself President is just asking for trouble."

"How about Austin?" he asked.

"Austin?"

"Yeah. Austin Sedgwick."

"It sounds like it should be the third."

"Third what?"

"You know, like Austin Sedgwick the third," she said with a posh English accent. "It's kinda stuffy, but if you want to play those kind of character roles, I guess it's okay. Can't you just see it as the credits roll up? Chones the Butler, dot dot dot, Austin Sedgwick the Third. Yeah, I guess I do kinda like it."

Alf suddenly disliked the name intensely. He had come to Hollywood to become *someone*. This was one of the major power centers of the country, perhaps even the entire world, and he was, by God, going to be someone powerful before he left. If your name was big in Hollywood, there was a good chance the whole world knew who you were. Alf didn't want the whole world to know that Chones the butler was played by Austin Sedgwick the Third.

"No," he said. "It's just not going to work."

"Why not?" she asked, obviously disappointed.

"Well, look at your name. Jessica Coolwater. It's perfect, for crying out loud! It says: I'm a beautiful, sultry, mysterious woman. And then, when people meet you in person, what do you know? You *are* a beautiful, sultry, mysterious woman. I don't even want to know what your real name is, because it couldn't sum you up nearly as well as Jessica Coolwater.

"Jessica Coolwater *is* my real name," she said. "I guess I got kinda lucky."

"Yeah, Kinda."

Jessica sat in silence for a while. Alf was not a nice guy and she knew it. That was okay with her, she didn't like nice guys. They were too boring, too predictable. Gimme a bad boy. The badder the better! But once in a while she wanted a little romance. Alf had just said something kind of romantic, probably an accident, probably wasn't even aware of it, but what the hell, it made her feel warm. She tilted her head down slightly and stared up at him with sultry bedroom eyes, the lids half closed. She wasn't blinking the strings away. Not even close! Rising sensuously from her chair, she moved slowly, deliberately toward Alf.

Even through his wine induced fog, Alf knew he was about to get lucky.

Jessica lightly kicked off her slippers and let her bathrobe fall to the ground. She brought her wine glass to her lips and took a gentle sip. Then she kissed him and he felt the tangy taste of wine enter his mouth from hers. He became aroused and, wrapping his arms around her, pulled her to him. For a few awkward moments they both fumbled with his clothes. He lifted her off the ground and placed her roughly on the card table. Poker chips and cards clattered to the linoleum floor. Alf had never been big on foreplay so he entered her right away and began thrusting powerfully. Her head hung over the edge of the table and her hair, nearly reaching the floor, flopped back and forth like an auburn theater curtain.

"Oh, Robert," she moaned.

Somewhere in the back of his mind, Alf could sense something wrong. He was much too overcome with passion at the moment to understand what it was, but definitely something was there, nipping at his concentration like a spiteful puppy. During one particularly powerful thrust, the flimsy card table gave up its rickety ghost and went crashing to the floor, with Jessica on top of it and Alf on top of Jessica.

Alf scrambled to his feet, dazed, shaking his head three or

four times until his vision cleared. Then he stared down at Jessica, who lay in a confused heap on the floor. "Who's Robert?" he asked.

"Robert? Oh, Robert," she said nervously. "Robert is... you...Robert Austin Sedgwick. I was just trying it on for size. I kinda like it, don't you?"

"Yeah, it's okay." He knew she was lying.

Jessica had indeed been thinking of someone else during their brief and desperate lovemaking. Robert Tornau, a producer, had been Jessica's former live-in lover and lately she had felt the desire to see him again. She missed him. He had a lot of money to throw around and he didn't ask too many questions. Robert Tornau knew how to show a girl a good time. Unfortunately, he had dumped her for a buxom horse groomer a few weeks before she had met Alf.

"Look, Baby, I gotta go," Alf said, pulling on his pants. "I just remembered something I gotta do."

"Now? What do you have to do at this time of night?"

"Just...you know... something," he said, backing out the door with his shoes in his arms. The door clicked shut and Alf strolled down the stairs, pausing on the last step to put on his shoes.

Alf never returned to Jessica's place after that night. He was done with her. She had served her purpose. Alf was now an experienced short-order cook. He could get a job anywhere. But he did decide to keep the name. Robert Austin Sedgwick would look great on a theater marquee. Whoever Robert actually was, Alf offered up a mumbled prayer of thanks.

2004

A thin beam of sunlight wiggled its way through the gently swaying trees and played on Xochitl's closed eyelids. Half awake, she tried to brush it away, as if it were a persistent insect. Slowly, and with great effort, she began to pry her eyes open. She was greeted with a bright, sunny morning, filtered through the checkerboard lattice of the gazebo. Stiffness gripped her joints as she struggled to sit up, but still she felt somewhat rested. Off in the distance a gas powered leaf blower performed its morning duty, rousing the neighborhood. The faint smooth hum hypnotized Xochitl and as her eyelids grew heavy once again, she felt herself leaning to one side. Slumber was about to swallow her when the events of the previous night whooshed into her head like helium into a dime store balloon. She bolted upright; eyes wide open.

Startled by her own recollections, Xochitl examined her hands and clothes to see if she had been dreaming. Dried blood assured her she had not. It was a long way across the park and an even longer way from the park to her house and Xochitl began to worry about being noticed. Walking the two blocks home incognito was going to be tricky. Not that she had done anything wrong, but she was very confused about the events of the previous evening. Until that was cleared up it would be a good idea to remain as inconspicuous as possible. But what to do about the clothes?

Xochitl could see the majority of the park from the platform of the gazebo and being still early, could tell that for the most part it was deserted. The only significant movement was from the man with the leaf blower who was a good city block away. A small, algae filled stream winding through the park gave Xochitl an idea. The stream was no more than a trickle, really, but it was flowing enough to accomplish what she had in mind.

Hopping from stone to stone along the creek bed, she found a place where the foliage was dense enough to afford some shelter, should anyone enter the park. Quickly removing her tank top and shirt, she soaked them in the cold, early-morning water. As she kneaded the fabric between her thumb and forefinger the stream began to run a pinkish-red. Gradually, the stains began to fade, but they were too firmly set in the fabric to disappear entirely.

Eventually the water ran clear once again, but the stains were still noticeable. Kneeling by the stream Xochitl had unintentionally ground the soft dark mud into the knees of her pants. It looks awful, she thought, but it does wonders for the bloodstains. She began to rub mud into the flannel shirt. When the shirt was thoroughly filthy she put it on, then she wadded up the tank top and placed it in her pocket.

On the way home Xochitl shared the sidewalk with a few joggers and dog-walkers, but thankfully her path was relatively unobstructed. She could feel the stares of the few people she passed, but did her best to ignore them, avoiding eye contact. Two or three houses from her home she encountered one of her neighbors, Mr. Lazlo, a stooped and wrinkled man, seemingly too old to be alive. He was in the company of a small, furry brown lap dog that had practiced and achieved, by far, the most annoying bark in the neighborhood. Xochitl had no patience for the thing, but tolerated it for Mr. Lazlo's sake.

"Whoa, young lady. What happened to you?" asked Mr. Lazlo.

"Aah, I was trying to jump across the creek and I fell in," she said.

The old man raised his index finger. "You've got to watch out for those loose stones," he said. "Why, I knew a man once broke his hip just stepping off a curb wrong. Walked with a limp till his dying day. It don't take much." The little dog began sniffing at Xochitl's mud and blood-encrusted knees.

"Yeah, well I guess I've learned my lesson. I think I'll just stay away from the creek altogether."

"Oh you don't want to do that," said Mr. Lazlo. "Deprive yourself the beauty of nature. You've just got to be more careful, that's all." The dog was licking Xochitl's knees. "Marlon, cut it out," he said. "Leave the poor girl alone, can't you see what she's been through?" Marlon was now barking at Xochitl's knees. He raised himself up on his quivering hind legs, took the fabric of Xochitl's pants in his pointed teeth and began to shake his head violently.

"OW!" Xochitl exclaimed. "Let go you little…"

Mr. Lazlo grabbed Marlon by the collar and yanked him away, tearing Xochitl's pants.

"Oh, I'm sorry, Xochitl," said Mr. Lazlo, giving Marlon a good shake. "I'm really very sorry. I'll get you some new pants as soon as I get my check for this month. I usually get it on the fifteenth."

"Don't worry Mr. Lazlo, they were ruined anyway. Look, I gotta get going. I'm all wet and I'm getting cold."

"Okay, but you be more careful next time, Xochitl. You're such a pretty girl. You don't want to walk with a limp till your dying day." He hobbled off, dragging Marlon, who was straining at his leash and yapping his annoying bark at Xochitl's now exposed knees.

1975

Chester, haunted by the humiliating laughter of the Stud Club that he had suffered that afternoon in the school restroom, frantically flipped through the channels on his television set searching for the ANYONE CAN! infomercial. "Anything from the mundane to the impossible" that's what Doctor Banders had said. Chester was particularly interested in that word "impossible." Short of some sort of unsanctioned foreign surgery, it was pretty much impossible for Chester McFadden to have two normal arms. But the good doctor had said "impossible" and, given his stinging circumstances, Chester was willing to take him at his word.

As he searched the channels, he came across a variety program presently featuring a Caribbean band, complete with strong-armed conga players and grass-skirted dancing girls. He imagined himself playing conga drums in such a band with two big powerful arms, a small group of half-naked Island girls rubbing his shoulders and egging him on as Elsa Starlighter gaped from the audience with unbridled yearning.

Chester was torn rudely from his fantasy by the appearance of a blue screen and the words ANYONE CAN! Flashing in yellow type. Groping for something to write with in the subdued television light, he began scribbling the address on the inside of his withered arm. A sense of relief came over him as he viewed his defaced appendage. He had the address! Tomorrow he would send away for the book and, not long after that, everything would change.

Chester had decided to keep his parents in the dark on the subject of his self-improvement plan. They kept him clothed and fed, but they were not what he would call sensitive, loving people and he was frightened of suffering ridicule.

Anticipating the books arrival, it turned out, was hard work. Each day Chester, nauseous with excitement, checked the mailbox before his parents got home. Every trip to the mailbox thrust him to heady altitudes of expectation, only to find him crawling into his bed each night crushed by bitter disappointment.

During the school week Chester did his best to avoid Elsa, hoping to impress her more completely once he became a full-bodied man. She would wait, he decided. After all, she had actually kissed him on the cheek. Elsa, he felt, deserved more than he was able to provide for her at the moment.

As Chester awaited the arrival of the book that would change his life, he sank into a world of fantasy, growing very close to the Island Girls. Wrapping them all in his big, bulging arms, he gave them names and assigned them personalities. Elsa, who was possessed of slightly Asian eyes, had somehow become an Island Girl, herself. The Caribbean band had become an ensemble centered around the conga drums that Chester led ferociously into musical battle, his mind filled with horns and steel drums and guitars and lots and lots of bass. Always, there was an enthusiastic audience cheering somewhere just beyond the blinding spotlight. He was self-confident yet humble. He was the new and improved Ricky Ricardo. Babaloooo!

Three weeks later when the book finally arrived, Chester breathed a sigh of relief, carrying it to his room and placing it reverently onto his bed. He stared glassy-eyed and motionless at the plain brown wrapper. "Okay, this is your big moment Chester, old boy," he said aloud, "The moment your whole life changes. Once you open that package things will never be the same." He began opening the package slowly, with great respect for its contents, un-taping the ends carefully, trying not to tear the paper. A minute into the process Chester's patience flew out the window and he began wildly ripping at the package, flinging wrapping paper to the four directions. And there it lay, with the powerful, confident face of Doctor Robert Austin Banders staring up at him from its cover.

Chester flipped through the book, taking his time to scan chapter titles and sub-heads. He closed the book gently and cradled it against his chest. Slowly, his soul began to shrink and a sinking feeling permeated his insides. He held the book at arm's length and, for a long time, stared at the face on the cover. Something was wrong.

Until now it had never occurred to Chester that he would actually have to *read* the book. Somehow that had gotten lost in the pounding of conga drums and the purring of Island Girls. He flipped to the back of the book, 563 pages of densely packed type. Good Lord! How was he going to get through all that? Somehow he had figured that when the book arrived his transformation would be instantaneous. Stupid, now that he thought about it. Chester laid the book gently on his nightstand, curled up in a fetal position and turned on the TV.

2004

Xochitl hoisted the receiver from the phone immediately after walking through her front door. She flopped onto the couch and pushed the auto-dialer, pressing the receiver to her ear.

"Hello." A soft, husky female voice.

"Marissa, I need to talk to you as soon as possible. Some really weird stuff went down last night and I'm not sure what to do about it." Xochitl's voice was quavering, high-pitched and stilted despite her efforts to keep it steady.

"Slow down, Honey, you don't sound so good. What kind of weird stuff?" A thick, intense pause. "Guy trouble?"

"No!... Well, yeah, but not that way. I mean, I'm pretty sure someone got killed and I don't know what happened to Ernie. Oh man, I don't know what to do. I don't have any idea."

"Xochitl, what are you talking about, baby? Who got killed? Are you alright?"

"Look, I got your message yesterday, why don't you just meet me for coffee and I'll try to explain everything. Maybe you can help me figure out what to do."

"Okay. Jitter Central? Is that okay with you?"

"Yeah, fine. Just give me an hour. I gotta take a shower. There's blood all over me."

"Blood...?"

"Yeah. I'll explain when I get there."

1975

Elsa, having learned the details of Chester's encounter with the Stud Club through the incredible machinations of the high school gossip grid, refused to speak to him, other than to inform him that, yes, he was in fact an idiot after all. Chester gaped as she delivered this bit of bad news in the main hallway surrounded by a group of close friends, after which she spun on her heels and stalked away. Chester had no idea what he had done wrong, though he felt that if he did know, it would probably not have improved his standing much. And if he couldn't figure it out on his own, Elsa certainly wasn't going to waste any breath filling him in.

Chester examined his situation closely. It seemed simple enough. One day girl like, next day girl no like. Girls were crazy. He'd made a complete ass of himself in the restaurant and she hadn't blinked an eye. Now he hadn't done a thing wrong, to his knowledge at least, and she wouldn't even speak to him. He turned to her and waved his withered arm grandly through the air as she hurried away.

"It's the arm, isn't it?" Chester called to her back.

"It's not the arm," she said flatly over her shoulder. "Idiot."

"It's the arm," he mumbled to himself as he turned and walked the opposite direction.

Elsa, hesitated just prior to rounding the corner at the end of the hallway. She turned and cupped her hands about her mouth. "GO PLOOP YOURSELF, CHESTER," she shouted.

2004

The steaming water brought Xochitl's body back to life. It occurred to her that this was the second day in a row she had returned home in wet, ruined clothes. Perhaps this would be a good time to ask Mr. Trundell for a clothing allowance, or maybe even a raise. She hadn't realized how chilled she had been until the hot water restored feeling to her skin. Stepping from the shower, she wrapped a large, fluffy towel around herself and, in a wave of dread, sunk gently to the floor, curling into a loose fetal position. Overwhelming fatigue enveloped her body, pleading with her to surrender to a rejuvenating slumber. Her eyelids had just begun to flutter when the phone rang in the living room, preventing her from slipping away.

"Shit!" she moaned, rubbing her eyes. "Ah well, I need to get up and meet with Marissa anyway."

The answering machine had just finished its outgoing message when she entered the living room. The voice of Albert Trundell boomed from the machine, filling the living room. "What the hell you done with Blanchard, St. James. He was supposed to be at his desk an hour and a half ago. I hope you two didn't go out partying last night. I need that story on Sporkin and I need the film you shot, too. Pick up the phone, St. James. I know you're there. Is Blanchard there at your place? Is that what happened? Don't tell me. I don't want to know. Okay, look, just call me as soon as you get this message. I've got a magazine to get out. I can't afford to have my employees sleeping off hangovers when they're supposed to be at their desks."

Xochitl placed her hand on the phone, but did not lift

the receiver. How odd, Trundell had no idea about Sporkin's murder. It should be all over the news by now. In fact, Trundell was the news. He should have known about the events of the previous evening almost as soon as she had. Surely the magazine maintained a police scanner and some sort of UPI wire. She wanted badly to pick up the phone and tell Albert Trundell everything she had seen, but just as it had the previous evening, her instinct told her to hang back in the shadows until she was in a better position to deliver some hard facts.

Her head was far from clear and she wanted to get some feedback from Marissa before she talked to anyone else. Xochitl's friend, Marissa, ran a small bookkeeping business from her home. She was used to gathering many confusing variables and placing them into some logical order. Xochitl trusted her opinion. Xochitl, herself, was generally more given to reaction and instinct, but the emotional impact of the night before had derailed her train, leaving a thousand possibilities for each question that flitted through her head like a cave full of startled bats. Her instincts felt dull, as though the edges had been filed off, her reactions sketchy at best.

Xochitl trudged into her bedroom and began sorting through her closet. She selected a clean pair of worn blue denim pants, a black T-shirt with the words "Small and Humble" printed on the front and a zip-up gray fleece sweatshirt. Stiff muscle pains shot through her back as she bent to lace up her sneakers. She sat quietly for a moment on the edge of her bed. Weezy walked silently across the floor toward her and rubbed his side against her leg. She reached down and gently stroked the cat's back. A soft musical purr rose from somewhere inside him and, despite all that had happened, Xochitl was flooded momentarily with a sense of well-being. She lifted the little creature up and held it firmly in her arms. The purring grew louder and higher in pitch. "You and me, kid," she said, burying her face in the creature's soft, warm fur. She placed him back on the floor and left the house to meet with Marissa.

1970

Over the next few years, following his parting with Jessica Coolwater, Robert Austin Sedgwick worked hard to further his career in the world of the cinematic arts. By the age of thirty he had won some small roles in low budget, mostly forgettable films, which debuted at drive-in theaters all over the country. The film's lack of longevity did not upset him. He had become interested in the process of making the films. He was astounded by the amount of work that went into making a film that disappeared from the theater nearly as soon as it premiered.

The actors on the set were treated with special favor and Robert quickly grew accustomed to the role. If he wished for a glass of water, there was water. If he wanted nourishment to clear his head, someone would arrive with a sandwich. Robert got pretty much whatever he wanted. Women were in huge supply and would sleep with him readily. A guy didn't even have to be famous, he discovered. He simply had to show some promise of fame. And Robert was showing promise by being in a film. Any film! Even a bad film. It was a perfect equation and women lined up accordingly.

The parties in Hollywood were like no other parties on earth and Robert Austin Sedgwick attended them all. He was approached by women whom he had, only a short time ago, considered vastly out of his league. He was offered drugs whose names he couldn't even pronounce, and drank liquor that, even at his present income level, he couldn't afford. He partied in mansions, on yachts, on exotic islands and once in a moving train car.

1975

When Chester McFadden got home on the afternoon of Elsa's painful and insulting departure in the hallway at school, he went straight to his room, closed the door and reached for the TV. But, the radiant face of Doctor Robert Austin Banders, staring up at him from his end table, forbade him to turn the television on. Chester sighed heavily and made himself comfortable. He cracked open the book, buckled down, and began to read.

At 5:00 the next morning he was still reading. Doctor Banders, it turned out, if nothing else, had been blessed with a great gift for inspiration. By the time Chester put the book down, at 6am, moments before his alarm went off, he was a believer. It was truly possible to do anything. Anything!

Doctor Banders stressed a focused mind and a strong, physically fit body. An eight to twelve week regimen of his prescribed mental and physical exercises was the key to ultimate success. This, along with daily readings of selected passages from ANYONE CAN! and his new book CAN DO!, due out in the fall. He presented examples of people instantly healing their own broken bones and curing themselves of hideous degenerative diseases simply by tapping into the previously unused portion of their minds. The book said that even the most intelligent among us use only 11 percent of the brain. Doctor Banders promised to teach him how to whittle into that unused 89 percent. A few months of physical and mental exercise and Chester would have a fully loaded moving and shaking muscle-machine hanging off his left shoulder. Hell, salamanders could grow new limbs and look how tiny their brains were.

1971

One night, during a Hollywood bash aboard the yacht of a successful producer, Robert Austin Sedgwick became captivated with a beautiful young woman who introduced herself as Lola Lorraine. She was sleek and muscular, with black hair to her shoulders, cut in the style of Elizabeth Taylor playing the part of Cleopatra; bangs terminating just above her plucked and tapered eyebrows. The tips of her ears poked through her hair giving her face a slight pixy-ish quality. She wore a low-cut white satin gown that accentuated her thin waist and ample bust line. Robert slammed into gear, wasting no time talking the mysterious beauty into an empty stateroom.

A half hour later, when they had finished their awkward, desperate floundering to the music of the creaking hull, Lola Lorraine sat on the edge of the bed, stoop-shouldered and aloof. In fact, Robert thought, she looked downright icy.

"Was it good for you," he asked tentatively?

"Yeah, it was okay," she said quietly, barely moving her lips.

"Is something wrong?"

"No."

"It's just that you don't seem very satisfied."

"No, I'm fine."

"You're sure?"

"Yeah."

"Well, it was great for me," he beamed. "I'd like to see more of you."

"You've just seen all of me there is," she said without smiling. "I can't get much more naked than this."

"Are you angry with me?" he asked carefully.

"No."

"With yourself?"

"Look, I've got to get going," she said, an edge creeping into her voice.

"Going? Where could you go? We're on a yacht, for Crissake."

"My husband will be wondering where I am."

Robert stared at the floor in silence as she put on her clothes and quietly left the room.

2004

Jitter Central was a typical modern coffee house, a converted gas station with lots of varnished pine and stained glass. A gas powered fireplace fluttered in the corner. Speakers on the walls blasted classic rock, which was occasionally masked by the sucking, whirring sound of an espresso machine.

The place was frequented primarily by college-aged people who found themselves unable to study in a quiet, confined environment, and older liberal artist-types who found in the place a sanctuary of like-minded armchair rebels. A few of the table-tops were painted with a crude representation of a chess board and were usually occupied by unshaven students with furrowed brows and their own sets of hand-carved chess pieces. A few boxy-looking booths on the corner contained computer workstations with high-speed Internet connections.

Xochitl felt at home in Jitter Central because she could almost always find a good conversation to jump into. The men here seemed to have a bit more substance. When she met men elsewhere in town, the conversation quickly turned sexual. She didn't mind that too much, it certainly had its place, but it was nice to have some place to go where the conversation at least started from somewhere else. Here people talked genuinely about things like art, philosophy, politics, or current events.

Xochitl was a good 10 minutes late as usual. With most of her friends punctuality didn't matter all that much because they were generally as late as she. But Marissa was different. She was an accountant and precision was her life. There were times in the past when Marissa seethed inwardly at Xochitl's tardiness, wishing all manner of pestilence upon her as she sat alone, waiting. As their friendship solidified, though, it became less of an issue. The truth was she actually envied Xochitl her spontaneity, and was secretly happy to have a friend who would pull her, at least a little bit, into the wild side. A few minutes sitting alone in a restaurant booth was a small price to pay for a good friend. But as Xochitl approached and made eye contact, Marissa made a show of looking at her watch.

"Okay, okay, I'm sorry," Xochitl whined.

"I can see all my lessons have fallen on deaf ears," said Marissa, wagging her finger.

"Deaf, but not dumb. Don't you know I've arranged my life so that I can lay down and sleep whenever I want?"

"You look half asleep now."

"Yeah, well, it was a long, weird night. And the weirdness continues as we speak."

"What happened, Xochitl, you said something about someone being killed."

"Yeah. Pretty weird, huh?" said Xochitl, fidgeting in the booth.

"I don't know if weird is the word I would have chosen, but give me the details."

"Well, I was supposed to take pictures of this guy, Doctor Sporkin," Xochitl began, wringing her hands, "and when I got to his house with Ernie, we found him dead in the kitchen and then I ran to a phone booth down the street and Ernie somehow disappeared and I called 9-1-1 and the cops never came and there were these guys in a van and I think they took Doctor Sporkin's body and Ernie was missing, too and they cleaned the place up all spotless as though nothing had ever happened and I'm not even sure exactly what did happen."

"Whoa! Slow down. Who was this Doctor Sporkin?"

"He invented this pill that you could take when you've been

drinking and it would make you sober again."

"Wow! No kidding? I know quite few people who could find a use for something like that. So who is this Ernie guy?"

"Oh, poor Ernie. I'm really worried about him. He was the guy who was supposed to do the interview and write the story. He's just a kid, really and he passed out when he saw the body. All the phones were dead, so I ran to a phone booth a few blocks away, well quite a few blocks away, really, and when I got back these guys were carrying what looked like body bags and putting them in a van."

"Did you ask them what they were doing?"

"No. I was afraid to. The whole scene didn't look right to me. It was all being done in the dark. And now that I think about it, they were being very quiet, as though they were making an effort to be as inconspicuous as possible. The cops wouldn't do that. Neither would a medical team. There'd be flashing lights and radios squawking all over the place. It would have been a circus. No, I just hid under some trees in the next yard and watched."

"Perhaps Ernie was frightened and ran when they showed up."

"That's what I thought at first, but the more I think about it the less likely it seems. Our company car was still there when I got back. But that's another weird thing, after the men in the van drove off, a tow truck came around the corner and hauled the company car off with all my best photography equipment in it. I don't know what I'm going to use for work." She took a sip of Marissa's coffee. "Trundell's always trying to get me to try one of their digital cameras. Maybe this is a good time to convert, though I like the film thing a lot better. Oh Marissa, I'm afraid Ernie has really disappeared. Trundell called this morning wondering where he was. He said Ernie wasn't in his office."

"Who do you think those people were?"

"I don't know who they were. They seemed to be operating outside the law. But if that's the case, why didn't the police show up when I called them? The doctor was supposed to meet with some of the pharmaceutical giants this week and make a deal with one of them. He needed someone to manufacture his pill. Maybe there was some crossfire between the companies that Doctor Sporkin got caught in. Maybe one of them decided to kill him and just take the formula. But that still doesn't explain the lack of police, though. Or maybe those corporations are more powerful than we think."

"That sounds kind of far-fetched. You weren't smoking any of that Aztec ritual stuff, were you?"

"No. I know it sounds bizarre, but the whole thing's been pretty bizarre. Whoever did this obviously has some money and organization behind them. It's not like he surprised a burglar and got hit over the head with a lamp."

"So how was he killed, a gun?"

"A blender."

"A blender?"

"Yeah. A heavy duty one." Xochitl looked over her shoulder. "Like the one over there behind the counter that they use to make smoothies."

"You're making this up. How do you kill somebody with a blender?"

"His arm was shoved into it up to the elbow."

Marissa's face went pale.

Xochitl paused, "Come to think of it, maybe it wasn't the blender that killed him. There was so much blood everywhere, particularly on the doctor. He could have been shot half a dozen times and I would never have spotted the holes. Maybe he was already dead and they were trying to grind up his body to get rid of it easier. Although getting rid of the body didn't turn out to be much of a problem for them in the end. I just don't know, Marissa. None of it makes any sense."

"Perhaps they were trying to remove identifying marks like fingerprints and tattoos. I don't know from experience, but I'm sure an unidentifiable body is easier to dispose of. Weren't you afraid that the killer might be hiding in the house?

After all, the job didn't seem to be finished when you found the body."

"Well, I was pretty nervous, but a car squealed out of the driveway just before we found the body, so, afterward I just figured that must have been the killer - that we had surprised him and he took off."

"Sounds reasonable." Marissa sat quiet for a moment. "Xochitl, have you been to the police?"

"No. Well, yeah - in a way. I called 9-1-1 from the gas station, but that's one of the weirdest parts because the police never came. That's not exactly true. One cruised by while I was hiding in the alley behind the house, but he didn't even stop, let alone go inside the house. It was like he was just out on a normal patrol."

"When you called 9-1-1, did you give them your name?"

"Yeah."

"So, you've reported a murder, given your name, and then just disappeared?"

"What do you mean?"

"I mean somebody must be looking for you. You don't just report a murder and then go home and live happily ever after."

"I phoned it in. What else could I have done, trudged over to the police station on foot, covered in blood? 'Excuse me, I'd like to report a murder, but don't bother going to the crime scene because there's no body. But look at all this blood. Somebody must have died. Right,' I needed time to think. I was kind of freaked out. I know you think my life's exciting, but that sort of thing doesn't happen to me every day, you know."

"I understand that you were confused, but you can't just report a murder and then drop the ball. Especially if you've given the police your name. You're surely a suspect. If you hide out, it just makes you look guilty. You have to call the police and tell them what you saw."

"But don't you get it? The police didn't come. They never showed up, and even if they had, there would have been nothing to show them - no body, no blender, not even a drop of blood. That place was so clean when I got back that, for a minute, I thought I was in the wrong house."

"Are you sure you weren't?"

"Yes, it was the same house. Everything was the same... except for the entire murder scene, which had somehow vanished. Whoever those guys were, they knew what they were doing. I could never have cleaned the kitchen that quickly even without a dead body and blood stains everywhere. Hell, it takes me longer than that to wash the dishes."

Marissa rose to leave. "Look, I've got an appointment with a client in 20 minutes. I still think you need to make some kind of police report. Why don't I meet you at your house at, say, one o'clock and we'll drive down there together."

Xochitl hesitated, and then sighed. "Okay, if you think that's best. I have to run by my place and feed the cat and then go to Trundell's office and tell him what happened. Maybe he'll know what to do. After all, he's sort of involved. I should be done by around one."

"All right," said Marissa. "See you.

1971

In the weeks that followed the opulent yacht party, Robert Austin Sedgwick was haunted with visions of Lola Lorraine. He had grown used to women being grateful for the experience of sleeping with a genuine movie star. Lola's aloofness had left him wanting. It had to be more than just a stupid husband that kept her from expressing her gratitude. The husband was surely of no real consequence. How close could they be if she was screwing Robert in a stateroom? Women like this always married men who were well moneyed and relatively oblivious for that very reason. Nor was she higher up the food chain than himself, so it couldn't be that. Robert must have done something wrong that night. He felt as though he needed another chance to show Lola what he could really do. He had neglected to get an address or phone number from her and now had no way of contacting her. In fact, he had no real information on her at all, other than the fact that she was married. His desire began to evolve into an acute frustration and then gradually boiled into a full-blown obsession.

1975

Having read ANYONE CAN! Continuously until dawn, Chester hadn't slept all night. The teacher in his first class was anything but interesting and he kept drifting off. He wasn't quite all the way asleep, nor was he fully awake, but occasionally the Island Girls were there with him, as were Elsa and Doctor Banders. Chester shook his head to clear the cobwebs. He willed the teacher to say something interesting, but, being as he had only read to page 87 in ANYONE CAN!, his strength of will was not yet of sufficient mettle to pull off a stunt of that magnitude. The teacher droned on and so did all his other teachers that day. The book called to him and he longed to be at home reading it and practicing the physical and mental exercises that would hack away at that unused portion of his brain.

2004

"Weezy," called Xochitl. "Weezy, come and get your lunch. It's tuna! Tooooonnaah!" Odd. No reply from the cat. Very unusual indeed. Weezy always appeared immediately at the sound of a can opening even if it wasn't for him. In fact, he usually shot through his cat door into the kitchen as soon as he recognized the sound of Xochitl's car pulling into the driveway. Food was essentially his reason for living, that and a good rub-down. But today, nothing. No squeaky little meow, no clicking of claws on linoleum, nothing.

A familiar fist-sized knot began to form again in Xochitl's gut and she sighed heavily. She didn't need this right now. Not with everything else that had happened. Weezy was as predictable as the dawn. He'd never missed a meal in his life.

Reluctantly, she admitted that there was a good chance he had gotten himself into some kind of trouble. A car immediately came to mind. A few cats had shared her living space before and it was always a car that ended it. Weezy was different, though. He stayed close to the house. He had been with her a long time and they had bonded. He had sat with her through some of her worst times and she had nursed him through some of his.

Xochitl opened the kitchen door and called the cat's name into the warm summer air. She went out into the back yard and did the same. Nothing. "Come on Weezy. I got better things to do with my time," she called. Back in the house she flopped onto the couch. Xochitl sighed heavily and rubbed her eyes with the heels of her hands. A few small tears reluctantly worked their way out the corners of her eyes as she began to imagine the worst.

Wait! What was that? Something...a noise? Yes, she definitely heard a noise. A muted thump. It appeared to be coming from the bedroom. "Wheezy," she called, running into the bedroom. A muffled meow came from somewhere in the room. Xochitl stood still for a moment, listening intently. Once again, a thump and a soft meow came from inside the linen closet. Weezy shot from the closet as soon as the door had opened enough to squeeze his head through. His face was already buried in the tuna bowl, purring loudly, when Xochitl entered the kitchen. "How'd you get in the closet, Bozo?" she asked, laughing. "How'd you close the door behind you? Talented cat. I ought to sell you to the circus. Maybe we'd get rich."

Xochitl stared back into the hallway for a moment and her smile slowly faded as a number of possibilities dawned on her. A sudden chill radiated from her spine to her extremities. Cautiously, she walked back into her bedroom and slowly looked around, taking in every detail. It appeared normal, except... something. Something wasn't quite right. An examination of each section of the room turned up nothing. Until... yes, there it was. A drawer in the nightstand next to her bed, halfway open. The drawer was her 'junk drawer'. She hadn't been in the drawer last night or this morning. In fact she hadn't used it in weeks. Or had she? Was it possible she had left it open and hadn't noticed it until now?

No, not likely.

Two things could instantly turn a room into a pigsty; loose coins on the floor and open drawers.

"Okay, stay calm Xochitl," she mumbled. "Panic is not your friend."

A second, closer look around the rest of the room revealed nothing else out of the ordinary. Perhaps she really was imagining things. After all, yesterday had been a very trying day. It was always possible she had moved the drawer a few days ago and forgotten about it.

Yes, it was possible.

Xochitl lifted Weezy and carried him into the living room. She took a few long, deep breaths and planted herself on the couch. She sat quietly stroking the purring cat's fur and staring, unfocussed, at the dark television screen. Perhaps she should give the house a thorough going-over.

A sudden blurred movement appearing across the television screen startled her. The television was off. What was happening? In a flash it dawned on her that the movement was a hazy reflection of something happening behind her. As the leather strip came slipping down over her face towards her neck, Xochitl was already raising her legs into the air. She gripped the leather strip with her fingers pulling outward as she wrapped her legs around the intruder's neck. With all her might she straightened her body, taking advantage of the intruder's bent-over position, and violently thrusting him forward over the couch, bashing his head against the edge of the coffee table. Blood sprayed across the table as the man went limp and slid to the floor. Xochitl hopped up, shaking. Standing on the couch, she examined him from a safe distance. He was big, Xochitl noticed, with short, stylish hair and an inexpensive looking suit.

Xochitl eyed the man cautiously for several minutes as he lay still. Tentatively, she reached for his wrist, felt for a pulse and found one. It was a little erratic, but it was there. Steeling her resolve, she turned the man over so that his face was to the ground. She pulled his arms behind him and wrapped the leather strip around his wrists, pulling tightly on the ends until his hands began to turn white. Duct tape was going to be necessary to keep his feet in place, and a little on the wrists wouldn't hurt either. There was a brand new roll somewhere in the garage and Xochitl sprinted through the connecting door to look for it. She found it right away in a box marked "Christmas Things" and returned to the living room. At least that had been the plan.

The man's head rammed her hard in the stomach as she walked through the door, knocking the wind out of her and sending her flying back into the garage. There was a loud clatter of cardboard boxes and paint cans as Xochitl fell backward. The intruder came charging into the garage, blood trickling down his face, searching wildly for Xochitl, who had flown backward into a pile of boxes.

She groped blindly behind her, exploring the box she had fallen into with anxious, probing fingers. Her hand closed around a solid object and she fished out a rotary handsaw. Staggering to her feet, she slapped her hand against its base to make sure the battery was securely fastened in place. Hopefully the battery had not gone dead since its last use.

The man huffed loudly and charged again. Xochitl squeezed the trigger and the saw whined to life. She ran the blade across the edge of a wooden workbench. Wood instantly became splinters and sawdust. For a moment she doubted the wisdom of using the saw as a weapon. If the intruder was able to wrest it from her grasp, he would surely kill her with it and it wouldn't be pretty.

But the man stopped.

"Put the saw down, Miss Saint James." The man's voice was thunderous, the voice of a man used to telling people what to do. " I'm here to help you."

"Yeah, I could tell. You just tried to kill me with that strap."

"I wasn't going to kill you," he boomed, "I needed to render you unconscious."

"Look man, I don't know who you are or who the hell you're working for, but the last thing I'm going to do is put this saw down."

"You're making things difficult, Xochitl. Much more difficult than they need to be. Now, put down the saw and untie my wrists." The man spoke with complete authority and Xochitl responded with a momentary self-doubt. He began to edge towards Xochitl.

She shook her head slowly and pulled the trigger again. The

man flinched almost imperceptibly.

"I'm with the State Department. Go ahead, check my wallet. My ID is in there."

Xochitl hesitated. "Pull it out and throw it on the ground."

The man wrestled with his tied wrists, trying to get his hand into his back pocket. "This would go much easier if my wrists weren't bound," he said angrily.

"Yeah, I'm sure it would, but easy for you is not something I'm concerned with right now."

After some breathy struggling, the man managed to fish his wallet from his pocket and turned around to offer it to Xochitl.

"Drop it on the floor," she said, "and then back away from it." The man dropped the wallet and took a few steps back. "Farther," Xochitl pointed to the corner of the garage.

The man walked reluctantly to the corner of the room and stood facing Xochitl. She squatted and lifted the wallet off the cement floor. The man stared at her, his eyes boring into her. She pulled out a wad of cards and spread them out between her thumb and forefinger. At a glance the cards looked much the same and Xochitl was forced to take a closer look. The instant her eyes were averted, the man was on her. He kicked the saw forcefully with his hard leather shoe and Xochitl felt a sharp pain shoot through her hand. But she managed to retain her grip on the power tool.

Examining her with icy coolness, the man prepared for a second kick. It came swiftly, barely visible, but Xochitl swung the saw around with all her force at the oncoming leg. In her haste she had forgotten to pull the trigger, but as the man's foot crashed into her hand her finger was forced onto the trigger anyway. Her wrist flipped up and the saw made a tearing sound as the blade ripped into the attacker's shin. Blood and chips of bone sprayed into Xochitl's face, blinding her. She leapt up and swung the saw about wildly, this time remembering to pull the trigger. There was a solid thud as the back of the saw made contact with the man's head. She heard him fall to the ground, his head making a disturbing smack, this time on the cement floor of the garage.

Wiping the blood from her eyes, Xochitl glanced around the garage, surveying the damage. The man was clearly unconscious and bleeding badly. She removed the leather strap from his wrists and tied a tight noose just above the gash in the man's shin. Then she placed his hands behind his back and wrapped his wrists with duct tape. She did the same to his ankles. Once she felt somewhat safe, exhaustion overcame her. It was as though every electron of current in her body had stopped flowing at once, leaving nothing to power her movement. Her knees buckled slightly and she sat down roughly on the floor. Weezy sauntered across the floor to her, tail in the air, purring. The cat rubbed its cheek against her leg. She gathered the little creature in her arms and buried her face in its fur. Blood and silent tears began to wet the little animal's fur. "Oh, what's going on here, Weezers?" she whispered. "What have I gotten myself into?"

1971

"Okay Rob, let's try that again," said the director, "but this time I need a little more anger out of you. Okay? I want you to really hate this man from space. He's evil. He's cold-blooded. He absorbed your sister, remember? Okay, we're rolling."

A man in a green rubber suit, something between an alligator and the Pillsbury Doughboy, lumbered up to Robert. "We mean you no harm," he rasped metallically. "We only want the girl."

Robert glared at the green creature. "Well, you can't have her. She belongs to the human race and with the human race is where she's gonna stay."

"We can easily defeat your puny human race," said the man in the rubber suit. "There are thousands of flying saucers exactly like the one you see before you poised for battle just beyond your human telescope range. We were hoping it wouldn't come to this."

Robert glared at the camera, raised his left eyebrow and bared his teeth in a vicious snarl. "I don't care how many of you are out there," he said, "You'll never defeat the human race while even one us still has a beating heart. You may bring on your legions and your superior science, but they won't stand a chance against good old American Know-how."

"Cut," shouted the director. "I'm still not feeling it. I'm not getting enough anger out of you, Rob. It's almost there, but I just don't quite believe it yet." He placed his hand on Robert's shoulder. "You seem distracted. Is something bothering you?"

"maybe."

"What is it?" asked the green creature.

"Is there anything I can do to help?" asked the director "....
Because I really need this scene."

"Do you remember the party on Sid's yacht a few weeks
back?"

"Mmm that was parties ago, but yes, I suppose, barely."

"I met a girl that night and I haven't been able to get her
off my mind. I don't really know anything about her, but she's
driving me crazy. I don't even know how to get hold of her."

"Women," spat the green creature.

"I should have known," said the director. "Which one was
it?"

"She said her name was Lola Lorraine. Which is the only
thing I was able to find out about her other than the fact that
she's great in bed. ...Oh yeah, and she's married."

"Married? Oh Robbie you're going to do something stupid,
aren't you? You know what the tabloids will do to you if they
get word of this. It could wreck your budding career. You want
to go back to being a fry cook?"

"I just can't help myself. I think about her all the time. Even
when I'm trying not to think about her, I'm thinking about not
thinking about her. And, in a way, that's kinda thinking about
her, too. You know what I mean, right? I'm hooked. And I'm
up against a fence because I have no idea how to contact her. I
don't know what to do." He was beginning to feel like Alf again.

Roger, the director, stood silent for a moment, examining
the backs of his hands. "All right, Robert. If it'll save my movie
I'll see what I can find out about her. You're useless to me in this
condition."

"Thanks Roger," said Robert. A sort of soul-borne lightness
crept over him that he hadn't experienced since the night he
first set eyes on Lola Lorraine.

"No big deal, kiddo," said Roger. "Now, more anger."

1975

As Chester entered the restroom between classes, he ran headlong into the full roster of the Stud Club.

"Hey Crab, did you ploop the little woman last night, give 'er some seafood?" asked one boy.

A malicious chuckle erupted from the group.

Another stood close behind Chester and spoke in low, threatening tones directly into his ear. "I plooped your mamma last night, Crab," he said, then laughed viciously.

Chester steeled himself and looked directly into the cold, compassionless eyes of the Stud Club boys. He squinched his face into a fair imitation of Doctor Robert Austin Banders on the cover of ANYONE CAN!. Thrusting his jaw forward as far as he could before it hurt and bulging his steely eyes like 100-watt bulbs, he generated what he assumed to be the threatening persona of a true warrior. However, Doctor Banders enjoyed the luxury of a strong square jaw and a pair of riveting green eyes, while Chester was blessed only with pudgy red cheeks and the sleepy eyes of a koala bear.

"Whoa, Crab, you're looking kinda whacko! You're not gonna swallow your tongue or anything weird like that, are you? You want me to get the nurse? You could maybe ploop her, too. She looks like she needs a good ploopin'. Don't you think? And you're just the man to give it to her."

Ferocious barks of laughter burst forth from the Stud Club. Unshaken, Chester continued to stare and added a continuous, full-body quiver to the mix in hopes of upping the intensity.

"I think he's gonna blow," laughed the first boy.

"Yeah, ploop you, Crab," said the other boy. "You better not blow up all over my clothes. This is my favorite shirt. You wreck it and I'm gonna find what's left of your ploopin' ass and kick it." They swaggered out the bathroom door and their laughter rang in the hallway for a small eternity.

Once the boys were gone, Chester turned and faced himself in the bathroom mirror, shocking himself back to reality. Instead of the handsome, intense features of Doctor Banders, he saw only the face of a jittering, pop-eyed lunatic. *Jesus! I gotta start those exercises right away.*

2004

Xochitl drove up to the back door of her house which entered into the kitchen. She pulled the intruder's unconscious body into the kitchen, leaving a red streak across her linoleum tile. Reaching beneath the sink, she found a roll of large sized garbage bags. Tearing a bag from the roll, she pulled it over the man's bloody legs, wrapping a length of duct tape around the top to keep it in place. With her swollen hand, Xochitl found it difficult to maneuver the big man's body into the back of her car, but with a little leverage and persistence, managed to roll him into an uncomfortable-looking pile by the tail gate.

As Xochitl pulled into the parking lot near the emergency room entrance to the Soda River General Hospital, the man in the back began to groan. "Shut up!" she snapped over her shoulder.

"I need . . . help," the man said, weakly, almost a whisper.

"You're getting help. Just shut up! It's more than you deserve. I should have dumped you in the river. Who are you, anyway? And none of that government bullshit this time, understand?"

The man was silent.

"Fine! I don't care who you are. The sooner I get rid of you, the better."

Xochitl crawled into the back seat of her car and removed the duct tape from the man's wrist. She opened the door and pushed the man out. Once he was outside on the ground, she tore the bag from his leg, crumpled it up and removed the tape from his ankles. She threw the whole mess into a nearby trash-can. A nurse met her at the door and together they brought a wheelchair for the man.

"I'll get him started," said the nurse, "you can fill out his paperwork at the admittance desk. Can you tell me a little bit about what happened to him?"

"Power tool accident," said Xochitl. "A rotary saw."

"He's dressed kind of formal for working with power tools," the nurse remarked.

"Yeah, well, he's kind of a formal guy."

"What's his name?"

"Uh, Robert Smith."

"And are you Mrs. Smith?"

"Oh, hell no."

"I see," said the nurse. "Are you related to the patient?"

"No, just a recent acquaintance."

"Is there a number where we could reach a relative?"

"Oh jeez I don't know. He's starting to come around, why don't you just ask him? I've really gotta get going."

"We'll need you to fill out some paperwork for him."

Xochitl began to edge her way toward the door. "Look, he cut himself and I brought him to the hospital, okay? You'll have to get the rest from him."

She turned and bolted through the door, leaving the puzzled nurse staring after her.

1971

A few days later, while working on the set of his latest film, Roger, the director, approached Robert waving a piece of paper in the air. "This is a list of all the guests at the party that night on the yacht. There's no Lola Lorraine."

"Let me see," said Robert, shoulders drooping. He searched the list and found there was indeed no Lola Lorraine. "Can I keep this?" he asked.

"Sure, what am I gonna do with it?" said the director. "Half those people I didn't want to see the first time."

During lunch break Robert sat alone at a table with the list propped up against a coffee cup. He studied it for clues. She had to be here somewhere. It wasn't likely that she crashed the party, not on a yacht and especially not with a husband in tow. She must have been using an assumed name. But then, in Hollywood, who wasn't? He searched for other names that began with LL. Nothing. He searched for contrived-sounding names, but that turned out to be nearly the entire list. Finally, he checked for males and females with the same last name. There appeared to be eleven married couples on the list. "Well, that narrows it down a bit," he mumbled.

After lunch Robert handed the director the list with the names of the suspect couples now underlined. "Can you get me some head shots of these people, Roger?" he asked. "I know I'll be able to concentrate much better if I can get this thing resolved."

"Some, maybe," the director said, scratching his head.

"They're not all actors, Rob. There are other kinds of people in Los Angeles, you know."

"Yeah, there's actors and there's people who want to be actors. Come on, Rog, my barber has a goddam head shot."

"Alright, I'll have my people look in the studio files tonight and see what we've got. I guess I could ask Sid if he's got anything, too. I'm not guaranteeing anything, Rob. But, meanwhile, I need some fire out of you. Understand?"

The next morning at breakfast Roger presented Robert with an envelope containing nineteen eight-by-ten glossy black and white photographs. "There were a few I couldn't find," He said. "I looked everywhere. My God, the things I do for you." Robert went through the photos, one by one. When he had finished, he went through them again. Nineteen head shots and not one picture of Lola Lorraine. Disappointed, he threw the pile of photographs on the table and walked stiffly out of the building.

He trudged wearily across the studio property to the parking lot where he slumped into his car, a classic MG Convertible. Robert was tapped out, beaten and depressed. He didn't feel much like working today. In fact he couldn't work, There was no way. Not in this state of mind. "Come on, Roger," he said to the empty air, "how can you expect me to remember my lines, much less show any emotion? I feel like the walking dead. Hey ya got a zombie picture? Sign me up." He turned the key and the engine roared to life.

Suddenly, an idea gushed into Robert's brain and he turned the key back the other way, killing the engine. Springing from the car, he sprinted across the parking lot back toward the studio, reaching the dining area just as a housekeeping girl was about to toss the pile of photographs into the trashcan. He tore the photos from the startled girl's hand and searched through them once again. He counted ten women and nine men. A smile slowly began to form on Robert's face. He walked off hurriedly, searching for Roger, whom he found talking to a cameraman.

"Roger, do you still have the list?" he asked.

"Yeah, it's on that table over by my chair."

"Can I get it?"

"Sure, help yourself."

Robert fetched the list and sat quietly, comparing each photo to the list. His heart raced as he crossed the names of ten women off the list, leaving only one underlined name. Eunice Banders.

Scrawling the name on a small piece of paper, he carefully tucked it into his wallet. Then he crumpled up the list and threw it in the trash.

He spoke the name aloud a few times to see how it sounded. "Eunice Banders, Eunice Banders, Eunice Banders. It's not exactly Lola Lorraine, but I guess it's got a certain something." There was so much power in a name. Look what a simple name change had done for him. Taken him from fry cook to movie star. He wondered if he would have been so eager to take Lola Lorraine into the stateroom if her name had been Eunice Banders. As he recalled her image with her white satin dress and shimmering black hair, he realized it wouldn't have made any difference at all.

That afternoon Robert began formulating a plan to locate Eunice Banders. He looked first in the phone book. There were seven people by the name of Banders, all male. One of them must be the husband of Eunice Banders, but which one? He needed to check it against the list. He hurried back to the trashcan where he'd thrown the list away, but the can had been emptied. "Damn!" He wrote the names and addresses from the phone book on a small piece of paper and, again, slipped it into his wallet. How could he do this? He couldn't just walk up and knock on their front doors. Or could he? What the hell, he was an actor. How hard would it be to get a delivery boy uniform from the wardrobe department and, as Jessica Coolwater would say, act like a delivery boy?

Shortly after sunset Robert donned a dark brown delivery boy uniform and casually strolled across the studio lot to the motor pool. There was a vast array of vehicles in the motor pool yard, but not many looked to be delivery vehicles. After a lengthy search he found a three-wheeled motorcycle with an enclosed cab and what appeared to be a refrigerated cargo box in the back. He entered a small building next to the fence that housed the attendant's office.

"Help ya?" asked the attendant, a tall, gangly man with thinning hair and missing teeth.

"Ahh...yeah, Roger needs that three wheeler out there in the yard for a scene in 'The Green Terror From Beyond'."

"Well, I dunno. Y'ain't gonna blow'er up or nothin', are ya?"

"No, no, nothing like that. There's just this scene where a delivery boy gets his spinal fluid sucked out by a man from space and we need the delivery truck to make it look authentic. We're going for realism here. See? We need the truck for believ-ability." He pronounced the last word slowly, with lots of ex-tended 'e's in it so that the attendant would make no mistake.

"You gonna get spinal fluid on 'er?"

"No, it's just a scene in the movie."

"I don't know, mister, she ain't really a movie truck," said the attendant, rubbing his rubbery face with the palms of his hands, as though all this thinking was wearing him out. "She's more of a catering veehicle."

"Yes, well, Roger will have it...ah, her back to you by tomor-row."

"We'll need her by noon. We gotta take a wax dummy over to Sherman Oaks. Gotta keep it cold. They filmin' somethin' on location and they need the dummy for a car crash scene. 'Sposed to get all burned up and ugly lookin'."

"She'll be back by noon."

"Best be, or it's mah ass."

1975

For twelve weeks Chester kept pretty much to himself, doing his mental and physical exercises religiously. He grew very excited when first he noticed his pudgy body begin to harden. It was difficult for him to believe that there were actually muscles under the baby fat that had insulated his body all his life. Muscles were just something some people were born with. And other people...not. As his right arm took on a lumpy, burly texture he waited patiently for the left arm to do the same. But alas, it remained the same shriveled pink anomaly it had always been. It steadfastly refused to imitate the right one and remained as understated and ill-defined as it had always been. Chester stifled his panic and decided he must concentrate more heavily on the mental exercises. The answer was surely hidden somewhere in that mysterious untapped portion of his brain.

As the book suggested, he sat in the dark imagining himself chipping away at a gray concrete wall. The key, the elusive eighty-nine percent, Doctor Banders had said, lay behind this wall. Many obstacles would be encountered while breaking through the wall, but answers would always be provided when needed if one remained in an open, meditative state of mind. Chester was pretty sure he was in the correct state of mind, but even so, progress was slow. It had been at least a couple of weeks and the wall barely looked touched. He began to lose patience. *Concentrate harder! Concentrate harder!* There was a burly left arm behind that wall with Chester McFadden's name on it and one way or another he was going to get it.

Then one day, just like the book said, the answer was provided out of nowhere. It was so simple that he felt stupid. *I'll use both arms and get a bigger hammer!* He realized he had been using a small geologist's pick to hack away at the wall. In his geology class at school he had recently used one of these small picks and apparently it had stuck in his mind. The tool was about the size of a carpenter's hammer with a point at one end of the head and a flat hammering surface at the other. All in all, a great tool for chipping away dirt and small rocks, but not much help while attempting to knock down the barrier to superior intellect and a perfect body. *I've been using this cheesy little pick because it was the first thing that came to my mind. That's the problem. I'm limiting myself. I'm thinking that it's all I can handle with my bad arm. Well, this is **my** imagination.... **My** land of **my** conga drums and **my** Polynesian girls. My mental and physical futures are at stake here. I can't afford to be wimpy about it.* He would imagine a strong muscled right arm and using both arms he would attack the wall with a large sledgehammer.

After days of pounding with the new bigger sledge hammer the wall began to give way. Just a finger-sized hole at first, but this eventually gave way to something he could get his small left hand into. No, wait, he'd decided to have two full-sized arms here. His full-sized hand wouldn't fit into the hole yet.

"Aw shit!" he said, "I've painted myself into a corner. I'll have to make the hole bigger still."

The imagined pounding for days on end caused genuine physical exhaustion in Chester until he was too weakened to continue. Dropping the hammer, he lay on his back and felt the cold dampness seep through his clothes from the eleven percent floor of his brain.

2004

Albert Trundell sat slumped at his desk, his head decorated with three yellow, number two pencils, one on the left and two on the right. He glanced up, startled, as Xochitl barged through his door.

"Jesus, Saint James, don't you ever knock? What if I was...?" He stopped short, gaping at the bloodstains on Xochitl's shirt. "What happened now? Are you alright?"

"I'm a little beat up." She held up her swollen hand. "I don't think it's broken. I can wiggle my fingers okay, but it hurts."

"Yeah, it looks like it hurts. Have you had someone look at it?"

"No."

"Why not? I can't be sending my people out on assignment looking like this - swollen body parts and all gimpy and shit." His voice trailed off, giving way to genuine concern. "Where'd all this blood come from, Xochitl? This is blood, right?"

"Yeah. But it's not mine though." Xochitl paused, looking wearily at her swollen hand. "I'm scared, Boss. I've got a hell of a story for you, but I don't know how it's gonna end yet."

"Well, let's hear it."

She hesitated, biting the back of her index finger. "Did Ernie ever show up?"

"That lazy bastard! I give him the chance of a lifetime and this is how he repays me. I'd assumed he was with you. I figured you two drunkards and a sober pill - hell, who knows what could happen. Maybe you drank more than the pill could soak up."

Xochitl didn't smile. She sat on the edge of his desk. "Something happened last night, boss," she said. "I'm afraid maybe Ernie's not coming back - maybe not ever."

"What are you talking about? I can't imagine anybody offering him more money at this point. He's still wet behind the ears. From the beginning, Saint James, tell me this story from the beginning."

"It's nothing like that, boss. It's something much worse." Half an hour later Xochitl had explained the saga, trying not to embellish anything. The story was bizarre enough on its own. Albert Trundell sat scratching his head with a fourth pencil. "So you haven't seen Blanchard since you ran to the gas station?"

"Right. I thought he'd just run off, but after you called this morning and after that man attacked me, it started to sink in that somebody is playing for keeps. I mean that guy really wanted me dead. It wasn't all emotional, like someone fighting for survival. It was calculated. He just coldly and calmly wanted me dead. He said he didn't, but he really did. I could see it. Do you know what it feels like to face someone who wants you dead?"

"I spent some time in Nam."

"So, you know! It's like nothing personal, just a job."

"I've been on both sides of that gun, Saint James. Neither side is pretty. The trigger side's prettier, but not by much."

Xochitl focused on Mr. Trundell, trying to imagine him willfully firing a lead slug into another human being. That must have been a long time ago. A different Albert Trundell sat before her now. Her boss had since become a very compassionate man. Compassionate enough to start AWARE Magazine and try to expose some of the dark, dirty corners of life in America - particularly corporate life. "Knowledge is power," he would say, and he truly believed it. Evil people only got away with things if they could keep them hidden in the dark, if enough good people didn't know about them.

The power of the people was unstoppable if they were organized and they could only be organized if they were well informed. Not by the claptrap propaganda of the mainstream press, whom he considered a gaggle of corporate whores, but by honest-to-God facts. Mr. Trundell was very concerned about the accuracy of the information his publication presented, and had fostered a reputation for high quality reporting. More than once Xochitl had seen him change his view when the facts for a given story crossing his desk were not consistent with his preconceptions. Most people would brand him as a liberal, but in truth, he was a man apart from partisan affiliation. His viewpoint was solely dependent upon the facts. Always.

"So you haven't been to the police about this?" asked Trundell

"No. Like I said, I called 9-1-1 right after we discovered the body, but nobody ever came. Even if they had, there would have been nothing there for them to see. I was afraid to call them after that. I couldn't believe how clean the place was after only thirty minutes. Anyway, my friend, Marissa, is supposed to drive me to the police station this afternoon so I can file a report in person."

"Why don't you hold off on that for a little bit, until we get a few things straight. What was in the guy's wallet?"

"The...Oh man, I forgot about the wallet. It's still in my garage."

"How could you forget about the wallet, Saint James? Its contents would probably tell us everything. Damn, I must have done have lousy job of training you."

"I'm a photographer, boss, not a reporter. I just take the pictures. At least I used to, all my camera stuff was in the car they towed."

Mr. Trundell pinched his eyes shut and rubbed his temples. "I'll see to it that your equipment is replaced. It was probably time for an upgrade anyway." Trundell went to his coat closet and began twirling the knob on a small black safe. Once the door was open, he took out a revolver and tucked it into his belt. "Tell you what, Saint James, why don't you and me swing by your house and see if we can't find that wallet. I don't want you going there alone right now."

1971

Robert Austin Sedgwick drove the little refrigerated delivery vehicle off the lot and, on his way home stopped at a hardware store for some paint, then at the market for some groceries. He placed the groceries in the refrigerated compartment in the back of the vehicle. A large patch on the back of the uniform he'd swiped from the costuming department said; "Chu's Big Oriental Market". The name patch over the left breast pocket read "Qwan". "I should have thought this out a little better," he said to himself, scratching his head. "Well, Qwan, old buddy," he mumbled, "it's a little late to turn back now."

He found a piece of cardboard in the kitchen and had a difficult time cutting out a stencil that said simply: "Chu's". It would be pushing his luck to cut the word "Market" into the cardboard, so "Chu's" would have to do. Then he went out to his driveway and, using the stencil he'd made, painted "Chu's" on both sides of the truck.

He gave the paint an hour to dry while he struggled into the ill-fitting uniform, and then drove off in search of the first Banders on his list. The names on the list had been arranged in order of distance from his house, closest to furthest away.

An overweight man dressed in his underwear and brandishing a beer can answered the door of the first house Robert approached.

"Chu's Big Oriental," said Robert holding two bags of groceries.

"Big Oriental what?" said the man, laughing. "You don't

look so big or so Oriental to me."

"Are you Mr. Banders?" asked Robert. "I have an order of groceries from Chu's Big Oriental Market."

"I didn't order no groceries. Say, you got any beer in there? 'Cause I'll take the beer if you got it." The man was wobbling side to side.

"No," said Robert, sympathetically, though all he felt was irritation. "I haven't got any beer. Perhaps Mrs. Banders placed the order."

"Well, if Mrs. Banders did, then you can just deliver it to Mrs. Banders the hell up in Yuba City, which is where Mrs. Banders took her useless ass after walkin' out on Mr. Banders."

"I'm terribly sorry to have bothered you," said Robert. "I seem to have been given the wrong address."

"Yeah, you're terribly sorry, alright. What kind of market ain't got no beer?"

Robert hurried back to his delivery truck and putted away as fast as the little vehicle would carry him to the next stop on his list. This was in a posh neighborhood and two Doberman Pincers chased him from the property before he could ring the doorbell. Luckily, he'd spotted a woman through the kitchen window and was relieved to find that it wasn't Eunice.

Robert's third stop was an 80ish year-old grieving widow who, although she hadn't ordered the groceries, offered to pay for them if he'd only stay for a little while.

No one was home at the next two houses Robert visited, which troubled him considerably. There was little chance he'd be able to get the delivery truck again after tonight. Old 'Corn pone Zeke' or whatever his name was, down at the motor pool, may have been a bit slow, but even he would start checking around if Robert took the vehicle again. He would have to return later tonight and recheck the two addresses.

The last two houses on his list were a wash. One was occupied by a physicist and his equally egg-headed wife. The other was a lifelong bachelor, who sat in the dark listening to recorded opera music. So, Eunice must live in one of the unoccupied houses that he'd passed up earlier in the evening.

It was around 11 pm when Robert pulled his little delivery truck into the driveway of the first unoccupied house, an expensive looking ranch home in the Hollywood Hills. He knew he was pushing his luck arriving this late in the evening, but he had no choice. There were a few small lights burning in the house that hadn't been on during his previous visit, but still he saw no movement. He had gotten tired of moving the groceries in and out of the refrigerator compartment and had taken to carrying them with him in the cab of the vehicle. The bags had gotten pretty badly beaten up and Robert was forced to hold his hands underneath them in order to keep the groceries from tearing through the bottom.

Robert stabbed his finger into the button by the door and waited.

Nothing.

He was anxious and the wait felt endless. He knocked on the door. There were subtle noises coming from within the house, still no one answered. Perhaps it was a dog clattering around in there. Eventually, Robert reluctantly accepted defeat. The door wasn't going to open. He turned to leave and walked straight into the barrel of a shotgun. A tall man in his fifties with perfect silver hair, wearing a dark green velvet bathrobe over white pajamas appeared out of the shadows.

"Who sent you?" he said. His voice was rich and liquid like that of a radio announcer.

"Chu's Big Oriental Market," said Robert, terrified. He jittered his hands to the sides of the bags and without support on the bottom the fatigued bags tore open, spilling groceries all over the porch.

"That's bullshit. Nobody delivers groceries at 11 o'clock at night and I sure as hell didn't order any Chinese food. Now who sent you? I'll bet it was Lenny. It *was* Lenny, wasn't it? How many times do I have to tell him, that part of my life is over? I don't do that stuff anymore. Come on, talk, or I'll use this thing. Don't think I won't. It won't be the first time."

"I swear I'm from Chu's Big Oriental." Robert squeaked nervously, now on his knees. He fumbled with the groceries, trying to collect the loose items, though he no longer had a bag to contain them.

"Keep your hands in the air where I can see them," said the man, poking the barrel into Robert's back several times.

Robert froze and raised his hands. "Go look at my truck. It has the name on the side. It even has a refrigerator compartment on the back," he said stupidly.

"Is that right?" said the man. He walked into the driveway, bent over to have a look and fired three shots into the little vehicle. "Now it has three holes in the side and a refrigerator that won't work. You call this piece of shit a truck. This isn't a truck. Come on, get inside the house."

Robert opened the front door and walked into the house, the man behind him with the gun at his back. He was ordered to sit in a wooden kitchen chair while the man tied his limbs. Then the man picked up the phone and dialed the police.

Half an hour later, as the police escorted Robert away in handcuffs, the man shouted, "When you get out of county jail, you tell Lenny that part of my life is over, you hear me? It's over!"

It took the police nearly a week to sort out Robert's story. He told them about the list, the girl, the party, the movie he was in. Nothing seemed to interest them except possibly the movie. All in all, it didn't look good for Robert Austin Sedgwick. He was using an assumed name and was driving a stolen vehicle, delivering groceries at eleven o'clock at night from a store that didn't exist. The more he explained, the guiltier he appeared. He had postponed his one phone call for a few days until his head was clear, eventually using it to get in touch with Roger. It would not be good when Roger arrived. Roger would explode when he found out about the stolen truck, but it had to beat the hell out of spending another night in the Graybar Hotel.

Roger took his time, but eventually came to Robert's aid.

He explained to the police that both the truck and Robert belonged to the studio and no charges were to be pressed on their account. Robert was informed that his silly antics had wasted five good production days, that the Sherman Oaks location shoot had to be postponed until another refrigerator truck could be found, and that he had started re-shooting Robert's scenes with a different actor. Robert would no longer be needed.

Robert was crushed. His movie career was surely over. Who would hire him now? As big as L.A. was, the actual film community was very small and close-knit. Robert's reputation, such as it was, would be ruined. His short brush with fame had offered him opportunities he could never have gotten elsewhere, a privileged position he had grown very used to. Being in the movies, as such, was not the end all, really, but it was status, it was his ticket to a damn good time. Now his ticket was being torn into little, tiny pieces right before his eyes.

As he was processed out of jail, Robert held his head low, avoiding eye contact with those around him, mumbling to the ones he was forced to interact with. Hands shoved deep into pockets, he slunk from the County Jail building a beaten man. The bright Los Angeles sun was painful after his days in the dark cell, but he placed his hands over his eyes in a double salute and took in the view, breathing in a sense of freedom. Suddenly, his heart leaped and his face cracked into a haggard, confused grin. There, across the street, stood a stately old theater and, miracle of miracles, on the marquee, in big red letters, were the words, "Revival Tonight, Reverend Eunice Banders".

"Holy cow!" shouted Robert, rejuvenated as he took the steps two at a time.

He dashed across the street to have a closer look. Several identical posters papered the wall outside the theater revealing, in a large black and white image, the severe, judicial face of the Reverend Eunice Banders. The face on the poster was only just recognizable as the sultry Lola Lorraine. This woman looked very conservative. Hair in a bun, she wore thick, dark rimmed glasses and no makeup. Something resembling a shapeless, satin choir robe was draped over her shoulders with a white collar like a ring of giant flower petals circling her neck.

This is too much, thought Robert. I've been chasing a preacher. Not the preacher's wife, but the preacher. Criminy! And how did she go from Jane Russle to Ethel Murtz? She could have strolled right by me on the street looking like this and I wouldn't have recognized her. In fact, I wouldn't have even noticed her. Robert was tempted to call the whole thing off, chalk it up to misconception, but he had already invested too much time and aggravation. Quitting now wouldn't get his job back. That was dead and gone. And he had already served a week in jail, pretty much for Lola Lorraine. No, there was no going back. He would forge ahead now, if only to see the look on her face when they met.

1975

The dawn brought an ethereal golden glow to Chester's room as he clawed his way toward wakefulness, feeling as though he hadn't slept at all. His eyelids were heavy and sticky. He sat on the edge of his bed and rotated his arms, discovering that both they and his shoulders were quite sore. Groaning, he got out of bed to brush his teeth. As he spat the toothpaste into the sink, it suddenly occurred to him that both arms were sore. **Both** arms were sore! His withered left arm was being exercised in his mental attempt to knock down the thick gray wall and was now sore. Sore meant that muscle tissue was increasing. Doctor Banders had said so. And Doctor Banders wouldn't lie! Would he?

For the next month or so, Chester felt a confidence he had never known before. It was only a matter of time now before he strutted, smiling and waving, down the halls of his school a normal young man. People would soon forget that he had ever been the Fiddler Crab. He'd acquire a new nickname. Something strong and full of authority, like Buck or Nick maybe. Or, oh! maybe people would call him Chet. Yeah, Chet, he thought, I like that. *Pleased to meet you. My name is Chet. Would you like to have dinner?* And best of all, his nervousness around Elsa would disappear. Assuming she would ever speak to him again. Of course she would speak to him again! How could she resist the new, improved Chet McFadden?

1975

Eleven weeks into the ANYONE CAN exercise program, Chester broke through the big gray wall. After a particularly energetic swing, the wall had simply shattered leaving a large man-sized hole. Exhausted, Chester stared at the hole in amazement, then, cautiously approached. This was the moment he'd been working toward. Eying the dark hole, Chester rubbed his still insubstantial left arm with his now burly right. He brushed his fingers lightly against the cold rough perimeter of the opening. It felt solid and tangible. Hallelujah!! Sweet normality lay just on the other side of this wall.

His left arm seemed to be growing bigger and stronger lately, but not by much. As yet it was not a normal high-school boy's arm. Could it be his imagination? Lately, with all the mental exercises and accompanying exhaustion, it had become increasingly difficult to determine imagination from reality. People at school still called him the Fiddler Crab, so he definitely wasn't completely normal yet. Still he had the feeling that, once on the other side of the big gray wall, he would be able to get the necessary repairs rapidly under way and have his new arm swinging in no time.

Without hesitation, Chester climbed through the dark hole and walked about ten paces into the untouched portion of his brain. The light was poor and it was hard to see. Something was there. He could just make it out. But what was it? Until now, Chester hadn't really considered what the answer to all the plagues of his life might look like. He stared harder, waiting for his eyes to adjust to the light.

Suddenly, Chester froze. As hazy shadows in the dark chamber hardened into a defined object, his heart sank. *No! it couldn't be!* Heavily and irresistibly. On the far side of the chamber stood a second big gray wall, every bit as formidable as the first. He sat down hard, gazing sightlessly at the dull gray surface before him.

Chester pulled himself from his meditative trance. Discouraged, he sat sulking on the edge of his bed, thumbing through the book for an explanation. In a small appendix toward the back he found a passage which stated that some people had a single big gray barrier housing a vast chamber containing all the answers they would ever need in various symbolic forms, while others had layer upon layer of these big gray walls to contend with. These were defensive walls, the book said, that the mind had built through the years to protect itself against painful experiences; roughly one wall for each extremely painful event in ones life.

"Ahh ShShshshit," he said aloud, tears forcing their way through his squeezed eyelids. "There must be hundreds of those things in there. It took me eleven weeks just to get through the first one. I can't do this. I can't!"

For the first time in three months Chester turned on the television and lay on his bed. The fetal position was comforting and familiar and soon he drifted off. He slept the sound sleep of absolute despair. There were no dreams, no big gray walls and no burly left arms or Island Girls, just precious emptiness. In the morning he gathered up the book and climbed numbly up the fire escape, rung by rung, onto the littered tar paper roof of his building. With his right arm he set the book down on a metal vent cover. With his withered left hand he struck a match and held it to the corner of the cover.

He watched as the chiseled, authoritarian face of Doctor Robert Austin Banders withered in the flame and then crumbled to ashes, along with a small group of Island Girls and a battered set of conga drums. All of them dissipating ceremoniously in the smoke.

2004

Marissa was parked outside of Xochitl's house as Xochitl and Trundell pulled up to the curb. They climbed out of the car and walked across the lawn toward the house.

"You ready?" Marissa called, trying to sound encouraging. She walked over and met them on the porch.

"Not just yet, Marissa. This is my boss, Mr. Trundell. Some stuff happened after I left you this morning. Someone tried to kill me." Xochitl fumbled with her keys, finally locating the one that opened the front door.

"What? Was it the same people?"

"I don't know. It seems like they must be related, but I don't have any facts. The guy who attacked me dropped his wallet so we're going to try to find it and see what it can tell us. He said he was from the State Department." Xochitl flung open the front door and froze. The first thing she noticed was that the bloody streak on the carpet was gone. She ran to the garage and threw the door open. Everything in the garage was perfectly in order. There were no signs of struggle.

"Saint James?"

"I swear, boss, the carpet was all bloody where I dragged the man through the living room and that's the box of power tools I crashed into. She went to the box and sorted through it, pulling out a rotary hand saw. "This is the saw." She examined it closely, but noticed nothing out of the ordinary. "I haven't been gone more than 90 minutes."

"Well, if what you told me about Dr. Sporkin's place was true, 90 minutes is overtime for these guys."

"So you do believe me then?"

"I'll tell you, Saint James, This seems pretty unlikely to me, but I'm out one staff writer and a company car. Add that to the fact that you're a lousy liar and that's not your blood smeared all over your clothes. I really have no choice, at this point, but to give you the benefit of the doubt."

Xochitl looked closely at the blade. "It looks pretty clean."

Mr. Trundell pulled an open-end wrench from the box of tools. "Gimme that thing, Saint James. I've got an idea."

"What are you going to do?" asked Marissa.

"You'll see," Trundell, placed the saw on its back. He rammed a piece of scrap wood against the blade and with the wrench began unscrewing the nut that fastened the blade. Removing the blade he peered closely at it. Then he looked at the spindle on the saw. "I thought so. Look at this."

Marissa and Xochitl stood on each side of Trundell, looking over his shoulders.

"What are we looking at?" asked Marissa, pinching her chin between her thumb and forefinger.

Trundell rubbed the spindle with his finger. It came away bearing a red streak. "They're good, but they're not that good," he said. "And look inside the safety housing. There's a little bit of red in there too."

"Interesting," said Xochitl, taking the saw from Trundell." Apparently it isn't as humanly impossible as we had assumed to clean up a crime scene in 90 minutes - not if you're willing to cut a few corners."

"Hold off on going to the police just yet, Saint James," said Trundell. "I want to do a little checking."

"Where should I go? I don't want to stay here."

"Why don't you leave town for a few days. I have no idea how deep this thing goes, but obviously someone is very upset that you saw Dr. Sporkin's body. Obviously they know what your car looks like. Come by the office and I'll loan you another company car. And don't lose this one! I think you'll be safer if you disappear for a while."

"I'll go with you, Xochitl," said Marissa. "We'll have a girl's holiday."

"No, that's probably not a good idea, Marissa. If I'm a target I don't want anyone else getting in the line of fire."

"But Mr. Trundell just said you'd be safe outside of town," said Marissa.

"Er," said Trundell, "safe - er."

Marissa stared at him, bug-eyed and silent, then back at Xochitl. "Where will you go?" she asked quietly.

Xochitl thought for a moment. "I don't know. Maybe down south. L.A. seems big enough to get lost in. Maybe I'll go there."

"Do you know anyone there?"

"No, but that's probably a good thing."

"Come on, ladies, let's get out of here. This place is starting to give me the creeps."

They walked out the front door just as the cat was walking in. "Oh Weezy. I forgot about Weezy. What am I going to do with him?"

"I'll come by and feed him." Marissa offered.

"That's not a good idea either," said Trundell. "These people came pretty close to killing your friend, here. I don't want them nabbing you and taking you somewhere for 'questioning', or using you as some kind of hostage." He made quotes with his fingers. Who knows what they're capable of? None of us should be anywhere near this house until this thing is cleared up."

"Maybe I could take him to my house," said Marissa.

"These guys don't do too well in strange houses. He'll just end up peeing on everything you own to mark his territory. I've got a travel cage. I guess I'll have to take him with me," Xochitl said, defeated. "He's not the world's best traveler, but it's only for a little while, and I'd rather do that than leave him here to fend for himself."

"At least stay at my house tonight, Xochitl. It'll do you good and you can make a fresh start in the morning."

"I guess that would be alright. What do you think, boss?"

"I'll follow you over there and make sure no one's tailing you." Trundell thought for a moment. "Let me give you my cell phone number. If anything happens out of the ordinary, and I mean anything, you call that number. Understand? Day or night!"

"You're the boss."

1975

Elsa was a kind, forgiving girl and had made several attempts to warm up to Chester in the past month. He had remained aloof, preferring to wait until his left arm was strong and masculine, until he could bring something of his own to the table. Now his only chance, and a slim chance it would be, was to beg for mercy, perhaps even use the arm as a sympathy ploy. Why had he been such an idiot? Why hadn't he let her into his life earlier, explained the ANYONE CAN! program to her, sought her help? She was definitely more balanced than he was, and overall, probably smarter, too. He might have avoided the last 11 weeks of self-delusion if he'd swallowed his pride and let her in.

Funny, it wasn't until this moment that Chester realized he had done the whole thing for Elsa. He'd assumed he was doing it for himself and that Elsa would be one of many positive rewards. He had foolishly pushed her away because he felt inadequate, horribly inadequate. He wanted to present her with something whole and alive. But she hadn't found him inadequate at all. She had liked him as he was, that was clear to him now, and he had pushed her away. Stupid!

At school Elsa was nowhere to be seen, though Chester had made a point of searching for her between classes. He'd heard she was at school but he hadn't run into her. Come to think of it, she had been scarce for the last few days. A sudden and paralyzing burst of bodily chemicals made Chester's limbs stop moving and his eyes go glassy. Somewhere off in the ether Chester felt tiny bonds, like fragile little strings, breaking, one by one. Elsa Starlighter was slipping through his fingers. The fingers of both hands.

After school, Chester walked to a nearby gas station to to call Elsa's house on the pay phone. He wanted to make sure she was all right, and given that, do a lot of groveling. With a large, hard knot in his stomach he fumbled the coins into the slot. A dial tone buzzed annoyingly into his right ear, while a deep, thunderous rumbling exploded into his left. He turned his head to look. The rumble was coming from the glass-pack muffler of a powder blue convertible '68 Camero, the slickest car on the road.

Through the smoking exhaust, on the passenger side of the car, just barely above the dashboard, Chester spied a pair of electric blue eyes. His stomach tightened even more than he thought possible and he was overcome with nausea. Elsa Starlighter turned away toward the driver. In the driver's seat, looking confident with a well-muscled left arm thrusting out the driver's side window, sat one of the boys from the Stud Club. Chester scampered into his all too vivid imagination, where he heard, plain as day, the stories that would be told of Elsa in resonant restroom voices. The lurid details, the hardened laughter.

A much more excruciating burst of bodily chemicals exploded into Chester's system with the suddenness of a sucker-punch, hitting him hard somewhere between his mid-section and his will to live. He stood frozen like one of the ice statues he'd seen in the Russian section of his social studies book.

If ever Chester thought that he knew pain, he was sadly mistaken. All the thoughtless name calling; all the times he had been attacked and beaten simply because he was different; all the stupid, embarrassing things he had done to himself in front of others, all of them were of no consequence when weighed against the blinding ache that he felt now. It was as though his sense of survival were a physical part of his body and someone had spitefully lopped it off, leaving only enough hope to keep the pain alive.

"Hey Crab," the driver shouted "You're lookin' pretty buff... at least on one side, Ha! You look more like a fiddler crab than ever."

The Stud Club boy gunned the accelerator and spun the rear wheels. Thick black smoke engulfed Chester and he heard the car speed away. When the smoke cleared Chester McFadden stood alone in the gas station holding the telephone receiver in his right hand. He heard the small, tinny voice of Mrs. Starlighter asking if anyone were there. "No, no one's here," he said into the receiver and hung up the phone.

Walking home the Fiddler Crab climbed down under the Mission Bridge - the troll bridge - and for the first time in years, cried out loud.

1971

Robert Austin Sedgwick rifled his closet for a suit. Something appropriate for attending the Eunice Banders revival meeting. His collection of tuxedos had served him well for film industry social events, but they seemed a little much for attending a religious function. Half an hour spent digging in his closet and he was ready to call it quits.

He drove to the Salvation Army Thrift Store, where he stole a dark blue suit. Removing the suit from the rack, he walked to the used book section, ducked behind a bookcase and put it on over his clothes. It was a bit bulky with his clothes underneath, but hopefully no one from the store would notice. Checking the suit briefly for hanging labels, he pulled them off, sauntered past the cashier and strolled out the front door. A few doors down Robert stopped and checked his reflection in a store window. The suit was okay. It was a little short, but it would do. The defuse reflection in the window failed to reveal the light stains that had probably led to the suit's being put out to pasture. He wore the suit home, where he made himself a sweet sugar sandwich on fresh, spongy white bread.

2004

Albert Trundell's office was his security blanket. Every time he sat his ample behind into his overstuffed swivel chair, he was bathed in familiarity. From behind his desk, facing the door, he sensed the placement of every object in the room. Everything except his pencils, which seemed to randomly disappear and then reappear in odd places such as the men's restroom or the middle of a hallway, or sometimes in his car. Pencils aside, this office was an extension of his person. Every paperclip, every pushpin. If a certain paper was three sheets up from the bottom of the stack in his inbox, he knew where to find it.

Trundell didn't enjoy mysteries very much, particularly mysteries where people he knew were being hurt. That was partly why he had founded AWARE Magazine. There were aspects of American society that had bothered him since his stint in Vietnam. When he had returned home from that conflict he had learned some bitter truths. He was not welcomed as a hero as he was led to believe he would be. He was cursed by some and treated like an unfortunate dupe by others. There were no jobs waiting for the veterans of that particular war. He had been lied to. Hell, everyone had been lied to and a lot of people had died as a result. Some of his Army buddies had taken to drinking heavily and abusing various drugs, becoming recluses or outcasts. Some had ended their own lives or the lives of their love ones. They had all been encouraged to commit horrible acts and had had horrible acts committed against them. And for what? For nothing. In the end, for nothing.

A short stint as a biker had given him a new sense of identity for a while. The recklessness appealed to him. The adrenalin felt familiar. But somewhere along the way, after too many barroom brawls over worthless women, bad drug dealings or, most often, too much alcohol, he lost interest. It had died suddenly, like a light going out in his head. One day it mattered if he had been sold some bunk weed, or his girl had ridden on someone else's bike, the next day it didn't matter at all. He was over it, and that day he simply climbed on his bike and rode away without saying goodbye to anyone. He rode all the way to California, to a beautiful little mountain town called Soda River.

Trundell sold his bike for more money than it was worth and started a small newsletter supporting Vietnam veterans, highlighting problems with their re-integration into American society. There were a lot of veterans, apparently, and a lot of families of veterans. His newsletter became popular in short order due to its high quality reporting and fair point of view. Eventually, with help from his subscribers, he was able to upgrade it to a full-fledged magazine. He had also broadened his scope to cover social injustice in general, primarily the transgressions of large corporations and the abuses of power committed by the US and state governments. People were still being lied to and hurt, just as they were during the Vietnam era and Trundell felt a duty to expose these lies to the general public. He had gone to war and killed people, seen his friends die, because he had believed the lies he had been told, from the recruiting office on up. There were several wars still occurring every day, a political war, a corporate war, an environmental war, and occasionally an international conflict. To present a new generation with enough information to make intelligent choices in these wars had become his mission.

Over the years Albert Trundell's magazine had become somewhat of an institution. The children of the first subscribers were now subscribers, themselves. Trundell never took his obligation to these people lightly. He would tell them the pure, unbiased truth whether or not that was what they wanted to hear. He was neither Republican nor Democrat and his magazine was unwaveringly neutral.

He remembered fondly the first day he had seen Xochitl Saint James. She had cornered him in the magazine's parking lot and shown him some photographs. Beautiful pictures, well composed, each one telling a story. Trundell had recognized her talent immediately. As he thumbed through the photos, he found himself possessed with the urge to crawl into each picture and look around, something he had rarely experienced with any of his photographers in the past. "Well, I can't deny you have quite an eye, young lady," he said "but I really don't need anyone right now." Then he had flipped to the next picture. It was a black and white of an overweight, middle-aged woman, dressed in rags, obviously homeless, sitting on the backrest of a bus bench with her elbows on her knees and her ragged boots on the seat. She was staring hard at two wrinkled vagrancy citations trying to comprehend their meaning. It was clear by the look on the woman's face that she was illiterate. Albert Trundell's heart had broken. The woman's face had made up his mind. "Alright," he said, "what have you done before?"

"Just this," she said, holding up the sheaf of eight-by-tens.

"You haven't worked anywhere before?"

"Well, yeah, but not as a photographer. I'm only 19. I went to Brooks Institute in Santa Barbara for a year, but I couldn't afford to keep it up. I think I'm pretty good, though. And I love your magazine. It's the only one that really slaps me in the face. Every time. I'm pretty sure I kinda have talent for this type of thing and I really want to use it for something good." She stared at his eyes. "I think AWARE Magazine is something good."

"Yeah," said Trundell, "I think it is, too. Like I said, I don't really need anybody right now, but, uh..." His words trailed off. Man, she's obviously some kind of a natural, he thought to himself. You don't find those every day. I better give her *something* or she may not be around when I *do* need somebody. "Look, why don't you come by tomorrow and I'll see if I can't find something for you to do."

"Thank you, sir," she said. "I really appreciate this."

He had put her to work in the development lab. It wasn't the front-end photography she was looking for, but at least this was related and would keep her occupied. The kid had been good, no denying it, but being a good photographer and handling a delicate assignment were two different things. There were people skills and strategy involved. Hopefully, with a little maturing, she would turn out to be an asset.

That had been four years ago and, although she was a bit of a loose cannon, he had never regretted his decision. She had more than earned her keep at the magazine, going to great lengths, even putting herself in danger, to get a particular picture that told a story. Xochitl had become somewhat of a surrogate daughter to him, a wild child, to be sure, but she had become an important part of his life.

And now his little girl was in trouble. No, Trundell didn't like mysteries, and this particular mystery was beginning to scare him. He had a dead doctor, an inexperienced reporter missing in action, possibly for keeps, along with a company car and all of Xochitl's camera equipment. That was big. The fact that they knew who Xochitl was and where she lived, that the crime scenes had been cleaned up impossibly fast, and that the police had never arrived after a call from a pay phone, all smacked of money. Lots of money.

2003

As Chester McFadden grew older, he often found himself on the sidewalks of his neighborhood secretly eying the happy couples strolling along beside him. Why he chose to put himself through this misery over and over again was a mystery to him. Perhaps it was the tiniest glimmer of hope still burning inside him, or perhaps the pain had become like an old reliable companion. Not a good friend, but someone whose presence he had grown used to. Either way he inevitably arrived at home feeling cold and empty with a familiar knot camped out in his stomach. Especially if the couples had been holding hands or walking arm-in-arm.

He was lonely and his fantasies frequently flew straight out of the bowels of desperation. *If I could somehow keep a girl on my right side, at least for a while, maybe until after she got to know me, well that wouldn't be so bad. Would it? Hell, she'd never know. True, it'd be a bit of work, but not impossible. Don't let the old right hand know what the old left hand is doing. Heh heh... Oh right! Like I'm gonna shove my right side in her face my whole life. Wake up Crab.*

But still...

But the years crept by and there was no young lover on the right side or the left. Chester realized that his chance with Elsa Starlighter had been a fluke, a miracle, a one-time deal. She actually had been the special girl he'd thought she was. As the severity of his situation came gradually into focus he sank into the dark crevasse of self-pity.

Chester had long been aware of a small neighborhood bar down the street from his place and had, for some time, entertained a certain curiosity about it. Sometimes he thought of venturing into the raggedy little building and getting drunk, really drunk, which was something he'd never done. *Just get shit-faced. Pissed enough to make it all go away. Just drown all those nasty memories in some sweet fizzy liquid ...* But as bad as things may have been, though, he refused to embark on a drinking career. That would just make matters worse. He knew this for certain. He enjoyed an occasional six-pack if there was a good game on the TV, but those were game beers, not pity beers. *Big difference.*

2004

Albert Trundell picked up the phone and punched in the numbers for the Soda River General Hospital.

"Soda River General," said a young and perky female voice.

"Hi, this is Albert Trundell over at AWARE Magazine. I wonder if you could give me some information on a patient that was admitted this morning."

"What was the patient's name, sir? Are you a relative?"

"Well, I don't know his name. He had an accident with a power saw. I'm sure they admitted him. I understand the blade went into his shin pretty deeply."

"Oh yeah, that guy. We actually ended up not admitting him. Some people came and got him while he was still in the emergency room."

"Who came and got him?"

"I don't know, sir. Some guys. They flashed some kind of badge and took him away."

"Was he conscious?"

"I guess. I don't really know. Unless someone's admitted into the hospital, they don't really go through me. I found out most of this stuff from one of the nurses who was working in the ER at the time. I wasn't in the room when they came and took him."

"I see. Do you know if they were able to get his name?"

"Well, there wouldn't be a record of it because, like I said, he wasn't admitted so he didn't come through me. I'm not sure if he mentioned his name to any of the staff. Most of the people who were working then have gone home, but I can ask them in

the morning."
   "Thank you. I'll call you in the morning then."

2003

One winter evening the cold, empty knot that personified Chester's loneliness began to tie itself so tight that it transformed from discomfort to physical pain. The Pepto Bismol bottle in his medicine cabinet held barely a teaspoonful of the bright, pink liquid. Not nearly enough to quell his symptoms. There was no replenishing his stock as the drug store on the corner closed at 5:00.

In desperation he wandered into an unobtrusive little black hole of a drinking establishment called Pinky's Bar, and ordered himself a pity beer. He sat down at the bar, glancing nervously over both shoulders. The top of the bar was a continuous sheet of pitted copper held to plywood with decorative brass tacks. Underneath the bar was a short wall of thick bamboo and Chester banged his knees against it as he adjusted himself on the stool.

"Ah Shit," he said.

"You got that right," said the bartender, a stocky, well-tanned guy, forty-ish, with short, spiked blond hair. He offered Chester his tattooed hand. "Pinky."

"Chester, but most people call me the Fiddler Crab."

"Which do you prefer?"

"Well," he eyed the colorful display of partially full alcohol bottles on the wall behind the bartender, "when I was younger I preferred Chester, but as I've gotten older I've discovered that I no longer have the patience or energy it takes to fool myself. It takes a lot of work to fool yourself, you know."

"What's that supposed to mean?"

"When I walked in here, obviously the first thing you noticed about me was my withered arm." He pulled his arm from beneath the bar. "Don't worry, everyone does. People call me Chester and, as long as there's no mirror around, I could be anybody, maybe a movie star or even a one of those Chippendale's dancer guys, anybody. But if they call me the Fiddler Crab, I know exactly who I am and exactly what the world thinks of me.

"That's pretty harsh," said Pinky, as he wiped down the bar with a wet, stained rag. "You shouldn't be so hard on yourself."

"I'm not being hard on myself," said the Fiddler Crab a little irritated. "In fact, it's much easier this way. I don't have to weather people's hollow sympathy or endure their cruel remarks. It's all in the voice, you know. It's not what they say, it's how they say it." The Fiddler Crab shook his head. "Sympathy is a deceptive thing. I hate sympathy worse than a direct insult. When a person gives you sympathy he puts himself on a higher plane than you, while making himself feel kind and generous. It's win-win for him. He can't give you sympathy unless he feels superior to you. It's impossible. You know who I admire? I admire the ones who just come up to me and say 'Hey, Fiddler Crab. What do think of this weather we're having?' To me, that's the ultimate compliment. I've been accepted for who I am. So if you don't mind, you can just call me the Fiddler Crab."

"Okay, Fiddler Crab, you're the boss. So what can I getcha?"

The Fiddler Crab fidgeted in his seat, then gestured with his chin toward the lone television above the bar. "Is there a game on?" he asked.

"What kinda game? This ain't really a sports bar." Pinky had tried many crackpot ideas through the years to turn this run-down bar into a gold mine but he was philosophically opposed to the idea of a sports bar. "I don't think it'd work for me. It'd be like having a religion bar, you know, Catholics on one side and Protestants on the other. Only problem is they wouldn't stay on their own side. And then you'd have a hell of a mess on your hands. Sports and religion, pretty much the same thing. And besides, sports bars bring in the wrong kinda people. Next thing you know you'd have a room fulla yuppies and there goes the neighborhood. You hear what I'm sayin'?"

At some point in the past, Pinky's had featured topless dancing. That had been a long time ago, another failed project, but all the trappings were still in place. A lumpy linoleum stage filled one side of the room. A small catwalk protruded from the middle along with a tarnished brass pole. On the wall behind the stage stood an ancient mirror whose glass had gone smokey with dried body oils. Occasionally, people got too drunk and crawled onto the stage and trying to do their own awkward version of a striptease, usually involving more comedy than titillation. Pinky lived for those moments and they were the reason he left the stage in place. "People are free entertainment," he would say, as his customers stumbled onto the stage to prove him right.

"I guess it can be any kind of game," said the Fiddler Crab. "I'm not very particular. I just need a game on while I drink."

"And you came in here instead of a sports bar?"

"The sympathy. At a sports bar I would have experienced the sympathy. So far you've spared me that humiliation. I'm in your debt for that."

"What are you fuckin' nuts," said Pinky? "You don't owe me nothing. So you got a little problem with your arm. Big deal! You're just some guy, you know, like any other guy that comes in here. Quit worrying about it. Around here, as long as you got enough mobility to get your glass from the bar to your lips, you're fine. In fact, you're a fuckin' Olympiad! That's the only sport we play around here. It's called Get the Beer in Your Pie-Hole!" Pinky turned the television to a football game.

The Fiddler Crab sat and drank and talked to Pinky. Hours went by and he found that he'd been smiling most of the evening. He'd decided immediately that he liked Pinky, which didn't happen to him very often. Pinky was good people. He was easy to talk to and, more importantly, easy to listen to. You could point him in some direction and he'd go on for hours. His stories were full of colorful characters and unusual situations, things the Fiddler Crab had never experienced in person. And the jovial bartender never seemed to run out of them.

Even though there was a game on the television, a little voice somewhere in the back of the Fiddler Crab's head knew he was drinking a pity beer. He did what he could to stifle the voice, shoving it back down into the murky depths from whence it came. After all, Pinky had made him feel good about himself. Something about this place made him want to stay and maybe even come back. He wanted to meet some of the people in the stories that poured out of Pinky in an endless stream. Perhaps they would accept him as Pinky had, as a man, as just the guy on the next stool.

The pity beer went down easily enough, but didn't have much effect, so he ordered second, and then third. Soon, as the warm glow of alcohol encompassed him along with Pinky's warm, inviting personality, he began to feel uninhibited and free to speak his mind on any subject. Throughout the evening Pinky introduced him to his regular customers and after several conversations the Fiddler Crab's tight core began to relax.

As the Fiddler Crab rose from his stool and fumbled with his coat, he was filled with good tidings for the world at large. *Man, what a nice evening. That's the last word I thought I'd use to describe a night in a bar, but I can't think of any other word for it but nice. My stomach doesn't hurt. I can't remember the last time the knot wasn't there.*

But when the Fiddler Crab walked out, glowing, into the chilly night air, the first sight that greeted him was a young, very-in-love couple, walking arm in arm. Even through his alcohol-induced daze the Fiddler Crab felt the knot once again begin to sink its claws into the lining of his stomach.

I'll have to do this again. Soon. This place felt like a haven tonight. I need to spend a little more time there and talk to people. Real People.

1971

As Robert Austin Sedgwick stood in the admission line for the Eunice Banders revival meeting, he once again had the urge to cut and run. This place was giving him the creeps. An ornately carved stone wall, which Robert found somewhat intimidating, fronted the theater. A long line of anxious worshipers disappeared into an arched, wooden door at its center. The line quivered and fidgeted with excitement. Most of the people wore a vacuous, glassy-eyed expression normally reserved for romantic situations. It was hard to get a handle on exactly what made these people different, but they were definitely not Robert's usual crowd. Everyone in line was well-washed, scrubbed ruddy, and pink. Some of the women were pretty, but somehow sexless. He hadn't known that was possible, especially in Los Angeles. Most amazing of all, he discovered, was that he could look anyone directly in the eye and they wouldn't blink the strings away. In fact, nearly everyone's gaze was open and inviting.

I may have gotten fired from 'The Green Terror From Beyond', but apparently it wasn't due to my acting skills, he thought. No one here has been anything but kind to me. Obviously, they think I'm one of them.

Standing in line, Robert felt obligated to say something, to make an attempt to be social. But what to say? He was only slightly familiar with the lingo of church people. He knew the "Now I lay me down to sleep prayer", but it didn't seem to apply here.

"Hello, brother." It was a man, thirty-fiveish, with a balding head and wire rimmed glasses. "I can tell you're excited about the meeting here tonight. I can see it in your eyes. The eyes don't lie, you know."

"Oh yes, I am, heh, I sure as hell am," Robert blurted. "I, um, pray the Lord your soul to take, ah...brother."

The man's grin cemented but his eyes took on a slightly puzzled expression. "Yes, well, ... thank you," he said, and drifted away.

When it was Robert's turn to go through the heavy, wooden doors, he pulled out his wallet, looked for a ticket agent, and finding none, discretely slipped the wallet back into his pocket.

Inside, he found a seat a few rows back from the stage and quickly surveyed his surroundings. The walls were decorated with long white banners every twenty feet or so, each one displaying a line drawing of a descending dove carrying an olive branch in its beak. The theater curtains had been covered with white satin. Hundreds of candles illuminated the stage. The decor was pristine, church-like, but the theater seats and floor were sticky with spilled drinks and discarded chewing gum.

From his position close to the front, Robert would be able to watch Eunice without being seen himself once the lights were dimmed. He wanted a chance to observe her, get a feel for what was going on, before he approached her. Lola Lorraine was somewhat familiar to him, but there was no telling whom Eunice Banders might turn out to be. Robert wanted to pick his time to reveal himself. An amplified voice boomed from the stage interrupting his thoughts.

"Brothers and sisters," said a man with thick black hair and a powder blue suit, speaking from a pulpit in the middle of the stage, "we are all here tonight to receive a message. A message that, in our hearts, we already know to be true. A message that, in the day-to-day pressures that tear us asunder, we often allow ourselves to forget. We, all of us, need to be reminded of the sad state of our priorities from time to time. I personally know of no one more blessed with the tools to bring us that message than the Reverend Eunice Banders."

Robert was momentarily startled as the audience sent forth a huge roar. Eunice Banders emerged from the wings carrying a folder full of loose-leaf pages. She strode quickly, almost self-consciously to the pulpit, placed the folder on it and began rifling through the papers as the roar of the crowd gradually diminished. Once the room was silent enough to for the Reverend Eunice Banders to be heard, she cleared her throat into the microphone. The remaining voices trailed off one by one until the hush was so complete that Robert could hear a single cough on the far side of the theater. The Reverend Eunice Banders raised her head and faced the congregation.

Robert realized with a start that the lights had not dimmed, nor were they showing any signs of doing so. He began to feel a slight panic and ducked his head behind the head of the man in front of him. He had a sudden vision of Eunice pausing to point him out while uniformed security men yanked him from his seat by his underarms. Of course, he thought, what an idiot. This is a church meeting, not a movie. They don't kill the lights in church, do they? Glancing over his shoulder he satisfied himself that the security guards were all in his imagination, then stealthily peeked past the ear of the man in front of him.

Eunice leaned into the microphone and began speaking in a low, even tone, not unlike the one she had used on Robert in the stateroom during the yacht party. Robert didn't listen to the words. He couldn't. Her tone was understated, lulling and hypnotic. He was drawn into a trance-like state, a comfortable place of complete trust and felt himself being tugged toward surrender. Unsure if it was love or demons, Robert looked around the theater and noticed that everyone wore the same expression as himself - a face frozen, with no evidence of emotion except in the eyes, which were wide and full of wonder.

"SALVATION!" Eunice barked suddenly, and an entire congregation of heads snapped back, startled. Then she relapsed to her monotonic, trance-inducing tone and continued on.

"The CROSS!" she shouted a little while later, and again the heads snapped back in a syncopated wave of flesh and hair. She drifted on, once more, in her soft, inoffensive voice. Robert began to sense a vague pattern, but, try as he might to guess where the loud bits were going to happen, they still took him by complete surprise every time and his head snapped back along with all the others.

An hour or so later a collection plate came floating down his row. Robert appeared to throw a few dollars into it, but when he pulled his hand away his dollar bills, as well as a few that had been in the plate, were tucked into his sleeve. He had a sudden craving for sugar.

"Excuse me," someone was bumping against Robert's knees, trying to work their way to the aisle through the sea of legs. Robert gradually noticed that people from all over the theater were walking down the isles toward the stage. They walked up onto the stage and knelt in a row before the Reverend Eunice Banders. She lay her hands gently on their shoulders and spoke to them quietly. Seeing his chance, Robert stood to make his way to the stage. He had been wishing for an opportunity and it wasn't going to get any better than this.

"Bless you, brother," said the man sitting next to him. Bowing his head low in order to hide his face, Robert walked down the aisle and ascended a short flight of wooden steps onto the stage. He dropped to his knees and bowed his head, hiding his face as Eunice worked her way down the row, lightly touching each person and mumbling encouraging words. Staring intently at the hard wood floor of the stage, Robert could hear her approaching, though he couldn't quite make out the words she was saying. He grew giddy with anticipation. Finally, Eunice was standing directly before him.

"Welcome brother. I'm glad you've decided to be honest with yourself and admit you have a need," whispered Eunice.

"Oh, I have a need, alright," said Robert raising his head and glaring into Eunice's eyes.

Eunice went pale.

BINGO! thought Robert. This was worth everything.

Eunice was silent for a moment as she gathered her composure. "Yes, brother, and I'm glad you've admitted as much. However, I sense a deeper conflict in you, which may require some additional attention. Perhaps you would agree to meet me later at my office where we could discuss the special circumstances of your situation."

"You got it, baby," whispered Robert so that only Eunice could hear him. "Where's your office?"

She whispered an address into his ear and moved on to the next person in the row. Robert hopped to his feet and faced the crowd, grinning like a lunatic.

"I'M HEALED!" he shouted, his arms spread wide above his head. "MY COMPULSIVE FLATULANCE - COMPLETELY GONE...COMPLETELY GONE! IT'S A MIRACLE! THANK YOU, SISTER! THANK YOU!" Walking down the stage stairs, Robert slapped a man on the back. "It's a miracle, brother," he said. "I found what I was looking for." He stared briefly into the man's eyes and farted loudly. Then he scurried away, up the aisle and through the big wooden doors into the cool night air.

2003

The morning after his first excursion to Pinky's Bar the Fiddler Crab awakened slowly and with great effort. As he pried his eyes open, his small, dark apartment came into view, hazily at first, then gradually solidifying into something he recognized. The yellowed walls began to shake as a freight train rumbled by just outside. A slight hangover poked at him, but it was nothing too serious. Mostly, he was just tired. He had spent the night tossing and turning in a sort of half sleep populated by a series of bright, visual selections of the previous evening's events. The visions, as far as he could tell, were fairly accurate, but they were out of sequence and seemed to end abruptly just as the story began to get interesting. He woke with a vague feeling of dissatisfaction.

The Fiddler Crab pulled the filter from a deformed plastic coffee maker and examined it for grounds, which he found. There was at least another day's worth left in them. He filled the thing with water and plugged it into the wall. It hissed and spat awhile, then a thin stream of brown liquid trickled from its underbelly. When the coffee was done he poured himself a cup and sat on the back steps facing the railroad tracks. The bitter liquid warmed his belly and soon his heart was pumping stronger. He felt blood flowing through his veins.

What did last night really mean? It was so out of context for me. I have nothing to compare it to. The whole evening had been pretty fuzzy, but he was certain of one thing. *Right now, at nine o'clock in the morning, I'd love to march straight back to Pinky's Bar and play another round of 'Get the Beer in your Pie*

Hole'. ...Obviously that wouldn't be the right thing to do. He didn't want to become one of those people who sat in a bar all day every day. They always had such lifeless eyes. *They look as though they've been living underground.*

...*But I was accepted there, dammit, I was accepted!* And that was addictive. He felt it already. Pinky had spoken to him with respect. Not that cheesy, exaggerated, respect that one used while addressing a new acquaintance or a movie star, but real man to man respect. ...*And the knot, the knot in my stomach was gone. It's always there and it was gone. I can't believe I actually talked to people with no knot in my stomach. I talked to people and they were interested in what I had to say.*

What part of this picture could be bad? Really, the root of the problem was that it was fun, really fun. And fun was something that didn't come knocking on the Fiddler Crab's door every day. *It's got a lot of pull, fun... Fun could be a drug.*

bottom line, he couldn't go there every night of the week. *I don't want to become one of those bar zombies. But, on the other hand the people I talked to were bar people and they weren't zombies.* Okay, so they weren't zombies, but he couldn't go there every night. ...Still, after last night he couldn't cut it out altogether, either. *I'm a different man after last night. I actually felt unencumbered by the arm. In fact, I didn't even think of it at all.*

All right, once a week, then. He'd allow himself that. *So... this is Thursday morning... I can go to Pinky's next Wednesday night.*

And he did. The Fiddler Crab sat on a Chrome and Naugahyde stool at the bar with a man on one side of him who was skinny everywhere but his belly, and on the other, a woman who was skinny everywhere but her chest. The man said his name was Darren and introduced the woman as "Tonsils". Pinky babbled about life as a chef in the Navy and made them all laugh out loud with his story of offering the Admiral fried rat as chicken. "What the hell," he said, "it all tastes like chicken, anyway."

The Fiddler Crab couldn't remember the last time he had laughed uncontrollably. He'd always been afraid someone would glare at him, as though, given his physical condition, he hadn't the right to laugh. Perhaps he never had laughed aloud. It felt good, glorious in fact, like pressure that had been waiting years to be released. He felt twenty pounds lighter when he laughed. It didn't even matter that an attractive woman was sitting right next to his withered arm. Hell, her name was Tonsils, for crying out loud.

Months went by, eventually joining hands to form a year, and at some point the Fiddler Crab, or Fid, as he had come to be known, began to make nightly excursions to Pinky's Bar. Sometimes he even went during the day. All of his fears of becoming a subterranean bar-dweller had proven groundless. The Fiddler Crab, it turned out, did not possess an addictive personality. There were no lifeless eyes staring back at him from the mirror behind the bar. He did not hide sullenly behind a hollow face pleading for answers to life's tough questions. Nor, it seemed, did anyone else in the place. Those people didn't last long at Pinky's. They were welcome enough, but the ground was not fertile for growing self-loathing and soon they would move on to a darker, more depressing location.

One thing the Fiddler Crab enjoyed immensely at Pinky's Bar was the celebration of birthdays. Pinky always made a huge deal about the birthdays of his regular customers. On your birthday, you could sit at Pinky's Bar and drink all day, from six in the morning until midnight and never pay a dime. Pinky had furtive, almost mystical ways of learning the birth dates of his customers. It was rumored that he had secret access to DMV files. Some said he was just plain psychic. Either way, when your birthday arrived everyone was aware of it and someone had always baked a cake.

The first time the Fiddler Crab experienced someone's birthday at Pinky's he couldn't believe the amount of emotion an ordinary person was allowed to exhibit in a public place. He had whooped and hollered and sang right along with everyone else, perhaps even a tad more than everyone else, as the celebrant wept tears of joy and acceptance. And no one looked at him funny. No one glared. In fact, no one paid much attention to him at all. Or to anyone else other than the birthday boy or girl. It was cathartic and when he arrived home that night he could barely sleep. The excitement had consumed him. It was too much. The dam was broken and he wanted to continue singing and yelling. Pushing out repressed emotion as though he were squeezing festering fluid from a lanced boil.

1971

"WHAT THE HELL WERE YOU TRYING TO DO?" shouted Eunice as Robert entered her office. "You might have ruined everything!"

Robert was momentarily stumped for words as he saw, not Eunice Banders before him, but Lola Lorraine. Once again, her hair was black and arranged in the Cleopatra style he had seen her wear on the yacht. She wore a short, tight-fitting red dress made of what Robert took to be some type of shiny oriental fabric. Angry eyes bulged from her, once again, stunning face. "God, what an idiot!" she growled. "Well, what do you want?"

"What do you mean?" asked Robert. "I just wanted to see you again."

"I don't believe this." Lola hissed. "What are you, sixteen?"

"Well, no. I enjoyed our little fling. I guess it must have meant something to me. I couldn't stop thinking about you."

"Oh come on! Grow up! I don't even remember your name. We had a quick, mildly satisfying tumble in the back room of a boat. We were together, what, thirty, forty drunken minutes? Big deal! What did you think, we were going to get married? I told you I was already married. Quit being such a fool. You could have done some real damage back there."

"I...I...I...thought perhaps you and your husband were, you know, having difficulties or something. After all, it wasn't that hard to get you into the stateroom on the boat."

"I love my husband."

"Well then how can you, why did you...?" Robert wanted

172

to ask something, but he wasn't quite sure what to ask. He wanted her to tell him where he stood, but it seemed fairly obvious already. It was the "why" of the situation that puzzled him now.

Lola's shoulders sagged. "Look, just tell me what you want," she said, her voice resigned and businesslike. "You know too much so I can't expect you to simply walk away without some compensation. You're going to want to talk, so what's your silence going to cost me?"

Robert stood pondering for a moment. A million thoughts were fighting for dominance in his head. It was true, he had her over a barrel. He could demand another night with her, and surely get it. He could ask for a good-sized sum of money. What to do?

"Show me how it's done," he blurted, breaking the silence. "I want to know the rules of your game. Everything. I want to do what you're doing."

"Impossible," she said quietly. "Pick something else." She had expected him to demand a repeat performance of the night on the yacht, which she would grant. This time she would let him down easy, apologize for shouting at him. She would make sure that he knew where he stood and send him on his way. Given time, she could charm him into leaving quietly, wrap this whole annoying episode into a nice, neat bundle and toss it on the trash heap. "There must be something I can do for you," said Lola, her voice suddenly soft and suggestive.

Robert felt a burst of strength as his position became clear to him. "No," he said with absolute Hollywood confidence, "You will teach me how to do what you are doing or not only will your followers learn some rather unsavory facts about you, but your husband will as well."

"We have an understanding, my husband and I. We go our separate ways at parties. It's what keeps our marriage fresh and alive. He was probably in the next stateroom with one of the starlets, dear. No, he's no threat. My people, however, that's another story. They can't know. But teaching you the business is out of the question. It's all very territorial. There's no room for you, understand? Any knowledge you might gain from me would be useless to you because there's just no room."

"Well, somebody better make some goddam room, because that's my price."

Lola sat down on the desk and buried her face in her hands. She began to whimper, gently at first, then in great violent sobs as the magnitude of her problem became clear to her. In the end she understood that there was no choice but to give in to Robert's demands.

2004

When the Fiddler Crab's own birthday rolled around, the old, familiar knot returned to his stomach. It was one thing to celebrate the birth of someone else, but the stakes got a little higher when the birthday was your own. *What if nobody even showed up?*

How was he supposed to behave when all the attention in the room was on him? *I haven't given that little detail nearly enough consideration. What do people do? I mean, I've spent most of my life trying to direct attention away from myself. Attention always leads to me being the butt of someone else's joke. Always.*

It had been big fun just celebrating other people's good fortune. Right out loud. That seemed like a big enough accomplishment, given his history. *My god! This was like watching Karaoke and suddenly being dragged onstage. Couldn't I just leave things as they were?*

Apparently not. During the few days leading up to his birthday the Fiddler Crab experienced a sense of impending doom. The personal network he had built over the past year began to feel like a house of cards built on a railroad track. In one sense it was a huge test. *Ultimately, this has got to be good for me. I hope. It's pretty rare that I get to be the object of positive attention.* Well, there had been that one date with Elsa Starlighter. *At least the beginning of the date was positive, and the little kiss on the cheek the next day, that was good, too, though it did lead to disaster.*

The Fiddler Crab's solitary life had left him ill-prepared to face the rigorous onslaught of positive human attention. The thought was terrifying. It would set a precedent he would be obligated to maintain. For once in his life people would expect something from him. What was he supposed to do? What if his reaction was not sufficient and he was forced to watch disappointment shadow the faces of his friends.

I'd never live that down. I'd be back in that fetal position with the TV and all. Oh, they'd still drink with him and talk to him, but that certain bonding something would be gone. Respect, maybe. There wouldn't be the respect.

The Fiddler Crab wanted to pack all his things and move to another city, or barring that, at least stay home from Pinky's on his birthday. *Maybe I could stroll into Pinky's a few days after my birthday and fake a stuffy nose or something. By then all the hoopla will have run out of gas and things will be back to normal.*

But if he didn't attend he would lose that budding amount of respect for himself that had come, almost as a gift, from the people at Pinky's Bar. The Pinky's regulars would be denied a chance to celebrate the life of their friend, Fid. A person's birthday, thought the Fiddler Crab, was a rare occasion when one's friends and acquaintances could say good things about him right to his face - a practice that didn't seem to be encouraged in ordinary daily life.

After all the time he'd spent at Pinky's Bar it was still difficult for the Fiddler Crab to accept the fact that he had real friends. He may interact with them on any given night, but he always harbored a sneaking suspicion that they were relieved when he left for home. Perhaps this allowed him to keep a little piece of his big gray wall up, to keep one foot always out the door.

It occurred to the Fiddler Crab suddenly, that this was the reason he wanted to avoid his birthday altogether. *If I celebrate this birthday with these people and they prove to be real friends after all, I'll have to knock down that little remaining piece of wall, no thanks to you Doctor Banders. And then what?* He'd have to trust them, lean on them when things were not going so well.

I'll be wide open. Defenseless... Somehow that was kind of attractive, but *...holy shit.*

Having identified these nebulous fears and brought them to the forefront, the Fiddler crab should have been relieved that he had finally faced his demons and been instilled with a new kind of confidence. *Oh, that's all it is? That's all this is about? Fear of friendship? Fear of intimacy? Hell, bring it on.*

But, in reality, his newfound awareness made him more frightened than ever. If public acceptance was the goal, his deformity once again became a huge issue.

In the end he solved the problem by employing a good old-fashioned cowardly compromise. The Fiddler Crab went to Pinky's, but not without first tying on a good, stiff drunk. He had never done anything like this before, getting himself fully hammered while the sun still shined through his living room window, and guilt overcame him in waves as he sipped on a twelve pack of beer throughout the day. In a way he felt as though he were cheating his friends. The object of a good night at the bar was not to drink one's self into incoherence, but to maintain a steady, friendly buzz, a social lubricant which the more regular patrons seemed to achieve somewhat simultaneously. Most nights everyone in the bar seemed to be on a mental par with each other, their emotional state dodging and darting in unison like a flock of birds or a school of fish. Everyone's drinking habits were pretty much common knowledge, and the social interactions took place accordingly, stilted at first, more cohesive as the night progressed. It was a fragile social arrangement and he feared the possibility of throwing a wrench in its gears, of insulting his friends by starting without them.

When the time came the Fiddler Crab staggered out of his front door, slamming it a bit too forcefully, and floundered down the sidewalk, banging his little pink elbow on the mailbox. "Ow, shit, man! I'm not drunk! I am *not* drunk! ... I'm drunk. ...Aww... come on, man, they won't be able to tell the difference," he mumbled, tripping on a crack in the sidewalk and going down on one knee. Ow! He staggered to his feet. *I'll just waltz on in there like it's a normal night. Hell, it is a normal night. It's just that I happened to be born on this day, that's all. So what? No big deal! So I'm a little tipsy... I'm sober enough to pull this off.* He banged his other knee on a lamppost. "Dammit!"

There was a good-sized bruise on the Fiddler Crab's forehead as he strode through the door of Pinky's Bar, and there were several new holes in his clothes. The place had a decent crowd tonight. A loud rumble filled the air. There were a few anonymous "What ups" and "Yo Fids" as he crossed the room. But, he noticed a bit nervously, there were no "Happy Birthdays". Not yet, at least. As he walked the gauntlet across the room, the Fiddler Crab hooked his shoe on the leg of a bar stool and fell flatly on his face. He rolled onto his back, shading his eyes with his forearm, embarrassed.

Pinky leaned over the bar, eternal washrag in hand. He stared quizzically down at the prostrate Fiddler Crab, his face turning alternately red and blue from a blinking promotional beer sign on the wall. "Hey Fid," he said, a touch of concern in his voice, as the Fiddler Crab hefted himself onto his favorite bar stool. "What's the poop?" Pinky pulled a glass from a sink full of dirty suds and began to wipe it dry.

That's it? Hey Fid? What's the poop? The Fiddler Crab was stunned. *What, does he not know it's my birthday? No way he doesn't know it's my birthday. He knows everybody's birthday.* True, the Fiddler Crab had no driver's license. He walked and took the bus to the few places he went. If Pinky truly had a friend at the DMV, The Fiddler Crab wouldn't be in the system and Pinky would never know. *But he should know, dammit, I'm a regular customer. I'm one of the gang. The people in this place are supposed to be my friends. My family, even.* His words were beginning to slur, even in his thoughts. The Fiddler Crab rose, clumsily and with some effort, to his feet and stumbled into Darrin, who was stretched toward the middle of the pool table, staring intently at the nine ball.

Darrin and Tonsils were playing a game of eight ball, with

Tonsils gleefully whipping Darrin's ass. He glanced up without moving his head. "What's up, Fid? You start without us tonight? What's the occasion?" He lowered his eyes and took his shot, missing the nine ball entirely.

"Yeah, well, I just got a little thirsty."

"It happens," said Darren. "But I can't say we're not hurt."

"Ditto," said Pinky. "How the hell am I gonna know when to cut you off, Fid? Damn, you're makin' my life complicated."

The Fiddler Crab hobbled as steadily as he could back to his stool, the stool that fit his butt just right. He sat down and worked his butt into the naugahide until it felt like home.

"So what can I getcha, Fid?" asked Pinky. Pinky always went through this ritual, even though he knew the preferred drink of each and every regular patron who walked through his door.

"Champagne," slurred the Fiddler Crab.

"Champagne?" Pinky scratched his head with a calloused, wet finger.

"Yeah, I said champagne, didn't I? You get hard of hearing all of a sudden?"

"Easy, my friend. You go changing drinks on me like that and I gotta take a minute to retrain myself."

The Fiddler Crab shut his eyes and rubbed his temples. Could this really be? All that worry and stress and these assholes, his "friends", didn't even know it was his birthday. *Shit! What a fool.* Sure, at first he'd hoped they wouldn't make a big fuss, all the embarrassing attention, the awkward response. But once he was resigned to having this silly-ass birthday celebration, he was actually anxious to get the thing under way. It would be a sort of rite of passage. He had battled himself, fighting his own reservations fiercely, in order to endure a party in his honor, and now he was bitterly disappointed when it was apparently not going to happen.

The Fiddler Crab sat at the bar, quietly brooding, sipping his drink for maybe half an hour. When he finished his third glass of champagne he slapped the delicate glass onto the bar, breaking the fragile stem. There was a clatter of broken glass and the place grew suddenly quiet at the universal sound of bar trouble. Everyone stared in his direction.

"You people call yourselves my friends? You're not my friends! You know that?" he said? "I have no friends."

"Calm down, Fid," said Tonsils. Her voice sharp like the broken glass, but drunker.

"Don't tell me to calm down. I don't have to calm down - and besides, I am calm."

"Oh, you're reeeal calm! C'mon, Sugar, tell ol' Tonsils what the problem is."

"There is no problem, okay? Everything is wonderful. Everything is just fucking grand."

"You shouldn't hide your feelings, Fiddy. It's not good for you. Talk to me. You can tell ol' Tonsils what's wrong." She gently rubbed his shoulders with her fingertips.

"Nothing is wrong!" he was shouting now. "Not a goddam thing is wrong!"

"C'mon, Darlin', just whisper in my ear. I promise I won't tell anybody," slurred Tonsils.

Pinky handed the Fiddler Crab a new glass of champagne.

"Maybe that'll cool yer jets, little feller," said Tonsils. She was cooing now. "Or maybe you've had enough to drink already. Is it another woman makin' you this way, Fiddy-widdy? You two-timin' old Tonsils?"

"Look, I'm fine, Okay?" He shrugged her hands from his shoulders, his voice a tight little growl. "In fact I've never felt better in my life. See - HA HA HA HA HA! In fact, I feel so good I'm going to go for a walk. Enjoy some fresh air."

"Who could you possibly have to see that's more important than us, your good friends, Fiddy?" said Tonsils.

"Friends, Ha! I have no friends." The Fiddler Crab stumbled off of his stool and strode stiffly toward the door. He turned and faced the wide-eyed crowd. "You know what? You're dead to me," he shouted. "Everyone here is dead to me! In fact, everyone in the fucking world is dead to me. The world is one big stinking cesspool of a garbage dump, and ... and your all just dead to me!"

The Fiddler Crab kicked the door open fiercely. It hit the outside wall with a thunderous crack. A startled yelp escaped a delicate young woman standing just outside the door. She wore a red, woolen overcoat and carried a large boom box under her arm. He stormed past her, barely noticing. The woman watched him go, then shook her head and walked into the bar. She placed the boom box on the pool table and removed her overcoat revealing a red satin teddy and three inch heels.

"Okay," she said in a voice, more breath than words, "which one of you boys is the Fiddler Crab? Sorry I'm late."

2004

Xochitl and Marissa were sitting on the couch in Marissa's living room with a large plastic bowl of popcorn. They had been watching 'On The Beach' and sat staring at the television screen as the credits made their journey northward.

"Well, that was depressing," said Marissa.

"Gregory Peck was kind of cute, though," Xochitl countered.

"Yeah, but he was too cold. I can't get into that whole duty before love thing."

"Marissa?"

"Yeah?"

"What do you think happened to Ernie?"

"Oh, I'm sure he's all right. He just..."

Xochitl held a palm to Marissa's face. "Seriously, what do you think happened?"

Marissa sighed and sat quiet for a moment, unsure what to say.

"I knew it," said Xochitl. "You think he's dead, don't you?"

"I...I haven't ruled it out, Xochitl," said Marissa hesitantly. "That man in your house was trying to kill you, and the doctor was very dead when you found him. You have to at least consider the possibility that Ernie is dead, too. That's why you're leaving town, remember?"

Xochitl bit her lip and her foot began to tap up and down. "It's not fair. Ernie's life was just beginning, you know. That was his first real assignment."

"I know, honey." Marissa placed her arms around Xochitl

and squeezed her gently. "Let's get you rested up for your big drive tomorrow." She got up and tugged on the couch until it unfolded into a bed.

Marissa walked to the television and was about to turn it off when Xochitl stopped her. "Wait, check this out Marissa. They're talking about those red light cameras. Did you know I got a ticket that day when you borrowed my car? You probably went through a red light and didn't even know it. It came in the mail today. What's he saying? Turn it up."

On the television screen a reporter was standing on a street corner with a microphone in his hand. He was saying that the city had been caught shortening the duration of the yellow lights in certain intersections in order to increase the likelihood of drivers being caught in a red light. Each of the intersections in question contained a red light camera. Apparently, a disgruntled city employee had blown the whistle resulting in an immediate spate of finger pointing. A spokesman for the city was forced to admit that the city had experienced a sudden need for cash. By shortening the yellow light, more people were caught in the intersection when the light turned red, resulting in more traffic fines. The hapless motorist was sent a citation, which he couldn't contest, since it contained photographs of both the driver and the license plate in the intersection. In fact, the whistle-blower said, the city had been steadily shortening the duration of the yellow light for some time. It was only recently that the light had become so short that people had begun to complain. The disgruntled employee had seized that moment to tell everything he knew.

"Ha!" said Marissa. "See, it wasn't my fault."

"Oh man, that is so cheesy," Xochitl moaned. "So what do we do with the ticket?"

"I guess I'll have to pay it."

"You're not paying anything," said Xochitl. "They cheated you. They cheated us both."

"Well, they did say the city is short of money."

"I can't believe you. The city's always short of money. It's not about how much money they have, it's about how much they want and what asinine things they choose to spend it on. Do you know how many police cars there are in this town? The other day I saw two squad cars and a motorcycle pulling over a guy on a bicycle. A bicycle! I'm not paying any bogus red light fines to fund that kind of behavior, and neither are you. It's just greed. There's never going to be enough money for them. The city's like a big badly run corporation. You're a book keeper, you should understand that." Xochitl stuffed a handful of popcorn into her mouth. "Man, things just keep getting weirder and weirder."

2004

The room was dark save for the blue and yellow glow of a television set spewing late-night commercial programming. The sound had been muted and the room was silent punctuated by an occasional groan. On the bed the Fiddler Crab had forced himself into the tightest fetal position he could manage, and there he lay staring at the soundless screen. "What a fool," he mumbled "God! I was so stupid." He had discovered in himself, now that it was too late, an aching need to be celebrated. He wanted to be defenseless and vulnerable before his friends. He wanted to learn to trust.

What would it be like to cry in front of someone who cared? I mean really cared. Someone who felt a need to cheer me up, wanted me to stop crying because my tears were hurting them, too.

He would never know. That was clear. He would never, ever know. Lying in this fetal position, the Fiddler Crab felt his skin grow a little thicker. In the end it was a calming thing actually, this thickening of the skin. It was a lowering of expectations, a reality check.

For a week or more the Fiddler Crab couldn't drum up enough nerve to return to Pinky's. Indeed, his first reaction was never to darken the doors of the heartless hellhole again. However, his first night at home was painfully boring. Television was, except for The Simpsons, inane, even though it kept him mercifully numb. He watched anything, staring at the screen intently, trying to feel the characters. Trying to make surrogate friends of them. But it was hopeless. Television characters were only as deep as the screen and the situations were too contrived. Life wasn't like that. Life threw you curve balls. It never promised you a happy ending. In some unhealthy way you could make yourself care about television characters, but you could never look them in the eyes and feel them staring back at you.

Gone was the feeling of glorious uncertainty that he experienced walking through the door of Pinky's Bar each evening. Anything could happen there, anything was possible. Sure, the setting was always the same, but the program played itself out differently every single night. Sometimes it was a comedy, sometimes a drama. There was never a central plot, just a variable cast of characters dragging in little fragments of the story from all over town and assembling the pieces in one place. You couldn't get that from television.

Now that he had something to compare it to, a week's worth of television was all the Fiddler Crab could bear. Obviously, if he was going to get on with his life he would have to return to Pinky's. He must get past that hurdle. Of course it wasn't going to be easy. He was experiencing the same sort of emotional turmoil that had plagued him before his birthday.

Should I apologize for being so snotty to everybody? Maybe I should be arrogant, make them apologize to me? Should I act as though nothing happened? But something did happen! He had denounced all of his friends. All of them. Everyone had heard it. *That's not nothing. That's something! A big something!*

He would have to figure out a way. He needed a plan. On the other hand, premeditation is what had gotten him into this mess in the first place. *Maybe I just need to let it happen naturally.* Planning simply caused expectations and if there was one thing people were good at, it was not living up to your expectations. *You say this, thinking they're going to say that, but instead they say something else and your next planned response is all shot to hell and doesn't make any sense. Better just to wing it from the start.*

These people were his friends. Surely they'd forgive one

little outburst. *At least I think they're still my friends. Oh man, I hope they're still my friends. I was pretty rude to them. But, hey, I couldn't help it. I was drunk. Right? I was drunk and pissed off! But then again, I started drinking without them. That wasn't a good idea. Bad etiquette. Kind of insulting to them. Ah hell, it was just a stupid birthday...what do I care.... what do they care?*

By the time the Fiddler Crab had finished alternately beating himself up and licking his wounds, he had decided to simply walk into Pinky's Bar and see what happened. And he would do this totally sober. Suffering the repercussions of his actions unprotected, this would be his penance. Whatever they decided to throw his way, he would take. He would hope for the best and expect the worst. "Right then, tonight..." he mumbled.

1972

Robert worked with Eunice for a little over six months, posing as an altar boy, an announcer, a healed cripple, anything that needed doing, and through it all he learned the day-to-day operation of a phony revivalist. He learned how to get people to the meetings, how to motivate them to empty their wallets, where the money went and how to avoid paying taxes on it. But most of all, he relearned something he had known long ago and had somehow, in his quest for a movie career, forgotten; that people simply wanted to be encouraged toward some dream. Now he understood that they would pay dearly for that encouragement.

One morning, having gleaned all the information he could from the Eunice Banders experience, Robert decided it was time to go. He went to Eunice's office and stormed in without knocking. "Good news, Baby Doll, you're free."

"Keep your voice down," she growled angrily.

"Oh sorry, Sweet Cheeks," he whispered. "I just got a little excited there. You see, it's graduation day for old Robbie Sedgwick. I think I've gotten about all I can from this little party, so it's time to go out into the big bad world and put myself to the test."

"I suppose you'll be in the same vulnerable position I am soon, so we should make an agreement. You don't talk about me and I won't talk about you."

"Don't even worry about it, Baby. I'm not thinking of going into the revival business. I'm thinking of something much more universal." He sat on the edge of her desk. "You see, when I was in high school, I learned that just about everyone has a dream. It doesn't really matter what the dream is, because it always boils down to the same thing. Everyone wants to be loved and admired. Maybe they want to be a movie star, or maybe they want to be the first person to reach the deepest part of the ocean, but whatever the dream is, it's just the way they've chosen to gain admiration from their peers. The dream itself is irrelevant. It's just a way to legitimize their longing for recognition."

He hopped up from the desk and began pacing. "And here's the kicker, they're scared to death to pursue their goal because, in their heart of hearts they know they're no Richard Burton, or that only one person can ever be the first to reach the deepest part of the ocean. If they seriously try to reach their goal and fall short, not only don't they get the recognition they crave, but also the way they define themselves to themselves has been destroyed. They don't know who they are anymore. There's just nowhere for them to go from there. As long as the goal is always out there, they can claim an identity simply by striving for it. It's the fear of realizing the goal that keeps them paralyzed. You see, they think they want to achieve their goals, but it's their own traitorous brains, fearing loss of identity, that keep building walls in front of them. If they keep the dream just over the horizon they have an identity, but they're always frustrated. It's kind of a no-win situation, but what if someone were to come up with a way around those walls? That someone might stand to make a substantial fortune."

"And you know a way around these walls?" asked Eunice sarcastically.

"Hell, no. But if I say I do, and I say it convincingly enough, with absolute confidence, a large number of people will jump through any hoop I put in front of them to find out my secret. And they'll stuff my pockets with money as they go. Thanks to you, darling, I now know how to get this very important message to the people who so badly need it. And, more importantly," he lowered his voice, "how to hide the money away. One last favor, there, Honey Cakes. I'll need a little seed capital. A couple of grand ought to do it, and then I'm out of your hair forever."

Eunice was relieved to be rid of Robert and his threat of exposure. Two thousand dollars seemed a small price to pay. She wrote the check with no argument.

2004

The five-hour drive to Los Angeles took Xochitl three and a half. She found driving long distance to be therapeutic. The scenery flying by had a hypnotic effect and the constant motion gave her a sense of genuine freedom. Driving long distance involved only one responsibility - to reach one's destination. Real world, shoulder-crushing responsibility was never an issue until the car stopped. So the urge was to keep driving, aimlessly and carefree, forever. Unfortunately, in this case driving forever was impractical.

A million random thoughts scurried through Xochitl's mind like a menagerie of little animals, having no desire for order or discipline. Faces from her distant past resurfaced, along with bits of old songs she had forgotten years before, playing like a stilted soundtrack to her own personal movie. Her emotions bounced all over the spectrum, visiting old lovers, friends and enemies. More than once she bellowed out a song, banging a rhythm on the cat cage and dashboard, causing Weezy to moan loudly. Occasionally thoughts of Ernie Blanchard surfaced, but she found herself wailing all the more boisterously, forcing them back into hiding.

Mr. Trundell had loaned Xochitl a small foreign pick-up truck with a basic camper shell on the back, power steering, power brakes and, unfortunately, no sound system. He had the maintenance crew remove the company logo on the doors out of concern for Xochitl's safety. All of her luggage fit in the bed of the truck with plenty of room to spare.

Trundell had taken her aside and insisted somberly that she take a handgun for protection. The thought of carrying a sidearm repulsed Xochitl. It made everything too real at a time when she was trying to retreat from her own harsh reality enough to get through a normal day. In a way, carrying a gun was admitting that there would be more trouble down the road, something she did not want to consider seriously. In the end she had told Trundell that she seemed to be doing well enough with the kickboxing and hand-to-hand training acquired as a hobby in the past few years. Besides, the whole idea of going to LA was to avoid the need for that sort of thing, wasn't it? Against her will, he had given her a cell phone and ordered her to call him twice a day, morning and evening, to keep him apprised of her situation.

"That's very sweet, boss, but I don't do cell phones. You know that."

"You will take this phone, and you will call me twice a day. Every day that you are gone. Do you understand? I've just entrusted you with a $25,000 company vehicle in a city 250 miles from my supervision. Are you beginning to get the picture?"

Xochitl had taken the phone, sensing that it was not about the safety of the truck. She kissed him lightly on the cheek, climbed into the cab and drove away.

Soda River was located in the western foothills of the Sierra Nevada Mountains. In order to intersect the I-5 freeway, which stretched straight down the middle of California through L.A., Xochitl had to travel a number of narrow roads on which people routinely drove too fast. No big deal, since she was possessed with somewhat of a lead foot and often felt the temptation to drive drive too fast along narrow roads herself. After a short layover in Kettleman City, a small collection of gas stations and fast food restaurants, to get food and water for both herself and Weezy, it was a straight shot to the City of Angels. Xochitl had never spent more than a day at a time in Los Angeles. Now, with no plans for room or board, she had no idea what to expect from the days ahead. The future seemed open to all sorts of possibilities and as she would soon discover, not all of them desirable.

1974

Even in the 1970s a full blown ministry of any type could get expensive. Robert started off small. He began with tent meetings (atmosphere is everything, Eunice had told him. You have to get them in the mood.) Essentially, the meetings were identical in all but content to the ones Eunice had fabricated. Each meeting began with a few moments of silence. Robert entered the stage from behind a curtain, lowered his head and raised his hands. Once the crowd grew respectfully silent and Robert's whisper could be heard clearly in the back, he slowly raised his head and began to speak. He spoke softly, forcing people to lean inward and strain to hear what he was saying. If they were leaning forward, he knew he had them. Suddenly, he would burst into a thunderous shout and watch the heads snap back, just as his head had during his first meeting with the Reverend Eunice Banders. He made it very clear that all of the information he was presenting was absolutely free. He had gone through years of hardship, traveling to the ends of the earth to collect the techniques he was presenting for their benefit.

Toward the end of each meeting, Robert would explain that his mission to spread physical and mental health through the achievement of goals was a rather costly enterprise that he had paid for up front, and if anyone could make a small contribution, the mission would be able to continue. "No more than you can afford, folks. Just ask yourself what true peace of mind is worth. You'll be making a great difference to the well-being of others."

By the age of thirty-five, Robert had collected a small fortune. It seemed that even more people were hungry for guidance than he had originally anticipated. Soon he bought a collection of expensive Italian suits and a foreign sports car. He began attending Hollywood parties again.

Everything was progressing very well until he was recognized at a party in Beverley Hills by a young man on the catering staff. The young man had given all of his savings at one of Roberts's meetings and was disappointed to see how his rent money was being spent. He filed fraud charges against Robert on the basis that, after completing all of Robert's exercises, he had not reached his goals. He had been bilked out of his money and he wanted it back, a hundredfold. The whole situation was no more than an inconvenience to Robert, who could afford a much better lawyer than the boy, but it did awaken him to the possibility of a serious threat. Suppose the boy had come from a wealthy family. The court case might have turned out quite differently. He resolved to take his show on the road, no longer working in the Los Angeles area. For safety sake, he changed his last name, once and for all erasing the existence of Alf Sedgwick. Just for the hell of it, he made himself a doctor, and as one final slap in the sultry face of Eunice Banders, he stole her last name - an act worthy of a particularly thick and grainy sugar sandwich.

Dr. Robert Austin Banders soon discovered that a traveling show was much more expensive than a stationary one. He was reaching more people and taking in more money, but somehow, at the end of the day, there was less in the kitty than there had been the day before. The fortune, instead of growing, was dissipating, drizzling away. Things had to change if he was going to survive. He needed something to sell them. The collection plate was fine, but it only went so far. He needed to keep them spending, even after he had moved on from their town.

A book!

A book would be ideal. He would begin by selling it at the meetings, but would also visit independent bookstores in each town he passed through, striking deals with the owners. He bought an old typewriter and began to spend all of his spare time writing. It took him a year, but in the end he had 563 pages of charts, diagrams, small intimidating print, and lots of pictures of Dr. Robert Austin Banders. He titled it: ANYONE CAN!, and it became the focus of his meetings. He referred to it continuously during the meetings so that people in the audience felt compelled to purchase it in order to keep up. A calculated break in the middle of the meeting brought them flocking to the sales booth in the back. Robert was deliriously happy. He was successful beyond his dreams and his power grew daily. For the first time, he knew exactly what he wanted to do with the rest of his life.

2004

"Hey Fid," said Pinky. He put down the glass he was wiping and reached into the beer cooler for a can of the Fiddler Crab's favorite beer. "How's it hangin'?"

"Well, it's been hanging pretty low for the last week. I guess I need to apologize to everyone here for my behavior."

Pinky made a farting noise with his mouth. "Apologize for what?" he asked.

"Well, I kinda bitched everybody out," said the Fiddler Crab, wadding his napkin into a tight ball.

"No big deal. We were kinda worried about you. We thought maybe we did something to scare you off. Tonsils wanted to go over to your place and see if you were all right, but none of us knew exactly where you lived. Then somebody suggested that maybe you had a thing about birthdays. I mean, you seem to get into everybody else's okay, but when it's your own, who knows, maybe it's a different thing. Maybe you had a thing about gettin' a year older. People are like that sometimes."

"You knew it was my birthday?" said the Fiddler Crab.

"Of course! We always know when it's somebody's birthday. I thought you knew that."

The Fiddler Crab was fidgeting in his chair. "But nobody said anything."

"Aaahh, so that's it. You didn't really think we'd let your birthday go by without doing something, did you? We were just waiting for the stripper to show up. She got here late, just after you left. We thought if we said anything it would ruin the surprise. I guess we shoulda just said something earlier."

"Man, I feel like an ass," said the Fiddler Crab. He was squeezing his beer can, making crackly, popping noises.

"I guess it was just your turn this time, Fid," said Pinky, picking up another glass and wiping it clean. "What would this place be if people never made asses of themselves? Hell, we'd have nothing to talk about."

The Fiddler Crab sat in silence for a while. Then a slow, distant smile formed on his lips. He had friends. Real friends! They hadn't brushed him off when he lost his temper. They had worried about him.

"Hey Pinky," he said. "I think I'd like to say thanks to everyone by buying them a drink."

"Aw, you don't have any money. You don't have to do that, Fid."

"No, no, I just got my check. I want to. You know, maybe it's just for me, but I want to do this. Drinks for everybody in the house."

"You're the boss, my friend."

As the Fiddler Crab sat at the bar, basking in the warm glow of new found friendship, he felt a light tap on his shoulder.

"Are you Fid?" It was a pleasant, breathy, female voice, slightly husky, but high-pitched and friendly.

Craning his neck to see who was addressing him, he said, "Yes, I...oh!"

Beautiful women had always made the Fiddler Crab nervous, but this one, with her long black hair, smooth olive skin, and startling blue eyes, took his breath away.

"Hi Fid," she said. "I'm Xochitl. I just wanted to say thanks for the drink.

1974

Robert Austin Banders had been a busy man, amassing a substantial amount of wealth through the sale of his book. Word of mouth remained long after he and his 'Dog and Pony Show', as he referred to it privately in his head, had left town. And word of mouth translated to sales. Orders for his book poured in constantly from bookstores in towns he had visited in the past. But still it was not enough.

Banders had become addicted to the money, to be sure, but the thing that really had him by the jugular was the respect he earned. People treated him with reverence bordering on worship. True, they were not the type of people he would associate with in his everyday life, but the fuel their adoration provided was very much like a drug. It was this as much as the desire for wealth that propelled him to seek ever-increasing heights in book sales.

It took Robert a while to grasp the concept of mail order. It just seemed too time consuming and complicated to fill as many orders as he was bound to get. Still, without it his empire would stay pretty much the same. So he began to leave piles of pre-printed order forms in conspicuous places during his meetings. It surprised him a little when people actually took them home for friends and relatives.

Then the orders arrived, and arrived and arrived.. Robert was completely unprepared to fill the quantity of orders that he received. At first he tried to fill them himself, but it took too much time out of his day, getting in the way of his tanning salon appointments and speech lessons. He set up an office in Los Angeles and hired a number of college students to handle the orders, but their hearts weren't in it. He began to receive complaints about missing orders and returned books from people who hadn't ordered them.

A direct mailing company turned out to be the answer. Robert had the orders sent straight to them and gave them access to order books in bulk from the printer. This system worked fine for quite a while, but eventually Robert again got the feeling that it wasn't enough.

Robert wasn't a big fan of television, preferring to read inspiring biographies from which he could glean little bits of wisdom usable in his Dog and Pony Show. Every hotel room he stayed in was equipped with a television, but he had an easy time ignoring it. One night, though, as he padded from the shower to the bed, he realized he'd left the book he was reading back at the auditorium where that night's Dog and Pony Show had taken place. Surly, the book was lost, and it was too late in the evening to purchase another copy. Reluctantly, Robert pushed the power button on the television. He was startled as the screen burst into life. Flipping through the channels, Robert saw sordid, distrustful relationships and people dying in ever more interesting ways. It appealed to him in a morbid fascination kind of way.

It was the commercials that really got his attention, though. If only there was a way to sell his book through television. Most of the commercials were obviously paid for by large corporations with lots of money to spend. Way out of his league. As the hour grew later, Robert noticed that the commercials were much lower quality and were advertising local and regional businesses. "How do I explain my book in a thirty second spot?" he asked himself aloud. His mind raced, trying to squeeze his over five hundred pages into thirty seconds. There was no way.

He flipped the channel again and came across a blue screen displaying an address and phone number in bright yellow type. The scene changed to a smiling man in a white lab coat standing before a table full of test tubes and beakers in a variety of colors, some of which were producing a sort of steam or fog. The camera cut to a small, but interested audience comprised mostly of women.

"A team of award-winning scientists worked for seven years to bring you Godiva hair coloring," the man was saying, staring earnestly at the camera. "Godiva will not only color your hair, it will make it more healthy. Here, take a look at these micro-photographs of a human hair. Can anyone in the audience tell me which is the before and which is the after? It's obvious, isn't it? The hair on the right was treated with Godiva. Now let's pan out and look at the beautiful head of hair this photograph was taken from."

The face of a startlingly good-looking woman filled the screen. "Who here doesn't want to look like this? Well you all can if you use Godiva once a week for a period of three months."

Robert was wide-eyed. This was it. This was the way to get his product into the minds of millions of people. He would no longer have to rely on the size of an auditorium to guarantee enough sales. In fact, if this worked out, he would never have to rely on an auditorium of any size ever again. He could record one scripted Dog and Pony Show and broadcast it into the homes of millions of people late at night. It was obvious to Robert that this sales technique was tailor-made for what he was selling. He was selling salvation to depressed people and depressed people were going to be in no short supply at this late hour. The target was perfect, just sitting there on their couches waiting for him. It would be like fishing in a barrel. He would get on it first thing in the morning, even if it meant missing his appointment at the tanning salon.

2004

Xochitl continued to stare into the Fiddler Crab's eyes. They were warm, comforting eyes and she felt safe and un-threatened there.

"So anyway, thanks," she said raising her glass and clinking it against his.

"Yeah, well, you know, heh, I'm just a big-hearted kind of guy, I guess," said the Fiddler Crab, his voice shaking slightly.

"Good. That's the kind of guy I need to be around right now," said Xochitl sternly. "Do you mind if I hang out with you for a little bit? I don't really know anybody here and you seem really nice. I haven't had a lot of pleasant experiences with men lately... although my boss, Mr. Trundell, did loan me his truck, and that was pretty nice."

"What happened? Guy get rough with you?" asked the Fiddler Crab, relieved to have a topic he could grab onto and run with. "I noticed you have a bruise on your arm."

"I guess you could say that," said Xochitl, drumming her

fingers on the bar and eying the bruise on the Fiddler Crab's forehead. "A couple of them over the last few days."

"You a hooker, or you just don't know how to pick your guys?"

Xochitl broke into a hardy chuckle. She slapped the Fiddler Crab lightly on the back. "Nooo," she laughed, "I'm not a hooker."

"Yeah, you don't look like a hooker. What do you do?" asked the Fiddler Crab.

"Have you ever heard of AWARE Magazine?"

"Yeah, I've bought it a few times. Why?"

"I'm a photographer for that magazine. What issues did you buy?"

"I don't know. There was one with a girl in a creek-bed, sifting mud through a screen. I ended up reading the article out of boredom, and it turned out to be really good."

"Oh yeah! That was an article about creek pollution caused by too many residential septic tanks squeezed into a small area. That was my friend, Marissa, in the cover picture. I just sort of posed her there in the creek to make a point."

"She's very pretty. I bought the magazine because of that picture."

"I'll tell her you said so, Fid. She'll be flattered."

The Fiddler Crab flushed and looked down at his beer.

Xochitl had a good feeling about this man. He seemed honest on the surface, an open book, but she didn't have complete faith in her powers of assessment right now. To be sure she decided to use a technique Her Aztec mother had taught her as a young girl that had been passed down through generations in her village. A technique for examining someone's essence. It was called 'holding hearts'.

Her eyes glazed for a moment while her heart reached into the Fiddler Crab's chest and made a gentle, silent connection. A flood of suppressed emotions entered her and she felt the senseless pain he had experienced through all his years of abuse. All the beatings, all the worthless sympathy, all the cruel remarks and averted glances, everything that added up to this blushing, gentle creature sitting next to her. She took it all in at once and examined it for a moment. Then she let it fade to a whisper, leaving only a memory. Her eyes cleared. They would be friends for a very long time. That was understood.

"Why don't you tell me about it, Fid?"

"Tell you about what"

"All this stuff that keeps you wrapped up so tight."

"What do you mean?" The Fiddler Crab tensed, studying Xochitl's eyes. He found no sympathy there, nor was there cruelty or anticipation. Only one human being asking another human being about his life. Her brow was slightly furrowed. But why was she concerned? Hell, he'd just met her five minutes ago. What did she care?

"Well," he said slowly, "there was a lot of senseless stuff early on, but I think the real trouble started with this guy named Doctor Robert Austin Banders. A very bad man."

"Yeah, my trouble started with a doctor, too. So, go on, tell me what happened."

PART TWO

CHAPTER 1

2004

Xochitl sat up violently. Her surroundings were completely unfamiliar to her. She found herself sweating profusely on a torn and dusty couch in a small living room, a thick blanket covering her. There was a loud rumble just outside the nearby window. Blinking several times in succession, she recognized the sound as that of a train, undoubtedly a freight train, judging by the length of it. It was daylight outside, but the walls were dim and yellow from the subdued light passing through the ancient water-stained curtains. Short, stilted scenes of the night before began to populate her fuzzy mind. She had gone to a bar. Nothing special, just a bar she had stumbled upon, and had a few drinks with her new friend, Fid. This must be his place. She hoped it was his place. It better be his place! Man, where was that sober pill when you needed it?

Recently, Xochitl had cut down on her drinking. She had driven home drunk one night and didn't remember a thing about it. No memory of whether she had driven alone or what route she had taken. It had occurred to her, then, that no one was going to stop her from doing that sort of thing until it was too late. Her luck wouldn't hold out forever. Someday she would hurt herself or someone else if she didn't stop. She may even kill someone. Short of getting pulled over, no one was going to take her keys and call her a cab, except herself. But last night was different. It had been nearly three days since she had felt safe, and as the alcohol relaxed her it became apparent to her that she had been much more tense than she'd realized. That funny bartender, Pinky, kept pouring her drinks on the house and telling her what a great guy Fid was. Things got a little blurred toward closing time. She had a sudden vision of an overweight woman trying to do a strip tease, but unable to operate the buttons on her blouse. A man had his pants down around his knees and was trying to walk like a penguin. What a night.

The Fiddler Crab came shuffling into the room in Bermuda shorts, a sweatshirt that read, 'I'm Going to Disneyland', and a pair of plastic, dime-store flip-flops. "Ah good, you're up. Want some coffee? It's pretty nasty, but it'll pry your eyes open."

"That'd be great, Fid."

"You remembered my name. I'm seriously flattered, especially after all those White Russians."

"Heh! I'm surprised I remember anything at all. Thanks for letting me crash here. I don't know what I would have..."

Xochitl froze.

"What is it?" asked the Fiddler Crab,

"Weezy!"

"What's a Weezy?"

"My cat, Weezy. He's in my car. Where is my car?"

"I think you said it was about a block away from Pinky's, but you didn't say where. We better get over there, though, because the meter maids start marking tires around nine and it's almost ten-thirty now. They give you ninety minutes from the time they mark your tires until they give you a ticket. Sometimes they even tow it. If they find an unfed animal in a locked car, you'll be in big trouble."

She pulled back the blanket and stood up wearing a yellow tee shirt and blue panties. "I don't care about the trouble. I just hope my cat's okay. Where're my pants?"

The Fiddler Crab was stunned into silence. He'd dreamed of having beautiful, half-naked women in his living room, but it had never really occurred to him that it might actually happen. "Wha...wha." he stated.

"Oh come on, Fid. A stud like you? Surely you've seen plenty of girls in their underwear before. Now, where're my pants?"

He pointed to the couch. "Looks like you were using them for a pillow."

She sat on the couch and wiggled her legs into a pair of blue, denim pants.

The Fiddler Crab stared at the floor.

"How'd we get here last night?" Xochitl asked, quickly tying her shoes.

"We walked," he said, remembering her charming drunken antics as they stumbled down the quiet streets.

"Ha ha." Xochitl began to remember grabbing him by both hands and trying to make him dance, singing "Guilty feet have got no rhythm."

The Fiddler Crab would forever remember the feeling of having a beautiful girl take his withered hand in hers as though there were nothing at all wrong with it. Even Elsa hadn't done that. And so he had danced...with a girl...a beautiful girl, for the first time in his life, down the sidewalk under a near-full moon.

Xochitl grabbed the Fiddler Crab's withered little claw for the second time and began to drag him out the door. It did not feel nearly as romantic the second time.

"Wait," he pleaded, "I can't go out like this."

"Sure you can, you look great."

He found himself flip-flopping down the sidewalk trying to match Xochitl's frantic gait. "I can show you where Pinky's is, but I have no idea where you parked your car."

"Well, at least get us that far, and we'll figure something out from there. Poor Weezy!"

Xochitl's voice was full of sympathy when she spoke of the cat. The Fiddler Crab reflected that she hadn't used that tone on him at all throughout the entire evening. Not even once. *There's no trace of it when she speaks to me, no pity at all.* His shell softened the tiniest bit.

A few minutes before 11, Pinky was just arriving at his bar. Fumbling with his keys, he glanced up to see the pretty girl from the night before, wearing the same clothes and dragging a badly dressed Fid down the sidewalk by his withered appendage. "Yo, Fid," he laughed. "Way to go, Romeo."

"Oh geez, Pinky," the Fiddler Crab blushed casting a worried glance at Xochitl. "It's not like that." But Pinky had already disappeared inside the gates of his own personal kingdom.

After searching several side streets, Xochitl found the truck that Mr. Trundell had loaned her. She scratched the paint with the key trying to get the passenger side door unlocked. A loud, throaty MEOW burst through the newly opened door.

"Oh, Weezy!" said Xochitl as she pulled the hapless cat from its cage. "I'm so sorry, little guy. I forgot all about you. Ugh! I'm an unfit mother." The cat was immediately flipped upside-down and cradled like a baby in Xochitl's arms. The Fiddler Crab rolled his eyes as Xochitl baby-talked to the animal. She squeezed him tighter and his purring grew in both volume and intensity. "Fid, is there a liquor store or a little market around here? I need to get him some cat food."

"Yeah, there's a little mom-and-pop market around the corner called Chu's or Wu's or something. It's been there for years. Hey, it looks like you got yourself a parking ticket after all."

"Ah shit!" Xochitl opened the driver side door and placed Weezy onto the seat. "Hop in, Fid, let's go."

The Fiddler Crab tore the traffic citation from under the windshield wiper and hopped into the truck. The cat arched its back and its fur stood on end. "Settle down, Weezy. He's a friend of ours." Xochitl scratched the cat's ears and the defensive feline began to relax.

"That's alright," said the Fiddler Crab. "That's the reaction I usually get from small animals and attractive women."

Xochitl paused with her hand on the ignition key. She

turned her head and stared at him inquisitively. "You've got to stop thinking that way, Fid. You're never going to get anywhere in life if you set yourself up as a victim. You're not a victim, you're an intelligent, sensitive guy. Which is more than I can say for a lot of guys, at least the ones I meet. You can't judge your worth by how other people treat you. I'm a pretty girl, and I know that. If I gave in to what society expects of me I'd be some rich guy's trophy-wife by now. But I'm not. I'm a professional photographer, and I want nothing more than to be a better professional photographer. I'm living my dream and I don't care what impression people have of me. I know who I am and I'm happy with that."

While the Fiddle Crab took the words in, Xochitl continued. "Something else, Fid. Something I haven't told you about yet. I have an ability that allows me to sort of feel people's souls. I can pretty much see what's in their hearts. It's sort of a gift passed down to me from my Aztec ancestors through my mother. She called it 'holding hearts'. I'm sorry for intruding, but last night at the bar I looked into your heart, Fid. You didn't feel me holding your heart, did you? You didn't even know I was there, but I was. I'm not just guessing you're a good guy, I *know* first-hand that you're a good guy."

For a moment the Fiddler Crab felt a little violated, but once her words sank in, he let it go. The results were good, so he couldn't complain. "How come you keep meeting all these bad men if you can see into their hearts?"

"I have a rule. If someone strikes me as a potential, uh, interest, I don't use my ability. It's an unfair advantage. You gotta trust someone before you can build anything."

In a strange way, that made sense, but it was bad news for the Fiddler Crab. Not that he had, in his wildest dreams, expected Xochitl to be interested in him romantically, but there was something very disconcerting about being told outright. It didn't even leave any room to dream. He sat quietly for a moment. "So this psychic thing is something all Aztecs can do?"

"First of all, I'm not a full blooded Aztec, only half. Second, it's not a psychic ability. It's more empathetic. I don't read your mind, so you can relax about that. I just feel what's in your heart. I sort of sense the overall mood of your life. It's almost like a warmth meter. Third, no, not all Aztecs can do this. Just some of the people in the town where my mom came from. It's a learned skill, not an innate ability"

It sounded to the Fiddler Crab as though Xochitl had given this little speech many times. The words rolled off her tongue mechanically, like the lines of a bad actor. The Fiddler Crab's reply was interrupted by a shrill, tweedly tune that they both recognized as the ring of a cell phone. Xochitl's brow creased. "God, I hate these things," she growled, fumbling in the glove compartment for the vile plastic offender. "But I promised Mr. Trundell that I'd keep in touch." She pushed the talk button. "Yeah boss?"

"Miss Saint James?" It was an unfamiliar voice.

"Uh... yeah," she said cautiously.

"Miss Saint James, my associates and I have reason to believe that the good Doctor Sporkin somehow passed part of a journal containing the formula for his sobriety drug along to you."

Xochitl's blood ran cold. "That's ridiculous. I never even met Doctor Sporkin. He was dead when I got to his house. Who is this?"

"That's not important. What is important is the formula. You have it, we need it. Perhaps we can work out an arrangement that pleases everyone."

"I don't know what you're talking about, man. I don't have any journal or any formula and I'm sure you have nothing that I want."

"Miss Saint James, reach down and feel under the seat. That's right, I know you're driving your truck. I also know you are passing through the intersection of Swensen and Pokeet."

She hung up the phone, swinging her head about wildly, searching for the caller. There were too many cars on the street. Spotting the right one in this congestion would be next to impossible. A powerful chill rumbled through Xochitl's body. She'd been in town one night and already someone was following her, watching her every move. She reached under the seat and searched with her fingers. There seemed to be nothing there. Then she felt her fingers slide across a slick surface- a small, stiff piece of paper. She pulled it out and looked at it, the car swerving back and forth across the road. It was a Polaroid photograph of Ernie Blanchard. Both his eyes were swollen and bruised. One of his legs was bent at an unnatural angle and there were small cuts all over his face and arms. The phone rang again, the pleasant, lighthearted melody a stark contrast to the somber atmosphere that had invaded the car.

"Are you ready to make a deal?"

"What deal? I have no fucking idea what you're talking about."

"Mr. Blanchard is here. Would you like to speak with him?"

Xochitl pulled the truck over to the side of the road and sat in silence.

"What is it?" asked the Fiddler Crab, "What's going on?" Xochitl held her palm up to the Fiddler Crab's face.

A voice barely recognizable as Ernie Blanchard came on the line. "Soach?" The voice was thin and quavering. His words were slightly unclear, as though his mouth were full of cotton balls.

"Ernie? What have they done to you?"

"It hurts, Soach. I think they're going to kill me." He began to sob. "I don't know what they want, man. I don't know anything about any formula."

"Where are you Ernie?"

"I don't know, I think I'm in some kind of a truck or van or something."

"Think, Ernie, that doesn't help me much. Are you moving or stationary?" Xochitl heard a muffled, metallic thump through the phone. Ernie was sobbing in the distance now.

"Well, Miss Saint James?"

Xochitl took a deep breath. "Look, why don't you be a little more clear about what it is you're looking for, then maybe I can help you find it. What does this formula look like?"

"Don't play dumb with me, Miss Saint James. I haven't got the time or the patience."

"I'm getting really pissed off here, mister. Believe me, you don't want to see me pissed off."

A purple service van shot past Xochitl's driver side window. She looked out in time to see a yellow smiley face decal on the door along with the words: Smiley's Catering. Through the phone receiver she heard a second thud, then the sound of Ernie Blanchard crying out again. The van rocked slightly sideways just as the sound of the thud reached her ears through the receiver.

"Bingo, you bastard," she said aloud and tossed the phone on the floor. Throwing the truck into first gear, Xochitl stomped the accelerator pedal to the floor and a cloud of thick gray smoke billowed from beneath the screeching tires as she sped off down the residential street.

"Will you explain to me what's going on?" demanded the Fiddler Crab. "This is getting really dangerous."

"I'll explain later, but yeah, things are going to get a little dangerous real soon. Buckle up, my friend, this could be the ride of your life."

"Or my death. Do we have to go this fast? I'm not used to this kind of thing. I don't even own a car."

"Fid, I need you to hold it together right now. We're kind of in a situation here. Yes, we have to go this fast. My partner has been missing for three days. He was abducted. I'm partly responsible for that. I've just discovered he's in that van and we are not going to let it out of our sight until Ernie, that's his name, Ernie, is in this truck with us. Is that clear?" She shot him a wild-eyed glance. "Just remember, my friend, it's not the speed that kills you, it's the sudden stop at the end. If we can avoid that, we'll be okay." Xochitl shifted gears and stomped the accelerator once more. Soon they were speeding neck and neck alongside the purple van. Xochitl fishtailed her truck into the van's left, front fender, producing a muted crunch. The van swerved, careening up a driveway onto the sidewalk, then through a picket fence into the front yard of a tidy, middle class home. The van's engine revved powerfully and it continued down the block, front yard by front yard, splintering fences as it went. Xochitl drove up the next driveway and followed the van through the yards. The noise was tremendous as engines roared, tires screeched and pieces of white picket fence flew in all directions.

The Fiddler Crab gripped the armrest on the door with all the fortitude he could muster. His seat belt suddenly felt inadequate. The fingers of his right hand began to turn white. Xochitl patted his shaking knee. "You're a hero, Fid. Anyone else would have been out the door by now." With much effort, he managed a weak smile.

The van slowed a bit, its tires screeching as it rounded the corner at the end of the block. Xochitl managed to smack it a second time from behind and set the thing wobbling as both vehicles, one after the other, flew off the curb into the street. The rear left wheel began to spin unevenly and Xochitl could tell the driver was struggling to control the vehicle. Eventually, the pursuit brought them to a bridge which spanned a narrow aqueduct, a concrete channel roughly fifteen feet deep and as many wide who's purpose was to guide a shallow trickle of water along with more questionable liquids to the sea. The van crossed the bridge and immediately turned sharply left onto a dirt service road paralleling the nearly dry aqueduct. Shortly, an entrance ramp for maintenance vehicles appeared and the van swerved down into the concrete riverbed, destroying a chain-link gate on the way. Xochitl followed, pushing the truck nearly to its limit.

"This guy's smart," she said. "He's moved the chase away from public view, and the channel is so narrow, we can't pull up alongside him."

Nodding his head stiffly, the Fiddler Crab forced a hollow grin and rubbed his knees together nervously. "Hooray for them," he said flatly. The cat, who had voluntarily scampered back into its cage, released a deep, frightening, tortured-baby sound.

"It's okay, Honey," Xochitl said in a high, singsong voice. "I know you're hungry. We'll get you some food in a little while." She reached into the glove compartment and pulled out a small pair of binoculars, handing them to the Fiddler Crab. "Fid, see if you can spot a young guy with a beat-up face through the rear widow of that van.

"Oh Jesus..."

As the Fiddler Crab raised the binoculars to his eyes, Xochitl saw the rear window in question smash to bits from the inside of the van. The dull-black barrel of a rifle made its way into the bright morning sunshine and after several seconds of searching, pointed itself in their direction. She slammed her foot on the breaks and turned left as far as she could go, running her left wheels three or four feet up the slanted, concrete embankment and narrowly missing a hail of bullets. The narrow gully afforded essentially no room to maneuver in. She had gotten lucky once, but Xochitl knew that, given her limited options, the gunman would easily out-guess her as he let loose his second volley.

"Get down, Fid!" she commanded, pointing to the floor.

"What?" The Fiddler Crab was miles from his realm of experience and was unsure what he was being told to do. Short of the television in his room, he'd never even been close to this much action.

"Pick up Weezy's cage and get on the floor. Switch places with him. Hurry!"

The Fiddler Crab scrambled to do as he was told. Xochitl once again saw the barrel of the gun emerge from the rear window of the van. She quickly ducked her head, leaving only her eyes remaining above the dash and stomped the accelerator pedal all the way to the floor. The truck shot forward as the gun began to fire. The windshield shattered, becoming an intricate spider's web of tiny glass crystals. Xochitl let up on the accelerator and drove her fist through the, now flimsy, opaque barrier. Thousands of little glass squares sprayed the inside of the truck.

The Fiddler Crab screamed. Xochitl looked at his huddled body and shook her head. "Men!" she shouted, slamming her foot, once again, onto the accelerator pedal. They both felt a heavy jolt as the truck slammed into the rear of the van. The rifle flew from the van's rear window, clattering across the hood of the truck. Xochitl jerked her head aside as the weapon came flying blindly through the broken windshield, into the cab. She felt the driver of the van abruptly apply his brakes, trying to slow the onslaught from behind. Her foot remained on the gas pedal. A heady feeling of power overcame Xochitl, as though her bloodstream had become pure adrenalin. "Come on, you bastard," she screamed. "Who's your Mamma? Huh? Who's your goddamn Mamma now?" She was up off the seat, with her full weight on the accelerator, pushing the van forward against its will. White smoke began to well up from the van's screeching tires and it wobbled uncontrollably, finally spilling onto its side. Xochitl applied her brakes and watched as the crippled van slid partway up the concrete embankment, then tumbled its way back down to the center of the canal. The shattered and dented purple box lay on its side, its front wheels still spinning mindlessly.

Xochitl's eyes were riveted on the van as she felt around the cab of the truck for the rifle that had come flying like a godsend through the windshield. Her hand found it and she pulled it into her lap. With her free hand, she fumbled with the door handle. "So much for that sudden stop at the end. You all right, Fid?" she asked, opening the door and squatting behind it.

The fiddler Crab was not certain whether he was all right or not, so he simply groaned, displaying some sign of life. "How's Weezy?" asked Xochitl, pointing to the cage.

The Fiddler Crab raised his head and peered inside. "He seems to be terrified, but I don't see any physical damage. Pretty much the same state as me. Are we okay, yet? Is it safe?"

He struggled to get up, huffing and grunting.

"Stay down, Fid. We may not be out of the woods yet," Xochitl, whispered forcefully. Turning toward the van, she cleared her throat and shouted: "Hey you, in the van, I've got you covered. Thanks for the weapon. I appreciate it. Now, open the door slowly and come out with your hands in the air." These words had always seemed hokey to Xochitl when she heard them in the movies, but now they simply made sense.

The back door of the van began to bulge as someone tried to open it from inside. Xochitl tensed. Looking closer, she realized that the bumper of the van had become bent during the chase, preventing the rear door from opening. A man began to crawl out of the shattered window on the upper rear door, heedless of the glass shards around the frame. Xochitl recognized the shirt and hair.

"Ernie!" she shouted, as he succeeded in pulling his entire body through the broken window falling in a heap to the concrete below. She threw the rifle onto the seat and ran toward the limp, bleeding pile. Gripping Ernie by the shoulder, she cautiously rolled him over.

"Soach," said Ernie, limply. "Watch out for these guys. They're really serious. They're like machines, relentless. Just get as far away from them as you can." His eyes glazed and then closed, his body went limp. Xochitl stooped over him and grabbing his wrist, frantically searched for a pulse. Locating a weak little thump, she breathed a sigh of relief.

"Fid, we've got to get him to a hospital," she shouted over her shoulder. A blur at the corner of Xochitl's vision drew her attention back to the van. A bloodied and battered middle-aged man appeared in the broken window. Xochitl was immediately aware of her vulnerability. Stupid, she thought, eyes darting frantically, searching for something, anything to use as a weapon. She sprang to her feet, but a pistol was pointed directly into her face before she could regain her balance. Her eyes locked onto the man's and she found herself engaging the riveted stare of a hungry predator. Great, she thought, a good soldier, the enabler of every stupid war that's ever been. The man was a robot. He would surely kill her if she didn't do something to protect herself very soon. He quickly lowered the pistol and fired a shot into Ernie Blanchard's prostrate body. Ernie jerked once and was still. Xochitl jumped back and screamed. The man instantly had his gun trained on her once again,.

Xochitl tried to scream again, but couldn't. Her whole body was paralyzed but for the shaking in her knees.

The man nodded his head toward Ernie, lying still in the trickle that passed for a creek in Los Angeles, little pools of mossy, pink water puddling around him. "I need you alive, Miss Saint James, but I also need you to understand that I'm very serious here."

Xochitl glanced at Ernie's bleeding body.

"You've given us quite a chase," The man continued. "As a result I have no choice but to incapacitate you a little bit." The man's voice was strained and it was evident to Xochitl that he was in a great deal of pain. He pointed the gun down toward Xochitl's knee. She cringed, then heard the shot and waited for the pain.

The pistol dropped to the ground beside her and she heard the booming, clattering sound of the man collapsing inside the hollow metal van. She swung around and gaped at the truck. A rifle barrel rested on the dashboard, pointed toward the van, with the shocked and contorted face of the Fiddler Crab peering from behind it.

"Thanks, Fid," Xochitl said mechanically as she began a hurried examination of Ernie. The pulse was still there, though even weaker. Apparently the bullet had entered his shoulder from behind and made a decent sized exit wound in front. She stripped off his shirt and tore it in two. She placed one piece on each of the wounds and laid Ernie on his back, applying pressure with her whole body.

"How is he?" asked the Fiddler Crab as he approached the scene. He felt strangely calm now, considering this was, without a doubt, the most surreal and intense thing that had ever happened to him. Somewhere in a dark, secluded corner of his mind a mad little voice was shouting that he had just killed a man, taken a human life. But the voice lost its voracity as it journeyed toward the surface. Like a drop of poison in a pond, it dissipated, seemingly harmless. Later he would pay, he knew that, but for now he felt a pleasant, functional numbness.

"We need to get him to a hospital, Fid. He's lost some blood from the gunshot wound, and who knows what they did to him earlier."

"Okay, let's get him in the back of the truck," said the Fiddler Crab, rocking back and forth on his heels. "Shouldn't we call the police about this? I mean, that man I shot is probably dead...and we haven't even looked at the driver. Aren't there papers we have to fill out? Is this murder? I don't even know."

"No police," said Xochitl as they hefted a limp Ernie Blanchard into the camper shell of the truck.

"Xochitl, we could go to jail for the rest of our lives if we get caught."

"I called the police the first time I walked in on a murder scene involving these guys and no one came. Think about it. I reported a murder and no one came! That's got to tell you something."

"Who are these guys, and what do they want?"

"I don't know who they are, Fid. Look, I need you to hop in the back with Ernie and keep as much pressure as you can on this wound. I don't know a whole lot about medicine, but I know it can't be a bad thing to stop his bleeding."

CHAPTER 2

As the, now battered, company truck emerged from the concrete flood-control canal, Xochitl opened the small, sliding window between the cab and the camper shell. She told the Fiddler Crab everything she could remember of the past few days. It felt good to her to review the whole chain of events. The situation began to make a little more sense to her as she spoke the events aloud. A pattern was beginning to emerge in the actions of her newly acquired enemies. It was clear to her, now, that she was dealing with a very powerful organization of some kind. It had to be someone with access to incredible resources, someone able to track her effortlessly from Soda River to L.A., despite her precautions. Perhaps a large conglomerate corporation with holdings in pharmaceuticals and personal data mining. Apparently, they could delve into her private life as deeply as they desired. She had no doubt that they were aware of her whereabouts at this very moment. The truck was almost certainly bugged and was probably being monitored on its way to the hospital.

"Fid, do you know any doctors?"

"Not really. Why?"

"I don't think it's a good idea to take Ernie to a public place. These guys seem to be able to find me very easily. I don't know if they're finished with Ernie, but if they're not, I don't want to leave him in a place where he's vulnerable. I don't want him getting snatched away again."

"I know a nurse from General Hospital. Not real well, but

I know her. She's a semi-regular at Pinky's. She's kind of an adrenalin junkie. I think she might help us."

Xochitl pulled the truck into a gas station and, pointing to the pay phone, asked the Fiddler Crab to call his friend. The episode with the cell phone had only confirmed her distrust of the evil little devices. She groped on the floor of the truck until she found the phone and tossed it into the garbage can next to the gas pump. The Fiddler Crab glanced over his shoulder, smiling. "She says she'll help us, but she's at work right now. We need to get him to her house."

"Okay, Fid. Here's what we need to do. We can't drive this truck to your friend's house. I think the truck may be bugged. It would be too dangerous. I think we need to meet your friend in the parking lot of the General Hospital. She and I will transfer Ernie to her car. She'll examine Ernie and make a judgment as to whether his wounds are something she can handle at home. If so, she'll take Ernie to her house and set him up. I'll drive this truck somewhere and abandon it. It's too risky to keep using it. The thing's probably bugged and, if so, they can track it everywhere it goes. I want you to make some excuse to stay in the Emergency Room waiting area at General Hospital for as long as you can hack it. Keep track of who comes in and who leaves." Xochitl opened the glove compartment and fished out a ballpoint pen. "Here, take this in case you have to write things down. Right now, though, I need you to write down your friend's name and address. We'll meet there at, say, seven o'clock tonight. Remember, pay close attention to who comes in the ER. I'm getting a feel for these people and I think someone will show up there looking for Ernie and me. They've undoubtedly tracked the truck to the hospital and I'm sure they'll assume I brought Ernie here for treatment. I'm pretty sure that they don't know about you, because you were on the floor most of the time. The only guy who got a good look at you is dead."

An hour later, Xochitl was walking out of a liquor store with a small pile of cat food cans and a forty-ounce bottle of beer. She opened the door on the side of Weezy's plastic travel cage and placed an opened can inside. A manic purring emanated from the cage as she slid into the driver's seat beside it. The bottle cap pricked her fingers as she twisted it from the bottle of beer. After sucking back a deep pull, she laid her head gently on the steering wheel.

She knew that the truck had probably been tracked leaving the hospital, but they would go to the emergency room first, anyway, to see if Ernie was there. They couldn't let Ernie live. He'd seen too much. Hiding him away in a back room somewhere wasn't going to be comfortable for him, but it might keep him alive. She put her face close to the cage breathing the fumes of good stout beer into the purring animal's face. "I'm so sorry, Weezy. I thought we were just going for a nice little vacation till this thing blew over. I thought I was going to get to show you what a beach looks like and Hollywood Boulevard, and man, just think of the camera stores they must have in a berg this size. In fact, my friend, that gives me an idea. Xochitl searched clumsily through a phone book hanging from a large metal ring inside the booth in front of the liquor store.

Following a short period of flipping pages back and forth, she located a large discount photo and electronics store. She wrote down the address and drove away in search of Mad Camera and Stereo, 'Home of the INSANE deal'. It turned out to be just what she was hoping for.

The store was extremely busy and thus the parking lot was huge, shared by only one other store, Huffing Brother's Paint & Decor. She found a parking space close, but not too close, to the building. The heavily damaged front of the truck was well hidden, surrounded by parked cars on three sides.

Xochitl entered the store and talked the clerk down to $257 for a used Cannon digital camera and a good-sized memory card that would enable her to save up to two hundred pictures. It broke her heart to give in to the digital tidal wave that was flooding the photographic world, indeed the world in general, but in the past few days she had become very leery of writing her name on any type of form, including something as trivial as a photograph development order. She hurried back to the truck. Sliding the cat cage across the seat she picked it up by the handle and placed it on the ground outside. Opening the latch on the camper shell, she removed her sleeping bag and placed it next to the cage. She locked the truck and began to lug the cage, along with her new camera and sleeping bag toward a residential area at the far end of the lot.

CHAPTER 3

In a corner chair of the emergency room's waiting area, the Fiddler Crab sat inconspicuously thumbing through a six-month-old tabloid. He had positioned himself so that he could see anyone who entered or left through the front door.

What the hell am I doing here? Is this really necessary? After all, it's not like I really know this Xochitl woman very well. Hell, I don't know her at all and I've already shot someone to save her. In my life, I never thought I would ever shoot anyone. But I did shoot someone! I did! I took a human life. That's not me.

Come on, man, just get up and leave. Just divest yourself of the whole situation and hightail it back to your boring, everyday life.

…Yeah, I should, but what kind of life is that?

Quiet! Peaceful!

Peaceful? Ha! It's a life where you practically peed your pants over a missing birthday party. Hell, you were sobbing like a school-girl. Do you remember that? You are not your own man in that life. True, it took you some courage to get to the point where you went out and found some friends and made a sort of family out of them, but you pretty much stagnated there. You never progressed. You got to that plateau and stopped.

Okay, also true, my life doesn't sound so rosy when I put it in those terms, but at least it's, I don't know…steady.

Steady is dull! Steady will kill you, my friend. Life must forge onward. In fact, I'm pretty embarrassed just sitting here alone thinking about the whole birthday fiasco. Okay, I mean if that's all there is, if that's all that's ahead, more of the same then ...what's the point? This is the first time you've ever had stories of your own to bring to the table. Don't be a fool. See how this one ends!

So he sat and watched the door.

The Fiddler Crab was unsure exactly what he was waiting for. The man he had shot was pretty average looking, somewhat on the big side, but not remarkably so. Or maybe not. The van had been on its side, the man could have been standing on something inside. Perhaps it was enough to simply keep an eye out for someone dressed similar to the shooter in the van. He sighed heavily, and stared at the door.

Guilt had begun to plague the Fiddler Crab as the numbing shock of the afternoon's action gradually dissipated. There must have been some other way he could have handled the situation besides killing the man. He reminded himself that the guy had already shot Ernie and was getting ready to shoot Xochitl. The world would be better off without him. But why did it have to be him, the Fiddler Crab, who made that decision? He barely felt qualified to make major decisions in his own life, let alone whether someone else lived or died. And yet he had done exactly that, without a moment's hesitation. Essentially, he had sentenced the man to death for his crimes. This, he knew, would plague him for the rest of his life.

The door opened and a man in a dark blue suit, light purple tie and immaculately shined shoes entered the waiting room. He looked intently around the waiting area, examining each person's face. Without looking up from his magazine, the Fiddler Crab felt the man's gaze settle on him like a spotlight. He flipped the pages of the magazine. Leaning his body toward the table, he flopped his withered arm about in an exaggerated and unsuccessful attempt to grasp another magazine. The man shifted his gaze to an elderly woman with blue hair and wrinkled stockings. He approached the receptionist and flashed a photograph from his breast pocket. The woman examined the photo then shook her head. The man returned the photo to his breast pocket. Without looking back he turned on his heels and walked mechanically from the room. Ten seconds later the Fiddler Crab rose to his feet and followed. A dark sedan pulled up and the man got in. As the car drove away, the Fiddler Crab memorized its license plate number. "GRB 147R," he said aloud, and he walked back inside to find something to write on. He tore a page from a magazine and wrote down the number.

CHAPTER 4

"**YOU** WHAT?" Albert Trundell shouted into the phone receiver.

"I ditched the truck, boss," said Xochitl into the receiver of a pay phone, her voice a strained calm. "It was pretty much wrecked anyway. They found us without any trouble at all."

"You wrecked the truck? Why didn't you call me like you were supposed to? That's why I gave you the phone. Was anybody hurt?"

"I'm pretty sure the phone was bugged, boss. They called me on it the first day I arrived. I chucked it in a garbage can. And I'm pretty sure the truck had some sort of locating device on it, too, because they knew where I parked it as soon as I got to LA. They must have bugged it before I even left Soda River. So I drove it to a parking lot and left it there. You probably should send someone down here to pick it up. But do it quick, I hear they like to tow people's cars away down here. Apparently, it's a big source of revenue in Southern California. Something you might want to investigate, boss. Anyway, all my stuff's still in the truck. I couldn't carry it all on foot."

"It sounds as though they are getting a great deal of their information from this end. My phone may be bugged, as well." Mr. Trundell was silent for a moment. Xochitl could hear the nasal whistle of his breath through the receiver. "Alright, Saint James, here's what we'll do. Do you remember who played center field for the company softball team two years ago? Just say yes or no. Don't mention any names."

"Uh, Yeah. What's that got to do with anything? " Xochitl remembered him well. Carson Wells, a long-haired loner, was the magazine's star photographer. He had an uncanny knack for spotting the one picture that would define a newsworthy event, not always the event itself, but often the affect it had on the people around it. Working together, it was always obvious to Xochitl that they had been seeing two entirely different scenes. He was a bit of a genius in that respect and Xochitl had always harbored a secret crush on him.

"Do you have that person's number?" Trundell asked.

"I think I could dig it up, yes."

"Good, I'm going to borrow that person's phone. For the next few days I want you to call that number. Make sure you call from a pay phone, so that it can't be traced to a residence or business. I'm going to wire you five grand. I want you to buy an old Junker, preferably from a private party. Don't bother to register it. You won't have it that long. Then I want you to buy a laptop computer. Nothing fancy, you'll probably only be using it for email. Go to a cyber-cafe, they probably have about a million of them in Los Angeles, and start an online email account. Once you have the account, I need you to email someone you know here in Soda River, again, no names, with instructions to hand deliver your new email address to me. I'm also going to start a new account. I'll email your new account from my new account. That should give us a clean line of communication. Email me from a different location each time, preferably a public place, just in case. Have you got all that?"

"Whoooo yeah. I guess so."

"Repeat it back to me." Xochitl repeated the instructions and was surprised to find that she remembered and understood them all.

"Oh, boss," Xochitl shouted, "I almost forgot to tell you the best news of all. I got Ernie back. He's in pretty bad shape, but he's alive. I don't want to say too much about it on the phone, but I think he's going to be all right."

"Thank God," sighed Albert Trundell as a great weight was lifted off his shoulders. "How the hell'd you accomplish that? Where is he? No, don't tell me. Is he in a safe place?"

"Well, he kind of found me. Someone with medical knowledge is taking care of him, but he's pretty well hidden."

"Don't even bother to give me the details until the next time we meet in person. I don't want anybody knowing where that boy is. Just keep him hidden away and make sure he gets good and well. Tell him I need him in one piece for his next interview. If you need any cash for his medical expenses, give me a call on the center-fielder's phone."

"Okay, boss. Thanks for everything. I better get going. I'm at a pay phone, so I'm in plain view."

"Alright, Saint James, call me tomorrow."

"Oh, oh, wait... Mr. Trundel?"

"I'm here Saint James."

"I got a license number from one of their cars. Do you think you could check it out?"

"Of course. What is it?"

Xochitl fumbled in her pocket, sorting through several pieces of crumpled paper. "It's GRB 147R."

"State?"

"Oh, California."

"All right, I'll run it and let you know what turns up.

CHAPTER 5

Sitting in the front seat of her newly purchased 1972 Plymouth Duster, Xochitl fiddled with her, also newly purchased, laptop computer, trying to get it to recognize the digital camera. She was familiar with the workings of computers, particularly in the area of photographic applications. At AWARE Magazine, all photos were scanned and digitized for enhancement and layout purposes. The laptop had come with a cheap, scaled-down version of a popular photo enhancement program, and Xochitl was trying to import the pictures from her digital camera into the program. After a few error messages and adjustments on both the camera and the program, a full-screen picture of Xochitl's out-of-focus face appeared in the program's document window. "Bingo," she said to herself and repeated the procedure a few more times, just to make sure it wasn't luck.

It was nearly 7pm and Xochitl began to wonder how Ernie was doing. Fid's friend had turned out to be a very likable middle-aged woman by the name of Molly Hernandez. Xochitl was aware that, if the woman was a nightly regular at Pinky's bar, there was probably a drinking problem hiding just below the surface, but after meeting her there was no question of her abilities or integrity. Molly was far from enamored by the concept of large corporations, particularly medical corporations.

The hospital she worked for routinely turned away prospective patients for lack of funds. Some of these people were able to qualify for social programs, but others simply suffered the ravages of their ailments. Molly found this unforgivable in an age where the technology for treatment of disease was progressing in leaps and bounds, while the average citizen was suffering a marked decrease in spending power and medical coverage each year. It seemed to her that they were killing their golden goose, pricing themselves out of the market. With fewer and fewer paying customers, they would have to keep raising their prices until no one but the ultra-wealthy could afford their services. Many people she knew couldn't even afford insurance premiums, let alone medical bills. It was a greed spiral that would inevitably come crashing down, but, until then, she would do what she could to help out.

CHAPTER 6

When Xochitl arrived at Molly's house, the Fiddler Crab was already sitting at the dining room table squinting over a paperback book on self-defense.

"How's Ernie?" she asked.

"Well, he's been through a lot," Molly replied, opening a jar full of tea bags "but he'll pull through okay. No broken bones or internal bleeding that I could find. The worst of it was the bullet wound. He lost quite a bit of blood. Fiddy's been telling me all about your adventure today. Do you think you might tell me what this is all about? After all, if my patient is prone to drawing gunfire, I think I'm owed an explanation. Would you like a cup of tea?"

"Yeah, please. I think that would hit the spot." Xochitl sat down at the table and glanced at the book the Fiddler Crab was reading. "I wish I could explain this whole situation to you, Molly, but I really have no solid idea what's going on, myself." Between sips of tea, she recited the story of the last few days to Molly, trying not to leave anything out. "So, anyway, I think were fairly safe, now, but it's probably a good idea if I stay away from your house till this whole thing blows over. If it blows over. The last thing I want to do is lead them back to Ernie, or to get you into any trouble. You've been nothing but kind and I'd hate to reward that by putting you in harm's way."

"Where do you think this formula is?" asked Molly.

"I don't know. I wouldn't even know what to look for. It could be printed on this teacup and I'd never even know."

"They must have a reason for thinking you have it."

"I guess. I've racked my brains and I can't think of anything. I didn't even know the doctor. I was just supposed to photograph him."

"Is there any chance that your employer, Mr. Trundell I believe you called him, is involved with these people?"

"No! Absolutely not." Xochitl's face darkened.

"That's pretty much the same reaction Ernie had," said Molly apologetically.

"Something's going on, though," said the Fiddler Crab, putting down the book. "People don't just hunt you down and try to kill you for no reason."

Xochitl sat quietly staring into her teacup for some time. "Is Ernie awake? Can I talk to him?"

Molly led the way into a small bedroom, lit only by a plastic night-light in the shape of the Virgin Mary. "This used to be my daughter's room," she spoke quietly, "but she lives with her father, now, down in San Diego. She doesn't visit often enough, still, I like to keep the room ready."

Ernie Blanchard's face was the only color visible in a vast, puffy sea of white pillows, sheets and comforters. He was awake, and smiled weakly as Xochitl entered the room.

"How you doing, bro?" she asked.

"I used to pay money to feel like this at Magic Mountain. It's not so much fun anymore. I must be getting old." Ernie coughed lightly and winced from the pain.

"Don't say that. You're younger than me."

"I don't understand why they think we have the doctor's formula," said Ernie, trying with difficulty to rise from the mountain of pillows.

"I don't either, Ernie, but obviously they have some reason for thinking we do."

"He was already dead when we interviewed him. Well,

I guess we never really got to interview him, did we?" He chuckled, wincing again from the pain.

"Ernie, when you passed out at the doctor's house, what happened?"

"I just got woozy. I'm not too good with blood, I guess."

"No, I mean what happened after that. I ran off to make a phone call and when I came back you were gone. What happened during that time? Did you see anything?"

"I was mostly unconscious, but I did come around a few times and there were a lot of people in the house."

"How many?"

"I don't know, maybe 20."

"Twenty?"

"Yeah. They were all doing things quietly and efficiently. A few were cleaning up the blood, some were putting the body in a bag, a whole bunch of them were searching the house."

"Were they looking for the formula?"

"I guess so. I heard a guy say something about some notes being missing. He asked me about it. When I said I didn't know, he started beating me and I passed out again." Ernie's face drooped and somehow grew smaller on the pillows. "Soach, I gotta confess something here. I ratted you out. That night they beat me up pretty bad. They kept asking if anyone was with me and eventually I cracked. I'm so sorry, Soach. I'm just not cut out to play the hero."

"Don't sweat it, Ernie. I've seen the way these guys operate. They would have figured it out at some point, anyway. Did you get any sense of who they might be, or maybe who they work for?"

"Everyone was wearing either a suit or a jumpsuit, but I didn't notice any kind of logo or insignia. I do remember a few names, though."

"You have names?"

"Yeah. They all called each other by last names but I only remember two."

"Hmmm," said Xochitl. Biting her lip. "Be hard to trace just a last name. What were the names?"

"Cortez and Schlatzski. Cortez seemed to be in charge."

"HA! Cortez, that figures."

"Schlatzski was the guy that shot me," said Ernie. His fingers lightly brushed his chest wound.

"Yeah well, Fid shot him, if it makes you feel any better." She poked her head out the door. "Hey Fid, why don't you come in here and meet Ernie."

The Fiddler Crab entered the room and introduced himself. Introductions made him feel uncomfortable, somehow inadequate and he stepped back and stood quietly behind Xochit.

"Okay, I think that's about enough." Molly began to usher them from the room. "This little boy's had a big day."

CHAPTER 7

"You know what worries me, Fid?" Xochitl asked. They were sipping Greyhounds in a dark booth at the back of Pinky's Bar. "I'm afraid these bastards have unlimited resources. What if we hold off all the guys that are on our trail right now and they just send more? And then, more? And more and more and more? What if they have more money than God? How do you fight against that?"

"Much as I can't stand Doctor Robert Austin Banders, he would have advised us to go on the attack. I think when you're threatened, that's the best thing you can do." The Fiddler Crab twisted his napkin into a rope-like column at the thought of Doctor Banders. "I saw you earlier today with very limited options and you attacked with great success."

"Oh Fid, that was just the Aztec in me. I lost my head. I'm lucky I didn't get us both killed. Besides, how are we supposed to go on the attack? We don't even know who these guys are."

A large handsome man in a casual sports shirt with a little animal on the breast pocket and pressed pants swaggered toward their table. He placed a beefy, intimidating hand on the table and leaned over until his face was directly in front of Xochitl's. He cocked an eyebrow. "Buy you a drink pretty lady?"

"You're blocking my view," said Xochitl flatly.

"Blocking your view of what?" The man feigned surprise.

Xochitl stiffened. "My good friend Mr. Fid, who you seem not to have noticed and who's a damn site prettier than you."

She turned her head and glared into his eyes.

The man turned and passed a disdainful glance over the Fiddler Crab, his expression hardening into disgust at the sight of the Fiddler Crab's withered left arm. He looked back at Xochitl, dismissing the Fiddler Crab as no competition "So, you're not only beautiful, but sensitive. What's this, a pity date?"

Xochitl brought her leg up slowly under the table. "No, tiger, you're the sensitive type and right now my foot's anxious to be introduced to your most sensitive part. Now, why don't you apologize to my friend here before I decide that you've insulted my taste in men?"

"Don't make me laugh, pretty girl. What kind of man has a woman fight his battles for him?"

The Fiddler Crab was straining to recall what he had read that afternoon in his book on self-defense. After the little speech he had given Xochitl only moments ago, he was aware that he must somehow go on the attack. Given his limited resources he was particularly intrigued with what he remembered of the chapter on pressure points. Apparently, there were quite a few places on the human body, which responded to slight pressure with intense pain. If only he could remember where they were. He had found one on his own wrist that caused him unbridled agony when he squeezed it, even with his weak, withered arm. *What the hell, let's give it a go.*

The man felt the pressure on his arm before he realized that anyone was touching him. It was very painful at first, and then it got worse. "Goddammit!" he yelled, falling to his knees. His chin struck the edge of the table and he bit his lip. Xochitl broke out in a hardy belly laugh.

"Yo Romeo," she laughed, "can I find you a woman to fight your battle for you? Because Fid, here, he can get pretty nasty if you piss him off."

The Fiddler Crab was elated, though he refused to let it show. He hadn't expected the pressure points to work this effortlessly.

The man jerked his arm away, fled from the table, and soon vacated the bar. Xochitl did not blink as she watched the man go. "Man I hate those yuppie guys. They just think they're the shit. They think that if they impress you with expensive clothes you'll just melt. They're all such slime balls. Everything about that guy was calculated to impress. He doesn't even get how creepy he is."

"So, I guess you weren't impressed," said the Fiddler Crab, feeling pumped up. He understood he'd said the right thing, but part of him was puzzled by her immediate revulsion to the physically superior man.

"I guess not," Xochitl replied.

"So what kind of guy turns you on?" He stirred his drink slowly with his straw.

"I don't know. I guess clumsy guys."

"That's it? Clumsy guys?"

"Yeah, a guy who doesn't know how to dress. Like you could wrap him up in an Armani suit and he'd look all wrong, out of place, all rumpled up."

"Why is that?"

"Because it's honest. If a guy gets up in the morning and just throws on some pants and a shirt, you can be pretty sure he doesn't have some dumb-ass plan for your day. Just some jeans and a flannel shirt, that does it for me."

"Like that guy over there?" The Fiddler Crab pointed to a young man with blonde, shoulder length hair standing at the bar, wearing a faded flannel shirt, jeans, and leather hiking boots. Though unkempt, he somehow appeared clean and well taken care of."

Xochitl stared for a good thirty seconds. "Yeah," she said, "like that guy."

The Fiddler Crab sat quietly for a moment. Xochitl felt awkward. She had decided immediately that she wanted to meet this man, but didn't quite know how to go about it. Other women seemed to have a natural instinct for this, but Xochitl, who lived each day guided by instinct, was, ironically, lost when it came to reeling in men. Fortunately, she was attractive enough to draw attention to herself, so generally they came to her. It wasn't that her instincts failed her during the crucial moments, she simply became overwhelmed with self-doubts and didn't listen to them. She felt that, had the man in question been seriously interested, he would surely have noticed her as soon as she entered the room. Given some preparation, she knew how to attract a roomful of men and then select the one she wanted. The problem was that an assault like that took some time. Securing the interest of an attractive man out of a crowd of strangers, particularly if he wasn't paying much attention to her, was simply beyond her scope.

"Don't be a snob," said the Fiddler Crab. "Go over and introduce yourself."

"Oh yeah, right."

"Come on. What guy wouldn't be flattered?"

"It doesn't work that way, Fid. He's gotta come to me."

"Well, okay. Suit yourself. I could use a another drink," said the Fiddler Crab. "How you doing? It's on me."

"Thanks, Fid."

The Fiddler Crab shuffled his way through the crowd to the bar, where he waited a few minutes for Pinky's attention.

"What'll ya have, Fidster?" asked Pinky, leaning across the bar.

"Well...let me see now..." The Fiddler Crab looked over his shoulder at Xochitl, who happened to be looking back at him. There was a look in his eye that was unfamiliar to Xochitl, a sort of round-eyed mischievous look. She saw him purposely move his elbow into the attractive man's drink, spilling it across the bar. The man tried to grab it, but wasn't quick enough. Xochitl saw the Fiddler Crab apologize profusely to the man, and then he turned around, pointing across the room to their table. Xochitl's cheeks reddened and she turned her gaze toward her glass. The man nodded. The Fiddler Crab turned toward Pinky. "I guess I'll have two more Greyhounds, and whatever this young man is drinking."

"Make it three," said the man.

"Three doggies in a bathtub coming right up," Pinky said as he set to work applying his knowledge of chemistry and magic.

The Fiddler Crab escorted the young man back to the table. He gestured grandly. "This is my good friend, Xochitl Saint James, visiting from Soda River, up in the Sierras."

"Hi, Xochitl. I'm Rick Sedgwick. Nice to meet you. So you came to our fair city to see all the tall buildings? Too much natural beauty up there in the Sierras? Must get tiresome after a while."

"I guess. Something like that. I'm kind of here on business."

"What do you do?"

"I'm a photographer for AWARE Magazine. Have you ever seen it?"

"I'm a subscriber."

"No shit? That's cool! What are the chances? A subscriber?" She felt the Fiddler Crab's foot kick her lightly in the shins. He stared at her steadily. Oh my God, she thought, he's telling me I'm babbling. The guy's been here like, one second and I'm already babbling. She took a deep breath, centered herself. "So, yeah, that's me. What about you?"

"I'm a musician."

"Flugal horn?" Xochitl cocked an eyebrow.

"I'm afraid I don't have the schooling for that. No, just guitar and vocals."

"Do you make a living at it?"

"Well, I limp along. I've got a little trust fund that helps me out if I get into trouble, though I don't like to use it."

"Do you play with a band, or just solo?"

"Both, really. Some songs just seem to sound better with a band driving them and others need to be able to breathe, so they sound best with just an acoustic guitar. I do club gigs with the band and then quieter coffee house type gigs alone."

"What's your band called?"

"Wicked Monkey Children. We're playing on Sunset tomorrow, at a new place called Slander. Maybe you could come and check us out. They have a great sound system and the drinks are pretty decent."

"We'll see what we can do," said Xochitl, planning what she was going to wear.

"AAARRGG!" shouted the Fiddler Crab. "Banders."

Xochitl and Rick followed his angry glare across the room, where it rested on a wall-mounted television. "Pinky, turn the TV up for a minute." Pinky reached up and twisted the knob until the booming voice of Doctor Robert Austin Banders reached their table.

"Friends," said the still handsome but now sixty-something face, from the screen, "ever notice that if you stand in one place for quite a while you get just plain dog-tired? Say you're at a good old American Veteran's Day Parade and at first you're having a grand old time watching all the tanks and trucks loaded with missiles go rumbling down the street, feeling secure and all, but at some point you realize that you just can't wait for the whole thing to be over. You begin to feel a little crabby and irritable because your legs are tired and sore. You're starting to feel a little... well, let's admit it, a bit unpatriotic on a grand American holiday. Well, friends, there's a reason why your legs are sore. You're working them out! You're burning calories just standing there! And burned calories, well that equals weight loss and who among us doesn't want to lose a few pounds? But if you're like me, you're busy all day. Who's got time for the gym? I certainly don't have time to wait around in the hope that some hormone engorged 'body sculptor' decides to take a break and let me on the exercise bicycle. I'm assuming you, too, have better things to do with your time than that. Suppose I told you that you could stand in the middle of your very own living room for hours at a time and FEEL NO PAIN as the pounds simply melt off your body. Did you hear that? I said FEEL NO PAIN. There are those who will tell you that there is no gain without pain, but I'm here to call them bald-faced liars. Besides, we're not trying to gain here, we're trying to lose - excess weight. My new book, 'You Can

Stand To Lose A Few Pounds', will guide you through twelve easy steps to weight loss without pain. Pain? Who needs it? Please stand by while Cindy gives you all the information you need to own your own copy of 'You Can Stand To Lose A Few Pounds'. Cindy?"

Cindy's face, and ample cleavage, filled the television screen. The Fiddler Crab couldn't help but notice that the new Cindy bore a striking resemblance to the one he had seen on the Banders infomercials eighteen years ago in high school. *He must be cloning them.* "I hate that bastard," he said to Rick. "He ruined my life. He dashed every hope I ever had."

"Yeah," said Rick. "At one time I hated him, too, but I got over it."

"You bought one of his books, too?" asked the Fiddler Crab, astonished. He had assumed that only lower life forms such as himself would fall for the doctor's elegant drivel.

"No, nothing like that," said Rick, obviously ashamed. "He's my dad."

CHAPTER 8

The Fiddler Crab sat devouring the remains of a rice and bean burrito at a wooden picnic-style table outside of Adolph's Cocina, his self-defense manual spread out before him. He loved Adolph's. The tiny, fixed income he lived on didn't allow him to dine out often, but when he got the chance, Adolph's was always his first choice. Financially, it was not good planning to be at Adolph's now, especially since he was scheduled to meet Xochitl and Rick at yet another, more expensive, restaurant later that afternoon. But guilt was rearing its ugly face by forcing a voracious appetite upon him.

Try as he might, he couldn't concentrate on his book and was reading the same line over and over. Ever since he had shot the man in the van, his appetite had become overpowering, as though he'd suddenly become the reluctant host of a tapeworm. Logically, he felt fine about the shooting, didn't consider it anything but necessary. Throughout the day, however, tiny telltale signs had cropped up to inform him that all was not right with the world. Somewhere, deep inside him, a voice was whispering that he had ended the life of another human being, and that, under any circumstances, that was not okay. It was a quiet voice, but persistent. For the most part he was able to ignore it, though occasionally a tiny seed of guilt would germinate inside him and sprout, momentarily spreading a sickly feeling throughout his entire body. So he ate. When the burrito was finished, he ordered a large bowl of chili, with extra onions. And then some taquitos.

The Fiddler Crab's life had taken some drastically interesting turns lately. Turns that, only days before, he would have considered so unlikely as to be considered fiction. Xochitl was very interesting indeed, but when she was around things tended to change faster than his sedentary brain could adjust. She seemed to handle drastic change without breaking a sweat, but it was scary for a guy who usually got his adventure from TV and other people's stories at Pinky's Bar. The car chase alone would have been something to remember for the rest of his life, but after that he had killed a man. He had *killed* a man! Little Chester McFadden, the butt of so many jokes had finally had the last laugh on someone. It surprised him how little satisfaction he drew from this. Had everyone who had ever one-upped him felt this sense of hollow victory afterward? Strange, then, that it had been such a popular activity.

CHAPTER 9

They were seated at a little chrome and glass table in the corner of a posh restaurant, called Cirque Du Fromage, located on the Sunset Strip. They were all going to see Rick's band play at Slander and the three had decided to meet here for a bite beforehand. There had been no disturbance in Xochitl's life for the last twenty-four hours and she was feeling secure enough to go to a public place to eat. And then to an even more public place to see Rick perform on stage. She had grown instantly fond of Rick after their introduction the night before. Conversation with him had flowed effortlessly and he seemed to possess just the right combination of weaknesses and strengths. Nothing about him seemed to be forced, and to someone as driven as Xochitl, this trait was like a big fuzzy pillow, and a powerful source of fascination.

The Fiddler Crab was not eating. He had done more than his duty at Adolph's that afternoon and was now beginning to feel the bloated pangs of gas. He glanced at Xochitl nervously as his intestines began to make long, drawn-out cat-like noises. The gas worked its way backwards and forwards through him, snarling and clawing at his inner passages. He found himself speaking too loudly in order to mask the embarrassing whine emanating from beneath the table. "I can't believe it," he barked. "I've carried this sort of smoldering hatred for Doctor Robert Austin Banders almost my whole life, ever since high school, and here I am having dinner with a member of his family. You just never can predict where life's going to take you." Xochitl and Rick bobbed and weaved, to avoid a collision with the Fiddler Crab's wildly gesticulating arm.

Rick was quiet. Eventually he cleared his throat. "I took the liberty of inviting my father here to join us," he said between dodges.

"You what?" The Fiddler Crab grew suddenly still, his eyes like saucers. A low rumble escaped from beneath the table. "Why the hell would you do something like that?"

Rick flicked the hair out of his eyes. "Well, I wanted you to meet him, Fid, so you would see that in reality he's just someone to be pitied rather than hated. Carrying around all that hate with you for years is not good for your body or your soul. I did it for years, too, but one day I realized that the more I hated him, the more power he had over me. I was just handing my personal power over to him in big, hateful handfuls. Don't get me wrong, I still don't like him much, and I haven't forgotten that he robbed me of a lot of my life, but I'm not seething anymore. It's kind of funny, when I stopped hating him, all the power seemed to dissipate from him. He no longer felt like a threat. I guess you can't have a war unless you have an enemy. Maybe today you can end your own personal war and let that poisonous anger go."

The Fiddler Crab's immediate burst of anger overwhelmed him as he struggled to control the pressure building in his gut, fighting to force his sphincter muscle closed as the forces of nature conspired to pry it open. Several times, he had excused himself to the restroom and relieved himself, but each time, as he returned to the table the pressure began to reassert itself. He tried to pay attention to the conversation and speak in a normal tone of voice, but the urgent situation in his bowels was clouding his mind, making his words jerky and loud. "That sounds easier said than done," he snapped. "Couldn't we maybe do this another day? You know, when everything's not so rushed."

"He's a busy man. It was now or never, so I took the plunge.

I hope you're okay with that." Rick was half apologizing, but in a patronizing insistent way.

"I'll live," the Fiddler Crab grumbled, though the pressure of pure dread began to grow in his head just as surely as the pressure of pure methane was growing in his gut.

Xochitl leaned over and whispered in the Fiddler Crab's ear. "If it was me, I'd kick the old man's ass," she said, lightly punching his arm. The Fiddler Crab smiled distractedly as he struggled to retain a gaseous flood that now seemed imminent.

A voice from behind. "Hello Richard." It was a stern, condescending voice. The voice of a master speaking to a servant. Everyone at the table looked up to see the spa-tanned, relatively unlined face of a well-dressed man in his late sixties. He was wearing beige slacks and a white turtle neck sweater. There was a dark blue dinner jacket tucked under his arm. "I trust this won't take long."

"Hi Dad. I just wanted you to meet some friends. One of them is very familiar with your work - or at least he was at one time," Rick said.

Xochitl noticed that, despite his talk of forgiveness, Rick had automatically adopted an inferior stance in the presence of his father. Xochitl silently sent the essence of her heart into the chest of the older man where she felt her presence spread out and engulf his heart. A dark, overpowering emptiness seized her and she let go immediately. The man seemed not to notice.

Doctor Robert Austin Banders surveyed the table, looking for anything that might be useful to him. Finding nothing, his expression turned cold. "A pleasure to meet you all," he said, "but I've got an appointment I really must keep." He turned to the Fiddler Crab. "If you'd like me to autograph a book for you young man, I think I could squeeze it in."

Through all this the Fiddler Crab sat mute. His fight with the evil gods of Mexican food had required his utmost concentration, but now all of his attention was focused on the bright, predatory eyes of Doctor Robert Austin Banders. The same eyes that had stared up at him from the cover of ANYONE CAN! so many years ago. *My God! Does he actually believe I would want his autograph?* He fought to recall Rick's words of forgiveness, but somehow their significance escaped him, lost behind the realization that his life-long enemy was standing directly before him. Many times the Fiddler Crab had dreamed of this very moment, but somehow, in the revealing light of reality, all of his imagined responses seemed childish, inappropriate, or even criminal. A sound emanated from beneath the table. *Fweeeeeeet!* It was the sound of air being forced from a balloon while pinching the opening shut. For a moment the Fiddler Crab sat frozen in horror at himself. The one scenario he had never imagined was one in which he sat farting uncontrollably, humiliating himself in front of his nemesis.

Against all the reason and restraint he could muster, all the well intentioned words Rick had spoken, the Fiddler Crab lunged, full force, up and over the back of the booth at Doctor Robert Austin Banders. He grabbed Banders by the throat. "You bastard! You ruined my life!" he shouted. The surprised doctor drew back his fist and punched the Fiddler Crab squarely in the gut. "Ugh!" *Furrrrrrffffff,* from the Fiddler Crab. Xochitl and Rick looked on helplessly as the sounds of violence and flatulence collided. Whack! *Ffffffffff,* Slap! *Plplplp!* Banders worked his muscular, well-tanned, movie star arms around the Fiddler Crab's middle and began to squeeze. "Yaaaaahh!" and "*Braaaaaaap,*" burst forth from both ends of the Fiddler Crab at once. He retaliated with a backhand across Banders' face. Smack! *Plap plap plap poooooh!* "You son of a bitch!" *Hisssssssssssss.....*

When it was all over, Doctor Robert Austin Banders and the Fiddler Crab lay in crumpled heaps on the floor sporting cuts and abrasions that appeared worse than they actually were. "You'll pay for this," said Banders between wheezes.

"I paid for it a long time ago," heaved the Fiddler Crab. "I'm just collecting my refund."

Xochitl bent over the Fiddler Crab, examining his wounds. "Nice work, Fid," she said quietly, next to his ear.

Rick was standing over his father, unsure what to do. Banders rose to his feet slid his arms into his dinner jacket. "I'll deal with you later," he growled at Rick and strode from the restaurant, brushing the creases from his coat.

"I'm so embarrassed," said the Fiddler Crab as he struggled to his feet. His instinct told him to make a break for it, to run as he'd always run in the past.

"Oh, get over yourself," said Xochitl, pushing him back down. "You handled yourself pretty well just now. You beat the hell out of an old enemy. You vanquished him. That's got to feel pretty good."

"I did, didn't I?" he said with glassy eyes. This was the first time in his entire life that someone had stopped him from running. What would his life have been like if more people had done that? What if Elsa Starlighter had refused to let him run from the little Italian Restaurant so many years before? Where might he be now? Married, with children?

"Hey Rick, I'm sorry, man," the Fiddler Crab said breathlessly. "I don't know what came over me. I didn't know what I was doing until I was already doing it."

"Forget it, Fid," said Rick quietly. "You're not the first to chew him a new asshole. Although, usually it doesn't involve me." His brow furrowed. "Actually, a confrontation with my father is probably a good thing. It'll force some things out in the open that need to be said. Well, let's head out, guys. We're playing from 9:00 to 9:30."

In the parking lot Rick got into the driver's seat of his car and closed the door. Just before he entered the car, the Fiddler Crab spied Xochitl's face over the roof. "Hey, Fid..." she said quietly. He stared across the top of the car into her expressionless face. Once their gazes were locked, she stuck out her tongue and made a loud farting noise. Then her shoulders began heaving in silent laughter. Her head disappeared below the roof and he heard the door click shut.

The Fiddler Crab remained outside the car for a moment. He stood, smiling to himself as he reveled in the strange feeling of acceptance.

CHAPTER 10

Slander was an old movie theater converted to a nightclub. The owners, two twenty-one-year-old entrepreneurs, had purchased the theater because it came equipped with a fully functional stage inside and a lighted marquee outside, figuring half their work had been done for them. However, the cost of leveling the floor, and installing and stocking three bars, on top of a liquor license, had left little capital for interior decorations. As a result, everything in the theater that hadn't already been flat black, was now flat black.

As the three climbed from of the car, Xochitl spied the marquee, which advertised the night's entertainment in varying degrees of importance.

TONIGHT: - **Bellview** – TANK'D – Snail Bait –

Flat Response – Camel Toe - Wicked Monkey Children

"Hmmm," she said, "I can barely read that last one, there. What does it say?"

"Okay, okay," Rick said, flushing. "So we're not at the Greek Theater yet but we will be one of these days."

Xochitl let the subject drop as they strolled around back to the stage door. "Don't you need a guitar or an amplifier or something? I'm no musician, but I know it takes more than an air guitar to please an audience these days."

"Yeah, audiences have gotten so much more sophisticated. The smoke and mirrors just don't fool 'em like they used to.

Thank God there are still a few slow ones out there or we wouldn't have a crowd at all."

"So?"

"I pay a kid to set my gear up for me. He wants to be a rock star when he grows up."

"So he drives down here early and sets your stuff up just the way you like it?"

"Well, in theory. It works much better if we're on first. That way he has some time to get it right."

"So there are advantages to being the last name on the list."

"Definitely. For instance, we'll be the only ones tonight who get an actual sound check. Everyone else has to just plug in and go."

"Why?"

"Time. We've got six bands playing here tonight in a five hour period. It's the only way to squeeze them all in. On the down side, though, the first couple of bands only get half-hour sets."

"Are you nervous?"

"About what?"

"You know, playing in front of people."

"Ha! Hopefully there'll be people here to be nervous in front of. The club's usually half empty until later in the evening."

They climbed a short concrete stairway and passed through a grungy hallway, littered with piles of beer-stained cables and old lighting equipment, finally emerging on to the stage, which seemed decidedly unglamorous in the bright light. Xochitl walked to the edge of the stage and faced the empty room. "So, this is what it's like," she said, raising her arms, palms out, engulfed in imaginary thunderous applause.

Rick ignored her, turning away toward his equipment.

A young man, around high school age, knelt in front of a large, Marshall amplifier, a confused look on his face. "So Rick, I forget. Does it go through the tuner first and then into the distortion pedal, or the other way around?"

Rick stood still, eyes closed, fists clenched. "Yeah," he

snapped. "The first one."

"Hey man, thanks again for letting me do this. I'm learning a lot."

"Yeah whatever."

Xochitl was a little unnerved at Rick's rudeness toward the boy, but thought it better not to bring it up. It was a side of him she hadn't seen before now. Marrisa had once told her that on a first date she always paid particular attention to how her date treated the waiter. The waiter was automatically in a subservient position and it revealed a lot about her date's character to see how he handled this little bit of power. "If you stay with someone long enough," she had said, "sooner or later, you're the waiter." Xochitl filed Rick's minor abuse of power under 'For further examination when more information is available.' Perhaps he was more nervous than he let on.

Twenty-or-so patrons had trickled in and were milling about in the subdued light, early birds who had no clue about the coolness of being fashionably late. Somehow the presence of the scattered crowd made the place feel more desolate than when it had been totally empty.

"It's weird starting with no crowd," Rick said. "There's nothing to draw energy from."

"I thought you guys were supposed to supply the energy," Xochitl said, turning her back to her audience.

"It seems like it would be that way, but it's actually a two way street. The audience feeds off the band and the band, in turn, feeds off the crowd's energy. If all goes well," he threw his arms up like an erupting volcano, "the energy keeps building to a nice big sloppy climax."

"Whew..." said Xochitl, fanning her face with her hand. "You must need a smoke after that."

Rick grinned. A tall portly man about Rick's age wandered through the door carrying a large black cylindrical object. "Hi Joe," said Rick. "This is Xochitl and Fid."

"Nice to meet ya," said Joe in a high-pitched, scratchy, overweight voice. "You guys playin' tonight?"

"No," said Xochitl. "We're here to see Rick."

"Ah," said Joe with a knowing grin.

Xochitl took note of the innuendo and pointed to the large container. "What's that?" she asked.

"Kick drum," said Joe, slapping the black plastic case with the palm of his big, beefy hand. "This here baby's the engine. It's what drives the music. Veerrry important piece of equipment, right here, little lady." He puffed his chest out, though it didn't extend any farther than his gut.

Xochitl grinned. "So, you only get one drum to play with?"

"The rest of the kit's in the car. It's just a small kit, though. When I was in my first band I musta had forty-two toms and a hundred and twelve cymbals, but then I realized I had to carry all that stuff around and set it up. And, what the hell, it wasn't getting me any more laid than a four-piece kit. So now I just travel light."

"So, that's the point? Getting laid?"

"Hell yeah, that's the point," Joe laughed.

Xochitl had a good feeling about Joe. She didn't have to examine his heart to know he was basically a good guy. It was all right there on the surface. The stage door creaked and slammed, followed by a series of bumping sounds. Soon a short, skinny man appeared dragging a large black speaker cabinet from the hallway onto the stage. He wore a rumpled, maroon shirt and blue jeans.

"Bass player," said Joe. Then turning toward the man, "Karl this is Sloe Gin and, Fizz was it?"

"Hi, I'm Xochitl, and this is Fid."

"Mmm," said Karl, disinterested. He turned away and began connecting cables to his amplifier, which was nearly as big as himself. A soundman appeared, seemingly out of nowhere, carrying a milk crate full of cables and microphones. He began wordlessly placing microphone stands in front of amplifiers and the places where vocalists would stand.

"You look bummed, Scratch," said Rick to the soundman.

"Chicks," said Scratch, shaking his head disgustedly.

"Aw, man... You didn't get dumped again, did you?" called Joe from his drum kit, now completely assembled. "Well, at least you still got a perfect record."

"Same old story," said scratch, trying to focus the guitar microphone directly at the edge of the speaker's voice cone. "She says I'm never home. I can't help it if it's an all-day, all-night kind a job. It's what I do, man. Aahh screw it. I'll live. Okay, guys, give me a minute. You know the drill. We'll do monitors first and then the house."

The sound check went smoothly and the band was able to kick back for fifteen minutes before the show began. Fid went to the sound booth and hung out with Scratch in order to give Xochitl and Rick some alone time. Rick went to the bar and ordered a Red Bull and two shots of whiskey. He pounded the first shot, guzzled the Red Bull, and then sipped the second shot for a few moments until it was all gone.

"Well, that oughta do it," Xochitl said.

"Everybody's got their formula," said Rick. "That's the one that works for me."

"I'd be talking a million miles a minute, without caring what I said."

"Yeah, that's pretty much what it does."

"So you are nervous up there."

"I don't know if I'd call it nervous. More like pumped. It's kinda like when you meet a girl that you like for the first time. Things just flow a lot better if you don't care what you say."

"So you drank your formula when we met?"

"Earlier, yeah. We had another opening slot."

"So you were drunk when we met?"

"Snockered."

"Hmmm..." Xochitl's eyes narrowed.

Rick felt her vibe. "I'm just kidding," he said. "Sober as a judge."

Xochitl didn't know whether to believe him or not, but decided to leave it alone for the time being.

"Well, it's about that time," said Rick. "I better get up on the stage."

As the band began to pound out their original tunes, Xochitl was immediately drawn to Rick's music, a melodic type of funk with a bit of a hard edge to it. It was one thing, she discovered, to be hooked on the music of a band, but it was another thing entirely when you knew the person who wrote the tunes. Certain passages and phrases reflected what she had learned of Rick's personality, while others made her wonder from what dark part of his soul they had emerged. All-in-all it was an educational experience and Xochitl felt that she had a little better understanding of Rick when the set was done.

Following Wicked Monkey Children's set, Rick paid the boy who had set up his equipment and grabbed Xochitl by the elbow, nudging her toward the door. "Let's go to my place where it's quiet," he said. "We can kick back and have a few beers"

"What about Fid?" asked Xochitl.

"I already talked to him. He wants to stick around for a while. He's interested in what Scratch is doing. I guess they're getting along pretty well. Scratch is showing him some mixing tricks. He says he'll catch a cab later."

"Okay," said Xochitl.

CHAPTER 11

Rick's apartment was sparsely, though expensively, furnished. Xochitl had expected something more cluttered, sloppier, with greater evidence of right-brain activity. The pictures on the wall were not rock star posters, but fine art prints, mostly Gauguin and Van Gogh, as well as some originals she didn't recognize. The floor was light-colored hardwood with several hemp throw rugs placed beneath the furniture legs. Overall, Xochitl got an impression of wood, chrome, glass, tidiness and wealth.

Rick went to the refrigerator and extracted two bottles of imported beer, opening them on an antique brass Coca Cola bottle opener fastened to the kitchen counter. "Cheers," he said, handing her a bottle.

"Nice digs," she said. "Local musicians live a lot better here than they do in my town."

"That pays for some of it, but the rest comes from a trust fund set up by my dad."

"I thought you said you didn't like to use your trust fund."

"I don't. It bothers me every time I pay the rent."

"Poor baby. Every time I pay the rent it bothers me that I *don't* have a trust fund."

Rick was silent, embarrassed. "It just ties me to him in ways I don't like. It gives him power over me. And, make no mistake, he's all about power."

"I thought you had forgiven him and you two were good

buddies now."

"I have. At least I think I have." Rick took a long slug off his beer. "Look, just because you forgive someone doesn't make you blind to their faults. Anyway, that doesn't have anything to do with it. It's not about forgiveness, it's about independence. I need to get my band signed to a major record label. Once I get a good amount of cash coming in, I can start making my own decisions."

"We did an article at the magazine, once," said Xochitl, "about how record companies treat musicians. It turns out that, as a general rule, they don't treat them very well. In fact, some people actually end up owing the company money after a couple of hits. You might be better off going the independent route, promoting yourself."

"Look, don't complicate things, okay?" Rick snapped. "I've already got my plans."

"Sorry, sorry," said Xochitl, palms up. "So... How 'bout them Dodgers, huh?"

Rick laughed, and Xochitl moved her face close to Rick's. Slowly, he leaned in, making up the difference, until they felt their lips touch lightly together. Just a mere tickle at first, then a little harder. Xochitl tilted her head slightly and opened her mouth. Suddenly there was nothing else in the whole world but two hungry hearts and a passionate kiss.

They stayed entwined for many minutes. Rick was gentle with Xochitl, passionate, but not insistent. Eventually, he pulled away and looked into Xochitl's eyes. "I want to make love to you," he said.

Xochitl stiffened slightly, tangling with her own scrambled passions. "I want to, too, but I don't think we should. Not until all this is over. This is obviously more than a casual thing and I wouldn't feel right getting that entwined until I know we're safe."

"Till what's all over?" Rick's brow furrowed. "What do you mean, safe?"

"I have no right to draw you into this. I should just leave

now."

"Draw me into what?"

"I better go."

"You're not going anywhere until you tell me what's going on." Rick had his hands clenched firmly around Xochitl's arms. "Are you in danger? Are you ill? Talk to me."

Xochitl struggled for a moment, then wilted. "Okay," she said, almost in a whisper. She laid her head gently on his chest. "You want the story? Well, here's how it goes."

CHAPTER 12

Stop yelling, boss," Xochitl said into the pay phone receiver.

"I don't believe this, Saint James! Have you looked at the cover of The Snitch today?" Albert Trundell's voice was over-powering, even through the tinny phone receiver. The Snitch was a sleazy regional tabloid focused primarily on the misfor-tunes of celebrities du jour and unsubstantiated stories involv-ing the supernatural.

"No, gee boss, I must be slipping. I don't know how that got by me. My subscription must have run out."

"Don't get smart with me, young lady."

"I love it when you act like a dad. Oh, wait. There's a bunch of newspaper vending machines outside this store and, what do you know, one of them is The Snitch. Hang on, I'll get one." Xochitl reached into the machine and pulled out a paper. Her heart stopped momentarily. The headline read: TOP DOC TUSSLES WITH FREAK IN POSH BISTRO. Beneath the head-line was a photograph of the Fiddler Crab and Doctor Robert Austin Banders slugging it out in an obviously trendy restaur-ant while surprised diners looked on. The most prominent surprised diners in the background, directly between the two opponents were Xochitl Saint James and Rick Sedgwick, star-ing straight into the camera. "Okay, boss," she sighed somberly into the receiver, "we have a problem."

"Yes, we do have a problem. You can bet that these people have seen this by now. They've probably already been to the restaurant where the picture was taken, asked questions, found out who Banders is and put a tale on him."

"Heh, yeah well, it's pretty early yet, boss."

"These are the kind of people who don't sleep, Saint James. I wish you'd take this a little more seriously. If, as you say, you've been seeing his son, they won't have to look too hard to find you"

"I'm not *seeing* him! We're just hanging out. Look, I *am* taking it seriously, boss, but I don't think that getting all sketched out about it is going to accomplish anything. We both need to think clearly, because I know, whoever they are, these guys are doing nothing so much as thinking clearly."

"Alright, Saint James," Trundell sighed. "I don't think it's a good idea for you to be *hanging out* with Bob Banders' son, or this physically challenged character in the picture, for that matter. How hard can it be to spot him?"

"That's not fair. They're the only people I know here, except Weezy - which reminds me, boss, if I send him to you, will you take care of him for me? The people at the hotel I'm staying at are complaining and I don't know where else to go."

"The cat? You want me to take the cat?"

"Yeah. He'll like you. He knows good people when he sees them, so he shouldn't be any trouble."

"It's not him liking me I'm worried about." Heavy sigh. "Alright, Saint James. Send me the cat. Anything to make sure you're safe."

"Thanks, boss." Xochitl was quiet for a moment, and in that moment a thousand thoughts populated her head. Was she doing something stupid, putting not only herself, but Rick and Fid in danger? A relationship, she knew, was a progression of small, almost imperceptible steps. A thousand tiny tendrils or strings, composed of interests and attractions, working slowly, in concert, to build a web and bind one person firmly to another. There was no one specific moment when two people realized they had crossed the line into 'relationship'. It was only evident in retrospect. Xochitl, in the short time she had known Rick, felt that line hovering somewhere off in the distance, just beyond the point of clear vision. True, they were brand new to each other, but something had hooked her firmly. It made her nervous, edgy. Traditionally, she had a less than perfect record when it came to choosing mates. Although she possessed the power to view the essence of any human heart in her vicinity, she steadfastly refused to exercise it in reference to her lovers, or even potential lovers. Perhaps it was fear of breaking someone's trust right at the start by using an unfair advantage. After all, she wasn't perfect, either. And, as she had discovered in the past, sometimes even a relationship with a good man could end painfully. A good man was no guarantee of a good relationship. Perhaps refusing to use her ability was akin to shooting herself in the foot, but what would a relationship be without some kind of trust?

It was unsettling. Rick seemed to be strong in the right places and vulnerable in the right places. In most social gatherings Xochitl had a distinct lack of patience and dislike for small talk which she tried, with varying degrees of success to keep under wraps. Rick, on the other hand, she was able to be with effortlessly. He was easy company. The progression felt natural and the thought of interrupting its flow made her frustrated and even more angry with her pursuers. But it was not just her own safety that was at stake here. Rick and Fid could both be facing grave danger through their relationship to her. That was not acceptable.

"I have to meet up with Rick and Fid at our usual watering hole tonight, boss. I'll tell them that for their own good they should maybe temporarily distance themselves from me a little bit."

There was another momentary silence. Trundell cleared his throat.

"Okay, not maybe. Absolutely. I'm sure they'll understand,"

she said quietly.

"What I'd really like is for you to come home to Soda River where I can keep an eye on you, but, hopefully, you'll have an easier time being invisible in LA, at least if you can manage to stay out of the newspapers. Can you manage that Saint James?"

"Yeah," she sighed. "I think so."

"That sounds less than convincing."

"All I can do is try, boss."

His voice softened. "Do you need anything?"

"You could send me a box of hand-made cigars."

"Cigars?"

"Forget it, boss. It's an Aztec thing."

"Anything else?"

"Oh, what about the license plate? Did anything turn up?"

"Nothing! It appears that the number you gave me was never issued. It's a counterfeit plate."

"Shit! Don't these guys ever screw up? Even just a little bit?"

"They're not gods Saint James. Remember the blood on the saw in your garage? That was a screw-up. They left a calling card that day."

"That's true boss. It gives me a little bit of hope anyway. Okay, I better get going. I'll call you tomorrow."

"Email me. It'll be safer."

CHAPTER 13

Banders sat stiffly at a large oak desk in his opulent study, flanked by a pair of thick, dark-suited men. Everything about the two men, save for their faces, was identical. They could almost be clones, he thought.

"I'll get right to the point, Dr. Banders," said one of the men, his fingers forming a church and steeple in front of his lips. "We're aware of your problem. We believe we have a solution we can all live with."

"Problem? What problem? What are you talking about?"

"It's come to the attention of my employer that during the early part of your career you, uh ...shall we say, neglected ...to file for a non-profit status. However, your actions, as regarding your tax obligations, were those of an organization which *had* filed for non-profit status. See what I mean?"

"I'm afraid I have no idea what you're talking about."

"You made a lot of money and you didn't pay any taxes on it," barked the other. "Clear enough, Dr. Banders, or should I say Mr. Sedgwick?"

Banders swallowed hard. "Who are you?" he asked softly.

"Need to know basis, Dr. Banders," said the first man. "First we need to reach an agreement. We're both in a position to help each other out here. If you play your cards right this could be win-win."

"What sort of agreement?"

"Though my employer is not necessarily affiliated with any

of the parties to whom you owe money, they are most definitely in a position to make all those financial troubles disappear."

"I'm listening."

"It seems you owe the good ol' U.S. of A. around two mil in
back taxes and fines."

Banders stiffened, gasping audibly.

"Calm down there, Doctor. Like I said, you play your cards
right, this whole thing goes away."

"What do you want?"

"It seems your son has met a girl. "

"Ah, the one with the little pet monster who attacked me."

"Right. Turns out she's not just any girl. This girl's got some
very specific knowledge. Now this knowledge is extremely
valuable to my employer. We need you to lead us to her. Once
the information is retrieved and is safely in the hands of those
who can utilize it, with all the leaks safely plugged, you'll be a
very free man, indeed. And a rich one! I know your son is probably full of youthful fire and idealism, but I also know what a
convincing man you can be when the situation calls for it. Get
that information for us, Dr. Banders. My people are willing to
pay off your tax debt and hand you another two mil besides.
How can you beat that?"

"Three," said Banders, poker-faced.

"Excuse me?"

"Three million. On top of the debt cancellation. If you can
afford two, you can afford three. I know they didn't send you
in here without some room to negotiate. This is going to cause
an irreparable rift between my son and I. Two million hardly
seems a strong enough salve for that wound."

"Alright, three. Once the information is in hand."

"Pleasure doing business with you," said Banders curtly.
"Now tell me the rest of the details."

CHAPTER 14

"**There** is no way I'm leaving you alone," Rick paced angrily, as Xochitl sat on the edge of his bed. "From what I understand, these men are capable of killing. I will not leave you alone with a bunch of trigger-happy thugs on your tail."

"It's for your own good," she shouted defiantly, "as well as mine. They can get to me through you, and they can get to you through your dad in order to get to me. If we sever the link, there won't be any reason for them to pursue you. Today we were all on the cover of a very popular regional paper. None of us is as safe as we were yesterday."

"Why don't you just give them this damn formula? It can't be worth your life." He was more reserved now, unsure, comprehending the undeniable logic of her words. They were in danger. All of them. Himself included.

"I don't have the formula. I wouldn't know what it looked like if it bit me on the ass. I have no idea why they think I have it, but I don't."

"They must have a reason. From what you've told me, whatever else they may be, they don't seem to be stupid. Think! Did you take anything with you from the murder scene?"

"No. I went in the kitchen, saw blood everywhere and ran out the door to the gas station."

"Look," said Rick, placing his hands on Xochitl's shoulders, "all I know is that we just met and we're both pretty clear about the fact that we like what we've seen. I don't want to toss that in the crapper because some faceless suits want to play rough. Let's get rough back."

"We don't know who to get rough with, Rick. We'd be swinging at empty air. And besides, there's no way we can get as rough as they can. Their resources are scary. Look, this doesn't have to be a permanent thing. When it cools down we can hang out again."

Rick stood silently brooding. In the end he simply nodded in half-hearted agreement.

"I've got to meet Fid for happy hour at Pinky's around six. The same thing applies to him. Why don't you meet us there and we'll have a last drink. It's just for a while," she said softly, touching his arm.

"All right," he sighed. "I'll see you then. I don't like it, but if your mind's made up, there's not much I can do about it.

CHAPTER 15

Rick's face was pinched as he drove down Sunset, mulling over his new situation. He liked Xochitl immensely. She was very different than any of the usual nightclub girls he hooked up with. She was easily as beautiful as any of them, but she was somehow deeper. It was like she could see right through him. Her scope was very wide and she absorbed the nuances of what was going on around her. She understood. Perhaps that was what drew him to her, the way she looked at him as though she already knew who he was and that it was okay with her. Whatever the reason, their attraction had been swift and merciless.

But was that worth dying for? True, he was in no immediate danger, but judging by the story she had told him, some kind of residual flack could come flying at him at any minute. What if she was one of those people who are constantly attracting trouble? She didn't really seem like that type of girl, but it was really too early to tell.

He tried not to admit it to himself, but a core fact kept trying to poke its ugly little face into his consciousness. He had been relieved after hearing her story, when she had talked him into keeping his distance. After all, he had worked hard to get his musical career to the level it was at. Every day was a struggle. Should he put all that at risk for someone he had just met?

Still, there was that undeniable attraction.

Eventually, he decided to let fate choose his path. If that light up ahead is still red when I get to it, I'll break it off with her, he thought. If it's green, I'll give it a go. But his foot, seemingly of its own accord, lifted gently off the accelerator pedal.

CHAPTER 16

"**You** don't have to like it, boy, you just have to do it."

"I couldn't. I know I just met her, but I have the feeling she might be, you know, the one."

"Oh don't be a horse's ass. There is no 'The One'. There're just those you happen to meet and it works out for a while. And then it stops working out and you move on. That's all there is. What, are you living in a Hallmark card? That's as good as it gets."

"You're just cynical. You're old and beat-up and cynical."

"Look, boy, this is about blood, and blood is in trouble here. We are blood, you and I, and what affects one of us, affects us both. This little tart is not good for me and is therefore not good for you. God knows I wish there were another way to handle it, but there isn't."

"She is not a little tart!"

"Oh stop it! You know nothing about her. I could pick up the phone and find out more about her in five minutes than you've gotten from her in the paltry few days you've known her."

"I'm not trying to get anything out of her. I've just been trying to get close to her."

"Good. Close is good. Keep your friends close and your enemies closer."

"She is not an enemy!"

"She is bad for this family. That doesn't exactly make her a friend. We are in big trouble. Get it? Big money trouble. We are facing ruin here. She is our ticket out of that money trouble."

"I can't."

"You can and you will! We are a clan, a tribe, and everyone in the tribe is called on to make sacrifices from time to time. It just so happens that this is your turn to make the sacrifice. You've known her for two or three days. Big deal. That's nothing. You are blood, and blood does what's good for blood. Listen, if I go to prison, life, as you know it is over for you. No more rock and roll band, no more late nights and even later mornings. No more endless party or elegant digs. You'll be flat broke and making lattes just to make ends meet. Maybe you'll even be a fry cook like your old man used to be. Carrying on the family tradition. I've worked hard so that you don't ever have to go through that. Are you just going to throw all that away for some bimbo you met less than a week ago? You understand? You are nothing without me. I go down, you go down."

Silence.

"No, you're not going to throw it away! Now you get home and glue yourself to your phone. If she's like any other woman she won't be able to resist contacting you."

Silence.

CHAPTER 17

"Can't I just buy him a regular ticket and put him in a seat?" Xochitl said to the woman across the ticket counter. "He doesn't make much noise. He rode with me all the way from Soda River and he hardly made a sound unless I was singing... I'm not a very good singer, I guess. I mean I like music and all, but I just can't...I mean I'm not...I'm sorry, I'm babbling."

"I'm sorry, ma'am. We don't allow unattended animals to ride in the passenger section of the bus. It's an insurance thing. He'll be fine in the cargo hold. We ship animals frequently and they do just fine."

"What if he needs something? What if he gets carsick? How's anybody gonna know?"

"The bus makes frequent stops. If there's an animal on board the driver or a baggage handler will check on it at each station. He'll be well taken care of."

Xochitl looked down at Weezy who was poking his nose through the little holes in the plastic cage. He seemed to be all right. Perhaps she was stressing over nothing. Still... she rubbed her temples, unable to quell the feeling of uneasiness that rose in her at the thought of turning her baby over to strangers. "Okay," she sighed. "You swear he'll be okay?"

The woman offered a sympathetic smile and held up her right hand, the palm facing Xochitl. "I swear," she said.

CHAPTER 18

As she drove her Duster toward Pinky's Bar, Xochitl felt a gentle weight settling onto her shoulders, gradually increasing as she considered her situation. Fid and Rick were the only friends she had in Los Angeles. She wasn't even sure she could call them friends yet. Sure Rick was a potential lover, but that didn't mean he was a great friend. She just couldn't tell yet. Fid, though, had certainly proven himself in a short span. His heart had felt warm, very lonely, but undeniably warm. He had killed another man in order to save her life, for crying out loud, and had put his own life on the line without complaint. Well, almost without complaint. That had to count for something. Whether he would hold up was the big question. There was no doubting his loyalty at this point, though, and the thought of cutting him loose was painful.

Rick was another matter. She was definitely beginning to harbor strong feelings for him, and to her way of thinking it was just natural not to trust someone you had feelings for, at least not this early in the game. They could hurt you, these objects of affection - without even trying. Rick seemed to possess a lot of great qualities, but that stuff had a tendency to melt away given enough time. Xochitl was being cynical and she knew it. It was a part of her she didn't really like. It had arrived uninvited after several of life's beatings and batterings, and she felt powerless to stop it. She was a beautiful woman and she knew it. Men desired her and there were battle scars all over her heart from their pursuits. They could be very cunning, silver tongued devils. Rick hadn't really given her any reason to distrust him, but he was a man and potentially guilty by association.

Xochitl had been alone for a while and had blamed it on such excuses as, "I'm focusing on my career right now." She wasn't really uncomfortable being alone, more bored than frightened. True, her skin had grown thicker, but in such gradual stages as to be nearly unnoticeable. Just a little layer (maybe an eggshell's thickness) at a time. In the long run this forced solitude would be more harmful than beneficial, but for the recent past it had been like a welcome, numbing drug. She had planned to crack the eggshell and remedy this situation once her life calmed down again. Rick had just sort of slipped in under the fence somehow.

Putting Weezy on the bus had not been easy for Xochitl. She had never been separated from him for more than a day or two since she had discovered him wandering around her neighborhood suffering from an obvious respiratory infection. He was very small and very dirty. It was clear he'd spent a lot of time crouching beneath parked cars for safety. The little creature had immediately bonded with her and Xochitl had gathered him up in her arms and driven him straight to the veterinarian for treatment. The cat, less than pleased with his visit to the doctor's office, somehow seemed to recognize that it was for his own good. He lay in a basket at the end of Xochitl's bed, recovering, for several days. Eventually, becoming mobile again, he began exploring his new digs, and since that day, had never left. Xochitl looked forward to what she called his unconditional lovin', each evening as she returned home.

CHAPTER 19

"What's yer poison, gorgeous?" Pinky growled.

"I think I'll have a Greyhound, Pinky," Xochitl replied, searching the room for familiar faces. "Have you seen Fid or Rick?"

"Haven't seen Fid, don't know who Rick is. Fid usually shows up around twenty after six. I think he's got a thing about being fashionably late. Builds the anticipation so he can make his grand entrance. Seems to work okay for him. This is LA, after all."

Xochitl chuckled at the thought of Fid primping for a grand entrance. "I guess I'll just grab a booth and wait for them," she said. "If you see them before I do, point them in my direction, okay?"

"You got it, beautiful. But before you go, I wanted to thank you for whatever it is you've done for Fid."

"What do you mean?"

"Well I've seen that little guy waltz in here with a phony, trumped up confidence, chest all puffed out and chin in the air. I've seen him scurry in here with his tail between his legs and I've seen him shatter like a piece of fine china. But what I've never seen him do until now is walk in with a genuine, satisfied liking of himself, the way any other normal guy would do. It started a few days ago when you showed up. I don't know what you did, but whatever it was, it's done wonders for him and I just wanted to thank you for it. Fid's not just a customer here, he's a friend, a good friend, and it lifts my spirit to see him doing well."

Xochitl blushed. "We've definitely had a few adventures the last couple of days. Maybe that's something he doesn't do regularly."

"Yeah, maybe," Pinky said quietly. He winked and turned away to take someone's order.

At exactly twenty after six, the Fiddler Crab made his entrance. Not a grand entrance by any definition, but Pinky was correct in his other assessment. Fid's confidence did seem real, not over-played or badly acted. He had the look of a man who was comfortable in his own skin. Xochitl watched him order a greyhound from the bar as Pinky pointed toward her booth.

"Hi good lookin'," he said, sliding into the booth opposite her.

"Hey Fid, how was your day?"

"It was okay."

"Just okay?"

The Fiddler Crab peered into his glass as though it were a thousand feet deep. "Well I can't help but worry about that guy in the van. I know he was a very bad man, and that it was a life-or-death situation, but it still bothers me. I mean, I killed him - I actually killed him! Couldn't I have just shot him in the shoulder or something?"

"Fid, that man was going to immobilize me by blasting off my knee caps, after which he would have raised his gun and blown your head into the next county. Hell yes, he was a bad man. In fact, he was a horrible man. You did us all a favor. Someone was paying him to do that, Fid. He was going to torture me and kill you for money. The world is better off without people like him. Think of it this way: If he'd lived he would be killing more people for money, so you're actually saving the lives of people you don't even know."

"Aren't you at least afraid that the police are going to come looking for us? We just drove away from the wreck. It wasn't like we cleaned up the crime scene or anything. They don't know it was self-defense. They're going to think it was murder."

"I don't think that's anything to worry about," Xochitl said. "If there's two things I've learned about these guys, one is that they don't like to leave a mess lying around. They are very thorough and very quick. The other is that they're either afraid to draw the attention of the authorities, or they have some sort of control over them. Either way, the police will never show up, and these people will clean up our mess along with their own. They don't take anything for granted. That van was probably disposed of, and the site of the wreck scrubbed clean before we even met Molly at the hospital. They seem to have a huge amount of resources available to them and, in this case, that's something that works in our favor. I'm more concerned about them coming after us - or at least me. That's why I wanted to meet you here this evening. Have you seen the cover of the Snitch today?"

"What's the Snitch?"

"The worst kind of rag, masquerading as a newspaper. But that doesn't matter. What does matter is this..." She lifted the paper from the seat beside her and held it up in the dim light of the bar. The fiddler crab's expression clouded.

"What the hell is this?" he said, a little too loudly.

"That's the wild card that blows our anonymity. Now they're not only looking for me, they're looking for everyone in that picture - you included. They'll assume they can get to me through any one of you. The worst case, of course, is Rick's Dad, because the paper already knows who he is. The article mentions that he was at the restaurant visiting his son who is sitting at the table in the background. Right next to me. You get it? Anyone could figure out where to go from there. It's a beeline straight to me. And look at you, right there on the front page of the paper. Under any other circumstances, I'd be patting you on the back and buying you a drink for making the front page while kicking that sorry donkey's ass, but this is different. If they find you, I don't even want to think about what they'll do to get you to rat on me. I like you, Fid. I like you a whole lot and I don't want to see anything bad happen to you."

The Fiddler Crab, staring in astonishment at the page, hadn't heard a word. "Freak? They called me a freak!" Anger boiled in his veins as he glared at the headline, dark primal anger, but at the moment of eruption, his shoulders shook slightly, and then sagged in despair. He had foolishly assumed that he was beyond this type of ridicule now. The events of the past few days had caused him to blossom into something he had never expected to be, a real man. It wasn't that he felt like some kind of superman. It was simply that the dull ache had disappeared. The constant specter of inferiority, residing daily in his gut since Elsa Starlighter had driven off with the boy from the Stud Club all those years ago, was gone. It had been usurped by a new feeling, one of lightness and possibility. Huge possibility. But now, with the advent of his new-found celebrity, the door had been slammed shut on his sense of possibilities and his lightness was rapidly gaining weight. New heights had only paved the way toward bigger, more public insults. "Maybe they're right," he sighed, "maybe that's all I am."

"Fid, are you listening to me? This is no time to start feeling sorry for yourself. There's nothing to feel sorry for, okay? So get outta that boat right now! I've already told you that this is the worst kind of rag you can buy. They'd like nothing better than to have one of us show up dead because of a story they printed. Hell, they could milk that for months, sell a jillion papers. The point is we can't let that happen."

"Freak! Oh man, that just makes me feel like crap."

"Look Fid, the whole reason I brought this so-called newspaper here is so that you could see the *photo*. Okay? Not the headline, the *photo*. Now take a good look at it and tell me what you see. Forget the headline."

The Fiddler Crab did as he was told, squinting in the dim bar light to get a decent view of the grainy halftone photograph. "If nothing else, I'll have irrefutable evidence that I vanquished the bastard who ruined my life."

Xochitl sighed. "What else do you see in there?" she asked, taking a good-sized gulp of her greyhound.

The Fiddler Crab stared a little harder, holding the paper up to a neon light advertising a popular domestic beer. "Oh, there's you and Rick in the background, sitting at our table. But look at me. I'm no freak. I'm like a tiger. Check out my face. I didn't know I could show that kind of ferocity."

Xochitl snatched the paper from in front of the Fiddler Crab. She jabbed her finger repeatedly at the picture. "It's you and me and Rick with Doctor Banders. Don't you get it? Banders is easily identifiable. He's famous! Hell, the paper knew who he was right away. That means our enemies know who he is, too. There seems to be no love lost between the Doctor and his son and we can be pretty certain he holds no affection for you or I either, especially you, after you tore into him like that. All these guys have to do is get to Banders and he'll happily beat a path to our door."

"So, you're saying it's probably a good idea that we split up for a while?"

"Haaalayloooooyah! Saints be praised! I can't believe the point got through." Xochitl tossed the paper onto the table.   "I just think we'll all be safer if we're not in the same location."

"I don't buy it," the Fiddler Crab growled. "That sounds like a cowardly solution to me and that's the last thing I'd expect to come out of your mouth."

"It's not just me. I'm worried about all three of us."

"I can handle myself," he said. "Look at this picture. I think I've proved that several times in the last couple of days."

"Fid, you're a total hero. I'm not denying that. But we got lucky the other day. Sure, we showed some bravado, but what if that rifle hadn't come flying through the window? I'd have no kneecaps and you'd be buried in a field somewhere! We can't count on that kind of thing happening all the time. We have to try to out-think these guys, which is all the more difficult because we don't even know who they are. I only know one thing for certain and that's the fact that these guys are not going to give up. We can't simply forget about the whole weird episode and go on with our lives. They *are* going to attack us again. Me, for certain, and you if you're connected to me or getting in their way. That's not an assumption, it's a fact."

The Fiddler Crab rubbed his temples hard and stared at the table for a moment. "You know that old saying: 'United we stand, divided we fall'?" he said. "There's a reason why that phrase has been with us for so long. It's true! What if you get into trouble and you have no one to call. It sounds more like you're setting yourself up as a sacrificial lamb to protect us." He raised his hand, pointing at the ceiling. "Well, I, for one, won't have it. I'm not going to cower if you get into trouble, and I know you'd do the same thing for me."

He plucked the offensive rag from the table and glared at it. "These people called me a freak in front of the whole world. Before I met you I probably would have accepted that. I almost did just now. I may not have believed it, but I would have accepted the hand I was dealt. I've been put through more tests in the last few days than I've ever had in my life and I have to say that I'm impressed with myself, with my ability to step up. The difference was that this time I had someone there in my corner who believed I could do it." He glanced at Xochitl. "I had someone to think about besides myself. The moment I began to fight for someone else's safety my strength increased tenfold. Okay, maybe not tenfold, but you get what I'm saying. I was part of a team, *our* team, and I was as much responsible for our survival as you were. I've never done anything like that before. It was important work and I pulled it off. The things we went through changed me and for that I'm eternally grateful to you. I'm not going to bale on you now, regardless of what you want. What we need to do is combine our talents. As you said, we know they are going to attack again, so, since we don't know who or where they are, the answer lies in being ready for any random situation they might throw at us."

Xochitl leaned across the table and kissed the Fiddler Crab

on the cheek. "You know, Fid, the first night I met you, man, it seems like a long time ago now, when I held hearts with you, I could tell you had an exceptionally pure soul. I had no idea I'd get to see it blossom like this in just a few days. I feel privileged. I can't make you go away. I just think it's a good idea because I really like you and I don't want to put you at risk."

Xochitl's thoughts drifted to Rick's apartment earlier that afternoon. How easily he had accepted the suggestion of separation for safety's sake, while Fid, on the other hand, was fighting her tooth and nail. Interesting. Where was Rick, anyway? He said he would meet with them around six o'clock, almost an hour ago.

"All right, here's what we'll do," she said. "Take twenty-four hours and think about this, and I mean really think about it. I'm pretty sure that in the end you'll see I'm right. I'll call you at home around this time tomorrow, and we'll decide how we're going to handle it."

CHAPTER 20

Later that evening Xochitl drove her Duster along Lankershim Boulevard in North Hollywood looking for a motel, the sleazier and more unobtrusive the better. The street was lined with small playhouses and theaters; many of them converted storefronts. She glanced at the play titles on the marquees. Most of them were somber names appealing to the depressed and paranoid. A few were comedies, but even they had a dark under-tone. The area was beaten down, but trying to make a comeback as an art district. Here and there Xochitl spied a small oasis of bright, new paint, a tire store here, a furniture store there, the owner's attempt to slap a happy face on the malignant decay the neighborhood had suffered. She felt a sad sense of community here as the residents banded together in an attempt to stave off the inevitable.

A dirty yellow sign caught her eye as she surveyed the metropolitan flotsam sliding by her window. 'El Cid Motel', the sign said, 'Cable TV – Ice – Wireless Internet.' It was perfect. Pulling her Duster into the parking lot, she squeaked to a halt. She got out, stretched her arms and walked into the office. The clerk, an obese woman with a flat, punched-in nose and a slight five-o'clock shadow, was dressed in a worn flowered muumuu. The dress was on its way from yellow to beige, with beige in the lead. Her massive, rippling arms occupied a good part of the counter-top, leaving little real estate for the registration book.

"Help ya?" the woman's voice was comprised of sandpaper and chain smoke.

"I just need a room," Xochitl said, eying the woman.

"Well, imagine that," the woman rasped. "I just happen to have one. Don't you love it when things work out? God knows, it don't happen every day."

"Yeah," said Xochitl. "I know all about that one."

"Well, everything happens for a reason," said the woman, handing Xochitl a key. "Room 204. Upstairs, in the back. You want to smoke? You gotta do it outside. It's not me, it's the law."

Xochitl removed her sleeping bag from the trunk of her car and found her room. The room was a sad, repulsive collection of cracked Formica and tarnished, rust-speckled chrome. She couldn't imagine anyone willingly staying in this place unless they happened to be running for their lives. The sleeping bag was longer than the bed, draping over the end and almost touching the floor. She flopped down and lay quietly, staring at the paint-peeled ceiling. At this moment she wished more than anything to have her cat curled up on her stomach, purring. His purring was a sign that all was right with her world. When Xochitl was happy, Weezy was happy.

Within twenty minutes, Xochitl was bored, a twitchy sort of boredom born of anxiety and uncertainty. The time was only ten o'clock and she was used to staying up much later. Flipping through the channels on the ancient, television, she was mildly surprised to see it broadcasting anything other than the I Love Lucy show, or the Ed Sullivan Variety hour. Plenty of programs were being aired, but nothing seemed to grab her attention. Surely, there must be something exciting enough to lose herself in. Nothing. Frustrated, Xochitl rose to her feet after an hour of exploring the airwaves.

This was crazy. She was like a prisoner awaiting execution. They would find her eventually, she was certain of that. But when? It was not Xochitl's nature to sit and wait. She wanted to lash out. But at who? At this point, her enemy was still some sort of faceless corporate entity with no name and no address.

She remembered spotting a small liquor store across the street on her way into the parking lot. Perhaps she could find something to calm her nerves, or at least make the TV bearable.

Back in her motel room, Xochitl pulled the tab on the first can of beer from the six-pack she had purchased and smiled as a foamy head grew from the little hole. In less than fifteen minutes the first beer was gone and that made it easier to drink the second, which made it easier to drink the third. Within an hour and a half the entire six-pack was history as Xochitl reveled in the sweet numbness that the alcohol brought to her troubled brain.

She sat quietly staring at the television screen, swaying gently back and forth. The programs on the screen still didn't entertain her, but at least they didn't annoy her too badly. Her mind had become deliciously blank, and somewhat euphoric.

It was completely without intent or forethought that she left the motel room and strode down to the street, where she dialed Rick's number on a pay phone. Something in the back of her happy, swimming mind told her that it wasn't a good idea, but what the hell?

"Hello?"

"Hi Rick, it's me."

"Xochitl! Where are you? Are you doing okay?"

"Yeah, I'm fine, just a little bored. Bored stiff, in fact."

"You sound kind of funny."

"I'm a funny girl."

"Have you been drinking?"

"Maybe."

"What does maybe mean?"

"It means a six-pack of Bud. Ha!"

"Where are you?"

"Oh man, I'm livin' large. But I really shouldn't say where."

"What do you think, I'm going to run out and tell someone?"

"I'm just trying to keep everybody safe. Supergirl! Know what I mean? If nobody knows anything, then everybody's that much safer."

"I'm a big boy. I can take care of myself."

"Didn't we already have this discussion?"

"Hey, it's me. I won't come out there if you don't want me to. I'd just feel better if I knew where you were. You know, just in case."

The line was silent for a moment. Xochitl began to giggle. "Ever hear of the El Cid?" Xochitl asked excitedly. "Sounds pretty grand, doesn't it, like something from Vegas. I can't decide if my favorite part is the chipped paint or the smell of bug spray."

"Sounds absolutely charming. Are you sure you don't want some company?"

"Any other time, I'd jump at the chance, but it's just not a good idea right now. I guess I kind of missed you, I wanted to hear your voice."

"I miss you too, Baby. I'm glad you called."

"Where were you earlier? You were supposed to meet us at Pinky's."

"Oh yeah. I'm sorry about that. Something came up with the band. I had to take care of it."

"Mmmm, I see. Well, I guess I better head back in. I feel pretty exposed out here in the street." Xochitl was fully drunk, now. She hung up the pay phone then, feeling a little safer since she hadn't been immediately struck down after her conversation with Rick, picked it up again and dialed the Fiddler Crab's number. The phone rang repeatedly with no response, then a beep. Hi, this is the Fiddler Crab. Don't worry. I won't bite. Leave me a message and I'll get back to you. It dawned on Xochitl that Fid was probably at Pinky's Bar, sipping a greyhound. "Hey Fid. It feels good to hear your voice. I found a place to stay out in North Hollywood. It's pretty shitty, but it's a roof. I was just hoping to say 'Hi', but I'll call you tomorrow."

Lastly, she tried calling Mr. Trundell, hoping that he had the center fielder's cell phone on him.

"Trundell."

"Hi boss."

"Saint James? What's wrong? Are you all right?"

"I'm just lonely, boss," Xochitl said quietly. "I need to hear a familiar voice. You wanna yell at me or something? "

"What are you smoking, Saint James? Are you implying that I always yell at you?" he yelled. "I don't always yell at you. Only when you deserve it, which is most of the time, or I'm worried you might do something stupid. Did you do something stupid? You don't sound like yourself. Have you been drinking?"

"How's Weezy?"

"He's right here, making a mess of my office. I don't think any of us got any work done today."

"Does he miss me?"

"I don't know Xochitl. He doesn't talk much, but he's getting a lot of attention around here. I doubt if he even knows you're gone."

"Ouch! Thanks boss. A real man would have lied to me."

"You're probably getting tired of hearing this, but do you need anything?"

"Just the Seventh Cavalry."

"Mmmm, I'll see what I can do."

CHAPTER 21

The Fiddler Crab had just returned from his nightly excursion to Pinky's Bar. He sat on the edge of his lumpy bed in boxers and wife-beater and resigned himself to nervous wakefulness. Part of him, a big part, was proud of his refusal to be stashed in the closet until this whole thing with Xochitl blew over, but another more survival-oriented part was concerned with the type of duty he had signed up for. At the rate things were going, he could conceivably end up dead before long. There was no mistaking the fact that Xochitl's enemies, now his enemies, too, were playing very much for keeps. If he were to bow out gracefully now, as she had insisted, he could probably look forward to a long, somewhat healthy life. But the Fiddler Crab knew that if his refusal to get involved caused any harm to Xochitl, it would be a long, guilt-ridden life, indeed. So, here he sat, with no real doubts as to his course of action, but definite doubts as to his sanity.

Eventually the Fiddler Crab rose from the edge of his bed and walked into his dimly lit bathroom. He splashed water onto his face and let it drip into the sink. In the mirror he saw a face on the cusp. Not the conquering hero he'd seen yesterday, but not the self-conscious loner he'd been in the past either. *Apparently satisfaction with yourself is not a permanent state. It looks as though you have to keep renewing your membership.* He returned to his bedroom and pulled on his pants and shoes. Xochitl's message had said that she was in North Hollywood.

He would go to North Hollywood and ...What? *I guess I'll just have to look for her car in every run-down hotel I can find.*

CHAPTER 22

Another soul-sucking hour passed in front of the television set and Xochitl, her perception fuzzy around the edges from a six pack of beer, set up her new laptop and putzed around on the internet for a while. Eventually, her vision grew blurry and she was bored enough to try to force herself to sleep. She lay on the lumpy motel bed and immediately began tossing and turning. How many people, she wondered, had slept in this bed? Hundreds? Thousands? Who were they? Drug addicts? Prostitutes? Fugitives like herself? How many of them had taken a shower before they had gotten into bed? And what type of sordid activities had taken place while they were there? Even through her drunken numbness, Xochitl's skin began to crawl. Rising from the bed, she placed her sleeping bag on the floor next to the door, and crawled back inside. As a child she was frightened of monsters under the bed or in the closet. To combat her fear she had reasoned with herself each night that if the monsters were truly there, they were going to get her whether she was asleep or awake. It amused her a little that, even though the threat was real this time, the feeling was the same. Soon she began to drift toward slumber. She would awaken in the morning with a marvelous feeling of well-being, having survived the monsters another night. Hopefully, she wouldn't have a hangover.

The door slammed hard into Xochitl's gut as it came crashing open. A dark-suited man, carrying a silenced machine gun, stepped gingerly into the room. Xochitl shot up, disoriented. The man's black leather shoe hooked itself into the bulky fabric of the sleeping bag and, waving his arms in the air, he went tumbling forward. Xochitl heard the gun clatter across the linoleum floor of the kitchenette. Though she was groggy and still drunk, instinct told her to vacate the sleeping bag as quickly as possible, to free up her arms and legs. She was on her hands and knees when a heavy foot sank into her abdomen, the same spot where the door had struck her. A gust of wind whooshed violently from her lungs and for a moment she couldn't draw a breath. The foot came again, but this time she saw it coming and caught it with both hands. She flipped her entire body over, twisting the foot outward as hard as she could and heard a cry of pain. There was no snapping of bones or tearing of cartilage, Xochitl noted disappointed, and knew that the man was only temporarily down.

Huffing, the intruder staggered to his feet and began to hobble toward the kitchen area. Xochitl had heard the gun fall in that direction. She quickly stretched her arm as far as it would go and hooked her hand around the man's ankle, yanking hard. It was just enough to cause him to tumble once more. A hollow bang rang out as his head struck the wooden cabinet under the sink. Xochitl slid her new laptop off the coffee table and heaved it at the man with all her strength. So much for that, she thought, as she heard the machine shatter into pieces against the cabinet door, missing the man completely. Instantly, she was on her feet, kicking the downed man as hard as her bare feet would allow. The man, using Xochitl's own tactic against her, grabbed her ankle and twisted until she fell to the floor. He bent over her and drove his fist into her face several times. Blood sprayed from her nose and she watched it pepper the man's shirt as consciousness began to fade. Xochitl fought the advancing darkness with every bit of will power she could muster.

But the blackness didn't swallow her whole, only chewed her up a bit and now was beginning to spit her back out again.

Awareness returned to her gradually, and she lay with her eyes closed, listening, trying to gain an advantage. She felt the man grab her arm roughly and then the feel of cold metal around her wrist. He's putting handcuffs on me, she thought. The man dug his large beefy fingers into her shoulder and tried to roll her over in order to snap the handcuffs together behind her back.

It's now or never, she thought. I'll be helpless if I wait any longer.

As she rolled over, Xochitl whipped the cuffed hand around at lightning speed, slashing the open metal restraint across the man's face. He jumped back, shielding his eyes. Blood sprang from a deep gash in his cheek. Xochitl leapt to her feet and slashed again. This time the cuff tore into the back of the man's arm, ripping the fabric of his suit. She lashed out a third time, but the man was ready for her. He caught the cuff in his hand and jerked Xochitl to her feet. Once more, he drove his iron fist into Xochitl's face. The cuff flew from the man's hand as Xochitl went flying backward. She flipped up and over the small draining board and, with a crash of shattering glass, disappeared through the kitchenette window. The fall was short, only one floor, and Xochitl was at the bottom before she realized she was falling.

CHAPTER 23

The roof of a parked car gave way, trampoline-like, cushioning Xochitl's fall as she landed on her back. Rolling off the car, she shook her head and sprinted toward the back of the parking lot. The little diamond-shaped spaces in the chain-link fence surrounding the lot were sized perfectly for Xochitl's small feet. Metal dug into her foot as she hefted herself onto the wobbly barrier, but there was no sensation of breaking skin. A dilapidated wooden fence paralleled the chain-link directly behind it, supplying some momentary cover. She leaped over the top of the fence and plummeted blindly into a dark alley on the other side. A small, pointed stone jabbed her bare foot as she landed, causing her knees to buckle. As she tumbled sideways to lessen the impact, a shower of bullets penetrated the fence. Xochitl flattened herself to the pitted blacktop, hearing no sound of gunfire, only the crack of dry wood splintering in what seemed to be a hundred places. She crawled, snakelike, using elbows and knees into the shadows of an abandoned car.

The man's head appeared momentarily at the top of the fence, then, as his head disappeared, the gun took its place. A shower of bullets impacted the car, but failed to penetrate through to Xochitl's hiding place. She heard the bullets trail off down the alley as her assailant held the gun above his head and fired randomly down the alley. On the ground in front of Xochitl were two bricks, one in front of each long-ago flattened tire. Xochitl grasped the brick blocking the front tire as the man hoisted himself up onto the fence. She advanced swiftly and silently the moment the man's hands were both resting on top of the shaky fence. It would be her only chance, she knew, the only time both her pursuer's hands were occupied with something other than the gun.

Ignoring the pain of the gravel on her bare feet, she burst forth from the shadows. The man, distracted by the wobbly fence, spotted her too late. The brick flew with all the power Xochitl could muster, directly into the assailant's face. There was a brief grunt of surprise and the sound of crushing bone as the man disappeared behind the fence.

Xochitl flew down the alley, sticking to the shadows in case her attacker had been working with an accomplice. "Stupid, stupid, stupid," she whispered to herself. "How could I have slept without shoes on? How could I have gotten drunk? I was expecting them to show up sooner or later. God, I'm an idiot."

The streets were well lit and Xochitl felt a pronounced uneasiness once she emerged from the alley. What now? She dare not return to the parking lot to retrieve her car. What if her pursuer had not been alone? Most likely he hadn't been. Also, there was no telling if they could identify her car by sight.

With no destination in mind, Xochitl began to make her way down Lankershim Boulevard, keeping to what little shadow she could find. The broken-down storefronts, rustically charming by the light of day, now seemed threatening, full of dark possibility. Each recessed doorway hid an imaginary assailant of some mysterious origin who existed for no other purpose than to take her life. *Were* they imaginary? Certainly the events of the last half-hour had given her reason to believe they were not. Struggling to chase these irrational fears from her mind, Xochitl strode on mechanically.

Unwittingly, Xochitl began to talk to herself aloud. "I need a plan," she said. "Fid was right. This is not like me at all. I don't run away. That's not how I do things. I need to go on the offensive, to present a show of force. But, who do I attack? I'd take the bastards out with everything I could muster, or die trying, if I knew who they were. There must be some clue. No-body's that good. Nobody's good enough that they won't leave at least one tiny clue, like they did with the power saw in Soda River." She shuddered as she recalled the last episode with her pursuers. "I know it's going to happen again. They definitely have one up on me, because they seem to be able to find me just about anywhere, on the other hand all I can do is wait for them to show up. I've just got to be prepared next time they appear." She glanced down at her bare feet and laughed bitterly. "Yeah, prepared."

A man dressed in a dark suit approached Xochitl on the sidewalk. Adrenalin flooded her system giving her a sense of clarity, but it was spiked with a reckless alcohol-induced bra-vado. She struck a menacing pose. "Yeah, bring it on dickhead. I'll do you just like I did your buddy back there," she shouted in a guttural growl, eyes riveted to the man like a cat intent on its prey. The pedestrian stiffened and drew a wide swath around her. The rapid clicking of hard-soled shoes faded to nothing be-hind her as the frightened man scurried away to safety. Xochitl examined her reflection in the dimly lit window of a thrift store. The face in the window was unrecognizable to her. The right cheek was swollen and a dark red streak of blood trickled down her face from a cut over her eye. The collar of her flannel shirt became dark and wet as it soaked up the red liquid. The hair on the right side of her head had become thick and mat-ted and was now nearly the same color as her shirt. Slowly, she sank to a sitting position in the darkened doorway of the store, her fingers tenderly probing her disfigured face, the handcuffs dangling from her wrist. "I need a plan," she repeated.

Following a brief rest, Xochitl began to move down the sidewalk again, trying unsuccessfully not to stagger. Across the street she spied a huge, multicolored metal hood-like struc-ture protruding from what appeared to be a large parking lot. At first, she took it to be some sort of art exhibition, but a small tentative crowd of people was gathered around it as though waiting for something. A man walked through the arc of the hood and began descending out of sight. With an explosion of glee, Xochitl realized what she was staring at. The subway! The LA Metro subway.

The street was fairly deserted and Xochitl had only to wait for one car to go by before venturing onto the asphalt and crossing the street. Half way to the far curb, the sound of tires screeching assaulted her ears. Xochitl broke into a sprint, not bothering to look over her shoulder. It wasn't necessary to look in order to know who was in the car, or to know that it had spun around in the middle of the street and was racing back in her direction.

Summoning strength from nowhere, Xochitl sped across the parking lot as fast as her tired legs would carry her, disappearing through the multicolored arch and down a brightly lit stairwell that led to the subway. She took the steps three at a time, ignoring the jarring pain in her unprotected feet. Arriving on the first level, she discovered a sort of information lobby. One entire wall of the room was populated with automatic ticket vending machines, lined up one next to the other. Xochitl ignored these, running past them toward the next descending stairway that would, hopefully, lead her to safety.

The alcohol in Xochitl's system allowed her to push her panic back just enough to let her process a few quick thoughts. I don't know how, she thought, but I'm going to take this one alive. I'm going to draw this bastard in and then I'm going to wring some answers out of him. I've had enough of this.

At the bottom of the stairs a large tiled platform awaited flanked by two sets of train tracks, one on either side. At present neither set of tracks contained a much hoped for train. Xochitl's heart sank and panic flooded through her in force. She kicked a wire mesh trashcan in frustration yelping in pain as she watched the can roll from the platform onto the tracks. An intense shower of sparks exploded from the spot where the can came into contact with the rails. Startled, Xochitl hopped back from the display holding her now throbbing foot.

From the stairwell she heard the click of heavy shoes,

shoes that meant business. Another suited man, as generic as the rest, leaped the last few steps onto the boarding platform. Xochitl crouched slightly, knees bent, arms across her chest, daring the man to attack her. She must have appeared formidable with her bloody, swollen face, bare feet and blood-matted hair because the man stopped and stared. In that instant Xochitl noticed that he had no weapon, at least no *drawn* weapon.

Staring at the man's unblinking eyes, she shouted, "What do you people want from me? I don't know anything about any stupid formula!" The man stood almost stoically staring. "Why don't we just end this thing? You tell me who you are and I'll swear to you that I have no knowledge of any formula. Fair enough?"

The man smiled slightly, a cold, penetrating smile. "You're a spunky one," he said. "It's a shame." Glancing over his shoulder at the sound of a second set of footsteps, he slid a beefy hand smoothly inside his jacket.

Xochitl's eyes grew wide and she leaped from the platform into the recessed trench that held the train tracks. How much more adrenalin could her body stand before her heart simply exploded in her chest. Knees buckled slightly as she landed, one foot on either side of the shiny steel rail. Judging by the smoldering remains of the garbage can, the train must be electric, Xochitl decided. One foot on the rail, especially a bare foot, and the life would be jolted out of her as she was cooked swiftly from the inside out.

Xochitl's assailant had drawn some sort of small, funny-looking pistol from his jacket. She studied it as he raised the barrel. A syringe. It's a small tranquilizer gun. The thought of being shot dead right here by this creep in the name of whatever hideous organization he belonged to was at least somewhat bearable, being drugged and dragged into their midst to who knows what end, was not. She ran down the middle of the tracks into the dark tunnel. Within seconds she had disappeared from view.

Once Xochitl was cloaked in complete darkness, she froze in position. Looking back toward the tunnel entrance, she saw the suited man jump gingerly into the trench, carefully avoiding the two metal tracks. As he stalked slowly but purposefully into the tunnel Xochitl had the advantage of watching her pursuer's every move from the cover of total darkness. She moved a little further into the cavern looking over her shoulder at the approaching specter. The tunnel made a gradual turn and Xochitl noticed several fluorescent lights mounted high on the walls ahead. If she proceeded she would be easily visible, giving her pursuer the same advantage she now held over him. Immediately, she reversed her direction and began to creep back toward the tunnel entrance. Through the back-lighting of the tunnel entrance she could see that the man was still a good distance from her.

Against all reason, at a time when she needed ice-cold reason more than anything, Xochitl's mind elected to go on a flight of fantasy. For a moment she was sitting at a warm wooden table in Jitter Central, sipping a mocha and talking to her best friend, Marissa, about guys. God, I wish I was there now.

A flicker at the tunnel entrance caught her eye and she snapped from her daydream, focusing on the little spot of light that now seemed so far away. Another man had leaped off the platform and was making his way into the tunnel. Thoughts of escape began to erode. The first man was getting uncomfortably close. Xochitl hated the feel of panic. It was such a useless emotion, compounding the situation, robbing the brain of its power to reason. Unfortunately, panic welled up inside her now and she was possessed with an unexpected urge to simply lie down and cry. She shook her head, clearing her thoughts.

Searching for the darkest spot, Xochitl decided that the space between the tracks and the wall would be her best bet. Straining her eyes in the dark, she stepped lightly over the rails. Carefully, she stretched out flat, wedging herself tightly into the spot where the wall met the tunnel floor. Forcing the shakes away, she lay completely still, holding her breath as she felt the man's tentative approach. Slowly, he plodded down the center of the tracks, hesitating briefly where she lay and, sensing nothing, moved on. Xochitl breathed a sigh of relief and turned her head to check on the other man. What an odd walk he has, she thought, as he hobbled up beside her. The plan was to let both men walk by, and then try to slip out of the tunnel while their attention was focused in the other direction. Not much of a plan, but it was all she had. As the second man executed his odd walk next to Xochitl's hiding place, however, instinct took over.

As she lay flattened against the side of the tunnel, her pursuer, sensing something, froze as he came alongside her. Xochitl knew he couldn't see her, but he was clearly aware of her presence, and fear overcame her once more. Slowly, the man began to turn his body in her direction, stretching his arms out, groping towards the wall. It wouldn't take him long to figure out that she was lying just below the spot on the wall that he was probing with his fingers. The man began to work his way down the wall.

"Fuck it," Xochitl said just loud enough for the man to hear her voice. He froze, snapping his head around, eyes probing the dark. The foot that hit him in the groin was as much a surprise to Xochitl as it was to her assailant. He doubled over in pain, but for some reason didn't cry out. Xochitl's foot lashed out once more in a panic-driven assault, striking the bent man in the face. He staggered backward, tripping on the rail, and suddenly it was the Fourth of July. Sparks flew in every direction and, through the explosion of blinding light Xochitl could see the man's terrified expression as the spark of life was overpowered by the fires of Hell and his life-giving breath sizzled forth from his lungs for the last time.

The first man dropped to his knees and began firing down the length of the tunnel. Those are not tranquilizer syringes, Xochitl thought, realizing that she was now in the same vulnerable, back-lit position that the man who was firing at her had been in earlier. Ducking as bullets flew by her, she crawled swiftly along the space between the rail and the wall toward the tunnel entrance, nearly touching the rail several times.

Xochitl burst from the tunnel and leaped to the boarding platform with adrenalin-powered legs. A train was at rest on the other side of the platform and she made a dash for the open door. There were, a half dozen people in the car, all of them staring in morbid fascination at Xochitl's wounded, bloodied face as she entered. Choosing a seat near the back, she ducked low, hoping the train would depart before the remaining gunman discovered her position. No such luck. The gunman strolled onto the train car moments later, just another businessman headed home on the downtown train.

The doors hissed shut as the train began to move smoothly away from the platform into the tunnel, slowly at first, then rapidly increasing in speed. The gunman casually walked the length of the car, searching each row of seats with the corners of his eyes.

Xochitl could hear the damnable clicking of his shoes as he approached. A mixture of anger and despair welled up in equal proportions and she closed her eyes, rubbing her temples with her fingertips. She just wanted all this to come to an end, regardless of how it turned out. The loose handcuff banged against her chin, distracting her. When Xochitl opened her eyes again the man was calmly settling into the seat beside her.

"Why don't you just cooperate, Miss Saint James?" the man said. His voice was surprisingly warm, the voice of a friend dispensing advice. "I think we can both agree that this has gone on long enough."

Xochitl slumped, her rough edges filed to a loose, sloppy smoothness by six cans of beer. "I don't know anything," she said weakly. "At this point, if I knew, I'd tell you just on the off chance you'd leave me alone. But I don't know anything." She turned and looked the man in the eyes. "What's your name soldier boy? You seem to know who I am and that puts me at a distinct disadvantage."

"That's not really important, Xochitl," the man said, looking out the window.

"**What's your name?**" Xochitl shouted, alcohol once more powering her engine. All eyes turned in her direction. "**You've gotta have a name! Maybe I'll just call you Dick. Is that okay with you, Dick?**"

"Voice down, Xochitl," the man said just above a whisper. "There's no need to cause a scene."

"**What's your name? Who do you work for and why do you people keep trying to kill me?**"

All eyes in the car were staring now.

"No one's trying to kill you," he whispered. A thin syringe appeared out of nowhere in the man's left hand and Xochitl felt it prick her arm. Instinctively, she jerked away, but not quickly enough to avoid a small dose of mystery liquid. This was a time to act quickly, to trust her instincts. In her condition even a small dose of a powerful enough sedative could put her out. And she had a strong feeling that these people wouldn't waste their time with weak sedatives.

Without warning, Xochitl brought her elbow up into the man's jaw. Grabbing his hand from behind, she pushed it away from her arm and, placing her fingers over his, rolled the fingers forward, then the wrist. The muscles behind assailant's wrist stretched to their limit and the man grunted at the pain that shot up his forearm. His wrist was now stuck in a position that afforded it no leverage at all.

He made a clumsy attempt to reach across his body and strike her with his right hand, but as the blow came, Xochitl raised his left hand, the one containing the syringe, causing the device to inject its full cargo into the fleshy part of his thumb. The man's eyes grew wide with sudden realization. Then the lids began to flicker and sink until the tiny pupils could no longer be seen. Xochitl released the man's hand and let out a small whimper, a cocktail of emotions surfacing at once.

The train came to a smooth halt at Hollywood and Vine. Xochitl stumbled from the train car, confused by the alcohol now coursing full bore through her bloodstream and the small dose of the mystery drug she had received during her tussle with the man on the train.

Hobbling onto the loading platform, she smacked solidly into a squat, roundish little body that tumbled backward on impact. "Look, I'm really sorry, man, but you need to watch where you're going," she slurred at the sprawled form. The little creature raised its head and stared at her fixedly.

"Fid? What are you doing here?"

"I was coming out to find your hotel. My God! What happened to you?" The Fiddler Crab hobbled to his feet.

"They found me."

"I guess. Are you all right?" He stared at the cuts and bumps on her face. "You know... I mean, in the greater sense?" He touched his index finger to her swollen cheek and she flinched.

"Hard to say. It just happened a little while ago, but it gets more painful as time goes by."

"Nothing looks broken at first glance. I'm not saying you're the picture of health, but if nothing's broken inside, I think you'll make it."

"Thanks doc. Yeah, I know I look like shit."

"So what now?" said the Fiddler Crab, glancing about nervously. "I don't think it's safe to go to my place, If they found your hotel, they may know where my place is by now."

"Yeah, you can count on that. We need to go someplace where I can just clean up a bit. Let's get out of the station first. I feel kind of exposed here."

The motley pair staggered up the steps of the terminal, toward the street level. Xochitl smiled weakly and pointed at a tiled wall decorated with brightly colored Mexican mosaic. "Aztec," she said.

The night air felt cool and refreshing as they emerged into the colorful intersection of Hollywood and Vine. The street was a jumble of brightly lit signs, some of them flashing, advertising lingerie shops, movie star souvenir stores, porn theaters, army surplus stores and odd little shops containing every sort of electronic device known to man. Xochitl leaned over a street-corner trash receptacle and wretched. "Note to self..." she mumbled, "Don't mix alcohol and drugs." Her muffled voice drifted up from inside the garbage can dressed in the smell of vomit. The Fiddler Crab flinched and turned away.

"What drugs?" he asked.

"The guy on the train injected me with something. Fortunately, I got more of it into him than he got into me. Still, I don't feel so good."

"Where is he now?"

"I left him on the train. He's probably on his way to Long Beach."

CHAPTER 24

But the man wasn't on his way to Long Beach. The syringe had been filled with a short term sedative. He had intended to render Xochitl unconscious only long enough to cuff her. Fortunately, he was nearly twice her body weight and consciousness returned to him only seconds before the train departed. Staggering to his feet, he dashed through the door as it began to close automatically. Once on the platform, he shook his head, breathing deeply and rubbing his temples. Frantically, he searched the platform. The train was at the Hollywood and Vine station, the station they were approaching when he was rendered unconscious. The girl had to have gotten off here. Darting up the stairs, he searched for signs of Xochitl. She couldn't have gotten far in her battered condition. He was reasonably certain that some of the sedative had entered her body. How much, he couldn't be sure. Hopefully she had received enough to slow her down a bit.

The brightly colored lights stung his eyes as he emerged from the underground station onto the sidewalk. Which way had she gone? Up Vine, to get away from the crowds, or Hollywood, to blend in with the thousands of tourists perusing the famous, star-studded sidewalks? A moment of indecision plagued him as he scanned the area for some sort of clue. No one passed without leaving some trace, however insignificant, no one. ...And there it was. A small drop of blood on the sidewalk. Pressing the toe of his shoe into the drop, he pulled his foot back, smearing it. Fresh. The drop might as well be a neon sign pointing down Hollywood Boulevard. The man straightened his jacket, sliding his hand inside near his left armpit. His gun lay snugly in its shoulder holster. The foolish girl had left him fully armed. Then he strolled off down the street, melding invisibly into the throng.

CHAPTER 25

Xochitl pulled her throbbing head out of the trashcan. The Fiddler Crab produced a handkerchief from his pocket and wiped her mouth and chin. "How do you feel, kid?"

"Like shit." Wavering, she stared fixedly at the curb, trying to orient herself. "Although, I feel like a higher grade of shit than I did a few minutes ago."

"Atta girl," he said softly. "Come on, we've got to keep moving. The sooner we get you out of the public eye, the better."

"I love you, Fid. You're the best!" Her words were slurred and sloppy, but they inspired the Fiddler Crab to press on.

He took her wrist in his good hand, wadding the loose handcuff and chain into a ball and stuffing them up his sleeve to avoid attracting any more attention than Xochitl's swollen, blood smudged face would draw. He began to lead her down the busy sidewalk with no hint of a destination in mind. Most of the shops they passed were closed or closing.

The Fiddler Crab cursed under his breath. "Where to... where to?" he mumbled, surveying the street for some sort of camouflage or hiding place. "They're rolling up the streets just when we need them most." His eyes came to rest on a large garish marquee surrounded by blinking pink and purple lights.

'THE NAUGHTY GIRL THEATER' the sign insisted. 'ADULTS ONLY! NOW PLAYING: MATE-TRICKS.'

"Let's go in there," Xochitl slurred.

"That's a porn theater, Xochitl," said the Fiddler Crab,

cheeks flushing. "We can't go in there."

"I know what it is. I'm not stupid. I may be drugged, but I know a good place to hide when I see it."

The Fiddler Crab's cheeks were crimson now. "Okay. I'm pretty sure we're not getting past the box office with you in your condition." He stood a moment, examining the front of the theater. "Stand around the corner for a minute. I'll see what I can do," he said hesitantly.

"Do I look that bad?" she said, her voice disoriented and hurt.

"Worse. You look beat to hell. If you try to buy a ticket with me, they'll wonder why you're going to the movies instead of the hospital. Besides, if someone starts asking questions, we don't want the ticket guy to remember seeing anything out of the ordinary... and you are definitely out of the ordinary tonight. I'll use my right hand and maybe he won't remember me either. I'm going to buy a ticket. You sneak under the window and join me at the door. Can you handle that?"

"Yeah, sure."

The Fiddler Crab had never been to an adult theater. He felt about them the way he had once felt about visiting a bar on a daily basis. It was something that spoke volumes about a person's self-image, something guys with no hope did, at least if they went to them alone. People who hung out in these places were "settling" in the worse way. This was different, though. Xochitl needed him to protect her for a little while, just until she got her senses back. And, sadly, this was the best he could do. He steeled his resolve and approached the ticket window. "One please," he squeaked nervously, sliding money through a slot in the window.

The man in the booth gave a little laugh, shaking his head and eying the Fiddler Crab's feeble attempt to hide his withered arm. "Here you go you poor bastard," said a thin, rasping voice from a tiny speaker. A ticket popped through the slot. The Fiddler Crab snatched it up and marched toward the door. So much for being incognito. At the door he prepared to stroll in with confidence when Xochitl shoved into him from behind.

"Wait for me," she said. "Man, you haven't even seen the movie yet and you've already forgotten all about me. I'm insulted."

It was true. The Fiddler Crab had felt such intense embarrassment simply buying the ticket, that he had momentarily forgotten about Xochitl. Part of him was curious to experience an adult film, but a larger part was anxious to find a dark place to hide his blushing face. He became slightly disappointed with himself. Pinky would walk into a place like this and not blink an eye. He certainly wouldn't blush. Hell, people would probably be greeting him as he walked down the aisle. Sitting in the dark, the Fiddler Crab realized that his aversion to this sort of place was perhaps more a weakness than a virtue. It wasn't as though he had tried it before and decided it wasn't a good thing for him. He had avoided exposing himself to places of this nature because it spotlighted his own lack of a love life. Something of which he was not so secretly ashamed. Now he was ashamed of being ashamed. It never ends, he thought.

They crept hesitantly into the theater, allowing their eyes to adjust to the darkness. Xochitl was beginning to feel a little stronger. She was still very high, floating down the aisle, but at least her nausea had subsided.

"Are you the plumber?" a breathy, female voice wafted from the screen.

"Yes I am, baby," replied a deep, male voice. "Looks like you might need a little help with your pipes."

"Oooh yes. Did you bring your snake?"

Xochitl guffawed through her nose, snorting loudly. "Oh yeah, break out the snake, plumber boy," she giggled.

"Shhhh!" The Fiddler Crab lead her to an aisle seat.
Sitting through ten minutes of the film, Xochitl spoke. "I need to get cleaned up, Fid." her voice stronger now, more lucid.

"That's probably a good idea. I wonder where the restrooms are in this place."

They made their way back out of the theater into the purple

velvet lobby. Xochitl spotted a restroom sign at the far end and they made their way toward it. Passing through a stained and faded curtain, they discovered a small hallway containing a single door. The door was held shut by a tarnished brass knob that was held on by a single screw.

"Where's the lady's room?" asked xochitl, immediately realizing the folly of her question. "Ah...yeah...no lady's room." She jerked her head toward the lone, tired bathroom. "I'm going in there, Fid. You guard the door."

The Fiddler Crab held up his good hand. "I'll check it first to see if...."

Xochitl barged by him, shoved the door open and disappeared inside. A moment later a short, bald man burst from the restroom and rushed past the Fiddler Crab, awkwardly yanking up his pants as he went.

CHAPTER 26

Xochitl's pursuer was feeling supremely confident. With his trained eye he had easily tracked the tiny drops of blood up the sidewalk. Moments ago, he had spied a small collection of drops at the foot of a trashcan. He had glanced inside and seen vomit covering the discarded hamburger wrappers and old newspapers.

"Excellent," he said to himself. She had been affected to some degree by the drug and that would work in his favor. If she were feeling nauseous, she would be moving slowly. He would find her not far ahead. A warm feeling began to glow inside him. Soon all would be right with the world. His perfect record would remain unchallenged. He had made the mistake of underestimating this skinny, frail looking girl before. And a serious mistake it was. That would not happen again.

The man continued to follow the drops up the street, eventually spotting another collection just outside a sad old porn theater, painted up like an aging whore. He stopped, leaned against the wall and stealthily examined the drops. There were no drops further up the street, but he had noticed one by the front door of the theater. He strode calmly to the ticket booth. "You seen a beat-up looking, black-haired broad go in here."

"No, man. We don't get too many chicks in here, if you know what I mean."

The man pulled a $50 bill from his pocket and slid it through the slot. "You seen her now?"

"No, man. I ain't kiddin' you. I ain't seen nobody like that." The man outside the window had the appearance of a heavy hitter and the ticket boy didn't care to aggravate him. He slid the bill back through the slot. Just then, a short, bald man came striding angrily from the theater, tightening his belt. Marching fiercely to the curb, he thought better of it, turned on his heels and continued his march in the direction of the ticket booth.

"I'll not be here again," he shouted in a thick British accent, shaking his fist angrily. "I was forced from the loo by a bloody woman. Don't you people have some way of preventing that sort of thing from happening?"

The boy in the ticket booth took the word 'bloody' for a British curse word, but the man outside the booth knew exactly what it meant. His girl was inside after all. He wouldn't even have to search for her. Thrusting the fifty back through the slot he asked: "Where's the restroom?" and strode purposefully inside.

CHAPTER 27

The sink looked remarkably like the toilet, except it was higher up on the wall. Both were stained with tenacious, fetid substances which could find purchase on surfaces even spiders and insects couldn't navigate. Xochitl dabbed at her chin with a piece of toilet paper when the restroom door slammed open and, to her utter crestfallen amazement, the man who had attacked her on the train barged in. Breezing past the Fiddler Crab, he effortlessly shoved the little man part way out the door. Wrapping a monstrous claw around Xochitl's tiny wrist, the man began to squeeze. Xochitl's knee shot up toward his groin, but this time the man was ready for it, turning slightly sideways, causing the blow to strike harmlessly against his outer thigh. He brought her wrist down hard on the edge of the dirty porcelain sink, causing the handcuff to dig into her flesh. She cried out as a sharp pain shot up her arm. In a brief instant of clarity, she realized, it was not the pain of a broken bone. Two fingers darted toward the man's eyes. He had anticipated this as well, and Xochitl's other wrist was in his hand before she knew what was happening. He brought this hand down, hard on the sink as well. Xochitl yelped as another sharp pain throbbed in her hand.

Xochitl's mind came to grips, almost calmly, that this could be the end. Weak and splintered, her reserves were flagging seriously. She needed hope to build her strength on. And hope was in short supply here. She pictured herself as a corpse lying on the floor of this filthy porn theater bathroom, with its stained bowl and cracked sink. One slip of the guard, one second of giving into the pain, and this vision would most probably become a reality. This man had been bested by her once. He would not let it happen again.

*Come on! Come on! You have to do this! You absolutely **must** do this! This is not how you are supposed to end!!*

Xochitl struggled fiercely with her captured wrists, trying to draw the man's attention there. As he struggled against her flailing arms, she raised her right leg and brought the heel of her bare foot down with all her weight on the arch of the man's foot. She felt a crack as the man's shoelaces dug into the skin of her foot. The room was overcome with a loud bellow. Instantly, her knee was in his groin, this time finding its mark. The man doubled over, sinking to his knees. Weakly, he reached into his coat and produced the gun Xochitl had neglected to relieve him of earlier. His hands were shaking badly and his first shot lodged into the frame of the door. The Fiddler Crab, who had watched the confrontation through the half-open door, regained his footing and rushed back into the restroom as the shot rang out. The door struck Xochitl squarely in the back and sent her sprawling onto the crouching man. Her right knee slammed into the kneeling man's nose and a spray of blood painted her already filthy denim pants a deep red. Pulling her leg back, she struck again, pummeling her knee into the man's hand.

"Shit!" shouted the man as the gun flew from his hand, clattering across the floor. The Fiddler Crab scrambled to retrieve it. Pointing the weapon into the man's face, he stared down the barrel with one eye. The man looked at him stone-faced, unshakable, assessing that the freak could not pull the trigger in cold blood. He could only respond to a physical attack. That was the advantage he had over the Fiddler Crab. Had the roles been reversed, the Fiddler Crab would already be dead. The Fiddler Crab lowered the pistol and fired through the fleshy part of the man's calf. The roar was deafening in the tiny restroom, startling the Fiddler Crab and Xochitl. The man cradled his wounded leg as the two fugitives fled from the room.

The Fiddler Crab managed to stash the pistol into his pants, covering it with his shirt, as they disappeared back into the dark theater. On the screen, the plumber was now visiting an all-girl's summer camp. The Fiddler Crab slowed his pace a bit as he stared at the screen. Xochitl's head had cleared considerably and adrenalin raced through her veins. The film seemed more surreal to her now than when she had been high on the sedative. "Come on, Fid," she said, grasping his elbow. "Let's use one of those exits down in the front."

"Yeah, sure. Anything to get out of here."

Supporting each other, they hobbled down the aisle toward a glowing green exit sign, a beacon in the dark. The Fiddler Crab pushed the heavy metal door open gently, hoping to avoid attention. The two shadows silently slipped through the dark exit.

CHAPTER 28

The man swore. He had told himself that he would not allow something like this to happen again. She was a small woman, hardly any muscle mass at all, but this kid just wouldn't go down. She had managed to drive her heel into the top of his foot so hard that bones were surely broken. And the wound in his calf was burning as though his leg had been injected with acid. Fortunately, the freak had no experience with firearms. It was only a flesh wound and would not be fatal. The bleeding would eventually stop.

He had paid attention to the level of force necessary to subdue the girl and she had surprised him. She was slippery. Once again he had underestimated her. You had to respect her radar for weak spots and her willingness to attack when the odds were against her. Any other woman her size would have shriveled and plead for mercy. What he really wanted, more than anything on Earth right now was to simply put a bullet into her and end it. There were so many places on the human body where one well-placed lump of lead would blow someone clear across the River Styx. But the boss had said, "No. Wound her if you have to, but nothing fatal, at least not until we learn the whereabouts of the sober pill formula." The pain in his groin began to subside gradually and the injured gunman struggled awkwardly to his feet, suddenly aware of his filthy surroundings. His damaged foot began to throb intensely with the rush of blood as he stood.

Pulling the restroom door open, he staggered through the lobby and into the theater. Immediately, his trained eye spotted the exit door easing slowly and silently into its frame. The man's leg began to throb in earnest, and he plopped himself into an empty seat. He pinched his eyes shut, willing the pain to subside. Reaching into his pocket, he produced a cell phone. "Yeah, hey, it's me. I'm on them," he said. "Yeah, she's with that gimpy guy who was in the newspaper picture... Behind the Naughty Girl Theater. It's a porn place on Hollywood...I'm going to need a little backup, I'm unarmed.... yeah, that's right. I got a little bit of a wound going, too, so you might want to hurry." The man replaced the phone in his pocket and, rising from his seat, lumbered down the aisle. Angrily, he kicked the exit door open, disregarding the pain in his injured leg.

CHAPTER 29

The alleyway behind the theater was a metropolitan box canyon, formed by multi-storied buildings with soot stained, graffiti-laden brick walls and dented metal doors. It was all shadows and dumpsters. Xochitl's first instinct was to exit from the alley onto the street and run for cover, but the Fiddler Crab disagreed.

"That's the first place they'll expect us to go," he said. "They probably have guys out there on the street by now. It's the first place they'll look for us. Let's crawl into one of these dumpsters. I'm sure they won't look too closely in there. If we pile trash on top of ourselves, they'll never see us."

Xochitl thought of all the open wounds on her body. "Not a good idea, Fid. Even if we manage to evade these guys, I'd die of infection before I could crawl back out. It's filthy in those things. There's got to be another way."

"Can you climb?" The Fiddler Crab gestured toward a nearby fire escape whose lower rung hung just below the second floor. He looked doubtfully at Xochitl. "It would take a bit of work to get up there."

"I don't care. Let's do it. I'm sure our friend in the bathroom won't be down for long. Looks like there's a door on each floor. Maybe we could duck into one of those. Or if we can get up onto the roof, maybe we can come down someplace unexpected, or at least stop for a while and get our bearings."

"All right, I'll boost you up. Stand on my shoulders and grab that railing," he said. "Once you're on the platform, reach down and pull me up. How are your wrists doing? It sounded like they took a pretty nasty crack back there in the bathroom. Can you hold my weight?"

"I don't know how they're doing. They hurt, but we don't have a whole lot of choice right now." Xochitl winked at the Fiddler Crab. "Besides, you're just a little feller."

The Fiddler Crab began to relax a bit. A sense of humor, dark though it may be, was beginning to return to Xochitl, which meant she was thinking clearly again, which meant that, thank God, he didn't have to make all the decisions. If her head were clear enough to make a joke, she would soon be wanting to resume her place in the driver's seat.

With his back braced against the wall, the Fiddler Crab locked his knees solidly. He crooked his good arm and tightly gripped the belt loop on his pants. Xochitl placed her bare foot into the crook of his arm and, with much groaning, hoisted herself up. Twice she lost her balance, tumbling onto the cluttered asphalt. The third time, on the verge of falling, her foot found purchase on the Fiddler Crab's shoulder and she flung herself through the air, locking her fingers onto the floor of the fire escape. Pain shot through her wrist, but refusing to honor it, she hauled herself up. Once on the fire escape, she lay, face down, on the metal grating, allowing her head to clear.

Seconds later Xochitl crawled to the edge and reached down with her left arm. The Fiddler Crab stretched his strong right arm into the air, grunting and groaning, but failed to do more than brush fingertips with Xochitl. Leaning from the edge, she hooked the backs of her knees over the bottom railing, as a child would do on a set of monkey bars, and hung upside-down. The Fiddler Crab was surprised that such small hands could grip so firmly around his wrists. Even now, in the midst of rising mental turmoil, he felt a little thrill at the touch of this beautiful young woman on his withered arm. Seconds later he was being lifted from the ground. The Fiddler Crab, even after their previous adventures, hadn't expected Xochitl to be so strong, but there he was with his feet dangling off the ground.

The Fiddler Crab scrambled self-consciously up Xochitl's dangling body and flopped, with a clatter, onto the metal platform. "Ow! Be careful. You just whacked the cut on my head." Said Xochitl, touching the wound on her brow and examining a bloody finger.

As the Fiddler Crab scrambled to his feet, Xochitl was half way up the steps to the next level. He darted after her and in moments they were five or six stories above the ground. Each landing contained a metal door and Xochitl felt a glimmer of hope, until she realized that each door they passed was lacking a handle. Of course. These were fire escape doors. There was no need to enter the building through them, only to exit.

Far below, the Fiddler Crab saw the man from the restroom limping through the theater door into the dark alleyway. Gently he grasped Xochitl's arm and pulled her to a halt.

"We've got company," he whispered. "Let's try to keep the noise down."

Xochitl stopped and peered through the railing just in time to see a tan colored, nondescript car pull into the alleyway. The injured man hobbled toward it. The door opened and two more men, identically dressed in dark suits, emerged from the other side. "Damn!" she said. "There must be a factory somewhere that produces these guys."

The men in the alleyway began to inspect the area around them. They held a quick conference, and struck off in different directions. One walked tentatively toward the entrance to the alleyway. Another began examining the large square dumpsters that populated the alley, cautiously glancing behind the large metal containers and then quickly tossing the lids up.

CHAPTER 30

The wounded man examined the back door of each business, hobbling from one to the next as quickly as his injury would allow. They must be around here somewhere. They were too frightened and in too bad a shape to have gotten very far. He wrapped his large, beefy hand around each doorknob, giving it a deliberate tug. Nothing. Thoughts of failure were beginning to torment him once again. This would be a hard thing to live down. A perfect record, shot to hell by some spindly little college girl and a freaky little gimp. He must be getting old.

He felt something, nearly imperceptible strike the back of his hand. In the dim light, he bent to examine it. A small red dot. He touched it with a finger from his other hand, smearing it into a pale red streak. Blood. It was a drop of blood. Tilting his head skyward, he began to scan the fire escape above him. A tiny drop of blood splashed against his cheek. The man's face hardened into a cold, satisfied smile. Of course. He hadn't considered the fire escape before. In his opinion, it was a stupid move. There was nowhere to go but up, until you ran out of up. And then you were trapped. He was used to working with professionals, someone who's moves he could reasonably predict. Perhaps that was the problem he'd had with this girl all along. She was an amateur, acting in desperation.

From her perch high above the ground Xochitl heard the man call out to his companions in muffled tones. All three glanced up toward the fire escape. A knot quickly formed in her stomach. The floor of the fire escape was nothing more than a metal grating, offering minimal protection from flying bits of lead. "Give me that gun, Fid," she said.

Expecting the men to take aim and fire at her perch, Xochitl huddled against the wall, offering as small a target as possible. She urged the Fiddler Crab to do the same. The first shot never came. Instead, she felt the metallic rumble of someone climbing onto the fire escape, then the dull, rhythmic clanking of footsteps as they made their way up the stairs. Were they stupid? Didn't they realize she had a gun? Surely the man from the restroom must have told them. Still, the dark-suited pursuers continued, apparently unconcerned. Did they know something she didn't know? The knot in her stomach grew tighter.

It gradually dawned on Xochitl then, that the grating was quite thick and from her vantage point she would be unable to fire an accurate shot unless the target were directly below her. Each landing on the fire escape was placed squarely above the one below it, with a steep metal staircase running left to right between them. Xochitl would only have a decent shot while the man was on the landing below her or on his way up the stairs, and even then she would have to poke the barrel of the gun through the grating, firing somewhat blindly.

The clanking continued, less rhythmically now, and Xochitl realized that there were more than one set of footsteps shaking the metal landing.

"Shit!" Xochitl exclaimed.

The footsteps came to a gradual halt two landings below the one on which she and the Fiddler Crab were perched. A thunderous shot sprang from below and a loud clang assaulted her ears as a bullet struck the grating, ricocheting into oblivion. Xochitl shoved the barrel of the gun through the grating and fired two shots blindly at the grating below. Silence. The pursuers ceased all movement for over a minute. Xochitl wasn't stupid. She knew that even if she'd managed, miraculously, to strike one of her assailants while firing blindly, the chances of having hit both of them were ridiculously small. The two fugitives sat in absolute silence.

Soon, a second shot exploded from the dark silence below, echoing several times across the man-made box canyon. This one produced no residual clang and Xochitl knew it had missed the landing entirely. She would not fire back until a solid target presented itself. Moments passed without a sound. The knot in Xochitl's stomach had grown tighter, making a meal of the alcoholic fuzz she had been peering through. She began to experience a hyper-awareness of her surroundings.

Another explosion. This one passed unobstructed through the landing on which they huddled, smashing metallically against the one above them. Both Xochitl and the Fiddler Crab flinched and automatically looked up as the impacted platform rang like a bell. The clamor of the shot died down and she felt a familiar rumble in the fire escape. Peering down through the grating, she saw one of the men dash onto the landing below her. Poking the barrel of the pistol through the grating once more, she quickly squeezed off a single shot. A barrage of shots rang out from the deck below. Xochitl rolled against the wall, staring at the essentially transparent landing, feeling naked and exposed.

"How you doing, Fid?" she asked nervously, more for her own sake than his.

The Fiddler Crab spoke through gritted teeth. "I don't have any holes in me yet, so I guess I'm doing all right."

More shots rang out, and the man below clambered noisily up the stairs. Xochitl shoved the gun through the grating, attempting to align the barrel with the top of the man's head. A bullet slammed through the grating close to Xochitl's hand and she yanked it away from the pistol. The gun flopped impotently back and forth in its hole in the grating, coming to rest more or less in the same position she had been firing it. She grabbed the handle and squeezed the trigger, but the man had moved on, further up the steps. Tilting the barrel forward, she fired another shot. The footsteps continued. Another volley of lead shot past her, some striking the landing.

The barrel of a pistol crept over the edge of the landing. Xochitl fired at it, narrowly missing. She fired again, but this time the pistol produced the loudest click Xochitl had ever heard. Instantly, she realized that she had been tricked into using up her ammunition. The gun belonged to the man from the restroom. Obviously he had known how many shots remained in the clip. "Stupid, stupid," she said aloud. Rising quickly to her feet, she prepared for the pain of kicking a metal object with her bare feet. But the Fiddler Crab had out-guessed her.

Before the man's head cleared the floor of the landing, the Fiddler Crab's shoe crushed his right hand and then kicked hard, wrenching the gun from his grasp. Shortly, far below, a clatter sounded, followed by a bang, as the man's gun struck the pavement and fired on its own.

The man came bursting onto the landing, charging straight for Xochitl. The Fiddler Crab tried to tackle him, but was, once again, easily pushed away. Xochitl snatched the pistol from its resting place in the grating. Long ago in a self-defense class, Xochitl had learned to throw a punch from waist level whenever possible because an opponent wouldn't see it coming until it was too late to block. Now, in the dim light of the fire escape, she brought the pistol up, barrel first, from waist level and jammed it as hard as she could into the man's mouth. She felt the cracking of teeth and he flew backward, bouncing off the railing, toppling down the stairs. As he tumbled erratically town the stairs and flew over the railing of the platform below, he managed, at the last instant, to snag the handrail with one hand, preventing an almost certainly fatal fall.

Xochitl grabbed the Fiddler Crab by the wrist and led him up the stairs. They ascended another three landings before they ran out of up. The door into the building was, like the others, exit only, with no way to enter from the outside. The clunking of shoe soles on metal grew more rapid, less rhythmic, and then stopped momentarily, presumably to assist the injured man as he clung to the railing. A low mumbling echoed off the walls as the two men discussed their options, though Xochitl could not make out what they were saying. Soon the landing began to shake once more. Xochitl realized that she had only a moment before the fully armed assailant was upon them. She looked around frantically for something to use.

A metal cable stretched from a heavy-duty bolt fastened to the wall just above the landing to the next floor down on the building directly across the chasm. Was it an electrical cable? She couldn't really tell in dim light. It would be stupid to climb out onto a wire only to discover it was a cable TV line or something similar, incapable of holding her weight. It looked thick enough, but she couldn't be sure. Slinging the loose end of the handcuffs over the line, she grasped the other wrist clamp in her hand and yanked down hard, pulling her knees up. The cable held.

"Bingo! Can you hold up the weight of your body with your strong arm?" she asked the Fiddler Crab.

"I guess I'll have to," he replied.

"All right, grab on to the top of my pants. And DO NOT LET GO! I don't need that on my conscience. Understand?"

They climbed awkwardly onto the railing, steadying themselves to some degree with the loose overhead cable. The clanging of the fire escape grew louder as the assailants approached the landing. "Hang on, Fid. Here we go." They sprang simultaneously from the railing and flew out into space. A wrenching ache shot up the Fiddler Crab's arm as his entire weight jerked to a halt at the end of it. Memories of ANYONE CAN! and his first attempt to support his entire body weight with his good arm came flooding back producing shock and dismay. It hadn't been easy then, and he was many years older now. The denim of Xochitl's pants dug painfully into his fingers. Only the terror of a hundred foot drop kept his grasp clenched firmly.

Their pursuer walked calmly to the railing and watched in silence as his prey glided away.

Xochitl felt a grinding as the chain from the handcuffs scraped along the cable. She prayed that the chain would hold. They began to pick up speed as the cable bowed downward under their combined weight. A feeling of elation rose in her as their speed increased, leaving their assailants behind. "I think we're going to make it, Fid," she said, just above a whisper.

The feeling began to fade.

The grinding noise above their heads grew quieter and more stilted, finally disappearing as the two fugitive's progress along the cable decelerated, eventually halting altogether. Xochitl looked down and saw the Fiddler Crab's panic-stricken face staring up at her, legs dangling, his single arm quaking as it struggled to hold on. The cable had bowed so far under their weight that the last quarter of their journey was steeply uphill. They had come to a dead halt eight stories above the ground.

"I'm letting go, Xochitl." The Fiddler Crab could barely speak the words around his clench-toothed grunts, all of his strength concentrated on maintaining his grip. "No use both of us going down."

"Don't be an ass," she snapped, her voice straining. "Look at me, I'm holding both of us up. If I can do it, you can do it. There's always a way out, Fid, There's *always* a way."

"I don't see a way out this time, Xochitl. I really think this is it. I can't hold on much longer."

"Force yourself! I have an idea. I need you to swing back and forth like a pendulum. I'm going to do it, too. When your legs get high enough, hook them over the cable. Do you understand?"

The Fiddler Crab nodded silently as Xochitl began to rock back and forth parallel to the cable. As his weight increased significantly from the centrifugal force, his arm felt as though the joint were no longer in its socket. A frightening numbness set in. Moments passed and eventually he felt the cable bump against his shoes. He kicked his leg up and momentarily panicked as his grip was torn loose from Xochitl's pants. He bent his leg hard to grip the cable with the crook of his knee, and then grabbed his ankle with his good hand, locking the knee in place. A human carabinier. Shaking, he slowly worked his other leg over the cable, careful not to lose his balance.

Once he was in place, Xochitl swung her legs up and crossed them over the cable. Looking back now, she discovered the fire escape landing was empty. She felt both uneasy and elated. It was good that her pursuers were gone, but where did they go?

"Fid, start working your way toward that building," Xochitl said in a soft, calming tone. "There's a window just under the cable. We can get in there somehow."

"I wasn't cut out for this," he whimpered. "I just want to be back at Pinky's drinking a greyhound."

"That's a possible outcome here, Fid, but only if you get your ass moving," she grunted. "Just imagine Banders is at the other end, bent over, waiting for you to deliver a swift kick to his ass."

Amidst grunting and groaning from the Fiddler Crab, wiggling his way awkwardly toward the window, Xochitl felt the vibrations in the cable trying to jar her hands loose. She followed him, sloth-like; hand over hand, leg over leg, trying to time her movements with the oscillations of the cable.

Movement in the cable abruptly ceased. "I'm at the wall, Xochitl. What now?"

She stopped, flopping her head down to view the wall. "I don't know. Wait till I get there. It looks like getting in that window might be a two person job." She worked her way to the end of the cable. Catching her breath, she relaxed her muscles as much as she could without losing her grip. The window was a good three feet below the spot where the cable was attached to the sooty, smog-stained brick wall. Getting in would be difficult, but not impossible. She scanned the alleyway below. "Where'd our friends go?" she asked.

The Fiddler Crab surveyed the alleyway. The car was gone. "They must have left us for dead."

"That doesn't sound like their style, but I don't have a better explanation." The cable began to dig into her flesh and she tightened her muscles once more. "At least it takes some of the pressure off."

The Fiddler Crab glanced at the filthy pavement cluttered with dented blue dumpsters far below. "Some," he said.

"I wish we had the energy to climb back up this cable to the fire escape," Xochitl said, sighing heavily.

"It's a long way, and all uphill. I'd never make it."

"Yeah. Neither would I."

"I hate to bring this up, Fid, but I think we're going to have to do the old trapeze act again. If you can grab onto my pants, I think I can swing you through that window. You'll probably get cut up a bit, but hey, welcome to *my* life. Once you're in, grab my legs and guide my feet to the window sill. I won't let go of the cable until I feel solid brick beneath my feet. You grab my belt loop and pull me toward the window. Then I think I can walk my fingers down these bricks and climb in"

"I don't know, Xochitl. I was about to fall the last time we did this. I don't think I could've held on any longer."

"You've had five minutes to rest. Quit thinking you're such a wimp. I have faith in you."

"Yeah, well... that makes one of us."

Xochitl gripped the cable with her hands and let her feet fall down below her.

Terror once again gripped the Fiddler Crab as he hung up-side-down by only his legs. He thrust his hand into Xochitl's pants and desperately grabbed a large handful of denim.

"Jesus, Fid. Leave me enough to wear."

Every muscle in his body tensed as he tried to bring himself to unhook his legs from the cable, losing his nerve each time. After several failed attempts, he hung completely still.

"Okay, I'm doing it for real this time." His voice was tight and squeaky, barely recognizable. "One...two...three..." Nothing.

"Okay kid, one more time. I'm getting really tired of this. All right, ready? For reals this time. One ... two ...*THREE!*"

Xochitl shot her long leg into the air kicking the Fiddler Crab across his calves.

"Hang on, Fid," she shouted as his legs flew over the cable and began to rock like a pendulum below him. "All right, here we go - at the window. Ready."

The Fiddler Crab was silent save for the huffing of his breath.

"Are you ready?" The Fiddler Crab heard from above. There was a desperation in Xochitl's voice that was new to him. She was not confident in this move at all. Maybe she doubted his willingness or ability to fulfill his part. Then again, he hadn't done anything lately to inspire her with confidence. He'd been whining since they climbed onto the cable. True, he could very possibly die if things went wrong here, but so could she. She was in no better position than he was, and she wasn't whining. The pain in his good arm began to diminish as he concentrated on the window. "Okay," he said, "Start swinging."

CHAPTER 31

The subtle ridges on the metal cable pushed their way into Xochitl's hand as her weight more than doubled from the dangling Fiddler Crab. She willed herself to hang on and began to swing her body back and forth. Centrifugal force from his movement increased the Fiddler Crab's weight by orders of magnitude and she felt her grip loosen a bit. Desperate, she summoned all of her will, clutching the cable. Ignoring the pain in her finger joints and aching wrists, she undulated her body to its extreme. The Fiddler Crab disappeared behind her and then came flying back toward the window. Inches from the glass, the window slid open and a pair of hands emerged from inside, seizing the Fiddler Crab's ankles, yanking him inside.

Xochitl sprang upward as her weight suddenly diminished by half. The cable snaked up and down for a moment and Xochitl bobbed with it, struggling to retain her grip. A burning in her palms from the ridges in the cable etched its way to the front of her consciousness, only to be upstaged by a stinging in her wrists from the brawl in the adult theater bathroom. She swung her legs up over the cable to give her aching hands a rest. Her breathing was labored and she realized it was as much from fear as exhaustion.

A confused relief came over Xochitl. The Fiddler Crab had gotten in the window without a scratch. But what the hell had just happened? Who had opened the window? And who's hands had grasped the Fiddler Crab? Relief caved in to dread. It had to be the men who were chasing her. Who else could it be? No one else would have known to open the window.

"Xochitl."

The voice was familiar to her. It wasn't the Fiddler Crab but she couldn't place it in this context.

She gazed across her dangling body at the open window. A long haired young man was leaning out, waving to her, motioning her toward the sill.

"Rick?" Was she delusional? Giving her head a good shake, she took another, more probing look. "What are you doing here?"

"Here, baby, hang by your legs and grab my hands. I'll pull you in."

Shimmying up to the point where the cable met the wall, she did as she was told, dangling by her legs in front of the window, stretching out her arms. As Rick wrapped his hands around her small wrists, she felt a warm burst of strength course through her system, the feeling of hope. Without a word, her legs dropped from the cable. Pain seared through her as her bare feet struck the side of the building. Her body was wracked all over with injuries, big and small. What did one more matter if it meant an end to all this. She was pulled toward the window by strong confident arms. Tumbling through the window into the room, she lay in a heap on the floor. Rick knelt over her, gazing down, saying nothing. Wrapping her arms around his neck, she closed her eyes and kissed him long and hard. For a time she lay silently, holding on tight to her rescuer until the fear and anxiety began to subside.

Gradually, Xochitl became aware of more than Rick's presence in the room. Slowly opening her eyes, she peered over his shoulder and immediately stiffened again. In a crumpled heap on the floor, The Fiddler Crab, lay motionless, a small pool of blood forming around him and a good sized gash in the side of his head. Standing over him, gun in hand, was Doctor Robert Austin Banders. Standing beside Banders was her assailant from the restroom.

"He'll be fine," said Banders, glaring at Xochitl "If I had my way, the little bastard would be dead by now after the way he humiliated me in public. You both would. But this is business."

Rick's hold on Xochitl grew limp as she sat up and pushed him away. He skulked away and stood behind his father. Xochitl felt sick, as though she had been punched in the stomach yet again. "Rick?" she said weakly.

"Ricky's a good son, as kids go," Banders laughed. "It's all in how you raise them. You've got to put the fear of God in them right from the start so they know when to do the right thing. Ricky knows when to do the right thing, don't you Ricky?"

Rick sulked, withdrawn. He stared at the floor. He would not meet Xochitl's gaze, nor his father's. Xochitl's mind reeled. "How can you be with them?" she said weakly. "You know they're trying to kill me, don't you?" Then she shouted, " HOW CAN YOU BE WITH THEM?"

Rick offered no reply as he stood gazing downward.

"It's a family thing, dear," said Doctor Banders. "Blood has an attraction all its own. God knows, the poor boy didn't want to act on my behalf. He simply had no choice."

"I don't get it," Xochitl said, letting her chin fall to her chest, then snapping her head up to stare at Banders, "what do you have to do with this?"

"Nothing, really. I have no interest at all in how this little drama plays out. I merely stumbled into a win-win situation. Your unconscious friend here made the unfortunate decision to attack me in a very public place. It didn't take these gentlemen long to find out that the young man in the newspaper picture was my son. I was approached, offered a large sum of money once the formula you are harboring is in their possession, and told that I could eventually do as I wished with the filthy little monster that attacked me. How could I refuse an offer like that? After all, it's my patriotic duty, isn't it?"

"Patriotic duty? What the hell does patriotic duty have to do with this?"

"Oh, is it possible you've been running so hard that you haven't paid attention to who has been chasing you?"

"I don't know anything," Xochitl said, her voice strained. "I keep telling these goddamn monkeys that, but they seem to have a comprehension problem."

"Now now, Xochitl, no need for name calling. We're all mature adults here."

Xochitl looked at Rick and laughed bitterly. "All right Doctor Banders," she said slowly, pronouncing the words with intent, "You seem to know the *'whole story'*, how about you fill me in?"

The suited man behind Banders shifted and cleared his throat. Banders glanced at him and he nodded his head almost imperceptibly. "Apparently, the way I understand it, you were the unfortunate witness to an assassination."

"I didn't arrive until after Doctor Sporkin was dead. I didn't see anything."

"Yes, well, that's unimportant," Banders continued. "What matters is that the good Doctor had the only known copy of the formula for his sobering drug on the premises at the time of his demise, however when the clean-up crew arrived, the formula was nowhere to be found. Now I don't suppose it just got up and walked away, did it? You are the only one who could have taken it."

"Why would I take it? I wouldn't know what to do with it. The closest I've ever gotten to chemistry is mixing a drink."

"Whatever your reasons, Xochitl, you must have taken it. Other than your friend, Mr. Blanchard who was out cold and was thoroughly searched, no one else was there. Now where is it? Your government needs to know. It's your patriotic duty to reveal the whereabouts of Doctor Sporkin's formula."

"My government? What are you talking about? These guys are from one of the big pharmaceutical companies, aren't they? What does the government have to do with it?"

Banders shot the suited man a sidelong glance. The man reached into his coat pocket and produced a small wallet. He opened it and flashed an ID card in front of Xochitl's face.

"Agent Cortez, Treasury Department," she read. "Figures. History repeats itself"

"Mmm... how can I put this simply so that you'll grasp the finer points?" said Agent Cortez, rubbing his chin. "You see, Miss Saint James, the various levels of government, particularly state and local governments, have a big problem. In fact they've had it for quite a while. Everything keeps getting more expensive. That doesn't just affect you and me. It affects the government, as well. They have to buy things just like we do. And just like you and I, when things get more expensive they need more money to buy them. City governments are fighting with county governments over who gets what share of the pie. County governments are fighting city and state governments for the same reason. And everyone looks to the Federal Government for an answer. No one has enough money. We've all seen stories on the news about this state or that state that will shut down unless a certain budget is approved within a prescribed time. In the end some form of budget is always approved and the state government carries on as usual. Imagine now, what would happen if there were no budget to approve? If there was just no money. Well, several states are approaching that status right now. They're getting dangerously close to having not enough money to cover their day-to-day expenses."

Cortez paused, rubbing his hands together. "So where is this money supposed to come from? They can't raise taxes. People, though they earn more money, have less spending power than they did thirty years ago. They certainly won't stand for higher taxes. They'd be rioting in the streets and we can't have that. So where do we get the money? It's simple really...fines. Much of the money comes from fines and penalty assessments and surcharges."

"I get the part about fines, but what are surcharges and penalty assessments?" Xochitl asked flatly.

"It's a sort of tax on the fine. For instance, here in California the penalty assessment on traffic fines is $24 for every $10 of your fine."

"That's ridiculous! It's more than the fine."

"Yes, nearly two-and-a-half times as much as the fine. California is a big, hungry state. That penalty assessment goes to the state's general fund. Most other states have assessments and surcharges that are lower than California, but they don't have as many people to govern. Their expenses are not as high.

There are many laws that carry a stiff fine if broken, speeding, driving without insurance, running a red light, or driving under the influence, for example. It's that last one that you're interfering with by hiding Dr. Sporkin's formula. And it's a big one, Xochitl. Many cities, counties and states have to add their own DUI specific surcharges on to their fines to pay for the cost of prosecution and driving education. People in many areas are ordered to pay for their own incarceration, so that the cost of jailing them is defrayed. That leaves more of the actual fine that can be applied to general governing costs. A portion of the surcharges or penalty assessment applied by cities and counties is usually handed over to the state to keep its wheels turning. It's a very necessary part of their income.

Plus it has a built-in advantage. If a citizen here and a citizen there are subject to a steep fine, they may grumble, but they pay it. Their friends sympathize with them, but they don't form an organized resistance because it's not that big of a deal. They blow up for a short period and then settle down to accept their fate. They did, after all, break the law. It's sporadic, you see, so there's an insular quality, a sort of buffer zone. But the good people in the world of law enforcement eventually get everyone for one thing or another. It doesn't make you a hardened criminal, just a normal citizen whose had a little brush with the law. It's like landing on the wrong square in a board game. And like I said, driving under the influence is a big square to land on. It's a big source of income for the state and city governments because it's a universally condemned crime and no one will argue with piling surcharge on top of surcharge.

Also this situation has, fiscally speaking, an added bonus. Since alcoholism is an addictive disease, it practically guarantees repeat offenders, who can be charged much higher fines and surcharges the second and third time around. You can understand why we can't allow a sobering drug to reach the general public. It would put too big of a dent in the income of cities, counties and states. It sets a very bad example. In order for this system to work there must be laws, and a certain number of people have to break those laws. We can't go around eliminating the situations that cause those laws to exist in the first place."

Xochitl had staggered to her feet and was pacing angrily. "Are you telling me that Doctor Sporkin was murdered by his own government to keep his drug off the market? That thousands will die at the hands of drunk drivers so that the government can maintain its present level of comfort? So it can grease the machine? That's hideous."

"It's just business, Xochitl. A large part of government is business. It has to be that way. We've, all of us, gotten ourselves into a big financial pickle and this is one of the ways we keep our heads above water."

"That's not fixing the problem," Xochitl shouted. "Any fool must realize that things are going to keep getting more expensive. What then?"

"There are very capable men working on that problem as we speak. They'll be ready to face it when it arrives. They're not stupid, Xochitl. They'll figure out a solution just as they have for our present crisis."

"Solution? You call this a solution? It's a stopgap measure at best. What are they gonna do, confiscate people's homes and sell them if they can't pay their parking ticket?" Xochitl inhaled deeply. "Maybe the question shouldn't be where is the money going to come from, but where does it go. Maybe we should be asking why it costs so damn much to run a government." She was in Agent Cortez's face now.

"I have a few friends in government jobs, just low positions, but they've told me some interesting things about how the system works. Like if a governmental department doesn't spend its entire budget, it receives less money the next year. In fact my friends are encouraged to overspend because then the next years budget is increased to compensate for it. They have no incentive to cut their spending. In fact they have every incentive to increase it. Now just imagine that wacky philosophy being employed in every little department from the city council all the way up to the White house. Not to mention some of the other ridiculous, unnecessary ways the money is spent. EVERYBODY SPENDS TOO MUCH!" she shouted suddenly. "And it all adds up." She pounded her palm with her fist. "That type of thing needs to be looked at before you go letting people die from drunk drivers."

"It's not our place to legislate, Xochitl," Banders chimed in. "We need to be patriotic citizens and do what's right. Do what's best for all of us."

"Oh my ass!" spat Xochitl. "What do you have to do with this anyhow? It's kinda out of your field isn't it? Shouldn't you be off peddling snake oil somewhere?"

"It seems I, too, have gotten myself into a financial pickle," said Banders. "Our good friend here has offered me a way out. And it's something I can feel good about. Something that's good for the country - good for the common man."

"That's the problem with people like you, Banders. You have no idea what goes on at the level of the common man. The common man can barely pay his common fine, while people like you send their traffic tickets to their secretary to take care of. You never even feel it." Xochitl remembered the traffic citation she had received when Marissa had run a red light in her car. She would have to spend her own money to prove her innocence, two or three hundred dollars that she could ill afford. And what about the fact that the city had shortened their yellow lights in order to cause more people to get stuck in the red light. Wasn't that pretty much the same thing that was going on here? Weren't the laws supposed to be in place to protect the people?"

Apparently some were not. Some, it seemed, were in place for no other reason than to generate revenue or had been subverted to that purpose. A list of these laws began to unfold in Xochitl's mind. This type of law suddenly seemed ridiculous to her, something she hadn't thought too closely about until now. Agent Cortez was right about one thing, it was like landing on the wrong square in a board game. It had nothing to do with criminality. You parked your car outside a store, you somehow got detained in the store, you got a citation because there was some silly-ass sign saying that you could only park for x amount of minutes. If you didn't have the money to pay the fine, the fine grew larger until you would never be able to pay it. Now your car was towed away and sold or squashed into a small metal cube. Now you're considered a criminal. The crime being that you didn't pay the fine that, by the way, you still owe, and you still can't afford, in fact, can afford even less because now you've lost your job because you've lost your car, didn't sell your first-born and rally like a good citizen, do what you were told by the mysterious powers that be. Now you're on the books, you have a record. You're a blemished citizen. And for what? What would happen if your car stayed in its parking space for more than the allotted amount of minutes? Would society somehow be damaged by that? Would it crumble? No! Society would not be negatively impacted at all - even if you parked there for two weeks. Nothing would happen. It was just a law to generate revenue. Xochitl imagined a group of mathematicians and politicians sitting around a table, working out the probable number of people who would forget to move their cars and the cash it would generate. "Well that's just not going to cover it, Ralph. The city needs more cash for that new overpass. Maybe we could shorten the allowed parking time by another five minutes."

Except this was worse. Much worse. This was a law that was created with good intentions, a law written for the public's benefit, being hijacked and turned into a political cash cow.

This law was created to alter a certain behavior that actually was harmful to society. The fines were stiff in order to send a strong message, to show the public that this was a serious problem. Now the fine had become more important than the crime. In fact, it seemed that the crime was simply an avenue to the money. There would be no influx of cash if the law were universally obeyed. But the accountants knew this would never happen. It was statistically impossible. Someone would keep breaking the drunk-driving law and the cash flow would continue. It had become beneficial to the government if its citizens broke the law, at least the laws that carried a heavy fine.

At some point there had been a turnabout in the judicial perspective. Xochitl wondered when this shift in the law from societal order to fiscal need had occurred. It must have been very gradual because no one seemed to have noticed. In the past few years it seemed that more and more of her friends had been slapped with excessive fines, but no one had thought to ask why. Certainly they were outraged, but they felt powerless to fight their citations and their anger was impotent and unfocussed.

Until now, she herself had not known where the laws had originated, or where the money was being funneled. Now she was getting it straight from the horse's mouth. No wonder there were more prisons being built and more criminals to fill them. Criminals were being manufactured as the focus of the law shifted and the definition of a criminal was altered along with it.

"Xochitl," Banders cooed, "you don't really think that drunk driving should go unpunished, do you?"

"Of course not," she said, exhausted. "What I'm saying is that the system is lop-sided. Here you have a chance to make the whole problem go away, and you can't afford to let it happen. You've painted yourselves into a corner. In fact you're willing to let people die to keep it from happening. That's the heart of your big financial pickle, right there. The logic is faulty right from the start." She glared at Rick. "God, you people make me sick."

Xochitl, suddenly overcome with fatigue, sank to the floor, limp, beaten. Wrapping her arms around her knees, she began to rock slowly back and forth. All the injuries she had suffered during the night, the small cuts on her bare feet, the bruised bones in her wrist, her swollen brow, began to hurt. As her spirits sank the pain increased. She looked at the Fiddler Crab, sprawled like a pile of dirty laundry on the floor. Oh Fid, she thought. What have I dragged you into? As Xochitl's last muscle went limp, darkness enfolded her. She struggled impotently to remain alert, but finally crumpled onto her side, surrendering completely to exhaustion.

CHAPTER 32

Xochitl's strained muscles and various wounds surfaced gradually, one at a time as she meandered her way toward consciousness. She noticed that her wrist was free of the handcuffs and brought her hand up to her face, examining it, balling it into a fist and gyrating her wrist. Not bad. Amazing what a little well-deserved rest will do for you. The air was unusually cold and she shivered, rubbing her hands together. With difficulty she rose to a sitting position and surveyed her surroundings. The room was unfamiliar, small, with tarnished metal walls and a damp concrete floor. A single bare, low wattage bulb gave the place a depressing, dreamlike quality. The Fiddler Crab sat in silence with his back to the corner, staring intently at Xochitl without really seeing her. "Hey Fid," she sighed, attempting a smile. "Nice day if it don't rain."

The Fiddler Crab focused his gaze on her, as though he were seeing her for the first time. "Looks like a freezer," he said mechanically.

"Freezer?" said Xochitl.

"Yeah, a walk-in. We're stuck in a walk-in freezer, Xochitl. Like they have in restaurants. I don't think it's turned up all the way, though, or we'd be statues by now. With any luck it won't get any colder."

"Well, that would explain the stiffness. My fingertips are kind of numb. But on the upside, my wrists don't hurt." She rubbed her hands together to generate some heat, but the attempt failed. "It looks as though the cold has reduced the swelling on some of our wounds. For what it's worth."

"Yeah, great, we'll make better looking corpses," said the Fiddler Crab.

Xochitl was silent a moment. "So, what now? Any ideas?"

"Xochitl, you must know where that formula is."

Xochitl clouded. "Oh, not you too. What, did they get to you while I was out? Of all the people in the world, I thought you'd believe me. Honestly, Fid, look at me. Do you really think I would have let someone do this to me, or to you, if I could have stopped it?"

"I *do* believe you. I just think maybe there's something you're overlooking. Maybe you saw something or moved something that seemed insignificant at the time. Maybe it didn't seem like anything special, so you didn't commit it to memory. That's all I'm saying. Obviously you didn't take the damn thing on purpose."

"Like what? I don't think I moved anything and I definitely didn't take anything. I may have knocked a few lamps over as I ran for the door, but I don't remember it if I did. I was pretty upset."

The Fiddler Crab stared at the ceiling and chewed his lip. "That's my point. Let's go through this step-by-step. What happened when you discovered the body?"

"Ernie passed out, poor guy."

"Then what?"

"I ran for the phone on the kitchen wall and slipped in a big puddle of blood."

"Then what?"

"When I got to the phone it was dead. Someone must have cut the wires."

"What did you do then?"

"I ran into the living room to look for another phone."

"Did you find one?"

"Yeah, but it was dead, too."

"Then what?"

"I ran out the door and down to a gas station."

"You didn't touch anything on your way out?"

"No, I...Oh, wait a minute. I sat on the couch for a minute to calm myself down...And I...Oh my God!"

"What?"

"I tore a couple of pages from a notebook that was lying open on the table. I thought they were blank. I just needed something to wipe the blood off of my hands. It was getting all sticky. I was starting to freak out. Do you think that's what they're looking for?"

"Pretty sure. What did you do with the torn pages?"

"I probably put them in my pocket."

"Your pocket?"

"Yeah! I have this habit from hiking in the woods. When I come across pieces of paper that people leave on the trail, I crumple them up and stuff them in my pocket, you know, to keep the trail clean. I think I might have done the same thing with the notebook pages."

"Bloody pages?" The Fiddler Crab sounded incredulous.

"It's a habit. I can't help it," she said. "It comes from a good place."

The Fiddler Crab let out a long sigh and sat still for a moment. "Well, there you are," he said with finality. "Where are those pants now?"

"I'm not sure. I probably threw them in my laundry hamper. Not that those blood stains are ever going to come out, but that would be the normal routine."

"Well, good...I suppose we can just tell these fellows where they can find their formula and we'll be on our way."

"It's not that simple, Fid. I found out some stuff while you were unconscious." Xochitl related her encounter with Banders and the government man, as well as her disappointment in Rick.

"Yeah, that guy kinda lost favor with me when he invited his dad to dinner," said the Fiddler Crab. "I didn't want to say anything because you liked him. It seemed like he had something missing. I couldn't put my finger on it, but something just wasn't there."

"Yeah, like his heart! Man what a weak-ass little bitch boy. I can't believe he would just turn on us like that. Anyway, the problem now is that as soon as they know where the formula is hidden, they have no more use for us." She watched the Fiddler Crab stiffen. "We've become very expendable. We're not just gonna walk out of here, Fid. They'd never let us do that. We'd be a huge liability. I'm sure the only reason they told me the whole story is because they have no intention of letting us live."

The Fiddler Crab's head sagged. "Yeah, I guess you're right. I don't know what fantasy I was living in, there. So I guess our silence is our ticket to a long and happy life," he smirked.

"Fid?"

"Yeah?"

"I just had a thought...What if this room is like bugged or something, and they've been listening to us the whole time?"

"Ah, yeah. I wonder. I mean why wouldn't it be? Seems like the smart thing to do."

"If it is, we pretty much just led them right where they want to go. Stupid, stupid! That was probably the only thing keeping us alive. Of course the room is bugged. Why wouldn't it be? If we were dealing with some petty thugs maybe I'd think differently, but these are trained government people. And it's not like they're going to run short of cash or technology for a situation like this. Of course they would bug the room."

An almost imperceptible click sounded in the room. The Fiddler Crab turned a paler shade of pale. He had squeaked past death several times in the past few days, sometimes by the skin of his teeth, but this time it felt like the real thing. He rose to his feet and examined the door discovering that the latch handle had been removed. He pushed hard against the door with his whole body.

Nothing.

The walls were steel, the floor was concrete, the window

was unbreakable and the temperature...was the temperature dropping? Yes, it definitely was colder than it had been a short while ago. His heart sank.

"Do you feel that?" he asked, rubbing his bad arm. "I'm having some serious doubts about our future, here."

"It's getting colder, huh?" Xochitl was curled into a ball with her back to the wall. Her voice was small and thin. "I'm thinking that maybe the walls are where the cold is coming from. If we sit in the middle of the room it might buy us some extra time."

"Who cares?" said the Fiddler Crab, dejected. "Don't you know when you're beat? What's a couple of extra minutes? Nobody knows we're in here and nobody's going to walk in by accident. Look around. This place is abandoned. I don't think we're going to make it this time, Xochitl. We've taken a lot of risks, but they always paid off. Now I don't even see a risk we can take, let alone a clear path. We're beaten. All we can do is lick our wounds and hope for a relatively painless end." He produced a deep sigh and began to shiver.

"Well, Fid, your biggest wound is that gash on the side of your head. If you can lick that you'll be real popular with the ladies," Xochitl said through a weak chuckle. She sat still for a moment, her smile gradually fading, breathing deeply to shrug off the advancing cold. Then, turning her head toward the Fiddler Crab, she wagged a shaky finger and said; "You know something, young man? I don't think I like your attitude one bit. This is no longer about us. We're in possession of some very incriminating evidence and if we don't use it a lot of innocent people will die needlessly in automobile accidents that could have been prevented. We have to get out of here. It's our duty."

They stared at each other, too numb to feel the tension between them. The Fiddler Crab sat down in the middle of the room, crossed his legs and draped his one good arm around his body. Xochitl rose to her feet with creaking difficulty, crossed the room and sat down beside him. She wrapped her arms around his pudgy little body and squeezed. The Fiddler Crab reached down and lifted Xochitl's bare feet off the floor, rubbing the soles with his good hand.

"Fid?" said Xochitl, her voice nearly a whisper.

"Yeah?"

"I'm sorry I got you into this. I didn't mean for any of this to happen. I just wanted someone to hang out with while I was in LA and you had a warm heart. If I'd had any clue what was coming I would have just had a beer with you and been on my way."

The Fiddler Crab felt only the faintest heat emanating from Xochitl's body. He wrapped his good arm around her and squeezed tight. "It's not your fault. You were just in the wrong place at the wrong time. I'm glad I was able to help out. I've had a pretty sedate life that, after a hellish childhood, is something I'm thankful for. But it's a case of 'be careful what you wish for,' because I've been bored for some time now. I mean really seriously bored, like depression kinda bored. You ever get that feeling where you want to do something, but nothing sounds interesting enough to get out of your seat for?"

Xochitl raised her hand with much difficulty and scratched her head. "No, not really, Fid. I've never had any trouble getting motivated. My problem is I usually act before I think. Sometimes it gets me into trouble."

"I think there can be such a thing as too much safety," he continued. "These last few days have been the most exciting thing that's ever happened to me. You taught me to fight. All my years I've just sat on my ass while other people took advantage of me or made me the butt of a joke. Believe me, a lifetime of that will suck the fight right out of you. I didn't know I could fight. But in the last few days I did - *we* did. I never felt so powerful. If I die in this freezer, I won't regret what's happened. This may sound kinda weird, but this is the first time I've ever felt alive enough to accept death. Don't get me wrong. I'm not looking forward to it, but…" His voice trailed off.

Over time the air grew unbearably cold. Xochitl held the

Fiddler Crab closer and a little tighter. "Never the less, Fid," she said, "I'm sorry."

Moments crept by in silence and Xochitl noticed how truly still the chamber was. The only motion was the shivering of their bodies. Neither spoke. There was nothing more to be said. The temperature reached a point where they could no longer feel it dropping, but neither of them mentioned it.

Simultaneously, both their bodies grew rigid as they heard a click from the door and then a slight thump. The Fiddler Crab spent several minutes struggling to his feet. Loping awkwardly toward the door, he pushed it gently with the palm of his hand. It swung open freely. He stared through the unobstructed doorway in disbelief. Xochitl gazed at him expressionlessly from her position on the floor. "Okay," he shrugged, "uh...I guess...let's go."

Xochitl was no longer sure that she was capable of movement, at least not upright movement. The Fiddler Crab was torn between rushing through the open door to precious warmth or going back to pull Xochitl to her feet. What if the door closed again? Someone, God knows who, had accidentally opened it from the outside. They would soon discover their mistake. It wouldn't do either one of them any good if the door were to shut again with both of them inside, but he would feel like such a coward scrambling through the door on his own. All these thoughts paraded through the Fiddler Crab's head in less than a second. Asking himself what Xochitl would do, he turned around and walked back into the room. Xochitl extended her arm and he grabbed her by the wrist, tugging until, reluctantly, she struggled to her feet. A wave of nausea came over her and she stumbled a bit, disoriented as though suffering a drug hangover. They were greeted with a glorious burst of life-giving warmth as they hobbled through the entrance, clinging to one another like a malformed four-legged animal.

Outside the freezer it was mostly dark, with only a few small, low-wattage bulbs lighting the far corner of a cavernous, warehouse-style room, filled with row upon row of deteriorating wooden workbenches. Must have been some kind of packing plant, Xochitl thought as she worked some flexibility back into her limbs. Running her finger across the surface of one of the tables, she discovered thousands of tiny knife cuts, confirming her suspicion. Bending over, she sniffed at the table. There was no smell of fish or meat. Staring intently at the far corner of the room, she could just make out several stainless steel industrial sinks. As her eyes groped the semi-darkness, she noticed a slight movement in the shadows by the sinks, or at least thought she had. Immediately, she crouched behind one of the worktables. Turning her eyes away slightly, she scanned the scene with her peripheral vision. Yes, there it was again. Someone was sitting on one of the cutting benches by the sinks. Here we go again, she thought. Her heart pounded, and she massaged her calves slowly, trying to generate enough heat to get her through any conflict that might arise.

Xochitl patted the Fiddler Crab's arm and pointed toward the corner. He nodded silently, squeezing the back of her hand. They crouched for a moment, letting their eyes grow used to the darkness and allowing the blood to flow back into their limbs. As the room grew gradually more visible, Xochitl scanned all four directions for the nearest exit from the massive room. The only obvious opening she could see was just beyond the spot where the shadowy specter sat hunched over, shoulders drooping. She could hear the figure humming softly to himself as he sat still. He seemed relaxed.

Xochitl realized that, even after rubbing her muscles, neither herself nor the Fiddler Crab were in any condition to fight, but they couldn't stay here. Steeling herself, she moved toward the figure. Perhaps they could take him by surprise. The Fiddler Crab followed, once again trusting Xochitl's lead. A few feet from the door, Xochitl stiffened. The Fiddler Crab could hear her breathing heavily.

Suddenly, she burst forth like a frozen tornado, sprinting at the lone figure, slapping him viciously across the face. The man's head flew backward, long hair cascading through the half-light. He rolled aside cradling his reddening face in his hands.

"Don't hate me," Shouted Rick. He looked frightened and vulnerable. For an instant Xochitl wanted to reach out and help him. Then her gut clenched.

"You! Oh, I hate you, all right! You make me sick," Xochitl hissed. "I can't tell whether I hate you more because you turned on me, or because you were weak enough to turn on your pathetic excuse for a father and open that door just now."

"I...I'm sorry, Xochitl. You don't know how he can be."

"Oh, shut up. I don't want to hear a bunch of lame-ass drivel from you. You're just spineless, plain and simple."

"You don't understand," he whimpered. "He's an evil man. He controls people. He controls me. I can't seem to refuse him. God knows I try, but I just can't. He always wins in the end." His hand dabbed gently at his reddening cheek, and he winced. "Blood is a strong thing, Xochitl. Even though I hate him, I love him, too. He's family. And you have to admit, he's doing the right thing for the country."

"Oh Hmmm where have I heard that tale before?" Hands on hips, Xochitl glared at him. "So what now? Are you gonna run and tell Daddy that we escaped, that you had nothing to do with it?"

"He's gone. He went with Cortez. They're on their way to Soda River. They left as soon as you told Fid where the formula was. Don't hate me, Xochitl. Please."

"God, you're even more pathetic than your Dad."

Xochitl strode icily past the pleading figure, towing the Fiddler Crab through the doorway by his withered arm. In the distance Rick's voice was small. "It's not my fault. It's family."

The building turned out to be a large warehouse-type affair, much longer than its width. Bright sunlight attacked Xochitl's eyes the instant she emerged. Her hands raced to her forehead automatically in a double-handed salute to shield her eyes from the piercing, 90-degree rays. The Fiddler Crab was squinting down at his shoes, giving his pupils time to adjust. "Man, is it really this hot?" he asked, "or does it just feel that way after the whole freezer thing?" Eventually they both felt comfortable enough to survey their surroundings. The parking area was mostly dirt and gravel. Once a paved employee parking lot, the potholes had gradually claimed the area as their own until only a few large chunks of crumbling asphalt remained.

"Where are we?" Xochitl asked.

"I don't know," the Fiddler Crab replied scratching his head. "This doesn't look familiar to me. But I think it's pretty clear we're nowhere near the alley behind the porn theater. We must have been out for quite a while."

"Yeah," said Xochitl, rubbing her eyes. "I kind of feel a little groggy, like I've been drugged."

"Me too. I've got a little bit of a hangover. Everything's kind of fuzzy. I hope we don't have to do any quick thinking any time soon."

"Well, we've got to figure out where we are," said Xochitl, "and then decide how to get to Soda River from here. Let's walk. This place gives me the creeps." They walked across the large parking lot through a chain-link gate and out into a narrow, deserted street that seemed to suffer from some sort of excessive grease buildup. Across from the parking lot stood a six foot cinder block wall adorned with spray painted territorial markings and beyond that a row of worn tract homes, which at first glance appeared to be lived-in, but upon closer examination were ragged and lacking in maintenance. A tiny ghost town. The sad legacy of a small society of long-dispersed factory workers. The whole place had a stark, feral appearance.

Xochitl glanced back toward the parking lot. A sign on the chain-link fence read: 'Vasquez Freshly Packed Vegetables - The Pride of Bakersfield Since 1951'.

"Bakersfield!" She grabbed the Fiddler Crab and pointed at the sign. "Shit, man, we're in Bakersfield."

"That explains why I didn't recognize the scenery," said the

Fiddler Crab matter-of-factly. "I've never been this far north."

"I don't recognize the scenery either, but I know how to get home from Bakersfield. Do you have any money, Fid?"

"Couple of bucks. How about you?"

Xochitl fished into her pockets and pulled out a small wad of bills. "I have the rest of the money Mr. Trundell wired me. Probably a couple of hundred dollars. I can't believe those guys didn't rob me. I know they're after much bigger fish, but you'd think someone like Banders would just rob you out of general principles."

"They're pros," said the Fiddler Crab, shivering one last time as warmth returned to his body. "They probably wanted to make it look like an accident, like a couple of dorks were playing around in an abandoned industrial freezer and locked themselves in. If there was no money in our pockets it would look more suspicious. I'm sure that's why they removed your handcuffs, too. All they had to do was come back in a couple of days and turn the freezer off. We may not have been discovered for years. If the authorities didn't look too close, nobody would ever suspect foul play."

"Yeah, maybe. Anyway, I think the best we're going to be able to do with this money is buy a couple of bus tickets. Soda River is about three hours from here by car which is probably what, about twelve hours by bus," she chuckled bitterly, "and they've got a good head start on us. Maybe we could rent a car, but my credit's pretty bad. How's yours?"

"I've never had a credit card," said the Fiddler Crab.

"That's probably a good thing in the long run, Fid, but we could sure use some instant money right now." They walked on in silence for a while, Xochitl's mind rifling through possible solutions. How hard could it be? All they had to do was get to Soda River, about a hundred and fifty miles away, before Banders and his buddies. True, they'd departed some time ago, but there had to be a way. As long as you're still breathing, she thought, there's always some way. And miracle of miracles, they were still breathing.

A slight but persistent buzzing, like a mosquito flying too close to the ear had, for several moments, been struggling to dominate Xochitl's consciousness. She had managed to ignore it while occupied with their transportation problems, but now the annoying sound grew loud enough to impose itself. A small plane, a bright yellow crop duster, sputtered by in the distance. She watched as the rickety aircraft performed a questionable landing on a dirt road that ran alongside a field of newly sprouted crops about a quarter of a mile away. A cloud of dust billowed from behind the craft as it rumbled and squeaked to halt. A young, thirty-ish man in a filthy, light-blue jump suit emerged from the cockpit. He kicked the wheel and strode determinedly up to the engine compartment, tossing open the hood. Xochitl could hear the man swearing even at a distance, though she couldn't make out the words. "Come on, Fid," she said, grabbing his hand as she began to run toward the downed aircraft. "Our salvation may have just fallen out of the sky."

The Fiddler Crab gulped hard as he witnessed the entire scene with mixed feelings. He was pretty sure he knew what Xochitl had in mind. He was not at all thrilled with the possibility of having to ride in the rickety-looking craft and his stomach once again turned to brick. As they approached the aircraft, the pilot was pounding angrily on the engine with what looked, from this distance, like a large, metal wrench. *Not a good sign... not a good sign at all.*

"Hi," Xochitl said, placing a hand on the man's back. "Having engine troubles?"

The pilot stiffened, bashing his head against the hood. "Ow! What the Holy Mother...? Where'd you come from? This is private property. You're not supposed to be here."

Xochitl held her palms up. "Oh, Sorry," she said. "Look, I'll be honest with you. We're in kind of a little bit of trouble. I know you have no reason in hell to help us, but we need a ride to Soda River."

"Soda River?" The pilot scratched his head. "Hell, you can

take a bus up there. Terminal's only just down the road, that way."

"We need to get there in a hurry."

"Aw jeez... just take the bus. I still got this field to spray." The pilot turned and buried his head back in the engine compartment.

Xochitl gripped the man's upper arm and he jumped, once again banging his head. "Ow! Aw jeez! Mother of pearl." She pulled him gently from the engine compartment and walked around to face him.

"What's your name, Mr. Flyboy?"

"Philo. Philo Schank."

"Well Philo, I've got a story to tell you," she said. "You like to drink?"

"Well, hell yeah I do! Whatcha got?" said the pilot. Then he recoiled, his voice growing somber. "That is...I've been known to indulge occasionally. But not while I'm working...so don't even think about offering me anything, 'cause I won't take it. Not while I'm working. You don't have nothin' right?"

"Look," she said, "how would you like it if you could go down to your favorite bar with your best buddies and have a great time, drinking like a fish all night, and then sober up, and I mean completely sober up, just before you went home?" She pushed her matted hair aside. "You could hop in your car and drive home just as safely as if you'd been at church all evening. And if you get pulled over for something? No problem. Your sober, man! Your wife wouldn't even be angry with you. Would you like that? Would that appeal to you?"

"Heh heh, that's kind of a dumb question, huh?" said Philo Schank, a sparkle in his eye. "Cept I ain't got no wife. I got a girl, though."

Ten minutes later Xochitl had finished telling the pilot her incredible tale. The man sat dumbfounded. "So this is real? This is a real thing? You didn't just make this up?"

"Look at my face. Look at my bare feet. Look at my swollen wrists. I didn't make those up, did I? All this happened. The whole thing is true. Ask my good friend, Fid." She gestured grandly toward the Fiddler Crab. "He'll back me up."

The Fiddler Crab nodded, slowly, wondering what kind of death trap he was talking himself into this time.

"Well, here's the deal," said the pilot, "I only got room for one passenger. Wouldn't even have room for that except this is an old converted trainer. A 152B. 1962. Got it from the flight school when they went out of business. Converted it to a duster myself." Philo's chest swelled. "We might could beat them fellas to Soda River, but I been having a lot of troubles with my fuel pump lately, as you've just seen. It's a risk. Around here there's plenty of open space and fields to bring 'er down in if anything goes wrong. We get up there in them foothills, there ain't nothing but trees and little strips of road. Could be dangerous, could be veeery dangerous."

"I'll do it," Xochitl said. "Look at me. It can't be any worse than what I've already been through."

The Fiddler Crab felt equal parts relief at being spared the perilous ride in this rickety tin mosquito and indignation at being excluded from the adventure. After all, he'd come this far and survived some close calls, even risked his own neck. Too much had transpired to even think about packing it in now. The thought of shuffling on back to his dark little apartment in Los Angeles, without even knowing what happened, seemed a horrible anticlimax. He'd come to believe in the cause. It really would be a good thing if the sober drug were to make it onto the open market. "I want to come along," he said, weakly.

Xochitl probed the pilot, searching his eyes for something she could use. "Is there no way my friend can come along? We've been through a lot together the last few days?"

"Well now let's see..." Philo was half mumbling, scratching his head. "You gotta go so you can get to your formula before them fellas do? And I gotta go 'cause I know how to fly the plane. That's one pilot and one passenger. Nope, that's all she'll hold, one pilot and one passenger. Your little buddy's out of luck."

"What if we get rid of the pesticide in the tanks, will that lighten it enough to carry two passengers?"

"Well now, as I understand it we're in a little bit of a hurry. Right? See, we'd have to fly back to the airstrip and pump this stuff back into the tank. We can't just dump it here. It's way too toxic and expensive."

The Fiddler Crab's heart sank and Xochitl saw it in his face. She reached into the pocket of her jeans and produced a small wad of bills, the remaining money that Mr. Trundell had given her. "Here, take this and rent a car. Shoot up to Soda River as fast as you can. You probably can't rent a legitimate car without a credit card, but I'm sure a town like this has some place where you can rent a wreck and they won't ask too many questions. If not, you'll have to take the bus."

"Oh great, I rent some wheezing old rattle trap and limp it up to Soda River while you soar through the clouds, in the lap of luxury, to the town's airport and then catch a cab right to your front door."

"The town doesn't even have an airport, Fid, and I don't know about the whole 'lap of luxury' thing either. No offense to Mr. Schank, here, but I'm pretty sure this plane doesn't have a first class section. I'm hoping he can put me down somewhere close to my house. I'll leave that part up to him."

"But I'm going to miss all the exciting stuff." The Fiddler Crab was pacing, talking mostly to himself. "I think I've gotten a little addicted to the adrenalin rush. These last few days have thrown me into high gear and I'm having a hard time coming down."

"Well, Fid, hopefully there won't be any more exciting stuff. With any luck, I'll get there with plenty of time to spare. I'll just walk in my room, find the scrap of paper in my pants pocket and...and..."

"And what?" the Fiddler Crab asked.

"And... I don't know. I guess I haven't really thought that far ahead. I've just got to get to the formula before Banders and his friends. The important thing, right now, is to keep that scrap of paper away from them." She pounded an open palm with the fist of her other hand. "There must be something more constructive we could do with it, something more final, or they'll just keep chasing us forever."

"Well, you work for a magazine, maybe you could just publish the formula."

"I don't think so," said Xochitl. "I mean we could, but the issues are planned out a good three months in advance. That's way too long. We'll need to think of something more immediate or we'll be dodging bullets until it hits the stands."

The small plane's engine roared to life and Philo hollered from the cockpit. "Come on," he said, "let's get along before this thing craps out on us again."

"There's a comforting thought," said Xochitl, climbing into the passenger seat. "Anyway, start thinking along those lines, Fid, and I'll see you when you get up there. Go to the Aware Magazine building and wait for me there. It'll be safer than going to my house and easier to find."

"Safe? What use have I got for safe?" he shouted over the roar of the engine, but the crop duster was already rumbling down the dirt road beside the field. He stood watching as the aircraft clattered its way into the sky. Soon the rumble diminished to a buzz, and the craft's details coalesced into a small yellow dot, finally disappearing altogether. Suddenly the Fiddler Crab felt very much alone. Everything was so damnably quiet. In the past few days there always seemed to be some kind of noise going on. If there wasn't enough external noise, they made their own. They talked, jabbered and joked, mostly. It was a great diversion and served to bolster their courage. Now there was nothing, not even the distant sound of a car or tractor. He turned in the direction of town and began to walk, painfully aware of the sound of his own footsteps.

CHAPTER 33

For miles the Fiddler Crab watched the heat ripples rise as he trudged wearily down a deserted, two-lane road. He had tried to hitch a ride with the few cars that passed him, and one had actually slowed down. Spying the Fiddler Crab's withered arm, though, the driver had sped away leaving him with only his indignant mutterings for company. Other than that, his journey was eventless until he happened upon a tattered old building with rippled windows and peeling yellow paint by the side of the highway. 'Ethyl's', a hand-painted sign outside the diner proclaimed, and in smaller letters underneath: 'James Dean Once Ate Here!' The Fiddler Crab's stomach lurched as it occurred to him that he hadn't eaten a thing in a good twenty-four hours.

He pushed the plate-glass door open. A rush of luscious cool air surrounded the Fiddler Crab as he entered the dilapidated building. The diner was straight out of the nineteen-fifties, all tarnished chrome and cigarette-burned naugahyde. The whole place had a jaundiced yellow appearance. It was easy to believe that James Dean actually had eaten here. In fact, by the looks of the place he could have eaten here yesterday. Ethyl's was not exactly a thriving establishment, the Fiddler Crab noticed as he approached the counter. He saw the tops of a few heads poking above the back of one sickly-colored booth and a depressed-looking fellow sitting alone at the far end of the counter, staring into his coffee. Otherwise, the place was deserted.

"What can I do for you, hun?" A heavy, middle-aged woman dressed in a plaid polyester uniform appeared behind the counter, seemingly from nowhere. She had a face comprised primarily of make-up which ended abruptly at her first double chin. "We got a great BLT. Hog farm's just down the road," she said, waddling to the other end of the counter to refill the depressed man's coffee cup.

The Fiddler Crab spied an ancient clock displaying an airbrushed painting of a child guzzling a cola. If the clock was right, it was 3:10 pm. The hours spent trapped in the freezer had seriously hindered his biological clock and he was unsure whether to order breakfast, lunch or dinner. Three ten, hmm, let's see...A BLT could pass as either lunch or dinner. "A BLT would be perfect," he said, a little too loudly. "You must be Ethyl."

"Indeed I am, handsome. I'm also Ethyl's daughter and Ethyl's granddaughter. A BLT it is, then. Hey Pete," she yelled across a stainless steel counter, "another one!" She turned back to face the Fiddler Crab. "Go ahead and find yourself a seat somewheres, hun, and I'll find you when it's ready."

He trudged his way toward a booth in the back, anxious to take the weight off his feet. Half way to his seat, as he passed the lone occupied booth, a large, beefy hand forcibly enclosed the wrist of his withered left arm. Startled, he found himself being yanked into the booth. He stiffened for an instant, but only an instant, because he had learned an important lesson from his time with Xochitl. The Fiddler Crab quickly grasped a fork off the table with his good arm, thrusting and lashing it about even before he landed sideways on the seat.

"Aaaah, you gimpy little bastard!!" It was a familiar voice. "I should have killed you outright when I had the chance," it hissed. The Fiddler Crab opened his eyes to the vision of Doctor Robert Austin Banders with a fork hanging from four neat little holes in his cheek. The Fiddler Crab squirmed, trying desperately to escape the vice-like grip, but the hand of Agent

Cortez was locked firmly around his withered arm. He lashed out again, yanking the fork from Bander's livid, bleeding face and thrusting it at the hand of the government man.

Agent Cortez squeezed the Fiddler Crab's withered arm in a bone crushing death grip. The Fiddler Crab winced and the fork flew from his grasp clattering across the floor. The room became fuzzy. It was only for an instant, but an instant was long enough. Bander's fist flew across the table, crashing into the Fiddler Crab's cheek. "Oh, come on, Banders," said Agent Cortez calmly. "There's no need for that."

"He stuck a goddam fork in my cheek! What are you defending him for?" He lashed out at the Fiddler Crab once more.

"This is not a personal vendetta, Banders. Think of it as a hunting trip. We're here to do a job, not to get involved with the prey." He turned to face the Fiddler Crab, "Looks like you and I need to have a little talk, Mr. Chester McFadden."

The Fiddler Crab froze in position. He hadn't heard anyone speak his real name in many years. His parents were the last to call him that, but they were long dead. Nobody knew that name. Nobody. The enormity of the deck stacked against him became very apparent. The Fiddler Crab stared at the man intently for a moment. Strength drained from him like water from a leaky bucket. Suddenly he was weak little Chester McFadden again, telling the boys in the Stud Club that Elsa Starlighter wanted him to "ploop" her. Embarrassment gushed into the cavity where his strength had resided only moments ago. Unable to look the man in the eye, the Fiddler Crab sagged into his seat.

"All right, Mr. McFadden, this can go easy for you, or it can be your worst nightmare," agent Cortez said, tearing a bite from his BLT and chewing fiercely as he spoke. "Obviously someone let you out of your intended tomb." He cast a sidelong glance at Banders. "I can probably guess who." He cleared his throat. "All I really want to know from you is what happened to the girl. Where is she?"

The Fiddler Crab's mind raced a mile-a-minute. "She didn't

make it," he said. "She froze to death in the freezer." Pain shot through his arm as the government man pinched a pressure point on the Fiddler Crab's shriveled arm. He screamed, unable to control himself and the man released his grip. He had no doubt that these men intended to kill him as soon as they got what they needed from him. And after him, Xochitl. It was going to come down to how much pain he could withstand?

"I see," said Agent Cortez, his voice a threatening rumble. "And you thought you'd stop off and grab a bite to eat on your way to...where? The police? Interesting that you didn't ask to use the phone when you entered the restaurant. Don't you think that would have been the sensible thing to do?" The man's hand shot out like lightening, gripping the Fiddler Crab once more around his withered arm. He shook the arm violently. "Where's the girl, Mr. McFadden?"

"I don't know," the Fiddler Crab gasped. "I don't know where she is by now, but she'll get to Soda River a hell of a lot quicker than you two losers."

"Hey what's going on here?" Ethyl croaked, BLT in hand, her chesty, wheezing voice cutting the pandemonium like a chainsaw. "Oh my God, look at the blood. Look, boys, we don't want any trouble around here. We're just trying to run a family business. Why don't you take this on down the road? I don't want to have to call the police."

With his free hand the government man reached into his jacket and produced a wallet-like folder. He opened it and thrust it into Ethyl's face. "I am the law, ma'am. This little fellow's wanted for a string of felonies. It was just our luck he walked in here when he did. Unfortunately, he put up a little bit of a struggle. I'll be happy to cover the damages, if any."

"He's lying," the Fiddler Crab shouted. "He's trying to stop the sober pill. He's from the government. The...the bad part of the government. Don't let him take me. Call the police."

"Sorry, ma'am," said the government man. "He's not quite right in the head. It's drug charges he's wanted for. We should be taking him in now so we'll leave you in peace." From inside the same coat Cortez pulled a pair of handcuffs and immediately slipped them over the Fiddler Crab's wrists. Rising to his feet with a slight groan, he pulled the little man, who was quietly sobbing now, from the booth.

"What about this?" asked Ethyl, waving the sandwich in the air. "Should I wrap it up?"

They marched from Ethyl's Diner single file. Outside, Agent Cortez opened the back door of his black government sedan and pushed the Fiddler Crab in. When he was halfway through the door, Agent Cortez grabbed him roughly, reached in with a key and unlocked the handcuffs. He pulled the Fiddler Crab's arms behind him and replaced the cuffs on his wrists. "Just in case you decide to do something stupid," he said.

CHAPTER 34

Xochitl was enjoying herself, in as much as that was possible, given the circumstances. Her window was open and the wind whipped her matted hair all over the inside of the cockpit. A slight odor of fuel and pesticide lingered which no amount of wind or scrubbing would ever eliminate. The engine purred loudly and to Xochitl's untrained ears sounded like it would push on forever. A thin black ribbon, a rural highway far below, was the only landmark dividing an otherwise unbroken expanse of green. Philo had told her that he wanted to keep the road in sight in case an emergency landing was in order. She had argued for speed, but in the end Philo, being the superior officer, prevailed.

"Look, I like a good drink as much as the next guy," he had shouted over the clatter of the engine, "but it don't do me much good if I'm dead, now do it?"

It was true, but Xochitl had grown impatient. She could feel victory in her grasp. They would surely arrive in Soda River far ahead of Banders and Cortez, but there was always room for the unexpected. Supposing they had phoned ahead to one of their agents who might have stayed in town. He could easily rummage through her closet and find the formula. If she could just get there quickly and do the job, whisk the formula away to, say, Mr. Trundell's safe, everything would be all right. It didn't matter what they did to her after that. She would have won.

Xochitl was torn from her thoughts by an uneven sputtering and the sound of Philo's timorous screeching. Aaawww, Dingers! Not again! I thought we was gonna make it all the way." The plane began to lose altitude and soon the engine plup-plupped its way into pure golden silence leaving only the rushing of the wind. Xochitl's good spirits plummeted to earth well ahead of the little yellow airplane. "Hang on tight, little lady," shouted Philo. "This might get a bit rough when we touch down."

"Touch down," Xochitl replied. "That sounds so reassuring. Especially for a plane whose engine isn't making any noise." Maybe he knows what he's doing, she thought. Maybe this will be nothing more than an inconvenience. Maybe he'll just float this baby right down to the ground, tap the engine with a wrench and we'll be on our way again. Maybe, maybe, maybe... But the ground was rising up all too quickly for Xochitl's taste. Small, insubstantial dots were acquiring visible details, becoming trees and boulders. Wire fences were becoming visible, as was the yellow line in the middle of the road. "Do you think the road is wide enough to land this thing?" Xochitl shouted to Philo over the whistling wind.

"It's wide enough," he said over his shoulder. "We just need to find a straight stretch of blacktop long enough to land in so we don't go rolling off into the bushes and break our landing gear."

"How much longer before we 'touch down'?" she said, making quotation marks in the air with her fingers.

"I think I can probably keep 'er up another thirty to forty-seconds."

"Oh great," Xochitl said, feeling her heart sink. She sat in silence, her mind struggling to compose some meaningful final thoughts just in case this turned out to be her last few moments on the planet. Nothing presented itself. Funny, she thought nervously, of all the times I've almost been killed in the last couple of days, this is the first occasion I've actually had time to prepare myself ...and I can't think of a damn thing.

Hell, I can't afford to die anyway. I love Fid to death, but there's no way my poor little guy's going to beat Banders and his uber-thug buddy up to Soda River and hide the formula. It's just not gonna happen. "Philo," she shouted, "bring this thing in, man. A lot of people are depending on us."

"Will do. Darlin'. Just hold on tight."

"Did you find a straight spot?"

"Well, not exactly. This stretch's got a long steady curve to it. It's pretty gradual so we might be all right,"

"Great."

The road was so close now that they could distinguish individual potholes, even an occasional road kill. Philo was struggling to keep the wings of the plane away from the oak trees growing wild along each side of the highway. Twice he yanked on the stick to lift the plane over protruding branches. Finally the little craft had no more flight left in it. The road whipped by just beneath them and soon the wheels bounced off the asphalt. Philo wrestled the stick, trying to center the plane over the yellow line in the road. They seemed to roll on forever, riding the gradual curve in the road. At first Philo had no real trouble steering the plane, but once it slowed down a bit and all its weight settled onto the highway he struggled to keep it on the blacktop. When the road curved a little more radically, Philo pulled every trick from his crop-dusting arsenal to make the plane follow without dipping the wings and scraping them on the ground. He not only wanted himself and Xochitl to come to a safe stop, he wanted the plane to survive, also. It had taken him a long time, working jobs he did not want to do, just to afford a down payment on this plane. He still had many payments to go and he didn't want to lose it now.

The plane slowed perceptibly. Details became visible out the windows and the rumbling under the wheels gradually diminished. Eventually the little craft slowed to a pace that Philo's strained decision making process could handle. He relaxed a little, letting the plane glide along, almost of its own accord.

His relief was short-lived.

"HEY LOOK OUT!" Xochitl's voice assaulted his ear.

It took Philo over a second to recognize the shiny object approaching him as the grill of a Mercedes Benz. Instantly, he whipped the plane into a radical right turn, off the side of the road, through a barbed-wire fence and into a fresh, green field full of startled cattle. He heard a syncopated hissing as the spinning tire was punctured by the metal barbs of the fence. As the tire lost pressure the plane wanted to pull itself to the right. Philo was losing control, afraid to apply the brakes in case the plane, still rolling along at a heady clip, took a nosedive. He had no idea how the plane would react with a flat tire. The wounded craft turned of its own free will and charged toward the herd of grazing cattle, which scattered in three of the four directions.

The plane finally came to rest on a green hillside populated by the bulk of the herd. A large agitated bull, multiple shades of brown and white, stood chewing its cud and eying Philo through the window. Philo cast the bull a stormy glance as he scrambled from the cockpit and got down on all fours to examine the damage to his plane. "Thank the Texaco star we didn't tear the landing gear off," he shouted up to Xochitl. "It's just a flat tire. No real damage."

Xochitl climbed awkwardly out of the plane and plopped onto the ground next to Philo. She bent over and placed her hands on her knees, taking a series of deep breaths. "So we'll be on our way...when?"

"Well I don't rightly know." He scratched his head. "I might could get the fuel pump running pretty easy, but I wouldn't want to try to take off with a flat tire. We'd never get up enough speed and we'd probably kill ourselves trying."

"So how long will it take to fix the tire?" Xochitl asked, growing uneasy.

"Well see, there's the thing... I ain't got a tire patch kit. It's just not the kind of thing you keep around on a plane. There's usually bigger things to worry about than a flat tire so I just never got one."

Xochitl grew quiet. She sat down on the sad-looking tire and rubbed her eyes. Sighing loudly she lowered her head and ran her fingers through her hair, catching them on the many knots that had formed during the flight. "So you're telling me we're through. We've lost. After all this crap, the week from hell, we're beaten by a flat tire. An ordinary everyday flat tire."

"Well it's not every day a plane gets a flat tire. In fact, I think it's kinda rare, on account of they're not on the road all that much."

"Come on, Philo. Don't you get it? We've lost. Thousands of people will die now. Drunk drivers and people who are hit by drunk drivers. We have no transportation. There's no way we can beat those bastards to Soda River."

"Well, I don't know if you were paying attention," said Philo with intent, "but there was a small town not too far back. I'm thinkin' that out here even a small town will have some kind of hardware store. These people out here probably fix their own stuff because there's no place to take it when it's broke."

"How far back was the town?" Xochitl asked.

"Hard to tell exactly from the air, but I'd say somewhere between five and ten miles. I might could run it, though."

"Right, Philo," she said. "That's half a freakin' world away. If it turns out to be ten miles, well that's pretty close to the distance of a marathon by the time you get back. Something tells me you're not that kind of a runner."

"Well, we gotta do somethin'." Philo was beginning to get agitated. "We can't just leave the plane here and hop on a bus."

"Yeah...maybe we can just..." Xochitl froze, becoming suddenly aware of a man in a dark suit walking across the field toward them. Her stomach immediately clenched, once again, into a painful knot. He had apparently come through the hole that the plane had left in the fence and was following its tracks to where they stood. As the man approached them Xochitl expelled a heavy sigh of relief. He was a little too old, too wide and a little too small to be one of those seemingly endless government clones. And besides, he was smiling.

"Hello," said the pink-skinned, portly businessman in a small, tentative voice that suggested too many female hormones. "Are you people all right? I apologize for running you off the road like that. I just wasn't expecting an aircraft when I came around the corner."

"Yeah, we're fine," Xochitl chirped. "Just a flat tire. Thanks"

"My name's Forest Langdon," said the man, holding out his hand for someone to shake. "Is there anything I can do to help, anyone I could call?"

"I'm Philo and this here's Xochitl." Philo took the man's hand and shook it vigorously. "I don't suppose you got a tire patch kit on you?" Philo could tell by looking at the man that he had most likely never set eyes on a tire patch kit in his life.

"No I don't. I'm sorry," said Langdon tentatively, "but the town of Willow is just down the road. I'd be happy to drive you there."

Philo turned and faced Xochitl. "Why don't I get a ride into town with this gentleman, while you stay here with the plane."

Xochitl brightened. "All right," she said, "but try to get back as quickly as you can. Here, let me give you my boss's number. Call him collect when you get to town. He won't like it, but he'll get over it. Tell him that the formula is in my pants pocket in my hamper. Tell him he has to get it and put it in a safe place. Okay? Got that?"

"Okay. Keep an eye on that fence while I'm gone. Make sure the cows stay inside. We're in enough trouble already once the rancher sees the hole we tore in his fence."

"Will do," said Xochitl, though she had no clue how to keep the cattle from charging through the fence. Fortunately, they didn't seem to be aching for their freedom, in fact, they seemed completely unaware of the break in the fence. Moments later she saw the silver Mercedes pull away from a dirt turnout beside the road and glide off down the highway. She picked up a downed fence post and tried to stuff it back into the hole. The dirt was crumbled around the hole and would not hold the post upright. This is stupid anyway, she thought. We still have to get the plane back out of the field. She plopped herself down on a small boulder and shot the herd a menacing look. "Don't even think about it," she said out loud.

CHAPTER 35

The Fiddler Crab stared wearily from the window of the speeding government sedan. The car was easily pushing eighty-five on the straight sections of road and a good sixty-five as it screeched around the curves. He felt himself thrust tightly against one door and then the other as centrifugal force tossed his Exhausted and handcuffed body around like a sock monkey in a dryer. Through all the tossing and turning he mulled over his experiences during the past week. He would never have attacked Banders or that idiot government agent before he'd met Xochitl. He felt good about defending himself, but was miserable at how it had turned out. He had always considered himself a simple coward, someone with no will to fight, even to defend himself. But it was much more complicated than that. Something in his makeup had always understood that he lacked the skills necessary to participate in violence, and had chosen other, less honorable, and less painful avenues when these occasions presented themselves. In the end, though, as a result of his cowardice, he suffered more violence. He was acutely aware of that dark facet of human nature that caused people to lash out at someone they perceived to be weaker than themselves. The weak often became the whipping boys, not only of the strong, but of anyone, even slightly more powerful, with any sort of aggression to express.

Xochitl had forced him out of that frame of mind, first in order to save her life and then to save his own. Even the fight with Banders at the Cirque Du Fromage would never have happened if Xochitl had not been there. It was interesting, in light of recent events, how that fight had turned out. At the time the Fiddler Crab had assumed that he had won. He had vanquished his life-long enemy and everything was going to be all right. Now he was a captive in the back seat of this speeding car as a direct result of that fight. He hadn't won at all. In fact, he'd doomed himself and possibly Xochitl as well. What was the secret? How did Xochitl know when to fight and when to run? Or did she? Perhaps she always fought, just as he had always run.

He was changing as a result of all that he had been through during the previous week. But events were flying at him much too quickly to analyze his new feelings. He felt different at his core, but couldn't quite put his finger on how. Life had been comfortably stagnant for many years and change had never been a welcome thing. It was something to be resisted, at least until some inevitable or safe direction became clear. Now things were changing too quickly to log any kind of personal growth. There was simply the situation and what needed to be done about it, and that was all. In the last few days, however, he'd begun to grow used to this new pace, taking things in stride. It was interesting how he had risen to the occasion, but the difference in his outlook, his gut feeling, was somewhat unsettling.

Now, as he sat helplessly in the back seat of a speeding car driven by two men who considered him nothing more than an irritating but necessary pawn, his thoughts were neither of escape nor revenge, but of who he had become. Obviously, he was stronger, more aware of his mortality than ever, but somehow less concerned about it. Little Chester McFadden, the mistreated boy he had been sheltering for so many years suddenly felt like a crumbling cardboard cutout that had only faintly existed lifetimes ago. If that ancient persecuted Chester were to die inside him, would that be a bad thing? No, he thought...no, it would not.

The Fiddler Crab was so completely engrossed in these

thoughts that he failed to notice the silver Mercedes Benz that sped by his window, going in the opposite direction.

CHAPTER 36

Xochitl smacked a large black cow loudly on its ass with the palm of her hand, and then jumped back to avoid any repercussions. The cow stared at the road, showing no sign that it had felt anything at all.

"Move," she said. "Get back in there!" The beast remained stubbornly in place. The cattle hadn't rushed the space in the fence as she had feared. They were not nearly organized enough. They were content, to mosey about the field without so much as a furtive glance at their new pathway to freedom, unless it turned up directly in front of them. Then they simply strode through it unaware that they were no longer held captive in the field.

Xochitl had been fooled by the cattle, lulled into complacency by their laissez-faire attitude and had allowed her attention to wander. She had lost two of the bovine monsters this way and now tried to prevent a third from traveling any farther from the field than it already had. The hefty black beast stood in the street chewing its cud and staring blankly down the highway. Xochitl expended a huge amount of energy trying to point it back toward the hole in the fence. "Look, man, just go! Okay?" She smacked it again causing pain to shoot up her arm from her injured wrist.

Striding angrily around to the front of the animal, she pinched its upper lip with her thumb and forefinger, tugging it toward the fence. The animal swung its head up, striking

Xochitl full in the chest and knocking her off her feet. She propped herself up on her elbows and glared at the cow. "I AM SO SICK OF GETTING KNOCKED AROUND! UNDERSTAND??" she shouted, then, calming herself; "Okay, look, I'm sorry. That was not called for, but you're the one in the wrong here. I'm just trying to help you out."

Xochitl lay down on the warm asphalt. Raising her arms, she shielded her eyes from the sun. "I can't believe I'm arguing with a cow," she said, her voice distant. "... and the goddam cow's winning." Another cow, this one smaller, brown with white spots, trotted through the hole in the fence and strode up beside the black one. She flopped over onto her stomach and buried her face in her arms. "Building a free world," she said, "one cow at a time."

CHAPTER 37

Philo had been telling Forrest Langdon Xochitl's story, as he understood it. He had embellished a few things and left out a few more, but most of the important facts were there. "So that's what we're doing, flying up to Soda River in a crop duster."

"That's extraordinary," said Langdon. "I wondered why she looked so disheveled. At first I thought it was due to the plane crash, but then I noticed that you yourself were unhurt."

"Yeah, it is kind of a weird story," said Philo. "I took a little convincing, myself. The little fella was with her when I met her, name's Lobster Boy or something like that, but there wasn't room for him in the plane. We turned him loose with some cash to see if he couldn't rent a car or something, maybe find his way up there on his own."

"Hmm, maybe a bus," said Langdon. "It doesn't sound as though he'd be able to rent a car. Or perhaps he'll hitchhike, though I don't like the thought of that."

"Yeah, me neither. He's kinda funny looking so I think he might have a bit of a time getting a ride. Might end up standing there all day."

"Well, the town of Willow is not far. We'll call the young lady's employer and buy something to fix that tire."

"That'd be great. I can't thank you enough. I really want to get that plane back in the ...SWEET LORD OF THE DANCE!! LOOK OUT!"

A dark, featureless sedan flew around the curve, edging slightly into their lane, nearly clipping the side view mirror as it passed. Philo estimated the speed of the sedan to be around seventy and he had just enough time to spot a little round orb jiggling like a Charlie Brown bobble-head in the rear window. "I think that there was the little fella in that car."

"You see? That's the problem with hitchhiking," said Langdon sagely, "you never know who's going to pick you up."

CHAPTER 38

Xochitl had pushed the escaped cattle from her thoughts. She lay face down on the blacktop, the warmth emanating from the dark surface slowly working its way like a sauna into the throbbing fabric of her body. Until now she had been able to push away the aching of her muscles and the stinging from open wounds. There hadn't really been time to clear her mind, to let the adrenalin dissipate and simply feel. But now in the soothing sunlight, pain. Dull throbbing pain that emanated from nowhere in particular and held her down like a playground bully. The warmth of the blacktop lulled her and she began to feel drowsy. Her eyelids fluttered uncontrollably, trying to close of their own volition. This is a highway, Xochitl, she thought, cars drive on it. You can't fall asleep here. Dull ache became true hammering pain as she made a pitiful attempt to sit up. "Okay, just a few more minutes," she said quietly as her head flopped back onto the pavement.

Gradually, she became aware of a persistent sound some distance away. It was not unlike the sound of Philo's airplane when she had first heard it buzzing through the air in Bakersfield. Except it was smoother, deeper, not as sharp. More of a hum. "Hmmm, interesting," she said as dream-like clouds touched her softly, inviting her into the warmth and comfort of slumber. The sound grew louder and Xochitl felt an infinitesimal dose of adrenalin enter her bloodstream. "Nooo," she groaned. "It's not fair." Her limbs instantly became more willing to move.

She rolled to the side of the road and was scrambling to her feet as a dark sedan roared around the curve. The cattle were not so quick. A screeching of brakes and billowing of smoke filled the peaceful air as the vehicle tried vainly to stop. A thunderous crash assaulted Xochitl's ears as two thousand pounds of metal plowed headlong into two thousand pounds of flesh and bone. The sedan came to an immediate halt, while the cattle, at least the largest parts of them, flew up and over the vehicle, landing with a sickening thump behind it. And then all was quiet again. Only the faint, bubbly hiss of a punctured radiator filled the air.

Xochitl looked on in horror. What had she done? No one was moving inside the vehicle. Were people dead in that car due to her carelessness? It was unlike Xochitl to be rooted to the spot. A thousand thoughts rioted in her head. Should she run to the car and try to help? Should she call someone? Call them on what? Should she put up some kind of warning to other cars coming down the road, or locate the rancher and accept responsibility for the dead cattle. All these thoughts and more paralyzed her.

A long, mournful moan reached Xochitl's ears and she turned to face the remaining cattle in the field. The low moan came again. "OOOOOOOOOOOUUUUGHHHHHHH." Surprisingly, the sound was coming from behind her, from the twisted wreckage of the car. She spun on her heels, staring trance-like at the steaming heap of metal. She rubbed her face nervously with the palms of her hands, her stomach knotted tighter as reality set in. There was no way out of this one. The wreck was going to have to be examined and the people inside given any aid she was capable of giving.

The stiffness that had settled into her body as she lay in the road had not dissipated and her gait was stilted as she walked tentatively toward the car. The moan filled the air once more and Xochitl could tell now that it was coming from the back seat. The button on the handle was broken but she yanked on the door anyway. Nothing. Running as best she could into the field, she located a good-sized tree branch and headed back toward the car. As she reached the edge of the blacktop the rear passenger door swung open and a squat little body toppled out onto the street. It staggered awkwardly to its feet.

"FID!" shouted Xochitl, running to his side. "Oh my God, Fid; are you all right?" Blood trickled from the Fiddler Crab's nose and he appeared a bit disoriented, but no bones protruded from his skin, no limbs faced the wrong way.

"Yeah, I'm okay," he croaked. "I got a feeling I'm gonna be real sore in the morning, though."

Xochitl wrapped her arms tightly around the Fiddler Crab's handcuffed body and hugged him until a pleasant, familiar warmth flooded through her, overriding her countless aches. "Oh Fid, I might have killed you with those cows," she said.

"On the contrary, I think you may have saved me. With any luck, though, those two guys in the front seat got what they deserved," said the Fiddler Crab, his mouth pressed against Xochitl's collarbone.

"Why? Who are they?"

"Banders and one of those government agents."

Xochitl let go of the Fiddler Crab and peered through the front passenger window. Doctor Robert Austin Banders was slumped forward against his seatbelt harness, chin on his chest. A slight rise and fall of his chest told Xochitl that he was not dead. "They must have gotten a good jolt," she said, "but they're alive. They could come around any time now."

"Yeah, weird. Shouldn't there be some kind of airbags or something?" asked the Fiddler Crab.

"Seems like it...Government cutbacks?"
As she spoke, the not-so-bright eyes of Doctor Robert Austin Banders struggled open. It was only for a moment, but long enough to seize Xochitl's gaze and flare in recognition.

"You," he hissed.

"We need to get the hell out of here, Fid," she said, her voice suddenly shaky. "I don't know how, but we need to get out of here now. Those guys may not stay unconscious for long. Banders is already starting to come around."

Xochitl sighed heavily and straightened her back. Making her way around the car, she threw the driver side door wide open. It scratched to a halt as the bottom of the door scraped on the pavement. Leaning into the wreck, she ran her hands over the driver's body, searching for a weapon. She wouldn't leave her opponent armed this time. It didn't take long. Reaching into Agent Cortez's coat, she pulled a pistol from beneath his left armpit. She studied it, and then turned it awkwardly toward the unconscious driver, holding it to the man's temple for what seemed like an eternity.

"What the hell are you doing?" shouted the Fiddler Crab.

"Just seeing what it feels like," she replied, staring down the barrel. Hands shaking, breath coming in spastic wheezes, she focused every ounce of her will on her trigger finger, imagining what it would feel like to pull the trigger on the man who had caused her so much pain and anguish.

The Fiddler Crab stared at her, motionless and silent.

She shut her eyes tightly. If only I could squeeze this trigger, she thought, imagining the jerk of the man's head and the splatter of blood on the broken window. God, wouldn't that be something?

The Fiddler Crab tensed visibly as a few seconds stretched into what felt like hours. "Xochitl, don't...*please* don't," he said, his good arm outstretched, the palm facing her. "I want to be on the side of the good guys."

Xochitl sighed and lowered the gun. "I could never do something like that, Fid. It's just not in me. I can see that now. It's different if they can't fight back." She lowered the pistol. "Come on. We can't stay here anymore."

Relieved, the Fiddler Crab deflated to his normal slovenly posture. Turning his back, he jiggled his handcuffed wrists at Xochitl. "Keys," he said. "I can walk okay. How you feeling? Can you walk?"

"I guess. Depends on how far, I'm not sure exactly where we

are. I never use this road. I know it goes to Soda River, but I'm not sure how far it is. I always go down the Southern Pass. It's quicker," she said. Returning to the battered sedan, she rifled through Agent Cortez's pockets, eventually locating his key ring.

"Well, I've never even been in this area, so that puts you a step ahead of me," said the Fiddler Crab. "You're right, though, we need to get out of here before the cops come."

"Okay, let's get hobbling and see what we've got left in us," Xochitl chuckled, releasing the Fiddler Crab's bound wrists.

They began to trudge down the rural highway, Xochitl with her barefooted limp, the Fiddler Crab, arm around her waist, supporting her as best his broken body would allow.

CHAPTER 39

"You've reached Justin Montrose, photoman extra-ordinaire. I'm not available to answer the phone right now, so leave a message and if you're lucky I'll call you back ....BEEEEP." Xochitl had informed Philo of the cell phone Trundell was borrowing in order to achieve a secure line.

"Hi, This is a message for Mr. Trundell. Mr. Trundell, you don't know me, my name's Schank, Philo Schank. I'm a pilot, a crop duster. I got a message from your friend Xochitl. Wonderful girl. She says what you're looking for is in her laundry hamper. There's some bloody pants in there and it's in the pocket. Uh - thanks."

Philo replaced the receiver into the cradle of the pay phone and walked into a small hardware store searching for something to patch his tire.

CHAPTER 40

Half an hour of determined trudging and many of the kinks had worked themselves from the joints of the weary travelers. They were almost able to walk normally. Stopping briefly at a shallow stream that trickled alongside the road, the Fiddler Crab scrubbed blotches of dried blood from his face and neck. An occasional car speeding down the road toward them caused the two fugitives to scramble into the nearby bushes to avoid being seen and associated with the wreck farther down the road.

Eventually the pair heard the mournful wail of a siren far off in the distance. It came from the direction of the accident. The ambulance would stop at the wreck. The paramedics would throw Banders and Cortez in the rear and scurry back the way they had come. Explaining the unattended airplane and the gaping hole in the fence would be another matter, something Xochitl was sure would interest the police. "Man, I hope Philo got his plane fixed before the police arrived," she said. "That would just make life so much easier for everyone.

CHAPTER 41

Philo Schank did, in fact, arrive at his crop duster before the authorities. A well dressed, portly woman, who's double chin spilled in ample waves from a yellowed foam neck brace, had offered him a ride from Willow. The ride was uneventful, other than the woman alternately offering him salvation and damning him to Hell.

"Yes Ma'am," Philo repeated countless times in reply to "Can I get a witness? Can I get an amen?" Philo paid for his ride by checking the woman's side-view mirrors for her, as she was unable to turn her head. They traveled at a moderate clip, something that annoyed Philo greatly. He wanted to get himself back into the sky and get this job finished. If they succeeded, he would be a hero. He knew that without question. And life didn't get much better than that. Explaining this to the woman driving the car, hoping to coax a little speed out of her, had not gone good at all. Indeed, it only initiated a new lecture on the perils of drinking and driving. The woman was set in her ways and preferred to glide along at a disturbingly safe pace, preaching the gospel and asking if there were anyone directly behind them.

"OH MY SWEET BABY CHEEZE-ITS!" shouted Philo as they rounded a bend, bringing them in clear view of the wrecked sedan and the butchered cattle. "What the blazes happened here?" He sprung from the woman's car before it stopped and hit the pavement running, glancing frantically in every direction for some sign of Xochitl. He ran to the car and looked inside. Shaking his head, he sprinted back to the woman's car.

"You got a cellular telephone, ma'am?" he asked.

"No sir. Them things'll swell your brain right up," she said. "I seen it on TV. I like my house phone just fine. Can I get an amen?"

"You mind heading back to Willow and telling the authorities there's a wreck out here."

"I can't say I don't mind at all," she said, "but it seems like the only right thing to do."

"It's what the Good Lord would do," Philo said.

"Amen," the woman said.

"And tell them they're gonna need an ambulance. This don't look so good."

The woman turned the big car about and glided off in the direction she had come at a pace no quicker than that of her arrival.

Philo opened the driver side door of the ruined sedan and felt the driver's neck searching for a pulse. It was there, slow and faint, but it was there. The man was bleeding slowly but steadily from several wounds, mostly in the area of his chest, where the steering column had punctured him. Philo had a small bundle of clean shop rags in his plane. They would be good for applying pressure to the wounds. He made a dash across the field to the airplane to retrieve the rags, calling Xochitl's name. He threw open the passenger door "Xoch..."

The pistol looked a mile long as Philo stared down its barrel into the bright blue eyes of Doctor Robert Austin Banders.

"You the owner of this thing?" Banders growled.

"Uh... yeah. Why?"

"Get in," said Banders. "Get us out of here."

Philo stood silent for some time considering his seemingly options, which right now seemed extremely limited. "Can't," he said cautiously. "Not right now anyway. We got a flat tire. Plane won't take off with a flat tire."

Banders had noticed the flat when he'd fled from the ruined

car to the airplane. "Fix it," he said.

"It'll take a little while."

"How long?"

"Maybe fifteen minutes if I hurry."

"You have seven."

"Look mister, I don't think that's even possible."

"Six and a half."

Philo leaned into the cockpit and reached under the seat for a tool kit. He scrambled to the landing gear and began frantically removing the wheel. In truth it took him about twenty minutes to repair the tire, but Banders was more interested in getting the plane into the air than causing Philo any real harm. A few forcefully barked orders accompanied by angry waves of the pistol were sufficient to light a fire under the simple pilot. Once he had completed the repair, Philo flew open the hood and banged on the fuel pump a few times with a wrench. Oh man, I hope that does it, he thought. The engine roared to life and they taxied out of the field, back onto the highway. Philo drove the plane along the blacktop in the opposite direction he had landed in order to avoid the dead cattle and smashed automobile, and there was that long stretch of straight road, back a ways, that he had used as a landing strip.

"That your buddy back there in the car?" Philo asked.

"Just a business associate," Banders replied flatly.

"He's still alive you know."

"Good for him."

"Jeez, man, don't you even care? He's banged up pretty good."

"It's a risky business."

Philo stared at the man mutely, then swallowed hard and turned back toward the windshield. He gunned the throttle as the long straightaway came into view. Once they were safely airborne, he turned his attention back to Banders. "Who are you?" he asked. "You look kinda familiar."

"No one you need be concerned with." Banders was growing irritated with the pilot, angry at his insistence on asking questions while Banders clearly had the jump on him. The man was afraid, Banders realized, but not terrified. It would be much easier if he were terrified. Five million dollars hung in the balance and right now, like it or not, this yokel flying the plane was an integral part of the plan. In a way it was fortunate that Cortez was too injured to carry on. There would be no argument over who went on to Soda River with the pilot. Cortez's absence left Banders in charge. He was free to handle the situation any way he saw fit as long as he produced the formula in the end.

"Where we going?" Philo asked calmly.

"You remember the young lady, Xochitl Saint James, whose name you were calling as you opened the door to the cockpit? We're going to her house in Soda River," said Banders. "The same place you've been going all along. That should be simple, eh? Even for you."

"You're one of them fellas she was talking about, ain't ya?"

"Just get us to the girl's house."

"I don't rightly know where that is," said Philo "See, she was gonna point it out to me when we got there."

"Just get me to Soda River. I've got the address in my head. I'll take it from there."

They flew on with only the droning of the engine to break the silence. Eventually Philo turned to Banders and a light of recognition flickered in his eyes. "I know where I seen you before," he said. "The Monster of Boggy Lake. I seen it just the other night. I couldn't sleep so I got up and turned on the..."

"Shut up and fly the plane." Banders was clearly angered by this. All his high profile work in dream realization through the years, his legendary goal-achieving seminars, all the television programs and magazine covers he'd appeared on and this buffoon could recall nothing more than The Monster of Boggy Lake. It was maddening.

"Course you was a lot younger then."

"Shut up!"

Philo was certain that Banders wouldn't shoot him while

they were in the air. It would be suicide. Once they were on the ground it would be a different story. He would have to be careful. But for now, fuel pump aside, he felt relatively safe.

CHAPTER 42

"Gimme here. Let me have a look through those binocs," said Coleman, engineer for the Far Western Railroad. In all the years that second engineer Sparky Dewhurst had worked with him no one had ever called him anything but Coleman. No first name, or perhaps that was his first name.

"I'm not done with them yet," Sparky said over the rumble and clatter of the moving train. "I gotta get used to these things. Come two weeks from now I'll be starting my retirement at the Florida seaside and I gotta know how to use 'em if I'm gonna take full advantage of the scenery." An exaggerated wink at Coleman, "If you know what I mean."

"Aw jeez Sparky, that 'scenery' will bring your floppin' old heart to a standstill. You'd be better off going down there blind. Now give 'em here."

Sparky reluctantly surrendered a brand-new pair of black, rubberized and waterproof binoculars to Coleman. "Man my age, can't do nothing but look anyway, so I want to make sure the view is good."

"Probably get your face slapped," said Coleman, pointing the binoculars through the windshield. "Good thing you don't have one of those digital cameras. I'd be bailing you out of jail." Suddenly Coleman went rigid. "Holy Cow, Sparky! Stop the train."

"What?" said Sparky, but he was already decreasing their speed.

"Stop it! There's cattle up ahead - all over the tracks." Coleman pressed the binoculars up against the glass, straining for a better look.

"Cattle? What are they, crossing over the tracks?"

"No. They're just kinda mulling around."

Sparky brought the train to a complete stop and Coleman leapt to the ground. He ran toward the small herd of cattle mulling about on the tracks fifty yards ahead. "Shoo!" he hollered waving his arms about wildly as Sparky blew the horn. The cattle, spooked by the sudden commotion, began to scatter on either side of the tracks as Coleman approached. Sparky began to move the train slowly forward, allowing Coleman to climb in while it was in motion.

"We better keep the pace down for a few miles," said Coleman. "Who knows where those things came from? Might be more up ahead." The cattle watched quizzically as the huge metal beast inched passed them, slowly disappearing around the bend.

CHAPTER 43

"We can't just walk all the way there," said the Fiddler Crab. "I can't do it, and I'm in a hell of a lot better shape than you are, and I've just been through a car wreck."

"Well we've got to do something," said Xochitl. "These guys are not just going to let it slide. The only encouragement I've felt so far is that Banders and good ol' Agent Cortez were trying to get to Soda River so quickly. I don't think they'd be in such a hurry if they were able to phone ahead and arrange for another agent to search my house." The thought of one of these strange men searching through her things gave Xochitl the creeps and she closed her eyes for a moment, balling her fists. "There may not be anyone waiting for us if we can get there in time. I'm pretty sure that they haven't called anyone since the accident. They were both pretty out of it. Besides, I think only the government man would even know who to call and between the two of them, he was definitely in the worse shape. Banders is just along for the ride. He's only in it for the money."

Eventually they stumbled onto a railroad crossing. There was a small silver structure off to one side containing the electronics for the crossing gate and flashing lights. "You mind if we sit in the shade for a few minutes, Xochitl?" asked the Fiddler Crab. "I'm pretty beat."

"Couple minutes. That's all," she replied. "I don't want our muscles to get too comfortable. We'll never get up again."

There were groans and the creaking and popping of stiff

joints as they sat down clumsily on the concrete platform. Neither of them spoke. Moments later, Xochitl tried to muster the energy to suggest they continue their journey when the tracks near her feet began to rumble and creak faintly. Instinctively she rolled around to the far side of the small building, out of view. A loud bell began to clang and the barricade arm descended jerkily across the road. The Fiddler Crab scrambled after Xochitl, plopping himself down beside her and peering over her shoulder. "What is it?" he said.

"Train," said Xochitl.

"We have to hide from the train?"

"I don't know who we have to hide from, Fid. I just think it's a good idea for us to stay out of everybody's way for a while, at least until we get where we're going."

"You're the boss," he said, burying his face in his folded arms.

Xochitl couldn't believe their luck. The train was traveling at a snail's pace, only slightly quicker than the average walk. Once the engine crawled by, Xochitl peered around the corner and saw a near endless stream of boxcars and flatbeds. She let the engine disappear around a bend, and then grabbed the Fiddler Crab by his good wrist, jerking him to his feet. "This is a gift from the gods."

Summoning all her strength, she launched herself into the first boxcar that rolled by them with an open door. Immediately she turned and popped her head out the door. "Give me your arm. Fid." The Fiddler Crab was trotting slowly alongside the boxcar. Xochitl wrapped her hand firmly around his wrist and summoned all her strength as she hoisted his flailing body through the door onto a splintered wooden floor.

The pair lay on their backs, exhausted, staring at the rusted, metal ceiling and feeling the bumps and rattles of the train, knowing that, for a little while at least, nothing would be required of them but to lie on the floor and try to relax.

The clacking of the wheels on the track became more frequent as the train gathered speed. Xochitl found the vibration comforting and her eyelids grew heavy.

"So, this train stops in Soda River?" asked the Fiddler Crab. "You're sure of that?"

"Well no, not exactly," she replied, snapping awake. "It's headed in the right direction, though, and there are railroad tracks passing through the town. It's a guess, but it's an educated guess."

"Oh man! What if it doesn't stop? What if we just whip right on through the town and out the other side? What then?"

"Don't get all uppity, Fid. I've noticed that trains tend to slow down when they go through town – I guess, you know, kids playing on the tracks and stuff. Maybe it's even a law or something. We can just jump off. I mean I don't think it'll be going quite as slow as it was when we got on, but way slower than it is right now."

"That's not very comforting," said the Fiddler Crab.

"Well it'll have to do," said Xochitl. "Jumping off a slow train is nothing compared to what we've been through up until now, anyway."

"I realize that. I was just hoping we were pretty much done with the whole cuts and bruises thing. I was hoping all we'd have to do was get the formula out of your house and take it somewhere safe."

"That's it in a nutshell, but how often do things stay in their nutshell?"

The Fiddler Crab rolled over and stared out the door at the moving landscape.

CHAPTER 44

"**Put** us down right there," said Banders, jabbing his finger at the windshield, "right there in that little clearing just outside of town. The one next to the river."

"I don't think that stretch is quite long enough," said Philo. "We do need some distance for the plane to slow down, you know. These things don't just stop on a dime. And we still got half a tank of poison in the back. Believe me, we don't want that stuff soakin' in all over us if we go for a tumble."

"Don't argue with me," said Banders, raising the gun. "I said put it down in that clearing, and that's exactly what you'll do. You understand?"

"Yes sir," said Philo mumbling a prayer as he pushed the stick forward. He carefully brought the plane down onto the highway just before the clearing, hoping to give himself a little more runway space. The wheels chirped loudly as they struck the asphalt, but Philo's tire repair job held and soon they were rolling down the road, approaching the clearing. Philo was immediately aware that the speed of the tiny aircraft was much too great to allow them to stop in time. He rolled into the clearing, applying the brakes as vigorously as he dare, but it wasn't enough. The little yellow crop duster overshot the clearing and, once again, tore headlong through a barbed wire fence. The tires were spared this time, but the wire from the fence whipped its way spastically around the left wing, then wrapped around itself forming a metal noose. A loud CRUUUNNNK sound of tearing metal flooded the cockpit as the plane, still traveling at a substantial speed, jerked quickly to the left. Philo watched as the wire tore the left wing from the fuselage. The plane rolled onto its right side, bending the right wing upward and finally snapping it off as well. Wingless, the fuselage tumbled a few more times before coming to a halt on the banks of the Soda River.

Banders wrapped his fingers around the windshield strut and pulled himself toward the shattered window. He was afraid to pull too quickly or apply too much pressure in case he had broken some bones or even, god forbid, severed his spinal cord. Slowly, he wormed his way through the windshield and tumbled from the wreckage onto the dirt. He sniffed the air, but found no smell of poisonous chemicals. Glancing back into the cockpit he saw Philo sitting limply, unconscious or dead, it didn't really matter. He'd outlived his usefulness anyway.

Banders stood up and checked himself briefly. He felt shaken, but, miraculously, not badly damaged. Giving himself a good hand-slap dusting, he strode with complete, unshaken confidence in the direction of the town. Apparently this was his lucky day.

CHAPTER 45

Xochitl found herself viewing Soda River from an unfamiliar perspective as the train lumbered through industrial districts and the backsides of housing tracts. Their speed had markedly decreased since entering into the city limits of Soda River, but they were still traveling about twice the speed of a hearty sprint. If they jumped at this velocity they would surely plant their faces into the rough gravel that ran alongside the tracks regardless how fast their legs were moving.

"I don't know, Fid, I don't think this thing's gonna get much slower. This might be all we get."

"We'll kill ourselves at this speed," he said. "What if we roll under the train?"

"That's a possibility. I was thinking, though, if we jump as far outward as we can, try to clear the gravel and land in the dirt and scrub brush, maybe we'll minimize the damage to ourselves. Not that that's saying much. We're pretty much damaged goods already, but it's all we have. What do you say? I'm willing to give it a try."

Xochitl moved to the door of the swaying boxcar and tried to assess the amount of thrust she would need to clear the gravel. "I'm just gonna back up to the far wall and do a running jump out the door. That's probably about the best I'm gonna be able to do. You don't have to follow me, Fid. Why don't you get off at the next stop and make your way back to my house."

"I'm not doing that! Don't patronize me. I didn't come all

this way to miss the action. I can't wait to stick it to Banders and these horrible government boys. I've got so many friends back at Pinky's that have gotten arrested for drunk driving. I'm not defending their actions, but this is a chance to make all that go away. If we succeed here, no one will ever again be faced with the decision of driving home drunk while they're too inebriated to even make the decision. It's a no-brainer to take the pill if it's available." The Fiddler Crab stood somberly for a moment, having said all he wanted to say. Then, quietly, he mumbled, "Besides, I have no idea where your house is."

"I honestly don't think there'll be any action, Fid. Banders and Cortez were pretty banged up when we left them."

"I'm going with you."

"It's not going to do us any good if one or both of us gets hurt. It's only going to slow us down."

"If both of us jump and one of us gets hurt the other can still retrieve the formula. I know you're no math whiz, but surly even you can see the numbers are better this way."

The boxcar began to produce a loud rumbling noise up through the wheels and through the ragged wooden floor and into the metal walls. As Xochitl glanced outside the clattering metal door, her concerned grimace transformed itself into a broad grin. She grabbed the Fiddler Crab by the arm and dragged him toward the rear wall of the boxcar. "On three run as fast as you can and jump when you get to the door," she shouted over the loud clatter.

"What is it?" asked the Fiddler Crab, scuffing his feet and preparing to run for his life.

"The river, Fid. It's the river," she said, absently patting Cortez's gun stuffed into her pants, hoping it would still fire once it got wet. "Ready? One....two....Three!" And they were gone.

CHAPTER 46

The shadows grew long in Soda River as the sun traveled away from the Sierra Nevada Mountains, across the San Joaquin Valley to the sea. In the town's one park, Xochitl's neighbor, Mr. Lazlo was sharing a late afternoon stroll with his constant companion, a nervous, fidgety little lap dog called Marlon. The scene had been tranquil until moments ago when Marlon began to bark incessantly in the direction of a large oleander bush. "Stop that yappin', Marlon. I'm sick of it. By gosh, yuh yap at everything in sight. Even when *nothing's* in sight, yer still yappin'. I'm sick of it, understand?"

Marlon paid no heed and continued to bark at the bush until, suddenly the branches parted and a man in a torn and dusty suit stumbled into view. There were traces of blood on the man's cuffs and collar and five tiny holes in his cheek. He was tall, in his sixties with a virile shock of wavy gray hair. When he spoke his voice was deep and purposeful. The voice of authority.

"Hello, I'm looking for Weldon Street," he said pleasantly, apparently unaware of his appearance. "I wonder if you'd be kind enough to direct me there."

Mr. Lazlo gaped in silence for a moment, then spoke in a guarded voice. "Well now, you go to the end of the park, in that direction there, and it's two blocks further down." He pointed with one hand and restrained Marlon with the other. "Where abouts you going?"

"Oh I have a friend who lives there. I'm going to drop in on her. It's kind of a surprise. We haven't seen each other for some time."

"It's not Xochitl is it?" said Mr. Lazlo, examining the man's torn clothes and abrasions. "Xochitl Saint James?"

A well-practiced edge crept into Bander's voice. "Well I hardly see how that's anyone's business but mine, sir."

Mr. Lazlo gazed unblinking into Bander's fierce, electric eyes. What was going on at that girl's house? Only a week ago he'd found her in this very same park in pretty much the same condition as the man standing before him. Come to think of it, he hadn't seen her since then. Was she all right? This man, despite his attempt at evasion and his intimidating body language, was obviously going to her house. The strength of his denial had made that clear. You don't accomplish ninety-four years of living without picking up a few things and Mr. Lazlo had bells and buzzers going off all over his insides. But what to do...

"I'll be on my way, sir," said Banders, returning to a softer, more cordial tone. "Thank you for your assistance." He strode off confidently in the direction of Weldon Street.

CHAPTER 47

He couldn't swim! It hadn't occurred to the Fiddler Crab until he plunged into the icy cold water of the Soda River that he couldn't swim. It had all happened so fast. In truth, he wasn't sure whether he could swim or not, having never before been in water deep enough to try. Even though he'd grown up not far from the ocean, the thought of wearing a bathing suit, had always prevented him from taking lessons. But now, engulfed in near freezing liquid, he began flailing his arms and legs wildly, struggling to reach the faltering light he could only assume was the surface. His head burst from the frigid liquid into the open air and he gasped spasmodically. Desperation began to seize him as cold water crept toward his mouth and he felt himself sinking once again. All his splashing and kicking seemed to have little effect and he gradually descended deeper into the icy chill. True terror set in. His thoughts gave way to blind panic, and he flailed aimlessly until a strong tugging at his collar jerked him upwards and once again his head burst through the surface.

"Calm down," said Xochitl as he continued to flail. "Stop it! You're making it worse."

Ironically a passage from "ANYONE CAN" flashed through the forefront of the Fiddler Crab's mind. "Separate yourself from your fear. Fear is simply a chemical message from your animal brain to your body, not unlike pain, requesting a change of behavior. It is not necessary to honor this request.

Simply feel the fear and then say to your body 'Thank you for your message. I appreciate your concern for my welfare, but I respectfully choose another path.' And then do what you wish."

Fear was a bit of an understatement for what the Fiddler Crab was experiencing. It had been full-throttled, blind panic until he felt Xochitl's grip and heard the familiar sound of her voice. Now, with a lungful of sweet, fresh air, recalling Bander's written words, he did his best to remove himself from his panic. It immediately threatened to boil up and pop the lid he had forced on it, but he was able to keep it squelched long enough to regain some measure of control

He went limp and Xochitl gripped harder to prevent him from sinking. "I said calm down, not drop dead. I could use a little help here." She wrapped her arm around his neck and began to drag him toward the shore. "Kick," she said irritably. And he kicked.

Soon they lay panting on the shore. "I was pretty sure you couldn't swim," said Xochitl, "but it was either jump in the water or do a face plant in the gravel."

The Fiddler Crab struggled to his feet, shivering uncontrollably as each wispy breeze passed through his saturated clothing. "Come on," he said. "We're wasting time."

CHAPTER 48

Having spent most of his life in big cities, Banders was having a bit of trouble finding Xochitl's address. In the city things were more symmetrical, much more orderly. Addresses were placed on a door or a mailbox in front of the house. That's just the way it was. Here in Goobertown people did all sorts of 'creative' things with their addresses. There were numbers painted on wooden signs, bird feeders, old wheelbarrows, wine casks, just about anything they could find that wasn't a mailbox or a front door. "God help them if they ever need an ambulance," said Banders, poking his way through the failing light. He walked by Xochitl's house three times before he spied the address, which he'd missed because it actually was painted on the mailbox. He strode confidently down the narrow driveway into the shadows behind the house.

CHAPTER 49

As Xochitl and the Fiddler Crab entered the park, Mr. Lazlo was trotting out of the park behind his jittering little dog. He was on his way to call...who? Someone. He hadn't figured it out yet, but someone needed to be alerted about that suspicious looking man. The sight of Xochitl limping into the park alongside the Fiddler Crab paralyzed the old man. Marlon scampered behind him, releasing a Munchkin-like growl. What was going on at that house?

"Xochitl?" asked Mr. Lazlo.

"Oh hi Mr. Lazlo," answered Xochitl pleasantly. "How's it going?"

Eying the soaking pair, all blood, scabs and torn clothes, Mr. Lazlo was lost for words until Marlon produced a muffled bark. "My God, are you all right, young lady?"

"Fit as a fiddle," she said, forcing a crooked smile. "Why?"

"You look terrible, Xochitl, and I couldn't guess what's happened to this fella'," he said, giving the Fiddler Crab's withered arm a sidelong glance.

"We're fine, Mr. Lazlo. We've just had a big day."

Mr. Lazlo shoved his hands onto his hips. "Well, not ten minutes ago, in this very park, I met a man who looked as though he'd had a big day, too. He was looking for directions to Weldon Street. Friend of yours?"

Xochitl's heart sank. Someone had arrived before them. If

they were in anything close to the condition she was in, it had to be either Banders or Cortez. But how had they gotten here? It had to be with Philo's plane, which was good news. At least it wasn't a fresh, new agent, straight from the factory and ready to go. Whoever was waiting at her house was in as bad a shape as she was.

"Black hair or gray hair?" asked the Fiddler Crab.

"More silver," said Mr. Lazlo. "Sort of like a news guy on the TV."

"Banders." they said simultaneously.

"Banders?" asked the old man.

"Thanks, Mr. Lazlo. You've been a great help," said Xochitl as they trudged off through the faltering light toward Weldon Street.

"Wait! Xochitl! Should I call someone? Who should I call?"

"It's okay, we've got it handled, Mr. Lazlo." It wouldn't do any good anyway, she thought.

Marlon produced a single deliberate, cough-like bark at their departing silhouettes. Mr. Lazlo scratched his head quizzically. "What's going on in that house?"

CHAPTER 50

Through the years Banders had confined the lion's share of his illegal activities to the realm of confidence and blackmail. He had never been attracted to situations requiring physical dexterity or more than a reasonable amount of risk. Somehow those things seemed beneath him. Breaking and entering, the task that stood before him now, required physical dexterity and a considerable amount of risk.

Arriving at Xochitl's house, he skulked around to the back door and tried the knob. Of course it was locked. What was he thinking? She obviously lived alone or she would simply have phoned a roommate long ago and had them retrieve the formula. Even silly young girls don't leave for a week without locking their door. Especially silly young girls.

The darkness had become sufficient to shield Banders from any curious onlookers, and to bolster his confidence. He steeled his shoulder and thrust it heartily against the door. Unfortunately, houses in Soda River were not constructed as they were in Los Angeles. The door steadfastly refused to budge, even a little. Cursing under his breath, Banders rubbed his bruised shoulder and examined the house for another approach. He slunk through the shadows to the front of the house and examined the garage door. The latch was in place, but no lock was in evidence. Banders yanked firmly on the handle. The bottom of the wooden door bowed out slightly, but sprang back and retained its position the instant the pressure was off. "Garage door opener," he growled.

On the flight to Soda River, it had occurred to Banders that both Xochitl and the little freak were missing as he crawled from the wreckage of the government sedan. The two of them had to be headed to the house. There was no doubt about that. He had no idea how they were traveling, or how much of a head start they'd gotten and now, having failed to gain entrance to Xochitl's house, it was beginning to make him nervous. A sense of urgency flared in the faux fitness guru and he reached a decision to throw stealth to the winds.

Returning to the back yard, he searched for a blunt instrument, something that would shatter a window efficiently, removing most of the glass in one swipe. A weathered redwood picnic table lay in the middle of the patchy, unkempt lawn and Banders hefted one of the benches over his shoulder.

Making his way toward the nearest window large enough to crawl through, he launched the wooden missile, splintering the glass into a thousand glimmering stars. Tearing off his coat, he wrapped it firmly around his forearm and brushed away the loose bits of glass, snapping off the few dangerous-looking spikes that remained imbedded in the wooden window frame. He unwrapped the coat from his arm and, laying it across the window frame, shimmied inside. He landed awkwardly, mashing his face into the rug covering the floor in Xochitl's bedroom and receiving a few minor cuts from the broken glass.

Dazed, he rose to his feet and, out of habit, attempted to smooth the wrinkles from his soiled and torn clothes. "No point in that," he mumbled and began to search for the bathroom, switching on lights as he went. The hamper would most likely be in there, and besides, he had to pee.

He searched the room briefly as he stood before the toilet bowl relieving himself. No wicker baskets, no fishnet bags, nothing. Zipping his fly, he marched from the bathroom and mechanically searched the rest of the house. The girl was twenty-three for crying out loud. Hadn't she developed any organizational skills? The hamper could be anywhere. What if there was no hamper? What if she was one of those young people who left dirty clothes strewn all over the house, like his son? No, she had specifically mentioned a hamper to the little freak when they were locked in the walk-in freezer. Banders had no idea where Xochitl and the gimp were at this moment, but he knew they were on their way. He didn't have forever.

CHAPTER 51

Xochitl spied the lighted bedroom window from half a block away. "Looks like Banders got inside somehow, Fid. I didn't leave the light on when I left."

The Fiddler Crab sighed heavily. "I'm thankful it's Banders and not that federal agent. Banders doesn't have the training to confront us. The best he could do is try to lie his way out of the situation."

"Let's not get too cocky, Fid. He's almost certainly armed. He stands to gain a great big pile of tax-free American samolians if he pulls this off. He's not going to scurry out the back door as soon as we come in the front."

"He's not the only one that's armed. We have a little protection, too," said the Fiddler Crab defiantly.

"Neither of us has any real experience with guns, man, other than what we've learned in the last couple of days. I don't even know what kind of gun this is. I know it's a pistol. That's all I know."

"You know how to point it and pull the trigger."

"Do I? What about the safety? Where's the safety? ...Is there a safety? They always mention it in the movies. Isn't that something we should know about? And don't forget we just climbed out of a river. The damn thing might not even shoot."

The Fiddler Crab had no reply. Suddenly, their situation

seemed much less of a cakewalk. All the points he had used to bolster his confidence had just been shot down with a dysfunctional gun. Were bullets waterproof? Would they still fire after the gun had been submerged? It wasn't underwater long, but how long was long enough?

"It's not like we can just fire it out here in the street to test it. We've pretty much got to go on pure faith," said Xochitl.

"I hope you're better at bluffing than I am." The idea of having to bluff somebody was more terrifying to the Fiddler Crab than the possibility of a gun battle. At least in a gunfight with Banders they would all, hopefully, be somewhat evenly matched.

CHAPTER 52

Xochitl fumbled in her pocket for her house key, trying to be as quiet as possible. A familiar sense of homecoming overcame her for a moment, only to be eclipsed by a sense of outrage at having her sanctuary invaded. This was her house, after all. It was supposed to be her safe haven.

The Fiddler Crab held the gun that Xochitl had handed him moments before. He couldn't get used to the feel of the thing. Though he'd fired one only recently, it felt bulky and strange to him, much heavier than he had anticipated. People in the movies waved their guns around as though they were made of balsa wood, with no substance at all. But this thing was solid metal, and he had only one hand to hold it with. If he were forced to fire it, the thing would probably go flying from his grasp.

Xochitl turned the key as carefully as she could manage, every muscle tense in anticipation of a loud click or rattle. The lock slid open smoothly, producing no sound. Xochitl gave the knob a slow, but deliberate turn and the door bumped slightly as the bolt gave way. The pair froze, senses primed for any response from the other side. A moment later, Xochitl eased the door open. A widening sliver of light illuminated their two tentative faces. An inch, six inches, a foot, fourteen inches, CREEEEEEEAK. Xochitl yanked her hand away from the doorknob, but the damage was done. She slipped into the living room, the Fiddler Crab hobbling behind her, dragging the weighty firearm. Reaching behind the Fiddler Crab, she silently eased the door shut. No use leaving trail markers for Banders to follow.

CHAPTER 53

In the garage, Banders rummaged through boxes and bags, somewhat distracted. It occurred to him that perhaps Xochitl's house, a rental, had come equipped with its own washing machine and dryer, which would surely be located in the garage. Unfortunately, that wasn't the case, but, once he entered the garage, many other possibilities presented themselves. He examined any sort of container large enough to contain dirty laundry. It was a bust. Nothing but Christmas decorations, power tools and photography equipment.

Was that a noise? Was someone in the house? He was getting jumpy. He knew that. Still, he should investigate, just in case. He crept through the door that led from the garage into the kitchen and peered over the counter into the living room. Nothing. He must be hearing things.

The bedroom. He'd only given that room a casual glance as he'd stumbled through the window and rushed off to examine the rest of the house. Stupid! He'd search the bedroom. Of course it would be in the bedroom.

Two wide-eyed expressions whipped around simultaneously to face Banders as he tore open the door to Xochitl's closet. Xochitl's hands were buried elbow deep in her laundry hamper, a stained oak framework supporting a fishnet bag. Startled, both Banders and the Fiddler Crab fumbled with their weapons, struggling to remove them from their waistbands and get them pointed in the right direction. Banders completed the relay first and had his pistol aimed threateningly at the Fiddler Crab's pudgy head. Immediately, Xochitl determined that Banders was actually intending to shoot. Banders' eyes spoke volumes, the hate, the anger, the embarrassment and humiliation of being subdued in a public place by this silly little gimp who had God-knows-what against him. It was the gaze of imminent death, of sweet revenge, penetrating the Fiddler Crab's now terrified face like a laser. One pop and the record would be set straight.

A finely polished piece of stained oak wood entered Banders' field of vision just before it exploded into his face. Banders stumbled backward out of the closet. Legs colliding with Xochitl's bed, Banders fell backward, rolled once and disappeared into the small dark space between the bed and the wall. With neither word nor glance, the two fugitives sprang to their feet and sprinted from the room, Xochitl clutching the hamper under one arm as she ran.

The pistol weighed heavily in the Fiddler Crabs hand as he dashed down the hallway, but he was determined to retain his grip on it. Banders listened to the frightening pitty-pat of five million dollars scurrying out of his life as he lay, crumpled and disoriented, in the dark, cramped corner. "Failure is not an option," he growled, aware enough to recognize this as one of those crossroads moments he'd written so much about. Staggering to his feet, he lumbered into the hallway that led to the living room.

As the Fiddler Crab dashed toward the front door, his withered arm outstretched to grasp the knob, the heavy, wooden barrier burst open from the outside. The Fiddler Crab was swatted back into the room like a ping-pong ball, flipping end over end, coming to rest near the fireplace. The gun, wrenched from his grasp by the impact, went clattering across the hardwood floor.

A large black man with rolled-up sleeves and, oddly, pencils in his hair charged through the front door into the room brandishing a weapon of his own. Albert Trundell immediately determined who his target was in the scene before him. The bad guy was the man chasing his favorite little girl with a gun. Still lumbering into the room, he pointed the barrel of his pistol loosely in the vicinity of Banders and pulled the trigger. Xochitl dove behind the couch seeking cover, an ostrich maneuver at best. Banders saw the shot coming the second he entered the living room.

Dropping to his knees, he flopped backward and rolled back into the shadows of the hallway from which he had emerged. The bullet lodged itself harmlessly into the wall. Thrusting the barrel around the corner, Banders fired blindly into the living room, toward the door. A shout of surprise and pain resounded throughout the house that could only have escaped from someone with the lung capacity of Albert Trundell.

A fuzzy warmth filled Banders' veins as he pictured his five million dollars coming home to him. All was not lost. A few random shots rang out harmlessly, but Banders could tell by their sporadic nature that the man was badly hurt, firing wildly, hoping to frighten him. A minute ticked by with no additional shots being fired. Then a minute and a half. Two minutes, and Banders grew bolder. He lay on his belly and, poking the gun from around the corner, pumped a couple of additional shots into the living room. No response. Peering around the corner, he spied Trundell lying on his back on the doorstep. Ecstatic, he sprang to his feet and dashed into the living room toward the couch, having seen Xochitl dive behind it.

"Stand up, you little bitch!" Banders commanded, but only silence came from behind the couch. Banders wanted to avoid leaning over behind the couch and physically pulling Xochitl out. He would be too vulnerable and he had seen how tricky this girl could be. Raising the gun, he took aim at the couch.

"I have more than one score to settle with you, young lady," said Banders, lightly kicking the leg of the couch. "And settle them I will. You seem to believe you have the right to waltz into my town and steal my son away and pervert his thinking. Do you really believe you have the right to prevent me from obtaining what's rightfully mine?"

Xochitl remained silent behind the couch as he scratched his temple with the barrel of the pistol. "It is rightfully mine, you know. I've done my part, and at a terrible price. My son may never speak to me again. Hopefully some sort of, uh... finder's fee, will help the poor lad get back on track. He's been so lost in the last week. Perhaps I've been too lenient on him. But, unfortunately, there's only so much of me to give."

A subtle weariness had worked its way into Banders' voice. "It's very taxing trying to perform one's patriotic duty in this busy world. And regardless of what you may think, it *is* a patriotic act I'm performing here. It's not just a California problem, you know. Nearly every state in the Union receives a part of its income from traffic fines and that's a system that absolutely must remain in place. If the states were to go bankrupt, who do you suppose would have to bail them out? I'll give you a hint...You and me. The American taxpayer. We will once again be asked to shove our bloodied and calloused workingman's hands deep into our threadbare pockets and fish out whatever bit of small change remains. We've got a system that's working, maybe not perfectly, but it's working. We simply cannot allow some little do-gooder tart to bring all that down just because she 'doesn't think it's right'." My God! How selfish can you get?"

Xochitl, huddling behind the couch, bit her tongue. She would not give this pompous ass the pleasure of a reply. Not only would an argument put her on the defensive, but also the sound of her voice would allow Banders to pinpoint her exact location.

"Fortunately for me, that system has provided an opportunity to do my duty and make a small profit as well. It's win-win. The American way. I deserve that reward. I've worked hard for it. I've sacrificed for it. But, unfortunately for me, I can't claim the reward without the formula. Sadly, that's where you come in. You see, there's really no way I can let you go free. It wouldn't be responsible of me. This absolutely has to be a nice, neat story with no loose ends. You've already witnessed the power my current employers wield over the local authorities. There won't be an investigation, at least not a successful one. Now if you'll please just stand and hand me the formula, I'll see to it that you and your, uh....friend go quickly and painlessly. I can't guarantee what will happen if I have to shoot blindly through the couch." Banders' voice grew quiet and breathy, just above a whisper. "I'm not a bad man, really. I don't like this any more than you do. Please, come out and save yourself the pain."

Silence.

His finger tightened ever so gradually on the trigger. Banders steeled himself. "Last chance," he said, his voice regaining its hard edge. "I know it's a dreadful cliché', but I'll give you to the count of three. You're either standing or you're dead. The choice is yours."

"One...........Two.......................Three!"

A deafening explosion filled the small room. The gun went flying from Banders grip, leaving him with a perplexed expression and a large hole through his right hand.

"Holy shit, it actually fired," mumbled the Fiddler Crab incredulously, the retrieved pistol shaking in his hand.

Banders bolted for the front door, his wide blue eyes glued to the Fiddler Crab.

"Don't!" shouted the Fiddler Crab, firing again. But Banders was already through the entrance. As the Fiddler Crab launched himself toward the front door in pursuit, he heard a startled cry from outside. Rushing onto the porch, he spied Banders, in a fetal position on the walkway, cradling his now broken knee in his bleeding hand, after having tripped over Trundell's still form. Shuffling tentatively toward Banders' prone body, the Fiddler Crab, in a sudden burst of rage, bent over, and shoved the hard steel barrel of his pistol solidly against his lifelong enemy's ear.

A thousand painful and embarrassing incidents flooded into the Fiddler Crab's memory at once, clamoring for attention like needy children. How many of those incidents were a direct result of the lies Doctor Robert Austin Banders had preached to the world as gospel? Enough, he concluded. He shoved the gun harder against Banders' head.

"You know, Dr. Banders, you spoke a lot of truth back there," he said, his voice high-pitched, quavering. "I especially like the part about there being no investigation. God knows I'm no genius, but it doesn't take an Einstein to understand that this whole ugly affair is meant to stay below the surface. You're right. There'd be no conclusive investigation, even if *you* were the one who died. I can see it now," he said, waving his withered arm through the air. "Top Doc Commits Suicide." It'll be presented as anything but a government related murder. Surfacing! That's the key here. Getting this formula up above ground and into the light of day. Once the existence of the formula is common knowledge, the damage is undone. There's no more reason for anyone to kill anyone."

Banders had lost confidence. This little gimp could actually shoot him. He could hear it in his voice. A flash of terror shot through him. Chastising himself, he hardened it into a ball of anger.

"And that's exactly what we're going to do. Our one and only goal once we leave here is to get that formula, and the story of its suppression, into the public eye as quickly as possible." The Fiddler Crab stroked his chin with his withered hand. "And a very interesting story it'll be. As soon as it hits the public domain, your people will slip into denial mode. It'll be all about damage control, all about the cover-up. The less said, the better. If all the principles are named, it's not going to look good for them if we start turning up dead. In fact, it'll be in their best interest to make sure we're as happy and healthy as possible. All we really want is to make the formula public. That drug is too important to be suppressed and right now we're in a position to keep that from happening."

The Fiddler Crab's eyes narrowed and his finger grew taught on the trigger. "My God, I get so pissed off every time

I think of the expression that poor doctor must have had on his face when he tried that drug out and it actually worked. The lives he was going to save..." The Fiddler Crab spat onto the lawn. "Surely, by now you must understand how much this means to us. Look at how much we've been willing to go through in the last week. How could we not be serious? You know, it's a simple game, really. The object on the one hand is to destroy the formula, or on the other hand, to bring it into the public eye. Once either of those things is accomplished, the game is over. There are no more points to be scored on either side. And for once in my life I am holding the winning card. No thanks to you and your bogus philosophies, by the way. "

The Fiddler Crab's voice trailed off and Banders tensed visibly. "But, you know what?" asked the Fiddler Crab, suddenly breaking his own silence. He shoved the gun harder into Banders' ear. "I'm being a little dishonest here. As much as I believe in what Xochitl's doing, for me it's very much about destroying you, the man who destroyed me. When I think back at the false hopes you fed me...oh God, I lapped them up like Demerol pills. ANYONE CAN! What a crock of shit." He clenched Banders' chin in his withered hand, spinning the fallen guru's head around, forcing a face-to-face confrontation. "NOT JUST ANYONE CAN!" he shouted. Banders began furiously blinking the strings away. "I wanted so badly to believe it was possible to change, to be normal, just like everyone else. You led me to believe I could be. Right up until the moment I admitted to myself that I was twice the fool I had been. I'd been suckered, and that was the moment my life began to really fall apart."

"It's not my fault you're a fool," Banders growled, suddenly seizing the strings and glaring arrogantly at the Fiddler Crab. "You were obviously desperate to find something to believe in. If not my lie, you would have believed someone else's." Banders chuckled bitterly. "It's not like anyone held a gun to your head."

The words stung. Their truth striking him like a balled fist, cracking the Fiddler Crab's stony shell. He was momentarily taken aback. Then, as he quickly patched the cracks in his armor, a more intense anger rose in him, an overwhelming desire to simply put this thing to rest. He had dreamed of this moment most of his life. One simple twitch of the finger and all would be right with the world.

He began to apply pressure to the trigger, a feeling that was no longer new to him. Would it be any easier this time? "You won't talk yourself out of this one. If they sweep your body under the rug, so much the better," he said fiercely. A loud howl burst forth from the Fiddler Crab's lungs and he forced the gun further into Banders' ear.

Banders screamed in terror.

CHAPTER 54

"No, Fid! Enough violence." Xochitl knelt on the porch cradling Trundell's head in her lap. She applied pressure to a large red spot on his shoulder. "No more, man. We have the formula. It's like you said, as soon as the formula's made public, it's over. We can make his story public along with the formula. He'll never fool anyone else again after that."

The Fiddler Crab's howl morphed into maniacal laughter, slowly dying down to a conspicuous silence. "Not again. Not you, too," he said. "This is the moment I've been waiting for since high school. Are you gonna rob me of that, the chance to set things straight?"

"That won't set anything straight." She took a deep breath, pressed down hard on Trundell's wound. "You may have dreamed about blowing Banders away all your life, but all you've seen is the moment before you committed the act. How good it would feel. But that dream doesn't tell you how bad you would feel afterward, probably for the rest of your life. If you pull that trigger now you'd feel great for about one second. Forever after you'd ask yourself if you could have handled it better. And in this case the answer would be a resounding yes."

"I still want to do it," he said.

"Of course you do. But, my God Fid, you've hated that man so long you've lost perspective. What would you fill that space with if he was dead? I'll tell you what...regret. Vanquishing him has been a passion with you since high school, maybe the only passion you've had. You kill him, you're killing the driving force behind your own passion. Your whole life. Let's just stick to the program...publishing the truth, okay? His life will be as shattered as yours ever was, and nobody has to bleed."

"Here." Without waiting for an answer she tossed him a roll of duct tape that she had retrieved from the kitchen drawer to fasten the towel to Trundell's wound. It bounced off his chest and fell onto the concrete beside him. "Wrap this around his wrists and ankles."

Sighing, he Fiddler Crab laid the gun on the walkway and retrieved the roll of tape. As he wrapped Banders' limbs, Xochitl called the hospital directly and requested an ambulance for a gunshot victim.

"They said we were lucky," she said, hanging up the phone. "Their other ambulance and practically all the police in town are taking care of a plane crash that happened just outside the city limits. I don't like the sound of that, Fid. I hope it's not Philo. Anyway, it looks like it may be a while before they're able to get here."

As the Fiddler Crab roughly taped Banders' limbs together, he realized that he could no more have pulled the trigger than could Xochitl earlier, at the scene of the accident. He'd meant what he had said to Xoxhitl, he really did want to be on the side of the good guys. Pulling the trigger would have eaten him alive. This was the thing that had been bothering him after shooting the gunman in the van. The gnawing thing he couldn't pinpoint. Shooting the gunman had been something he had had to do. It was absolutely necessary, and still it tortured him. It was permanent. Shooting someone was permanent.

Banders struggled halfheartedly, squealing as the tape pressed against his shattered knee. Soon he lay still, realizing he was beaten. "I couldn't have shot him any more than you could," the Fiddler Crab said to Xochitl over his shoulder. "I know that now." With Banders bound, he felt secure enough to admit what was now going through his head. "You know, you get swept up in something like this and a whole new set of rules kicks in, but at some point you find your limits. Life gets a little cheaper when people are trying to kill you and you somehow feel like you have the right to do it back. You forget you're still living in a supposedly civilized society where two wrongs actually don't make a right. So I guess there was something good about this, after all. Banders actually did teach me something. He showed me where my limits are."

"You're a good man, Fid. I know that for a fact. I've seen your heart. And killing that amateur philosopher wouldn't have been a good thing to do. Most people crumble under way less weight than you've had to bear. But I think that shooting Banders would have been the thing that pushed you over that line. It would have made you weaker, not stronger."

"My God, and you call *me* an amateur philosopher," Banders spat in contempt.

The Fiddler Crab tore a final piece of tape from the roll and placed it over Banders' mouth. He tossed the roll back to Xochitl. "How is he?" he asked, staring at Trundell's outline on the dark porch. A siren began to wail in the distance.

"He's lost a lot of blood, but he's got a pulse," she said pressing hard on the wound. "God, I'm so thankful for that. This man has done so much for me."

Trundell groaned.

"Hang in there, baby," she said, stroking his hair, now absent of pencils. "The ambulance is on its way."

CHAPTER 55

Xochitl pointed a camera she had fished from a pile of photography equipment in the living room and clicked off a few shots as the paramedics loaded Trundell into a brightly lit ambulance. Perhaps it seemed a bit callous under the circumstances, but she knew he would be proud of her for documenting the incident. This was going to be a hell of a story in which he played a major part and the more explicit the photos, the better.

Xochitl and the Fiddler Crab went back into the living room to await the arrival of the police, snapping a few photos of the bound and gagged Banders, propped in a corner where they had dragged him. She retrieved the laundry hamper from behind the couch, having managed to stash it there during the scuffle. Rummaging through the fishnet bag, she yanked out a pair of bloodstained, black denim pants. Shoving her hands into the pockets, she emptied the contents onto the coffee table. Several scraps of paper, a handful of change and a ballpoint pen formed a small pile on the table. She pulled the pen from the pile. "Man, I'm glad I found this before it went into the washing machine."

"Concentrate, Xochitl," said the Fiddler Crab. "This is what we came for. We need to get this done in case there are any more guys like Banders or Cortez on the way."

She frowned, opening the scraps of paper one by one, examining them for something resembling a formula. One was merely a tiny gallery of doodles, primarily of nude women. The next was a list of pharmaceutical companies. The third contained nothing but a single website address.

"No formula," said Xochitl.

"I was kinda wondering about that all along," said the Fiddler Crab. "I'm no chemist, but it seems like something as complex as a drug formula would be too big to fit on a scrap of paper. But this has to be it. Either that or everyone's mistaken and the whole thing's been for nothing."

"No, Fid. These guys are very thorough. They knew what they were looking for. It's gotta be something to do with that web address. Let's check it out." Xochitl moved to a small desk in the corner of her living room and fired up her computer. She called up her web browser and typed in the address: http://www.sobertrol.net. A plain gray website with ordinary black text filled her browser's window.

"I guess the guy wasn't real big on style," remarked the Fiddler Crab.

"Apparently. Too much left brain. Hmmm... Looks like a sort of diary or manifesto or something. Plan for the world, political views, history of ecological disasters, genetic engineering. No formula, though. He was trying to start a bidding war over this formula. Why would he put it in a place where anybody could find it? That doesn't make sense. They could just steal it."

"Well, we can't seem to find it, so it must not be too obvious. Click on the photo gallery," said the Fiddler Crab. "If we know what kind of guy we're dealing with, maybe it'll give us a clue."

Xochitl clicked on a plain text link to the gallery page. The same type of dull plain page appeared in the browser, but this one was peppered with badly taken photographs above off-center captions. "Looks like Sporkin in paradise," she said. "Every photo is of him with a different pretty girl in what looks like a different nightclub."

"How does a guy with a nose like that get himself surrounded by super models?" asked the Fiddler Crab, dismayed. "I mean, that nose is almost as bad as my arm and I'm not surrounded by super models."

"Hey. What am I, chopped liver?"

"Oh no. Sorry, I didn't mean...I just meant..."

"He's probably got money," She said sarcastically. "They're probably just stupid money girls."

"Do I detect a smidgen of bitterness?"

"Don't get me started."

"Well, he must have had some kind of stash if he paid for all of his own research. That's not cheap." The Fiddler Crab examined the screen more closely. "Wish I had money."

"So what does this tell us?" asked Xochitl.

"That our man was a party boy?"

"Maybe he had an alcohol problem of his own."

"Possible."

Xochitl dragged the cursor across the screen to click on page two of the gallery.

"Wait. Go back," said the Fiddler Crab. "Do that again."

"What?"

"That one with the blonde, drag the mouse across it again."

Xochitl did as she was told. "I don't see anything."

"I thought the picture was a link. I could have sworn the cursor turned into that little pointing finger thing for a second there."

She swiped the cursor across the picture once more. "Nope, I don't see it."

"Here, let me try." The Fiddler Crab took the mouse and began to drag the cursor slowly back and forth across the photograph, in a grid pattern, from top to bottom. Suddenly, for a mere instant, as the cursor passed over a tiny martini glass that Sporkin held, it transformed into a small hand with a pointing finger. "There!" he exclaimed. "It's not the whole picture, just a little tiny link on that glass. Man, that was a bit of luck." He clicked the mouse button and a new page filled the screen. The page, filled with line after line of procedural instructions and chemical symbols, seemed to go on forever as he scrolled downward. "I think this is it, Xochitl."

"Yeah, it kinda looks that way." Xochitl pressed 'control A' on her keyboard, highlighting the entire page, then 'control C' to copy the contents. She opened her word processor program, pasted the contents into an empty document and saved it as theprize.doc. Pulling a blank CD from her desk drawer, she inserted it into the machine and saved the document to it. She grabbed the Fiddler Crab by the shoulder. "Come on, Fid."

"Where we going?"

"To Aware Magazine. I have an idea."

"What about Banders? The police should arrive any minute."

"I wouldn't bet on it." Xochitl hurried toward the door, then stopped and turned on her heels. She took a piece of paper from her printer and wrote on it with a marker pen. Retrieving the roll of duct tape from the front porch, she fastened the paper to Banders's chest. It was a sign reading: BREAKING AND ENTERING. Xochitl, using a tee shirt from her laundry hamper, carefully lifted Banders' gun from the floor and placed it next to him. Banders made a muffled sound and swore at her with his eyes as she lifted her camera and clicked off a few more shots before disappearing into the night.

The door was left unlocked as they departed on the off chance that the police actually would arrive this time.

CHAPTER 56

Arriving at the offices of Aware Magazine, the pair made their way immediately to the computer maintenance department. The overhead lights were dimmed and a low hum emanated from the perpetually running machinery, the sound of information and climate control hovering in the large room full of padded cubicles.

"Everyone must have gone home already," said the Fiddler Crab.

"Yeah," said Xochitl. "It's just after seven. I have a hunch, though. Follow me."

Navigating a sea of cubicles, they approached an office at the far end of the room. The sign on the office door read: 'Marcus Loam - System Administrator'. Xochitl lightly pressed her ear to the door and remained there for about thirty seconds. She looked at the Fiddler Crab and nodded. The Fiddler Crab stared back at her, confused. Placing her hand on the knob, she turned it gently, and then pushed the door open. A thin, nervous looking man in his early thirties with a haircut somewhere between Alfalfa and Hitler sat facing a computer screen, headphones covering his ears. From over his shoulder, Xochitl viewed the contents of the screen. The man was placing bets at an online casino. He jumped visibly as Xochitl tapped him on the shoulder.

"My God, Xochitl. You nearly scared me to death." He made a closer examination of Xochitl and the Fiddler Crab. "Holy

Shit! What happened to you?"

"Long story. I need a favor, Marcus."

His eyes narrowed "What is it?" he asked.

"I need you to send an email to all the customers on the subscribers email list."

"Are you kidding? I can't just send personal emails to the recipients on the subscribers list." He pushed himself away from the desk and spun his chair around. "That list has a very specific purpose. We can't compromise its integrity or nobody would open our emails. Besides, I'd get fired. It's not as though no one will find out. There're fifty thousand people on that list. Somebody's going to complain."

"Marcus, I promise you won't get in trouble."

"You don't know that. Hell, I'd be in enough trouble if any-one found out I was placing bets on a company computer. I wish I could just do it at home, but the wife's a software en-gineer and we share a computer. She'd kill me if she found out. And she *would* find out."

"Personal problem, Marcus. Besides, everyone knows you place bets on the company computer. How do you think I knew you were here? Look, I can promise you that you won't get in trouble. Mr. Trundell would be in total agreement with me on this."

"Well, I haven't heard from him." He picked up the phone and handed it to Xochitl. "Here, get him on the line."

"I can't. He's in the hospital. He's been shot."

"Shot?" Marcus rose from his chair, incredulous. "What are you talking about? I think I would have heard about that."

"It just happened. Like...half an hour ago." Xochitl filled Marcus in on the details, with the Fiddler Crab piping in occasionally.

"How is he?" asked Marcus, concerned.

"I don't know. The paramedic said Mr. Trundell was lucky they were able to get to my house so quickly. He said it wasn't going to be fatal, but wasn't sure how much damage was done."

"Man," said Marcus, "I would have been jumping up and

down if that had happened to most of the bosses I've worked for, but not Albert Trundell. He's easily the best boss I've ever had. More like a friend or a dad. God, now I'm bummed. Such a good man."

"You're talking about him like he's dead, Marcus. He's gonna pull through. He's a very strong man and we'll do everything we can to make his recovery as painless as possible."

"Yeah, sorry. It's just a shock."

"I know." Xochitl stood somberly behind Marcus for a moment, letting the mood settle. "All right, my friend, about that list."

"What do you want the email to say?"

She handed Marcus the CD. "This is a copy of the page that held the formula from Sporkin's website. Put that in there somewhere. Also include a link to the procedural page on the good Doctor's website just so everyone will know how to get there. Then a few lines asking them to copy the formula to their own hard drive and then email it to as many friends as possible. Explain that it's a story in the making and they can be a big part of it. Tell them that once thousands of copies of the formula are spread throughout the world, there will be no suppressing it. Tell them that this is an act of civil disobedience. I think most of our readers will rally behind that call."

Marcus sighed heavily, turned to face his desk and began typing the letter.

CHAPTER 57

Within moments, around the country and around the world, people of conscience, opened an email from their favorite publication, Aware Magazine:

Dear Reader,

Thank you for taking the cause of fairness and equality in both business and politics upon yourselves. In a world fueled by greed and soulless corporate policy this is often a thankless task.

Recently we have come into possession of information that is evidence of great wrongdoing toward the American people, indeed all peoples of the world, perpetrated by the current administration of the United States government. There is an attempt to withhold something that could save millions of lives in the future. The recently murdered Doctor Anthony Sporkin has created a drug which will neutralize alcohol in the blood, causing a sobering effect. An attempt is being made to withhold this drug in order to increase government revenues based on the fines incurred from drunk driving, drunk in public, etc. Below is a link to the late Dr. Sporkin's website: http://www.sobertrol.net/procedure.html

If you would like to help prevent the formula for the sobriety drug from disappearing out of the public domain, please copy and paste this page into a word processor document on your personal hard drive and save it for future reference. If you feel comfortable doing so, please pass it on to your friends and urge them to do the same. The more copies of the formula that end up in public hands, the more likely this formula will find a manufacturer and become available to the public. Thousands of people die each year from alcohol related accidents. This is a chance for all of us to band together and erase that statistic once and for all.

This is but a request for a voluntary act of civil disobedience and should only be done if you feel comfortable with it. A detailed account of the events leading up to this action will be forthcoming in the next issue of Aware Magazine. Thanks again for your attention to this issue. Attached you will find the contents of the procedural page from Dr. Sporkin's website.

Vote your conscience,
Xochitl Saint James.

"It's a little flowerier than I would have written it, but it gets the point across," said Xochitl staring at the screen.
"It's just the way I write," said Marcus.

"No, don't get me wrong...it's perfect....I just meant..." She took a deep breath, holding her hands out, palms down. "Thank you, Marcus. It really is perfect. Much better than I could have done. I guess it's just that I'm only now realizing that this is it, the reason we've been getting the crap kicked out of us for the last week." She tapped the palm of her hand against her forehead. "Man it feels like a year. And now it's done. Nothing can stop it now. It's not just that the formula is safe, we're safe, too." She turned and grasped the Fiddler Crab by the shoulders, shaking him violently. "At last, Fid, we're safe. No more running. No more hiding. No more dodging bullets. God, that feels good. There's no reason for anyone to hunt us down now. We won the game."

Having grown somewhat used to the sensation of adrenalin pumping through his veins twenty-four hours a day, the Fiddler Crab was only half relieved at having survived the adventure of his life all the way to its conclusion. "Wonderful," he said flatly. A large part of him was sorely disappointed that it was all over. He had been plagued with cuts and bruises, humiliation and insults, but at least it wasn't boring. In fact it was worth every ruptured capillary and ego bruise, but where could he go from here? Could he really satisfy himself simply sitting at a barstool in Pinky's Bar? He would have some great stories to tell at Pinky's, but what would happen once the stories grew aged and rusty, and creaked when he told them? Would he sit at his stool, eyes on the door, eager to pounce on any new patron willing to engage in a, by now, exaggerated tale describing the high point of his life?

The Fiddler Crab's sudden mood change was lost on Xochitl. She picked up the phone and dialed information. "Soda River General Hospital," she spoke into the receiver. "Thank you." Her fingers danced over the number pad. "Yes, I'm a friend of Albert Trundell. He was admitted a couple of hours ago. I wonder if you could give me an update on his condition. ....Uh huh....uh huh.....I see. And the plane crash, I think that might have been a friend of mine, too. Is the patient's name Philo Schank? I see, well can you tell me his condition? Okay, thank you." She hung up the phone, turned and faced the Fiddler Crab. "He's gonna be alright. But it's gonna take a little while. We can't visit him for three or four days. She wasn't allowed to tell me the name of the pilot, but he's alive, too. She wouldn't give me any details."

"Thank God," said the Fiddler Crab, rising from his corrosive funk. "Both of those guys are in there because they tried to help us." He took the receiver from Xochitl's hands and began dialing.

"Who are you calling, Fid?"

"Molly Hernandez."

CHAPTER 58

"Pick a number between one and ten," said Xochitl as they pulled into her driveway.

"What do you mean?" asked the Fiddler Crab.

"Just pick a number between one and ten,"

"Why?"

"To see who gets to use the shower first."

"That's not fair. You already know what the number is."

"I'll be honest."

"Yeah, sure. We're talking about our first shower in what, three days...four days...five days? Man, I don't even know," he said, sniffing his armpit. "And it's not like we haven't been sweating. I can't even tell you what was happening to me up on that cable behind the porn theater. I'm just glad I didn't pee my pants."

"I'm glad you didn't, too. Otherwise I'd be happy to let you use the shower first."

"Did I mention I peed my pants?"

"Nice try. Pick a number."

"Five."

"Sorry, seven. You get to watch Banders while I wash the remnants of this whole stinking ordeal off my tender young body."

"I'm sure I can find a way to entertain myself. Maybe I'll stick pins in him." The Fiddler Crab poked at the air with the fingers of his withered hand.

"Ha! It's not like he wouldn't deserve it."

Xochitl stopped the 4runner and pulled the keys from the ignition. She fumbled for her house key, and then remembered she had left the house unlocked. "Ah shit!" she exclaimed as she entered her living room. A small pile of duct tape lay on the carpet, the edges cleanly cut as though with a sharp knife. The paper 'Breaking and Entering' sign was torn into small pieces and strewn about the room. "Someone got to him."

"Yeah, looks that way. It's not like them to leave a mess like this, though," said the Fiddler Crab, glancing around the room suspiciously. "We better give the house a once over."

"God! I thought we were done with this."

"We probably are, Xochitl. I'm pretty sure they just cut and ran. Anything else would be stupid."

They walked together through the house, inspecting the bedroom, closets, bathroom, every nook and cranny they could think of. In the kitchen, Xochitl eyed her counter with puzzlement. On the draining board lay an open loaf of bread and, turned on its side, a half empty box of sugar.

"I know I didn't leave that there," she said.

"Mmmm, takes all kinds. Maybe he's hypoglycemic or something," said the Fiddler Crab, running a finger through the spilled white powder. "Anyway, the house seems clean."

"Yeah. Okay, I'll be in the shower. Keep an eye on the place."

The Fiddler Crab returned to the living room and plopped himself onto the couch. The cushions felt luxurious and soon his lips were blubbering in a loud snore.

CHAPTER 59

The Fiddler Crab felt no embarrassment or self-consciousness as he gave Xochitl an extended one-armed hug
while his other arm dangled impotently at his side. "I'll never
forget this week," he said quietly, his voice trembling slightly.
The odor of diesel fuel and fast food mingled in the air.

"Me either," said Xochitl between muted sobs.

"Aw, I bet you do this kinda stuff all the time."

"I get myself into a scrape once in a while, but not like
this...And never with a companion this cool. Listen, you better
stay in touch, Fid," she said gripping him tighter. "I wouldn't
have made it through this thing without you. You saved my
life. Not to mention some of the stupid things you kept me
from doing."

"I think we're pretty much friends for life," he said, shaking his head. "I can't begin to tell you how my perspective's
changed. I was a whole different man just a week ago. Damn,
has it only been a week?"

"Yeah, this whole thing's given me some pretty solid slaps
in the face, too. I don't think I'll ever look at things quite the
same way again...especially government things."

"I was talking more about internal stuff."

"I know." She pulled him away and stared into his eyes
at arms length, "I'm just not very good at talking about that
kinda stuff." She gazed over his shoulder, focusing on a fast
food menu. "Let me just say you're a life-changer, Fid. After all

this, you deserve a nice quiet life at home…and at Pinky's Bar."

"I'm not sure I can settle for a nice quiet life now. I've developed a taste for adrenalin, more than a taste, really. More like a hunger. I like it. I don't know that I'm physically equipped for it, but I like it,"

"You're physically equipped just fine, Fid. Don't let that stop you from doing anything."

"Well, I'll have to do some serious thinking when I get home."

A mechanical voice filled the room drowning their conversation. "Now boarding for Fresno, Bakersfield, San Fernando and Los Angeles!"

"I guess that's me," said the Fiddler Crab releasing his grip on Xochitl's arm. "I like being with you. I don't want to leave."

Xochitl began to sob in earnest. Thrusting her arms around him, she gave him one more tight hug, then kissed his cheek. "You better go or we're just gonna keep doing this all day."

A tear sprouted in the corner of the Fiddler Crab's eye and wound its way slowly down the side of his face. He turned and trudged through the glass door toward the bus. On the bottom step of the bus he turned and offered a small, wide-eyed wave, then disappeared inside.

Xochitl watched as the bus drove out of the lot. She walked slowly to her car and got behind the wheel. Everything was fine for about a block, and then it all came out at once. Wracking sobs, loud moans and buckets of tears. Waves of pain as she missed him already. She pulled the red 4runner into an alley and placed her head on the steering wheel, letting the sobs come until she was cried out. "Alright, get it together. It's not like he died. He's just going back to LA. You can see him again sometime."

She exited the alley and drove down the busy street toward her house.

CHAPTER 60

"Christina Aguilera."

"Britney Spears."

"Christina Aguilera."

"Britney Spears."

"No way, man. Christina's way hotter. She knows how to move." Philo Schank gyrated wildly in his hospital bed.

"Oh, and Britney doesn't?" Ernie Blanchard waved his arm in the air, his I.V. tube wiggling like a startled snake.

"Sure, she moves okay, but not like Christina. Christina really means it when she moves. Britney's too staged."

"Staged? Staged? All right, well what about the Madonna kiss? You didn't see Christina involved in that, did you? And she was right there. What a lightweight."

"Obviously staged! What, do you think they just walked up to each other in front of a billion people and said, 'Hey this would be a great time for a girl-girl kiss. Let's just try it and see what happens'?"

"Will you two just can it?" Albert Trundell's thunderous voice engulfed the chorus of young male squeaks like a blanket. "We're supposed to be trying to recover. Besides, that's not music. Haven't you two ever heard of Etta James?"

"Etta who?" asked Ernie.

"Is she hot?" Philo piped in.

"My God, whatever happened to the music?" Trundell shook his head and turned the television from MTV to the jazz channel.

"Awww, Maaan," the two young patients droned in unison.

The three men had landed together in the same hospital room through a small circus of red tape and faulty logic. After conferring with Xochitl Saint James, the administration person had made the erroneous assumption that, since all three parties knew Xochitl and had been injured during the same adventure, they must be acquainted with each other as well, indeed, must be good friends. Since they were all suffering from internal injuries, it made good sense to put them together. It would be a positive thing for them to heal alongside their friends.

The first few days were lost in relative silence as the three men vegetated in their beds, quietly licking their wounds. But as their flesh began to knit itself back together, the men gathered strength, which first manifested itself as a propensity to fidget, then to mumble, followed by conversation, and finally, constant argument. During the past two days the three found innumerable subjects to disagree on. Sports was the first to go. Everything from football to professional wrestling. Then the best automobile ever, which led to airplanes, a subject Philo clearly aced, historical Playmates of the Month, the best looking nurse, which one of them was being given the most bad-ass drug, and most recently, pop divas.

"Nice to see my boys looking so good," said Xochitl, snapping pictures as she entered the room with Marissa. "How we all doing?"

The two younger men nodded and mumbled. Albert Trundell immediately gave Xochitl a probing look. "What's this I hear about an email, Saint James?"

"Oh yeah," Xochitl replied, hesitating. "I know I didn't have your authorization to use the subscription list, boss, but it was the only way I could think of to make sure the formula was so widely disbursed it could never be gathered up again and suppressed. I mean, I have an email list on my computer, but it only has about twenty names in it. I wanted to get it out to as many people as possible. And what better way to find sympathetic minds, than to sent it to Aware readers. I hope you're not mad, Mr. Trundell."

"I....I'm actually very impressed, young lady." Trundell thumbed a remote control and the head section of his bed rose with a hum. "That was a bit of quick thinking. You may have put the reputation of Aware magazine in a little bit of jeopardy, but the reward we all stand to gain is enormous. You succeeded in making the formula public, and gave Aware readers a chance to get involved, promising them an explanation in the next issue. I have a feeling that the next issue is going to be one of our biggest sellers. Brilliant instincts, Saint James."

Xochitl breathed an audible sigh of relief as Marissa patted her on the back. For the last four days she had been on pins and needles, worried about how Mr. Trundell would react to her unauthorized actions, wondering if she still had a job. Eating at her just as badly was the inability to visit her boys and find out how they were recovering. The doctor would not allow visitors until he felt they were strong enough to handle them. Apparently all her worries were in vain. It had turned out to be payday. Not only did she still have her job, but the boss was singing her praises.

It was a bit of good news that was welcome and sorely needed after the disappointment of returning to her house to find Banders gone. That night and the next, Xochitl and the Fiddler Crab had spent at Marissa's place. They told each other that the house was too cold with the broken window in Xochitl's bedroom and they should wait until it was repaired. It was fairly certain that Banders wouldn't attack them now. His reward was lost, so he had no reason. Except one, revenge, which was enough to keep them in hiding for a few more days. He had been spitting mad when she'd left him bound in the living room, but it would be a stupid move on his part to seek revenge now. And Doctor Robert Austin Banders was anything but stupid. It wouldn't serve him in the long run to do something impulsive that might get in the papers. It certainly wouldn't improve the big picture for him, and the big picture was something Robert Austin Banders always kept his eye on. A few days later, after retrieving Weezy from Trundell's house, they had confidently returned to Xochitl's, now safely repaired digs. Banders would eventually turn up somewhere, she knew. He couldn't stay out of the spotlight for long. She wondered how he would handle the publicity he received when the story appeared in Aware Magazine. He would probably find a way to turn it to his own advantage.

"The story, boss." Xochitl stared solidly into Trundell's eyes.

"Hmmm?" Trundell said, raising an eyebrow?

"Do you think Ernie could write it? After all, he was there."

Trundell was silent for a moment. "Well, he has done good work. I felt confident putting him on the Sporkin story, though I wouldn't have if I'd had any idea of the consequences. I'll tell you what. This is going to be a huge story for us, so how about this ... Blanchard, you co-author the story with one of our more experienced writers. You'll receive a byline along with the other writer, so you'll have full credit for your part. I think you've earned your stripes on this one."

"Damn! Thanks, boss. I won't let you down."

"How's your plane Philo?" asked Xochitl.

"It's pretty much done for. Wings are tore off. Landing gear's gone. It's just a big yellow tube with a broken propeller on the front now. The good news, though, is that she didn't spew bug spray all over the place."

"What're you gonna do?"

"Well, she's insured, so I guess I can walk away from it. Mr. Trundell, here, says it's time the magazine had its own small plane, and that someone would be needed to fly it. What do you think? You saw me in action. You think I could handle it?"

"Philo, you're amazing. You'll be perfect. I'm so stoked you'll be working with us."

"Where's the little fella?" Philo asked.

"Fid? I just put him on the bus this morning. He went back

to L.A. He's not really big on meeting new people. I think it made him nervous being in a town full of people he didn't know. He's got a bar down there, Pinky's, where he knows everyone. It's his home away from home. We promised to stay in touch, though."

"Damn," Trundell grumbled. "I wanted to thank him personally for taking care of my little girl."

"He did, too, boss. He saved my life on a couple of occasions."

"Mine too," Ernie added. "I would have bled to death long ago if it wasn't for that guy."

"I'll have to call him when I get out of here," said Trundell.

Xochitl chatted a while longer, then, pulling Marissa by the hand, exited the room, giving her boys a chance to rest. On the way home, after dropping Marissa off, her mind danced with a hundred clear images of life over the past week and a half. She felt lucky to be alive. True, a few times it had been her skill that had pulled her through, but most of the time it had been luck or someone else's actions that rescued her. Clearing her mind, she pulled into her driveway and lifted Weezy into her arms as he ran to greet her.

CHAPTER 61

"**Then** this guy smacks me on the head with a baseball bat as soon as I fly through the window. I didn't go down right away, though. I managed a couple of swift kicks to his balls before I went down. I gave as good as I got. He knew he'd come up against the Fiddler Crab." The Fiddler Crab's eyebrow cocked. He gazed intently at an assemblage of rapt listeners as he pounded the last tepid swig from his beer. He plopped the empty mug on the bar and another immediately took its place.

"Damn, Fid, I can't believe all that stuff happened to you in one week," exclaimed Tonsils, slurring only slightly. "My little Fiddy." She leaned in and kissed him on the cheek.

The Fiddler Crab flushed

"Tell us again about the car crash with the cow guts and everything," someone shouted from the back of the room.

There was no doubt in the Fiddler Crab's mind that he had arrived. He had become the hero of Pinky's bar. Those who had been friends were now devotees. But as the stories grew larger and more diffuse with each telling he felt less and less loyalty to the facts. Gradually, he began to consider his accomplishment a somewhat hollow victory. After the first few tellings reality no longer got in his way and he found himself, like a drug addict, escalating in order to achieve the expected reaction from his audience. The words tumbling from his mouth were a complete surprise to him as they bore a diminishing resemblance to the truth.

And thus the Fiddler Crab was faced with a choice. Should he let his adventure with Xochitl, which had clearly been the most exciting thing ever to happen to him, remain the pinnacle of his existence? How could he top that? How could he forge new heights on his own? His friends, with the exception of Pinky himself, had all distanced themselves as they placed him on a pedestal, and quite frankly, it was getting lonely up there.

Then there was the issue of the truth itself. Didn't he owe it some sort of allegiance? After all, it hadn't been simply a random adventure for adventure's sake. Some very important things had been accomplished at the expense of cuts and bruises, both physical and emotional. Real people had been badly hurt and some even killed to bring about these changes. He felt cheap, like a television network, diving ever deeper to achieve new popular heights. But popularity was a sudden, unexpected addiction, and so for now, he expounded and expanded, keeping only a wandering eye on the truth.

One night as he sat on the edge of his bed, the Fiddler Crab considered his options. As he saw it, there were three. One: he could go out in search of adventure, once again placing his life on the line for the sake of applause. As great as his adventure with Xochitl felt in retrospect, this option did not appeal to the Fiddler Crab's basic nature. Truth be known, he was a mole of a man and quite comfortable with it.

Option two involved stretching the truth until it snapped. There would come a day, he knew, when his audience would know the stories better than he did, and his credibility would come crashing down around his head. This option didn't appeal to him much either. At his current rate of exaggeration, that day was not far off.

Option three had a very warm and human appeal to it, though it involved a substantial life change as well. He would go the other way. He would humble himself in the eyes of his new-found followers and reestablish himself as an ordinary, everyday guy, thus winning them back as friends.

But how do I go about doing that? Get up on the bar and moon everyone? No, not humiliate, humble. Big difference. Not so distinguishable in my life so far, but maybe this is the time to draw that line. Okay, so who's the humblest person I know… The Fiddler Crab brought up the faces of Pinky's regular customers, examining them in his mind, one by one. Finally, his thoughts settled on the image of a well-dressed, middle-aged man sitting quietly in a torn naugahyde booth. *Mr. Carmichael. I don't even know his first name, but everyone respects him, no one doubts his word. Ever. He sits in that same booth in the back of the bar, doesn't say much, but when he does everybody listens. He's not concerned with whether we believe him or not because he knows he's speaking the truth. So how do I get from here to there?* He glanced at his feet, wiggled his toes. *Baby steps, baby steps. What makes him a humble man? Confidence in his point of view? A job? A job would give a man certain amount of freedom to make his own decisions. Mr. Carmichael seems to have a job that he goes to every day. You can tell it's not a high paying job, but he's not going hungry either. He's neat and well-dressed but not ostentatious. He does the best with what he has without trying to seem like something he's not. Obviously, he's not concerned with deriving any status from it.*

The Fiddler Crab brightened visibly.

He began to think out loud. "Maybe that's it. Should I get a job? I'll get a job!" He leaped to his feet and paced the room. "God, how scary is that? I've never worked for anyone in my life. How will I survive without my monthly check for my handicap?" He faced the mirror on the wall. "I could do a job if I had to. If I'm honest with myself, I have to admit that the check has been more for the state of mind caused by my arm than any actual inabilities caused by the deformity." He raised his good arm and pointed a finger at the mirror. "You've been more of a mental cripple than a physical one. You've been afraid of change your whole life." He sat back down on the bed. *This ordeal with Banders and Xochitl has opened my eyes to all sorts of possibilities. Change was forced on me in a lot of the situations and I handled it pretty well. And change is change. Once you're there you can't go back.* "I guess that's where I am right now," he said, punctuating the air with his finger, "ready for a big change."

Okay, then...a job. How do you get one? What do you do? It's not like there's a job store. Or is there? I don't even know. I'll have to ask Pinky. He's a man of the world. He'll know.

CHAPTER 62

Doctor Robert Austin Banders glared down from the wall-mounted television into the bustling chaos that erupted nightly at Pinky's Bar. The Fiddler Crab glanced up at the screen, then, as he turned his attention back to the bar a giggle escaped him. He thought of Banders bound with duct tape on the floor of Xochitl's living room, swearing furiously through the strip of tape across his mouth, bearing no resemblance to the authoritative, distinguished gentleman on the screen.

"Hey Fid, isn't that the guy? The guy you fought?" asked Tonsils.

"That's him," the Fiddler Crab said, dipping a handful of beer glasses into a sink full of soapy, but questionable water.

"I'm proud of you, Fid. You kicked that guy's ass. He had it coming and you gave it to him."

"Yup, guess I did."

An uncomfortable silence filled the distance between them.

"What'll ya have?" asked the Fiddler Crab as he wiped the tarnished copper bar with a damp, stained rag.

"Oh Fiddy, you know what I drink," said Tonsils. "A screwdriver. It's good for you. It's got orange juice."

"I'm just practicing," said the Fiddler Crab as he thumbed through a tattered paperback mixology manual. "I just want to hear myself say it. How was I? Did I sound authentic?"

"Well, you're not quite in Pinky's league yet, but keep it up, it won't be long."

He handed the drink across the bar to Tonsils and stood for a moment ... just feeling. What was it? Just a touch of it, ever so slight, but there it was.

Peace.

The beginnings of humility. He was doing a job, maybe not particularly well yet, but he was doing it. A job that involved serving his friends. And his friends appreciated his efforts. And he got paid. And it felt good. Giving up his government check had been very scary, a big step. But supporting yourself was something that everyone else in the place did every day. They weren't looking for an easy answer. They just did what was necessary, and more often than not, it worked out. No intimidating hardcover books to plow through. No grueling physical or mental exercises to subject himself to. Just good honest labor. Cause and effect. Peace.

"I'll bet Xochitl feels like this all the time," the Fiddler Crab said aloud, reaching into the refrigerator for a beer to satisfy his next customer.

CHAPTER 63

As far as she knew, mountain lions were afraid of people. So what was the problem with this one? Apparently, they hadn't read the same magazine articles. Climbing a tree to escape a lion was foolish behavior. That was common knowledge. But there was the lion, and there was the tree, and what were you going to do? So up the tree she went, managing to snap a few shots over her shoulder as she climbed.

A large branch appeared before her and Xochitl hoisted herself onto it, scurrying toward the narrow end. As the branch became thinner beneath her, it sagged under her weight. The lion sprung lightly onto the branch and cautiously edged its way toward her. As the creature approached, the branch sagged more radically, the angle too great for her to remain standing upright. It was also common knowledge that, when faced with a mountain lion one should try to make one's self appear larger than the animal, thus scaring the beejeezus out of it. Despite this, she lay down and hugged the branch with her arms and legs to keep from falling off.

"What an idiot," she grumbled. "Why don't I think before I act? Fid…. Where are you when I need you?"

The lion crept forward, producing a low, guttural rumble. The branch bent further toward the ground. Xochitl gripped tighter, sharp edges of tree bark digging into her hands. The lion began to lose its footing as the branch reached an angle too steep to proceed. It retreated slightly and lay down near the trunk end of the branch. Breathing a heavy sigh, the creature draped its legs from the branch like little anchors to keep itself steady. The lion cast an expressionless gaze at Xochitl for some time, then closed its eyes and went to sleep.

Possibilities, she thought. I can't hold on forever. If I let go, I'm gonna fall a good twenty-five feet and, at the very least, break a leg. The lion will feel the vibration, wake up, climb down and eat me. Maybe if I move back toward the lion... and... What? Kick him? Ha! My kickboxing teacher never mentioned mountain lions...or trees. It's pretty much just geared for male attackers.

Xochitl's eyes opened wide with a sudden revelation. "Male attackers... Holy shit! That's it!"

The little canister of pepper spray on her key chain. She suddenly became aware of it digging into her thigh through her pants pocket. But how to reach it? She would have to shimmy back up toward the cat where the branch would better support her weight. She would need to grip the branch with only her legs in order to get into her pocket.

Without opening its eyes, the animal growled, a casual but threatening sound, as it felt the branch begin to wiggle. The beast was confident, aware that its prey had nowhere to run. Xochitl moved as gently she could, though the branch still wiggled substantially. Reaching a spot that felt solid between her thighs, Xochitl found herself five feet in front of the now watchful predator's nose. Her new position had taken much of the bow from the branch and the lion was beginning to feel more secure.

Xochitl thrust her hand into her pocket and felt the small, tubular canister in her fingers. The lion rose to its feet and assumed a hunting stance, shoulders raised, head lowered, legs bent. Xochitl jerked on the canister, but the keys on her chain caught on the fabric of her pockets. Growling, the big cat inched toward her, swiping at her with its front paw, claws extended. She could feel the cat's breath now and tugged frantically on the canister, feeling the fabric of her pocket binding into a wad as the keys dug deeper.

The canister was out of her pocket now, but the bound key chain prevented her from raising it any higher than her waist. The lion crooked its back legs, poised to pounce. Xochitl's sense of balance began to leave her as she struggled to pull the key chain loose and raise the canister to a level where it would be of some use.

The lion rocked back, cocking its hind legs. The chain broke and Xochitl whipped the canister to face level and sprayed. An intense burning sensation overcame her as the pepper spray shot into her own eyes. "Goddammit," she shouted, her eyes burning horribly. Spinning the canister in her hand she fired blindly as the lion pounced. The cat screamed in pain as it slammed into her chest knocking her loose from the branch. Briefly, she felt herself falling, the cat's screams mingling with her own.

The ground felt soft beneath her as she landed on her back, softer that she had anticipated. Then the ground moved. She had landed on top of the cat and now the creature was in a state of panic flopping about in agony. Xochitl rolled to the side, and then rolled again, and again. She kept rolling until her back thudded up against a tree trunk. Through her blind stupor, she heard the cat sprinting sightlessly off into the forest, screaming as it ran. She pulled herself into a fetal position and lay quietly, concentrating on peaceful things, waiting for the pain in her eyes and the pounding of her heart to subside.

An hour later Xochitl Saint James climbed wearily into the cab of her aging Toyota 4runner and turned the key. As the engine roared to life, she removed the strap from around her neck and placed her camera on the floor between the seats. She patted the camera case fondly. "Okay boss," she said aloud, "I better get a raise for this one."

THE END

Thank you for coming along on the Sober Pill journey. It was a blast to write and I hope you enjoyed reading it as much as I did writing it. It would mean the world to me if you'd pop on over to Amazon and give The Sober Pill a quick review. Thanks again for your participation. I hope this book gives you inspiration to go out and jump into some adventures of your own.

RocMo Brown.

www.ingramcontent.com/pod-product-compliance
Lightning Source LLC
Chambersburg PA
CBHW031942260626
47157CB00017B/2086